TAKE A RISK BUNDLE

COMPLETE SERIES BOXSET

ROBIN BIELMAN

WORTH THE RISK

Entangled Publishing, LLC
2614 South Timberline Road
Suite 109
Fort Collins, CO 80525
Visit our website at www.entangledpublishing.com.

Indulgence is an imprint of Entangled Publishing, LLC.

Edited by Adrien-Luc Sanders and Stacy Abrams

Manufactured in the United States of America

First Edition April 2012

For Greg ~ my happily ever after!

Chapter One

Somewhere between the first and third floors of the high-rise office building, Samantha Bennett leaned against the wall of the elevator and willed her rising temperature to cool it. She couldn't show up to her job interview looking like she'd run the six blocks from her hotel.

The strangers filling the elevator on their way to work weren't helping to ease her anxiety. And she really wanted to figure out who had decided to douse himself with cologne and tell him that less was more. Instead, she slid one sweaty palm down the skirt of her new black suit while the other squeezed the handle of the umbrella she'd bought this morning. Thank you, gloomy Idaho sky.

Five floors and a few deep breaths later, the nerves bunched across her shoulder blades had finally drifted away. But when the elevator doors opened and her gaze fell over the shoulder of the woman crowded in front of her, her legs shook. The man squeezing into the front swept a new kind of panic over her.

Dean.

Quivers traipsed down her spine. She angled herself for a better look, but hopefully one where he wouldn't notice her.

God, he looked good. Better than she remembered. His caramel-colored hair was streaked with lighter shades, indicating he still spent a lot of his time outdoors. It hung a little longer now, more surfer-chic than Indiana Jones. Shoulders broader and a chest more developed hid behind a thin khaki T-shirt. Longing overcame panic. Her body tingled. Everywhere.

All the women in the elevator were eyeing him.

His nearness made everything she'd fought to forget come roaring back to the surface. Samantha worried her bottom lip. She wavered slightly, her hand twitching around the umbrella stem. The elevator doors shut, and—

The umbrella opened.

"Oh my God! I'm so sorry!"

The expanding nylon whacked several people in the back as bodies bumped. Gasps of annoyance filled the tiny space. Flustered, Samantha took a few seconds to close the damn thing.

Once the umbrella shut, she snuck a peek in his direction. He'd turned his head, but a swift duck while she'd gathered her dignity saved her from meeting his gaze.

"Sorry," she muttered again, feeling her cheeks heat and perspiration slide down her side.

His face was the same. The same one she'd dreamed about countless times over the past five years: the square jaw, slightly crooked nose, piercing aquamarine eyes that never wavered during a conversation. The tiny smile that had passed over his lips had her itching to see if he was still ticklish in that little spot on his hip.

Get a grip, Sam.

At this moment, if he asked her, she'd forget all about the job interview and once again follow him from Yosemite to the Badlands.

No, she wouldn't. She was indifferent to him now. And she needed to focus on the meeting, on landing the contract, or she might not be going anywhere but the unemployment line.

It should have been a done deal. The World Heritage Fund was the largest international nonprofit organization dedicated to preserving historical sites. Global climate change contributed more and more to the organization's plight, and they were looking for a partnership with another environmental company to preserve Route 66. The famous highway, stretching over two thousand miles from Chicago to Los Angeles, had been replaced by an interstate highway system a long time ago, but a recent bill signed into law to preserve and restore historic features like gas stations, cafés, and trading posts along the route had put it back on the map.

Samantha's employer, Global Site Preservation, wanted the job. It meant national exposure. It meant an unprecedented alliance. It meant Samantha's freelance position with the company could turn into something more permanent. If she didn't come through with the account, she feared they'd start looking for someone more established.

That could *not* happen. She needed to keep this job more than she needed anything else. It would prove to her father that she could make it on her own. His scathing words when she decided to leave his law firm still flooded her with sadness. And doubt.

The elevator doors chimed and people exited. Her body tensed at the loss of barriers. At the next floor, the woman she'd been trying desperately to hide behind abandoned her, leaving her feeling exposed. Naked. Uncomfortable in her own skin. She prayed Dean wouldn't turn around.

He'd left World Heritage Fund a year ago to start his own preservation company—Monument & Heritage Recovery—and Samantha hadn't been able to resist keeping track of the California-based organization. Dean had gained a great deal of respect in a short time. So why was he in town? If she'd known he'd be here, she could have prepared herself. Or better yet, done everything possible to avoid him.

The risk he posed to her was too great, even after all this time.

Dizziness swooped in as she realized they'd be getting off the elevator at the same floor. She blinked back the disorientation to glance at her watch. Was there time to pass her floor and circle back after he departed?

Nope.

He'd probably come to town for a simple visit. His father owned World Heritage Fund, after all, and while everyone in the field knew Dean's departure had strained the father-son relationship, she imagined he still came to Idaho now and then.

Dean. His name conjured up all sorts of images she needed to extinguish from her mind. Pronto.

"Thank you," a woman said, exiting the elevator while he held out an arm to hold the doors open.

"No problem," he replied, his familiar voice causing all

sorts of flutters in her stomach. Dammit. The smooth texture of his tone still affected her in ways she was powerless to control.

You don't care about him, remember?

She focused on the metal doors closing. If she didn't, she'd slide down the elevator wall like hot fudge on ice cream. There were only two more floors to go, so she needed to buckle down. She could do this. She *had* to do this. Sure, his presence rattled her, but she was meeting with his father, not with him. Besides, five years had passed since they'd seen each other. Reason indicated they could offer each other friendly hellos and be done with it.

Unless Samantha took into account the broken heart he'd left her with. The broken heart she hadn't let anyone else come close to healing.

Suck it up, she thought. *The job matters and nothing else.* She'd dedicated the past few years to getting herself to this point, and she had no intention of blowing it now just because Dean Malloy stood three feet away from her.

Finally they arrived at the twenty-third floor. She waited, pretending it wasn't her stop, so that Dean would exit first. After he did, she followed, catching the closing elevator doors with her trusty—not!—umbrella.

Hanging back, she watched him greet the receptionist before moving deeper into the office and disappearing from view. The sight of his broad shoulders, nice-fitting khakis, and easy swagger sent her entire body into an unwelcome mess of memories. She wondered what it would be like to touch him again, to hold his hand, to kiss him.

"Good morning," she said to the receptionist, her voice more strained than she would've liked. She cleared her throat. "I have a nine o'clock appointment with William Malloy. I'm Sam Bennett."

The fifty-something woman with warm eyes moved a mouthpiece away from her lips. "Yes, Miss Bennett. Have a seat, please, and I'll let him know you're here." She gestured toward a sitting area with dark green couches.

Sam willed her body to relax as she grabbed a magazine off the table beside the couch. It wasn't easy in her suit, the skirt riding up a little higher than she'd realized it would. She pressed her knees together, sat taller, and tried to pull it down. No luck. With a defeated sigh, she opened the magazine to a photograph of a backpacker on a mountain.

The image immediately reminded her of Yosemite, and the first time she'd met Dean. She'd decided to take a month off before law school to journey around the western part of the country, wanting to see the great outdoors that her uppity father had deemed too incidental for their family vacations. On her second day there, she'd bumped into Dean at the top of Vernal Falls.

Fresh off graduation ceremonies at Harvard, Dean was the daring adventurer she'd always dreamed of meeting. Not to mention his adorable charm and irresistible smile made her eager to follow him wherever he might go. Left to her own devices, she would have stayed on the straight and narrow, covered the routes most taken, and missed seeing anything out of the ordinary. Dean had offered more.

Her stomach knotted at the memory. She'd been unable to resist him.

"Hey, Gloria?"

His voice shook her from her memories, and she scrambled to lift the magazine in front of her face.

"Do you think you could get Henry O'Neill on the phone? He's supposed to meet Dad and me for lunch today."

With trepidation, Samantha peeked from behind her magazine. Dean stood at the reception desk—all calm, cool, six-foot-two-inches of him. His approachable posture, his muscular biceps, his confidence, were an irresistible combination that made her want to jump up and shout, *Look over here!*

But she didn't. She couldn't. The way her heart pounded in her chest, the way her body warmed in all the wrong places, the way she still daydreamed about him...it wasn't indifference she felt. And she'd promised herself to forget any feelings of attachment where he was concerned.

Damn him for being here.

She tried to drag her eyes away, but she failed. Honestly, looking at him was better than looking at a sunrise, or a rainbow, or a snow-capped mountain. He must have sensed her heated gaze, because he turned to look in her direction. With about the swiftness of a three-year-old, she whipped her face back behind the magazine, lowered her chin, and squeezed her eyes shut.

"Henry," Dean said a moment later, saving her, she hoped, from discovery. And major embarrassment.

Samantha didn't dare look at him again, and she prayed his conversation would be short, because her arms were beginning to get tired from holding up the magazine. It was a good thing her pre-adolescent dream of becoming Nancy Drew hadn't panned out. She sucked at covert operations. Even at twenty-seven.

Thankfully, Henry quickly agreed to the time and place for lunch. Sam opened her eyes to read about "35 Dream

Jobs: Turn Your Passion into a Paycheck" and wondered if someone were trying to tell her something. Footsteps, she assumed Dean's, sounded, then quieted, relieving her once again. Sort of. Just knowing he was in the same office created nervous tension inside her. No way would her mind win over her body's reaction to Dean, so she'd have to do whatever it took to stay away from him.

This was supposed to be a done deal, she thought again, willing her mind back to the task at hand. Then her body stiffened. Was Dean the hotshot environmentalist World Heritage Fund was also accepting a proposal from?

She dropped the magazine into her lap.

"Sam," Dean said, sitting across from her with a smile that slayed her.

Chapter Two

It *was* her. His girl of summer all those years ago. *Samantha.*

The pair of powder blue eyes he couldn't look away from made his gut clench. Her startled expression amused him. Her floral fragrance immediately unlocked memories he'd tried not to think about, and a smile he couldn't contain spread across his face. Lingered.

He'd noticed her the second he'd stepped back into the lobby. No. That wasn't true. He'd noticed her on the elevator, but he hadn't thought it possible she was the girl he'd spent a few summer weeks with. Now he knew.

To his surprise—and delight—her close proximity quickened his pulse and stimulated blood flow to all sorts of body parts. A rush of feelings bombarded him—heat, joy, desire, fear. The simple act of seeing her again stirred far too many complex feelings, emotions he thought he'd left on mountaintops and hiking trails of national parks years ago.

"Dean," she said, so softly, so innocently sexy, that his groin tightened.

They stared at each other. Speechless.

She still looked like an angel with a devilish edge he knew could be coaxed out with the right words. Her luscious heart-shaped lips spoke to him without movement. Honey-colored hair neatly pulled back indicated a more manicured appearance, yet there was no mistaking her youthful spirit. Her hiding behind a magazine confirmed that.

"Wow. It's good to see you." He stood and leaned over to kiss her cheek. The contact sent a jolt of electricity through him.

"Oh my gosh. It's good to see you, too." The corners of her mouth pulled upward to reveal a killer smile that brightened her almond-shaped eyes.

He carried her sweet smell back with him as he sat, and images of the two of them assaulted his mind. Like a thirty-second film clip, memories bombarded his brain in rapid succession: he and Samantha holding hands, laughing, touching, kissing, undressing.

Pausing for a moment before speaking, he *really* looked at her. God, she was even more breathtaking now. He couldn't believe he was seeing her in the flesh.

He could tell by the way her eyes narrowed that she was sizing him up, too. The trance between them filled the air with wonder and…curiosity? Was she as interested in him as he was in her? It honestly felt like no time had passed since he'd last seen her, and suddenly he wanted something lengthier than a brief *hello* and *how are you*.

Wait.

What the hell was he thinking?

He'd come to town to get a job. A very lucrative job that would catapult his company to the top of its field and give him the distinction he craved. His father wasn't handing over the partnership for Route 66, but was making Dean work for it. *And* adding competition from Global Site Preservation, a renowned environmental company based in Chicago with a much longer track record and better-known reputation than Dean's.

Hooking up with Samantha would be a really bad idea. He didn't need or want any distractions. Besides, the last time he'd seen her, she'd broken his heart.

"How've you been?" he asked, snapping the charged tension between them.

"I'm really well, thank you." She cleared her throat. "And you?"

"Good. Really good." He relaxed into the couch, his gaze stuck on the flecks of green in her blue eyes. "I'm surprised to see you here."

She squirmed a little, her hands gripping the magazine. "I could say the same to you. I'd read you started your own company in California, contributing to the preservation of important sites and striving to guarantee future generations get the privilege of knowing their history."

"Wow. You sound pretty knowledgeable on the subject. Have you been influenced by all the hype over environmental issues and climate change, or are you just keeping tabs on me?"

Her cheeks reddened and he imagined he'd caught her off guard with his directness. He remembered seeing her blush on several occasions that had been much more intimate. *Shit.* If he weren't careful, he'd get a hard-on right here in front of her.

"Last I remember," he continued, "you were headed to law school and then a career with your father's firm, doing contract law, I think it was." He had deliberately changed the topic of conversation to her.

"Actually, I'm in environmental law and preservation now." She sat up taller, straightened her back. "After law school I did work for my father, but then decided to go to night school to get my MBA in Environmental Policy and Management, too. Some guy I'd met really made an impression on me, and I didn't want to be stuck doing estate contracts the rest of my life." Her flat tone left no doubt that she wanted to keep her distance from him.

"Sounds like a smart guy."

"I've met smarter since."

"No doubt." He deserved that. He knew he'd broken her heart when they'd parted ways. *I'm sorry* sat on the tip of his tongue, but he couldn't bring himself to say it. Not yet. Not when she'd broken his heart, too. He'd known he'd never meet anyone else quite like her. So when he lost his cell phone—the only connection he had to Sam—after they split up, he'd foolishly tracked her down to surprise her. Only he was the one who'd been surprised.

And just like that, he remembered he didn't want a long-term relationship. That work came first. Was what he looked forward to every day. The look on her face when they'd said good-bye had hurt him down to his core, but a few weeks later she'd reminded him to never waver on wanting his independence.

So why was jealousy nearly choking him now? Why was he clenching his hands? When he'd noticed her gripping the magazine, he hadn't seen a ring on her finger, but only a fool would think she'd stayed single all these years. In his case, just looking at her made him ache to get lost somewhere remote so they could spend all day and night touching each other.

"I work for Global Site now. I'm here to meet with your father. You're not here for the same reason I am, are you?" She tilted her head and narrowed her eyes, but she looked more apprehensive than confident.

"So you're my young, gorgeous competition." He watched her cheeks redden further. "My contacts at Global Site speak very highly of you."

She shifted her weight, crossed her legs at the ankle. "I doubt they included those exact adjectives, but thank you anyway. And you're the hotshot environmentalist who's going to give me a run for my money."

"That your assessment or does my reputation precede me?"

"Considering I didn't know it was your company after the account until a few minutes ago, you can rest assured I haven't given *you* any thought until now." A smirk crossed her face, entangling him in a situation he both relished and regretted. Dean excelled at what he did. And nepotism aside, he was the best man to tackle the Route 66 project. After all, he'd learned from the best, having worked for his father for so many years. But he wished it wasn't Samantha he'd beat.

And he'd bet it all she *had* thought about him over the years. He'd certainly thought about her.

With more clarity than ever before, he recalled picnicking with her in Jasper National Park. They'd eaten slowly, sipping on champagne after every bite. When Samantha dropped tortellini covered in red sauce down her white shirt, he'd quickly suggested she take it off. It wasn't the first time she'd dropped something down the front of her shirt, and he'd always tried to coax her out of the messy article of clothing.

At the sight of her silky skin he'd reached out, touched her shoulder, traced his fingertip down her arm, and circled back up her abdomen before landing at the generous swell of her breasts. She was curvy in all the right places, and over the course of the month they'd spent together he'd memorized every slope and angle. Navigating her body with his fingers had sent a rush of heat through him. The only thing better was tracing her with his tongue.

She was always so susceptible to his touch, her body responding to him like he'd had a magic wand. He wondered if he'd have the same power over her now.

"Dean?" Snapping fingers broke him free from his recollection. "You still with me? I completely understand if you need to gather your thoughts and prepare for your presentation. Don't let me keep you."

"Presentation?" He leaned forward, elbows on his knees, back in the present where, goddamn it, he'd stay from now on. "I was just thinking maybe you'd like me to give you a few pointers on what to expect from my old man. I could fill you in on what he's looking for. Level the playing field." Teasing. He was teasing.

The look of betrayal on her face told him she didn't think he was needling her. "I don't need any inside information from you. In fact, I hope you won't have any objection to my kicking your ass and securing the job for my employer."

"Have at it," he said. This Samantha was feistier than before. He liked it. He liked it a lot. But it also made him a little nervous. Sam was smart, persuasive, capable, and if he weren't on top of his game, she'd win the contract.

The chance to work with his father again, to mend some of the hard feelings between them, was the biggest reason he was after the deal. He knew he'd never get another chance like this one.

"I mean, I'd hate to think you'd use your family ties to get the account. And I'd like to believe your father wouldn't have invited me here if I didn't have a chance of landing the deal."

"You're right—"

"So you can keep all those thoughts to yourself, Dean. I'm perfectly capable of getting down and dirty on my own."

Blood rushed to points south. No way in hell did he want her getting down and dirty on her own. He wanted to do it with her. Preferably without clothing. *Shit.* In the course of five minutes, Samantha Bennett had emotionally and sexually hijacked him, and he didn't know what to do about it.

"You're right that my dad wouldn't meet with you unless he thought you offered something top-notch." He fell back against the chair, relaxing. At least on the outside. Inside, he felt tied up in knots. "And for your information, I had to fight for the chance to give a presentation. My dad was ready to—"

Damn. He'd said too much. He didn't want her knowing how close she'd been to a done deal before he'd convinced his dad to give him a chance. He'd shamefully used his mother's birthday on Sunday as a reason to visit this weekend, and then told his father that while he was here, what harm would there be in hearing him out? His ideas for Route 66 were good. Incomparably good.

Sam's eyebrows lifted in a most appealing way. Not the look she wanted, he knew, but every move she made seemed to capture his interest in a seductive manner. "Well, I'm sorry to disappoint you, but if you think I had your dad committed over the telephone, just wait until I get him in person."

This time confidence radiated off her in waves, making him admire her more. He gulped. She'd not only gotten prettier, but much more brash.

"Excuse me, Miss Bennett?" Gloria said from behind the reception desk. "Mr. Malloy apologizes for the delay, he was stuck on an international phone call. He'll be right out to get you."

"Thank you," she responded, moving her gaze over Dean's shoulder for the first time since he'd sat down and gotten her attention.

"Well, I can surely attest to your charms in person," Dean said. "I remember many a day we wiled away in various stages of—"

"Dean!" The way her face alighted with delight, passion, and embarrassment all rolled into one convinced him she remembered everything, too.

He lowered his voice to a husky whisper. "Come on. Remember Vernal Falls? The truffles we had for dessert?" He hadn't been able to look at one since without remembering the way he'd straddled her hips, nudging the bulge in his boxers between her legs and pulsing ever so slightly while he'd rolled the chocolate down her neck, then bit it in half and poured the liquor inside down her bare upper body, aiming between her breasts and trickling down to just below her belly button.

Her eyes darkened, and he noticed her chest rise and fall. "I remember."

While his tongue had lapped up the warm liquid spread over her skin, he'd slid her panties down, haphazardly discarded his boxers, and slipped inside her. Outside. Under a blue sky littered with puffy white clouds. The memory stood as crystal clear now as it did then.

"I haven't had one since." Or wanted one. Not without *her*.

"Me neither." She looked at him with such intensity, he suspected she could see into his soul. "I also remember eating some disgusting fish you caught and some weird berries that you insisted were an aphrodisiac."

"Hey, I was young and trying to charm the pants off you however I could."

"I seem to recall you didn't have much difficulty in that department." She batted her eyelashes—he knew it was unintentionally, because whenever she'd gotten a little nervous with him during that summer, she'd blinked repeatedly.

Her adorable anxiety had melted his heart then. As it did now. Maybe she wasn't as immune to him as she'd like him to believe?

"You had a few tricks up your sleeve, too," he said coolly.

"I did not!"

"Really? You don't remember the time we skinny dipped in Lake—"

"Sam Bennett. Sorry to keep you waiting. It's a pleasure to meet you."

Samantha quickly stood and reached out an arm to greet the deep, masculine voice coming from behind Dean. The magazine she'd scrunched in her lap fell to the floor and

Dean couldn't help but take in every inch of her tall, curvy-in-the-right-places frame.

"Mr. Malloy. It's so nice to meet you in person."

Dean rose with a little dodge to the side so as not to intrude on their handshake. He stepped back, then turned to face his dad.

The old guy looked surprised to see him. "Dean? What are you doing out here?" He looked from him to Samantha, his brow furrowing. "You haven't been bothering this young lady, have you?"

"I don't think so, sir. Just a little friendly conversation. I understand she's ready to knock your socks off with a killer presentation." He winked at her. He truly wanted her to do well. Knew she'd do well. But knew he'd do better. If he didn't take the cocky approach, he wouldn't stand a chance against her.

Samantha graced him with an appreciative tight-lipped smile, her eyes sparkling, before returning her attention to his dad.

She'd dazzle his father, Dean had no doubt of that. But worse, so help him God, he wanted her again. He thought after five years he'd purged her from his system, but truth be told, she still held a special spot inside him, her effortless ambush of his body and mind testament to that.

Dean was in deep shit.

"Worried?" his dad asked him, a bit of playfulness in his tone.

"Just a little."

"Well, I'm anxious to hear what she's got to say, so let's head on back to my office, shall we?" He gestured Samantha to his side. "And call me Bill." The two walked away without a second glance back at Dean.

When they reached the reception desk, Dean decided he had to do something. "Hold on." They paused, looked over their shoulders. Dean stepped beside the desk. "Mind if I have a quick word with Samantha?"

For a moment Dean thought he'd be denied. His father wasn't the most patient man, and a frown worse than a dagger to the heart crossed Sam's face.

But when his father said, "That's up to the lady," in a warm voice, he knew Sam couldn't deny him a moment without looking inconsiderate, rival or not.

"Sure," she answered with less enthusiasm than Dean would have liked. Of course, she had to be businesslike in front of the president and CEO of World Heritage Fund.

"Why don't you bring her back to my office when you're finished?"

"Will do." Dean turned to Gloria as his father stepped away. "Can I use your pen?"

"What in the world are you doing?" Sam whispered as he took her elbow to steer her away from the desk, and from listening ears.

Dean steadied himself on the back of the couch. Touching her sent impossibly hot pulses through his veins, knocking him completely off balance. "I wanted to know if you'd have dinner with me tonight."

"Dean." The sound of his name on her lips made him determined to get his way.

"Look, I know we're competing against each other here, but I'd love to spend a little more time with you. Catch up." Her worried eyes told him she didn't know what to do or say. He couldn't blame her. He'd hurt her when they'd parted ways. He would hurt her again when he got the contract.

"How about a drink, at least? There's a great bar I go to when I'm in town."

She kept him waiting for a few torturous seconds, their eyes tangling with memories, regrets, anxiety…and questions. Finally she said, "Okay. One drink."

"Great." He lifted her hand and, pulling the cap off the pen with his teeth, wrote a set of numbers on her palm. A breathy chuckle left her lips before he replaced the pen into the cap with perfect precision.

"That's my cell phone number. Call me a little later and we'll work out the details."

"All right."

They walked back to his father's office in silence, but the electricity in the air between them crackled. Dean knew he was being a fool, knew he needed to stay focused on the job and landing the contract from his father. Not landing in bed with Samantha.

Unfortunately, he couldn't help himself.

Samantha Bennett still took his breath away. Still stirred a desire in him that no one else had come close to duplicating.

He heard her take a deep breath as they reached the office door.

"See you later," she said, then disappeared before he had a chance to wish her luck.

As the door gently shut, he remained rooted to his spot, thinking and breathing in the scent of her that lingered in the hallway. He didn't regret walking away from her five years ago. How could he? He'd traveled the globe and worked hard for something he strongly believed in. He'd gleaned the experience and knowledge to move on to bigger and better things. Had established his own company at the age of twenty-eight. He'd always wanted nothing more than freedom and self-reliance. His mantra? Never surrender. And that applied to both his professional and personal life.

But as fate would have it, the beautiful blue-eyed girl who he'd impulsively trekked through half a dozen states with, all while falling head over heels for, was back in his life.

He was older now. Wiser. Or maybe not, considering that while he knew it wasn't the best idea, he still wondered if she'd agree to rekindle things for the entire weekend. A reunion of sorts. But if she consented, could he walk away from her again?

Chapter Three

"Sam, this is Keats McCall, my president of field operations. He'll be sitting in on our meeting," Mr. Malloy said, standing and moving around his glass desk as Sam walked into the expansive, clutter-free office.

"Nice to meet you, Mr. McCall." Samantha extended her hand and tried not to give away her surprise. She'd read up on Keats McCall because she'd wanted to know everything about World Heritage Fund. At thirty, with movie-star good looks and enough article bylines on heritage protection to garner international recognition, he ranked high on the short list of environmental preservation wonder boys. But she hadn't expected to meet in person the man who'd taken over Dean's position. Not yet, anyway.

"No Mister necessary," he said. "I go by McCall. And it's nice to meet you, too." He released her hand and gestured to a small conference table situated beside a floor-to-ceiling window. The view from the twenty-third floor revealed rays of sunshine peeking through the gray clouds.

The three reached the table, McCall pulling out her chair. She gave a small smile in thanks and couldn't help but notice his gaze linger on her longer than necessary. While his interest flattered her, Samantha had only one man on her mind.

Remember the time we skinny dipped... Oh, she remembered all right. She remembered *everything* about her weeks with Dean Malloy. Every moment was etched into her psyche in high definition 3D.

"Sam," Mr. Malloy said, "before you launch into your presentation, I'd like to ask a couple personal questions. It's procedure on my part. I like to know who I might be working with."

"Sure," she said, pushing away any and all thoughts of Dean before they screwed up her meeting. Damn him for stirring emotions inside her she'd long kept tucked away.

She put her leather folio case on the hardwood floor so it leaned against her chair leg. Her hands weren't so easy to figure out. She clasped them in front of her, forearms on the table, but a second later slid her arms down to her sides and wrapped each hand around the edge of her seat.

"Don't be nervous," McCall whispered, leaning into her personal space. "He started the same way with me."

"I'm not nervous. But I have a feeling Mr. Malloy already knows everything about me." Samantha had done her research—she'd bet money he'd done his. Did he know about her brief relationship with Dean? Had Dean ever mentioned her?

Her sister and cousin knew about that summer and had helped wipe away more tears than Sam cared to admit. But she hadn't told anyone else. When her father had pressed her for reasons why she wanted to pursue work in the non-profit world of environmentalism, she'd kept to herself the man who had changed everything for her, the man who had opened her eyes to the really important stuff. She didn't want her dad soiling Dean the way he'd soiled everything else in her life.

As Mr. Malloy considered her words, he relaxed into his seat and laid his palms flat on the table in front of him.

"Tell me the one spot on this planet that means the most to you," he said.

Simple words. Not a simple answer.

She immediately felt her face flush as snapshot after snapshot of her escapades with Dean flashed in her mind. The adventures they'd had in some of the most beautiful spots in the country and the places where they'd stood hand in hand in awe, marveling at the scenery, were memories she'd carry with her forever. Nothing meant more to her than those few weeks.

She glanced around the office, feeling no discomfort at taking time to contemplate her answer. Framed photographs of architectural projects from around the world decorated the charcoal-colored walls. While Samantha hadn't been to any of them, she recognized the Taos Pueblo in New Mexico, the Funchal Cathedral in Portugal, Westminster Abbey Sedilia in the UK, and the Great Wall of China.

"Boundary Springs in Crater Lake National Park." The spot where she'd realized she was hopelessly in love with Dean.

"That's interesting." Mr. Malloy's gaze matched his tone of voice—curious, but not quite suspicious. "My son says that's a favorite of his as well."

A woman less skilled at concealing her feelings would have cracked, but not Samantha. No matter how telling this piece of information was, she'd long ago replaced adoration for nonchalance where Dean was concerned—and she would cling to that decision no matter what.

"Have you been there as well?" Samantha asked. "It's a spectacular place."

"I haven't. But I'll be sure to make a mental note of it." If he'd caught any sort of connection between herself and Dean, it didn't show on his face. "And the one place you must see before you die?"

"That's easy. Machu Picchu."

"Ahh. The Incan settlement in the Andes Mountains *is* breathtaking. I was there many years ago when the Temple of the Sun made it onto our Watch List. We sent a team to reinforce the infrastructure and to help the people there come up with a conservation plan."

Samantha sighed. She wanted to visit Peru and so many other places around the world. If she could make her job with Global Site permanent, it guaranteed she'd travel far and wide as an advocate for the preservation movement.

"I imagine you've been to hundreds of out-of-the-way places." She reached for her portfolio, nervous about answering more personal questions. She didn't want to appear rude, but the sooner she started with her presentation, the better. She'd poured her heart and soul into the proposal, and she knew her ideas were good. But even with the full backing of her bosses, she still hadn't been in the business as long as Dean. An unwelcome feeling of doubt had wormed its way into her thoughts after their exchange in the waiting area.

"Too many to remember." He looked to McCall. "But I'm not getting any younger, so this guy's racking up the frequent flier miles now."

"With pleasure," McCall said.

"Well, Route 66 will probably add more driving miles than anything else. Would it be okay if I shared Global Site's vision for how we can work with you to revitalize the highway and landmarks along the historic route now?"

"Sure," Mr. Malloy said.

Samantha pulled out two reports and handed them to the men. "Since you added Route 66 to your Watch List of places in jeopardy, Global Site has taken an active interest in it as well."

Despite the cool office temperature, a trickle of sweat slid down Samantha's lower back. She had to land this contract. Had to keep her job and paycheck. She stacked her own papers neatly in front of her and sat up taller. The deep breath she tried to be discreet about didn't go unnoticed by McCall, and he gave her a closed-mouth smile. The gesture reached his pale green eyes and gave her the silent support she needed to kick some cultural heritage ass.

"Let's hear what you have in mind." Mr. Malloy didn't bother with the report. He sat back and gave Samantha his full attention.

"We'd like to start in Chicago and head west. By combining our forces with yours, we estimate covering the two-thousand-plus miles will take approximately twenty-four to thirty-six months. We can't possibly cover every mile, so we propose targeting abandoned and fire-damaged original buildings, bridges, and highway remnants that can once again open to transportation independently or by incorporation into current highways."

Mr. Malloy nodded. "That sounds logical. You think tackling the project in a linear fashion is best?"

"We do. We'll reach out to local preservation organizations as well as community groups in a piggyback method that we believe will result in greater and greater word of mouth and state participation as we make our way to California. Sort of like a Conga line."

Both men chuckled. Samantha had debated over whether or not to use that line, but a coworker had told her not to forget to add it just before she'd left the office for her flight. She was happy to find her belief that environmentalists had a good sense of humor to be true.

"How do we decide which areas to skip?" McCall asked.

"We'll give our attention to the more populated sectors, but also to rural spots with currently dilapidated markers or signs that may attract attention. If we can resurrect some of the charms of the route, we think we'll get more people interested in exploring the country from the road less traveled." Samantha pulled several photos and diagrams from her pile and spread them across the table. "For example, we'd like to repair the Twin Arrows Trading Post in Arizona."

She singled out the picture of the structure as it looked now and introduced a drawing detailing her company's ideas. "We see huge potential to attract tourists with families here. We've researched the family vacation, and expensive airfare combined with a tough economy means people are sticking closer to home and exploring nearby states by car rather than traveling to tropical destinations or overseas." Samantha paused to catch her breath. "I remember when I was young how wonderful it was to stop at these interesting posts and find souvenir treasures that took me forever to decide between."

"I was partial to rocks and fossils myself," McCall said, his hand smoothing over one of the photos like he could wipe something away and see beyond the trading post.

"Dean loved to collect arrowheads." Mr. Malloy grinned at the memory. "He'd get one, come home, and immediately hunt for a rock so that he could try his hand at carving a matching one. I think my wife still has his collection somewhere."

At the mention of Dean, Samantha's heart thumped with longing, as if an old habit—a really good, never-want-to-give-it-up habit—had returned. "Some things are hard to part with."

"Indeed they are."

Samantha heard the hurt in Mr. Malloy's voice as well as felt his regrets, as if an invisible wave of emotion fluctuated between them. Dean's departure from World Heritage Fund still pained him, yet his love and admiration for Dean was obvious. She didn't want to think about how much their father-son relationship had suffered because of Dean's business decision. Not when her own father had made it clear that once she left his company, she meant nothing to him. In truth, even before she left, she'd meant little.

"Global Site envisions resurrecting many, if not all, of the trading posts along the historic highway," she said. "Roadside culture is as important as the highway itself, and for those posts still operating, we see sending a team of specialists to assist in helping to design a conservation plan and strategy."

With a project as large as Route 66, Samantha could only give an overview of Global Site's plans, and she hoped she'd struck a chord. Her report went into great detail and she imagined both men would give it careful consideration over the weekend, making the many sleepless nights and countless hours she'd spent perfecting the written presentation worth it.

World Heritage Fund *had* to agree to a partnership with Global Site. The project would not only pump life back into Route 66, but into her own existence as well.

Silence filled the office space as the three of them studied the pictures and plans strewn across the table. Samantha had flown to many spots along the famous highway to see firsthand what challenges lay before them. With her camera around her neck and a notepad in her hand, she'd explored miles and miles of land. A shiver raced through her as she remembered finding old alignments of Route 66 in sparse desert brush a few hundred feet from existing highways. Every discovery was part of her own treasure map and with each, she wanted more and more to land this contract.

"You all right?" McCall asked.

"Yes." She took a deep breath at his notice. "Just remembering a few of the places I scouted and how excited I was to find parts of the Route."

"So you're the great photographer behind these pictures," Mr. Malloy said, studying a shot of Canyon Padre Bridge, a monument not far from the Twin Arrows Post.

"I am." Samantha gave a silent thank-you to her photography class. Her teacher had urged her to sign up for his advanced course next month, but she hoped to be in the field and unavailable by then.

McCall pushed back from the table. "I'd venture to say we're only seeing a glimpse of your talents, Miss Bennett."

"Please, call me Sam."

He smiled. "Sam."

The first person to call her Sam had been Dean. She'd been adamant about using her full name since kindergarten and would correct anyone who did otherwise, but when Dean had shortened her name, everything inside her went soft. She never knew which version of her name he'd use — how exhilarating that was! — and forgot all about her preference. When she'd started law school, she'd discovered "Sam" garnered less unwanted attention (and a few gender mistakes, which didn't hurt in the competitive world of law), so she'd kept the abbreviation in business as well.

At the moment she longed to hear Dean say it. To whisper it in her ear. To tease her with it while his hands slid to places that hadn't felt a man's touch in far too long. McCall's pronunciation paled in comparison to Dean's.

"And thank you," she said, forcing thoughts of Dean away. "I think you'll find a convincing and top-notch proposal in your report. I know I speak for everyone at Global Site when I say we'd be thrilled to partner with you."

"I wouldn't have invited you here if we weren't serious about partnering," Mr. Malloy said, "but I do have another presentation to consider."

Samantha swallowed the lump in her throat. "Of course."

"I'll read this carefully over the weekend and have a decision by Monday morning." Mr. Malloy lifted the report and then stood. "Are you free to come by at ten?"

"Absolutely." Samantha rose to her feet. When she'd agreed to the interview, she had been told she'd get her answer on Monday, so she'd already planned to stay the weekend. But the next seventy-two hours would be torture.

"Great. I'll see you then. McCall, would you mind seeing Sam out? I've got to step down the hall."

McCall nodded. "No problem." He helped her gather her materials, then put his own report under his arm.

"Thank you," Samantha said, stepping through the office door McCall held open. She wanted to ask him his initial thoughts on her presentation, but she held her tongue. It wouldn't do any good to appear too eager, not when her arm accidentally brushed his and he looked pleased by the contact.

"I've got some free time this weekend," he said as they walked toward the lobby. "How about I show you some of the best-kept secrets in Idaho?"

Samantha wasn't sure what to make of McCall's overture. Was he simply acting on behalf of World Heritage Fund and extending courtesy while she was in town, or was his interest more personal?

Either way, it didn't matter. She had no plans to drop her defenses around good-looking men who devoted everything to the environment. She'd read enough about McCall to know he was just like Dean. He traveled the globe finding and preserving treasured sites, and if a woman happened along who sparked his interest, then great. McCall's online friends included far more women than men. Not that she'd checked up on his personal as well as professional life.

"That's really nice of you, but I'm behind on an outline my boss has been asking for, and I really need to finish it. Thank you, though."

"Dinner, then? You've got to eat, and I know this great

sushi place."

His voice was a mixture of sexy and sincere that made for a killer combination. Plus, she loved sushi. But… "I really can't," she forced out.

McCall paused and plucked a business card and pen from the reception desk in the lobby. He flipped the card over and wrote something. "Tell you what, here's my cell phone number if you decide you need a break from work." He handed her the card. "Feel free to call anytime."

Samantha almost—*almost*—caved under his incredibly charming smile. But then without her permission, the smile she most longed to see ambushed her thoughts. And once again memories of Dean made it difficult to move on.

"Thanks. I'll keep that in mind." Samantha stepped toward the elevator, retrieved her umbrella from the metal bin, and pressed the down button. "'Bye, McCall."

"'Bye, Sam."

The elevator doors opened and Samantha stepped inside. When she turned she found McCall still standing at the desk. She smiled at him, but just before the doors closed, she caught sight of Dean. Their eyes met and her heart skipped a beat.

Chapter Four

"She's off limits, bud," Dean said, putting a hand on McCall's shoulder. He didn't know where the words came from—he had no claim on Samantha. But seeing her with McCall had triggered a goddamn volcano to erupt inside his chest, the idea of the two of them together threatening his very survival.

McCall's body shook with amusement under Dean's hand. "Really? Why's that?" he asked, swallowing down the laughter Dean saw in his eyes.

"No reason other than it's a bad idea."

"Hell, Dean, she's the best bad idea I've come across in a long time."

Gloria cleared her throat from behind the reception desk. She raised her eyebrows and shooed them away with a flick of her hand.

Dean grinned at her and started toward his—or rather McCall's—office. "No doubt. But are you planning on showing me the sites this weekend as well? How do you think the old man will react if he finds out you're not playing fair?" Dean stopped and lifted the leg of his khakis to show off his calf. "Have you taken a look at these lately?"

"Not bad, Malloy. But the legs that just left this building could stop traffic. Yours might stop a convoy across the Sahara, but only because they've run out of gas."

"Funny. You know if this gig doesn't work out, you could do stand-up." Dean didn't bother letting McCall lead them into the office. He strode right on in and for half a second thought about sitting behind the desk. He settled for standing near the six-foot totem pole that had been a token of appreciation from the province of Victoria, British Columbia, some years ago. Dean had left everything of value—and sentiment—in his old office.

McCall filled the high leatherback chair at his desk and narrowed his eyes at Dean. The two had known each other a long time, and McCall liked to think that because he was older, he was wiser. "You *know* her. And you've never liked anyone interfering in your business."

"I got you this job, didn't I?"

"No. You *recommended* me for this job. I got it on my own." McCall kept his unsettling gaze on Dean. "And I see regret written all over your face."

Dean put a hand on the totem pole and concentrated on the grooves as he circled the piece.

"That's why you're here, isn't it?" McCall added. "To get back in."

Yes and no. Dean's company was thriving. He didn't regret going out on his own. But he did wish his dad hadn't taken his decision so hard. Now the chance to work with the leading international preservation organization *and* to mend fences with his father was an opportunity he'd sacrifice everything to achieve.

"I'm here to get a contract that will help my company as well as my father's. I want a partnership. Nothing more."

"And if you don't succeed?" McCall lifted his eyebrows.

"I'll succeed."

"I don't know about that. From what I just heard, your competition is going to be damn hard to beat. Plus, she's a lot easier on the eyes."

Samantha. Dean hated McCall's interest in her and headed for the office door before he said something he *would* regret. Hell if she hadn't capsized his even keel when it came to his temper. His body thrummed with tension, but while he wanted to lash out at McCall, he wanted to do something entirely different to Samantha.

"Guess I'd better go seal the deal, then. You coming?"

McCall shook his head. "Can't. I've got a conference call this morning. I think your dad wanted to meet with you himself. He'll fill me in later."

"Okay." Dean closed the door behind him and took a deep breath. He knew better than anyone what a hard-bitten man his father was. They'd tiptoed around each other for months, and now it was time to prove himself valuable once again. With the Route 66 deal his, he'd work side-by-side with his dad and take steps to eliminate the strain between them.

He strode into his dad's office without reservation. "Hey, Dad. You ready for me?"

"Sure. Have a seat." He put aside the report in his hands. Dean took the chair across from the desk and decided to spare any small talk. "Thanks again for giving me the opportunity to get the 66 deal. I know our joint efforts will revitalize the Route like no other two companies can."

"I see you're cocky as ever, but Global Site's been around a long time, son."

"Exactly. That's why you need me. My staff is young, energetic. We're looking at preservation in new ways. The climate is changing, and I mean that philosophically as well as environmentally. We're working on and applying cutting edge ways to preserve monuments with sustainable resources." Dean tried not to bounce in his seat, but talking about this got him fired up. "I've got interns with innovative course concentrations in architecture, project planning, advocacy, and fieldwork. The ideas they're flinging at me are phenomenal."

A small smile spread across his father's face. "I never doubted you'd lead us into a future that keeps tradition but sets new standards."

The compliment—the first in a long time—reminded Dean that when his dad wanted to, he could motivate anyone. Employees worldwide looked to him for guidance and respected his vast knowledge.

"I learned from the best," Dean said.

"That you did." He leaned forward onto his desk. "Now tell me the specifics."

"The PowerPoint's in your inbox. Want to pull it up?"

"I'll read it over the weekend."

A moment of disappointment hit Dean. He'd hoped for a quick answer. A "you're hired" before they'd finished speaking. But that wasn't realistic. Samantha had probably supplied a written presentation and it was only fair his dad give equal attention to both.

"We want to kick off in Texas with teams heading east and west simultaneously. With additional cooperation from the Route 66 associations in Arizona and Missouri, specialized teams will hit every National Register site, building, structure, object, and district."

"You see fanning out as the best way to approach it?"

"Absolutely. By commissioning crews to work concurrently, we'll draw more attention to our efforts. In addition, the scope of work will benefit from communication between teams on what's working and what might not be."

"You're talking about a lot of manpower."

"I've got advanced apprentices and graduate students chomping at the bit to work with experienced and skilled preservationists to restore sites. Taking the Route off the Watch List *is* going to take time. Especially when you consider we can't neglect other cultural heritage sites around the world. But this project will garner us national attention the likes of which no other preservation effort in this country has seen. The shit load of time we dedicate to it will pay off in spades for both local and state economies *and* bring huge consideration to our industry."

"It's the oddest thing," his dad said, the lines around his eyes deepening and the corners of his mouth lifting ever so slightly. "Hearing some of my words come back at me."

Dean smiled. "It might not have seemed like it at the time, but I was listening. There's no way I could have started my own company without taking with me everything I learned from you."

"What else?"

"I've got two phenomenal restoration ecologists

working for me. Have you heard of them?" Recos were the up and comers in the preservation movement, and Dean didn't think World Heritage had any employed. Yet.

"I've met a few but haven't had a reason to hire one."

"They'll reverse any damage to the ecology in the areas we focus on and repair and replant where necessary. The Route is more than just a road, and we want to paint with broad strokes." Dean leaned back to let those last words sink in. "Paint with broad strokes" was a phrase his mom used all the time. She'd say it when she wanted to remind someone—namely Dean or his dad—that it's important to look beyond what's right in front of you.

"Not a bad idea." Light danced in his father's eyes, and Dean wondered if it were his pitch or the way sunlight slanted through the office window.

His dad always got excited at the start of a new project. Every beginning added years to his life because the older man felt personally responsible for protecting the sites his company helped.

"We also propose limited relief to the Salton Sea. We think lending assistance to the abandoned, salt-encrusted structures along the shoreline is worthwhile. Some buildings aren't historic, but it's worth a look."

"You've always had a soft spot for water."

Dean tried to hide just how true that was as a vivid picture of Crater Lake flashed in his mind. Samantha's arms were around his neck, his hands on her lower back, nothing between their hips but clothing Dean had silently cursed. They'd stood in a secluded spot along the lake's rim early one morning, and the emotion he saw in Samantha's eyes that day had been far deeper than the breathtaking blue water of the lake. He'd never seen it in another girl's eyes before, and he guessed it was love. The racing of his own heart confirmed he'd felt the same way. But they never said the words.

"Yeah, I guess I have."

"And now that you're in California, there's no shortage."

"You should come with Mom the next time she visits." Dean meant it. His mom had visited several times over the past year, but his dad had always claimed prior commitments. Dean and his mom didn't discuss it because they both knew he stayed behind to make Dean feel guilty. Still, Dean desperately wanted to show his father his new life.

His dad undid the top button of his polo shirt. "That's the first time you've asked."

Dean's gut clenched. "I figure you should see the company you'll be partnering with." *Screw you, Dad.* If his father wanted an invitation, then he'd get one in the form of a business proposition.

"Being a cocky sonofabitch isn't scoring you any extra points."

"It's called confidence, and I'm confident my company is the best one to support the core programs you value most here at World Heritage while setting newer standards that will catapult us beyond recognized methods. I know how you work, Dad, and I can take my people and contacts and seamlessly integrate with yours."

"You're not using nepotism to get the job, are you, son?" He raised a wrinkled hand to his chin. The thin gold wedding band—which his father had gotten repaired several times because he refused to take it off while working in the field— gleamed as if it had recently been polished.

Since when did being William Malloy's son score him an advantage? "Just stating the facts. Whether you like it or not, I know this company as well as my own. I'm sure Samantha Bennett gave an excellent presentation, but Global Site can't compete with what I can offer you."

Something flashed in his dad's eyes, but Dean hadn't a clue what it was. He pushed aside the heart-sinking thought that in his dad's mind, Samantha had sealed the deal for her company. "I think they can. Sam Bennett's got passion for this project in spades."

No doubt. Dean remembered her passion like it was yesterday. She'd turned him inside out with her enthusiasm for their travels and their lovemaking. And despite the reason for their paths crossing, damn if he didn't crave to touch her again. "Are you telling me you've already made a decision?"

"No, I haven't. Despite our past year, I plan to carefully consider both presentations and have an answer Monday morning. There's no room for hard feelings in business. I'll make the best decision for WHF and Route 66. Period."

"Sounds fair." Dean edged toward the end of his chair. "The PowerPoint includes every gas station, motel, café, trading post, and drive-in theater threatened by urban development or abandonment and decay in the more rural areas. I'll have my phone on, so call me if you have any questions over the weekend."

"Will do."

Dean stood. "We're meeting Henry at one. He's made a reservation at Café Vermecci."

"Some things never change, huh?" His dad pushed his chair back and met Dean eye to eye. His shoulders relaxed and Dean was reminded of how effortlessly his dad slipped into different modes of operation.

But more than that, his dad's words stirred up a bothersome revelation: Dean hadn't gotten Samantha out of his system. Not by a long shot.

"Yeah. Pain in the ass that can be." Dean turned. "Leave at twelve forty-five?" he said over his shoulder.

"Sounds good."

Dean followed the hallway to a small office available to business associates when they were in town. The chair behind the desk squeaked as he landed with a *thud*. He lifted his hands and laced his fingers behind his head while he leaned back.

After a moment, his body sagged with heaviness, as if sludge ran through his veins. He refused to believe Samantha meant anything more to him than a quick slip between the sheets. It had to be his libido protesting lack of action lately. Nothing more than lust jumpstarted by a pretty face. But he knew that wasn't true. *Pretty* didn't begin to describe her charm and how without even trying, she'd commandeered every thought in the back of his mind. And not just today.

Dammit. Giving in to his selfish need for her would be the stupidest thing he could do. But resisting her would be worse.

Maybe she wouldn't call. Maybe his ego had read more into her reaction than was there. He hoped not. Because he knew his response to her had been anything but subtle.

The buzz of his cell jolted him from his deliberations. He pulled it from his pocket and checked the screen. Not Samantha.

"Thayer. What's up?" Dean said to his VP, his voice

rougher than usual.

"You tell me. Thought you'd call in by now. Everything okay?"

Shit. Nothing about his morning had gone as planned. "Fine. Just finished up my meeting. We'll know Monday morning."

"Gut?" Thayer asked, squeezing hopefulness into the tiny word.

"Not sure. Global Site left a pretty big impression."

"I doubt it was as big as yours."

Dean heard the wisecrack in his friend's voice. Yeah, Dean had definitely delivered a personal as well as professional impact. "Listen, I'm a little preoccupied at the moment. I'll call you back this afternoon."

"It's the hot environmentalist from Global Site, isn't it?"

His lips spread into a weak smile. Thayer's sixth sense had pegged it. The guy had been telling Dean to get laid for weeks. "It's not what you think."

"It rarely is. But my hunches are pretty accurate. Whatever you do, Dean, don't screw up the contract."

"Hanging up now." He tossed the phone on the desk, his body tensing much as it had with McCall. Thayer only meant to remind him of his priorities, but at the moment, a sexy-as-hell woman who now shared his devotion for the environment took the top spot on his priority list.

Idiot flashed in his mind in neon green lettering. No matter how bad an idea it was, he realized that if he let the weekend go by without pursuing Samantha, he'd regret it forever.

Chapter Five

"I'll have a fuzzy naval," Samantha said, looking past the waitress to see Dean arriving. *Please make it a strong one.*

"Hey, I'll take whatever you've got on tap," Dean added quickly and slightly out of breath. He took the seat across from her in the crowded bar.

The waitress smiled brightly at him and nodded before rushing off.

"Sorry I'm late. It took longer to get out of the office than I thought it would." Settled in his chair, he looked around then pierced her with a look that made her entire body tingle. He stared into her eyes for several long seconds. "You look beautiful."

Samantha gazed at the sexy man whom she'd spent the entire day contemplating. Just looking at him made everything inside her melt. She'd had every intention of canceling their date for a drink when she'd called him, but upon hearing the desire and good humor in his voice, she'd caved.

"Thank you." She'd changed into jeans and a white V-neck T-shirt, and she'd let her shoulder-length hair down.

"And can you repeat that?"

"Thank you?"

"No. Fuzzy naval. I like the way your cheeks flush when you say it." The grin on his face and the sparkle in his eyes told Samantha she wasn't the only one enchanted.

That only made her feel worse. If she let Dean get the upper hand, she'd lose what little confidence she'd managed to muster on her way to meet him. Throw her into a room with top executives from around the world and she could fend for herself. Throw Dean Malloy at her and he zapped her of every coherent thought.

"Sh-shut up," she sputtered.

"Oh, I see it works with those words, too."

"Still a big tease." She eyed him suspiciously, wondering if he flirted with all the girls he met, but secretly pleased they'd immediately fallen into an easy banter. Their competition for the Route 66 account obviously wasn't on the table this evening. And now that she sat here with him, away from anything work related, she stupidly figured she should make the most of it.

After all, she'd wondered for years what it would be like to see him again.

"Only with the people I like. And I didn't tease you that much, did I?"

"No, not really. If I remember correctly, I think I rather enjoyed it. Considering my family has zero sense of humor, your fun-loving outlook on life was a refreshing change of pace."

"I remember lots of things we enjoyed." He studied her face as if wondering whether she was thinking the same thing.

She was. "Me, too." She pulled her eyes from his and looked around the bar. The happy-hour crowd laughed and flirted, the sound of enthusiastic voices making its way to her ears. Something sizzling passed by—fajitas?—and her stomach growled.

He leaned forward with his arms on the table. "Seeing you again, it feels like just yesterday we were hiking mountains and navigating rivers. That was a great summer, wasn't it?"

"The best. And I haven't had one like it since. Once I got back to reality there wasn't any more fun and games. But I'm sure you've had plenty of adventures." She scooted her chair a little closer to the table, propped her elbows up, and placed her chin on top of clasped hands.

"I imagine you've seen and done more things these past five years than I could ever dream of." She had little doubt that Dean had continued to live life on the edge. He wasn't afraid of anything. He'd leap when others wouldn't. That mentality had rubbed off on her and propelled her to try new things over the years. She wondered if she should thank him for that.

"Oh, I don't know. Why don't you share a dream or two with me?"

"You first. Tell me what it's been like preserving some of the world's most iconic sites and garnering World Heritage Fund—and now your own company—an amazing record of success."

"Wow. Do you always cut right to the chase now, or are

you just happy to see me?"

"Both." She punctuated her answer with a look she hoped was more Marilyn Monroe than girl next door, because as much as her mind shouted, *Get away from him! He hurt you!* her heart pumped with more life than it had in years.

"Glad to hear it. Because I'm very excited to see you, too." His incredibly bright blue eyes stayed on hers with such intensity that they held her captive.

The exchange took her back to the first night they'd made love in his tent. He'd looked at her like she was something to be cherished and compared her to glacier lilies bursting through the snow banks in spring. "They spread warmth and sunshine," he'd said. His gaze — and the line — had worked.

The connection broke when their drinks arrived.

Like a scene out of a late-night comedy, as the waitress put down Dean's beer, Samantha somehow managed to knock it over with her arm, causing the frothy liquid to spill toward him. Dean pushed back his chair, jumped out of the way in the nick of time, and laughed all the while.

"I see some things haven't changed," he teased.

"Oh, I'm so sorry! I can't believe what a klutz I am. Is it all over you?" She stood to help in some way, but a busboy rushed over with towels to wipe up the mess.

Samantha plopped back down in her chair, embarrassment gripping her in a chokehold. Why was it that whenever she felt nervous, she seemed to grow another appendage that went out of control?

"Bet you haven't missed that," she said.

"Actually, it makes me want to do a little investigating of my own, find out what else about you hasn't changed." He resumed his place at the table before asking the waitress to bring him another drink. "I never shy away from a challenge, you know that. And you, Samantha, make every moment anything but dull."

He could make a wilted flower bloom, she decided. The combination of his smooth tone and generous words quickly lifted her from her fluster. "Thanks. What better way to re-connect, huh?"

"I could think of a better way."

Holy crap. Even a Dodo bird would know that was a come-on. Samantha quivered as Dean's eyes grew dark. And his stupid sexy smirk had her ready to drop everything. He still made her feel good in all the right places, but *holy crap*, how could she even think about getting horizontal with him again? What was wrong with her?

For the past three months she'd worked her ass off at a job she wanted to keep long-term. Nothing mattered more to her than turning her freelance career into a permanent position with Global Site. She needed the money. She needed to prove to her father she could succeed on her own.

"I'm sure you can. But I'm not interested." She'd never been a good liar and hoped he didn't detect the gut-wrench-ing pain it took to speak those words.

A brief grimace passed over his face before he shrugged. "So tell me about your new career choice. I know our in-dustry will greatly benefit from someone like you. Have you been out in the field?"

So they *were* going to talk about work. Her stomach tightened.

"I have. I love visiting individual sites and assisting local teams. I learned from you how great the outdoors is, and how much there is to appreciate in the architectural gems that many people take for granted or don't even notice beyond a quick glance."

With leisure, the corners of his mouth lifted in an entirely too endearing manner. His smile could melt coal. "I'm happy to hear I left such an impression on you."

"Yeah, well, don't let it go to your head." Samantha grinned in return. Despite the heartache he'd left her with, Dean was the reason she'd decided to pursue something with deeper meaning, something that could make a difference in the world. Even though it meant defying her father. Even though when she'd told him of her intentions, he'd belittled her, yelled at her, told her if she walked out, she wasn't welcome back.

Dean leaned against his chair. "I always knew you had a mind for seeing the great beauty in our earth. You proved it to me over and over again during our jaunts that summer. I loved the way your eyes lit up when you saw something for the first time. Like you never wanted to forget it."

"That summer held a lot of firsts for me." *First time roughing it in a tent, first time going without a shower for days, first time in love.* Samantha stared at Dean, and without her permission, the same feelings she'd had all those years ago came flooding back.

"So, no more daring adventures? No more hands-on experience for the fun of it?" he asked.

"No, not really. Since that summer I haven't had much time for a social life. Nothing to speak of, anyway."

He looked pleased by her admission but stayed quiet.

"Tell me about you," she said. "How is it having your own company?"

"It's great. I've done a lot of traveling, met the most incredible people, learned there's still a hell of a lot to be accomplished. My dad wasn't all that happy about my leaving, but he taught me a ton, and I'll always be grateful to him for giving me the opportunities I've had."

"Are you getting along better with him now?"

"Not exactly. But I'm trying to mend things. Without his guidance, I wouldn't be in the position I'm in today. Of course I don't have much time for a social life either." He paused to catch his breath. "So, what about your dad? I seem to remember you telling me he ruled with an iron fist. How'd he take your defecting?"

A lump lodged in her throat at Dean's question. Chills settled on every inch of her skin. "He's cut me out of his life and is certain I'll fail."

"Sam, I'm sorry." Dean's hand reached out to hers and held it protectively atop the table.

The gesture calmed her like nothing else could. She'd felt so safe and secure with Dean during their summer together. Felt appreciated for the first time in her life. He'd protected her fiercely—from the weather, from treacherous terrain, even from a bear. But most of all, from her own fears. He'd given her more that summer than she thought she'd deserved.

"It's okay. I'm fine. I'm happy with my decision, and that's all that matters." She blinked a few extra times to push back the tears forming. "So, is Monument and Heritage Recovery strictly focused on historical preservation?"

He squeezed her hand before releasing it. "No. We plan to venture into urban planning and include newer sites that have become dilapidated due to conflict or Mother Nature."

"Well, from what I've read, you're off to a stellar start." Dammit. She hadn't meant to remind him she'd been aware of his success.

"It's hard work, but I love it." He took a long sip of his drink, never taking his attention off her.

Samantha loved it, too. Which meant it was time to finish her drink and be on her way. If she risked spending any more time with Dean, come Monday morning she might regret winning the Route 66 contract. Because she *would* win it. The consequences of losing—both personally and professionally—were too devastating to think about.

You'll fall flat on your face. Make no name for yourself. You're nothing without me. The last words her father had spoken to her still stung. A shiver rolled through her, and she again fought back the moisture threatening to fill her eyes. She'd make it on her own, prove to herself she didn't need her dad's help to succeed. And prove to him his expectations were dead wrong.

"You okay?" Dean's concerned voice freed her from the painful thoughts she couldn't let go of.

But it also reminded Sam that she didn't completely trust the man sitting across from her. He might look and sound sincere, and she hated the thought that this meeting might be professional and not personal, but maybe he'd only invited her out because he wanted to soften her up so she'd spill Global Site information.

"Fine, just tired. I think I should head back to my hotel now."

Dean lifted his glass, drank down the ale in two large gulps, then wiped his top lip with a brush from his hand. "I'll walk you."

"That's not necessary. It was great seeing you again. Good luck with everything." Despite her parting words, she stayed glued to her seat.

A moment of charged silence passed between them. Was she really going to walk away from him, just like that?

She hated him for leaving her all those summers ago without a second thought. Hated that he hadn't called to say hello or asked to keep in touch. He'd simply hopped on an airplane never to be heard from again. He'd left her ruined. Her heart in shambles.

Contemplation crossed his face. His eyes held hers with something that resembled regret. "Look, Sam. I don't want to say good-bye. Not yet. I was wondering—"

"Dean, buddy! How's it going?" A casually dressed guy with handsome features approached their table, slapping Dean on the back.

Dean looked up, his lips pursing at the interruption before acknowledging the man with a smile. "Hey, Joe, it's good. How about you?"

"I'm great, man." He looked from Dean to Samantha. It looked like curiosity, or perhaps surprise, that crossed his face before the corners of his mouth rose to meet his big round eyes. "Sorry to interrupt, but some of us are having a drink and thought you might like to join us."

"Well, uh…"

"Come on, dude, we haven't seen you in what, six months?"

"It's okay with me," Samantha said, not wanting to keep him from his friends. She'd politely excuse herself before he could get out whatever it was he'd been ready to say.

"Maybe just for a few minutes." His eyebrows lifted, and

he looked at Sam expectantly.

"Great. Joe Kincaid." He thrust out his palm toward Samantha.

"Samantha Bennett," she said, shaking his hand.

When Joe released her, Dean rose from his seat and picked up her hand without giving her a chance to argue. As they stepped away from the table, he waggled his eyebrows in a display of flirtatious affection and total disregard for her wish to leave.

She thought about speaking up, but only for a split second, because much to her chagrin, she relished the feel of his fingers intertwined with hers. The contact sent a zing of pleasure ricocheting around her insides. The gesture was intimate and comfortable, like they'd held hands thousands of times before.

Samantha liked it. She liked it a lot.

Dean led her to the other side of the bar where a group of young men and women was busy talking, drinking and… kissing.

"No social life, huh?" she asked, eyeing the couple making out.

He looked back at her with a little-boy grin that shouted mischief-maker. "Really nothing to speak of. That's just a kissing game that Joe and his friends like to play."

Her own words coming back at her made her chuckle. "Kissing—"

"Hey Deany boy!" Shouts from a couple of the guys rang out as he and Samantha joined the group. The delighted looks on the women's faces didn't go unnoticed by Samantha, but she also observed disappointment when they saw his hand clasped around hers.

"Hey everyone, this is Samantha."

The small crowd smiled and greeted her with hellos and waves. There was only one vacant seat left, so Dean sat and pulled Sam down onto his lap.

This was so not the position she should be in. But all eyes had swung to them, and she would not falter in front of strangers. Not completely sure what to do to keep her balance, she put her arm around Dean's neck.

Being so close to him, touching him, sent a rush of warmth through her.

Crap, she was in trouble.

Dean wrapped one arm around her waist while the other fell across her thighs. They looked at each other, their faces only inches apart. If Samantha had to guess, she'd say the grin he wore meant he was pretty happy with their position.

"Two minutes, fifteen seconds," someone shouted, drawing Samantha's attention away from Dean.

The group shifted their eyes to the couple who had just finished kissing. They were each guzzling a glass of water while cheers and jeers passed among the witnesses. When they finished drinking, sly smiles spread across their faces.

"Not the best time, not the worst," Joe's booming voice acknowledged as he stood and looked around. "Who's game to try next?"

Samantha leaned her head to Dean's ear and whispered, "Try what?"

"How about Dean and Samantha?" someone shouted, followed quickly by more votes for the pair.

"What do you say, Dean?" Joe looked at them with raised eyebrows. "Up for a little hot-sauce challenge?"

"I'm game if she is." Dean regarded Samantha's quizzical

expression then added, "Hot sauce is a kissing game where we each get hot sauce on our tongues, then make out to see how long we can last."

Samantha gulped and looked at his lips. They were sinfully appealing, but she had no intention of connecting with them again. "No, thanks."

"Aww, come on!" someone from the crowd shouted.

"You chicken?" Dean asked.

"What? No. I just see no reason to kiss you if I don't have to."

"I'll do it!" a female voice shouted.

Samantha tried to stand, but Dean held tightly to her waist. "I'm not doing this with anyone but you."

She relaxed against him. He always knew exactly what to say. This time, though, so did she. "Sorry, Dean. I've got to go."

He cupped her cheek and looked deep into her eyes. "One kiss, Sam. I dare you."

Damn him. If she didn't agree, he'd think he won something here, and she couldn't let that happen. She couldn't let him beat her over a silly kiss. Especially if he thought his kiss would distract her from the reason she was in town.

"Fine. I'm game."

Whistles and sighs echoed around their corner of the bar while Joe grabbed two bottles of hot sauce off the table. "The rules are"—he looked at Sam as he spoke—"time starts when I say go. Your lips must stay in contact. Tongue is optional. As soon as you part, time stops. Ready?"

With eyes stuck on each other, they nodded. Joe stood over them with a bottle of sauce in each hand and they simultaneously tilted their heads back to receive several drops on their tongues.

"Go!"

The second Dean's lips touched hers, she immediately forgot about the hot sauce. Not that it bothered her to begin with. She loved spicy food, but the burning sensation on her tongue held no comparison to the burn sweeping through her body as his lips pressed against hers.

The kiss started off slow, a gentle connection that reminded her of the first time he'd taken her mouth to his. Just as they'd paused to catch their breath while hiking up Yosemite Falls Trail, he'd gingerly leaned in for a taste. Something about the way the perspiration glistened on her lips, he'd told her, had drawn him in.

This time they weren't alone, but as Dean's mouth rubbed against hers, she lost all sense of time and place. His lips tasted sweeter than sugar. His touch awakened an eagerness she never wanted to give up.

She opened her eyes to take a peek at him and found his electric baby blues on hers. She blinked, hoping to communicate how much she was enjoying this, and felt the corners of his mouth lift.

The hand Dean had around her waist smoothed its way up her back, stroking her spine. It came to a rest at her neck, his fingers playing with her hair before they inched up to cup the back of her head. She closed her eyes as Dean brought her face tighter to his and parted her lips.

The thrust of his tongue in her mouth made her breasts tingle and a feel-good vibration settle in the pit of her stomach. He stroked the inside of her mouth, the combination of his taste and the hot sauce setting off pulses of pleasure from her head to her feet.

Dean continued to dictate the tempo of the kiss, pulling his tongue back so their lips could close for a quick breath before opening wide again and kissing her like he couldn't get enough.

Music Sam hadn't noticed before touched her ears. The soulful sound with a steady bass line influenced their rhythm. The swirl of their tongues, the tilt of their heads, the lean of her body into his, followed the soothing hum of the music and washed over her. Everything else around her faded—the voices, the bodies, the clinking of glasses, the smell of fried food—the only thing in the room was the two of them. So much for thinking Dean meant nothing.

Never letting up on the sweet pressure of the kiss, Samantha steadied her hands on Dean's shoulders while she lifted her body from his lap. His eyes flew open, but she could see the confident, trusting stare he imparted.

That, and a good dose of lust.

His hands skimmed down her sides to her waist as she turned her body to face him. A moment later his hands were splayed around her bottom as she widened her stance and sat back down on his lap, now in a straddle position.

She relaxed her hands, let her arms fall around his neck. She shimmied in close, eliminating any space between their hips and torsos. The bar music that created a synchronized trance wafted back to her ears, and now with their bodies tight against each other she could feel their heartbeats in harmonious union.

As if he could feel it, too, Dean sucked harder. The gentle roll of his tongue disappeared. A whimper escaped her lips, a groan his. Her heart rate sped faster as their mouths entertained each other's with a deeper connection.

His body felt so good that she didn't care if she ever came up for air. She wanted this kiss to last forever. She knew after this weekend she'd never see him again and wanted to linger on his mouth for as long as possible, hoping he'd remember her taste as much as she'd remember his.

Oh God, how she wanted more, though. She wanted to nibble and feast on much more than his mouth. And she wanted him to devour her. A craving to have his naked body atop her, under her, moving inside her, intensified, and it sent potent heat waves down her spine. If she could lock them in a time warp right now, she would, forever losing herself to his hold.

Because this wasn't a kiss between strangers.

This was a kiss between long-lost lovers becoming intimately familiar with each other again, desiring not only the physical contact but also something *real*. Samantha's mind became a blur of happiness. Her brain registered a surge of rapture. She couldn't have moved her body away from his if her life depended on it.

Forget being turned on. This man, this kiss, encompassed everything she ever wanted. The exquisite touch sent her mental faculties colliding with her sexual desires. She thrust her tongue deeper, pressed her mouth firmer, tried to extinguish any space between them. She kissed him with her entire heart and soul.

Somewhere in the back of her mind she heard, "Four minutes, fifteen seconds."

They both shifted, as if they'd held their breath underwater and needed to finally come up for air. Knowing they'd significantly beaten the last couple's time, they broke the intense suction and the buzz holding her body hostage faded.

Then with eyes heavy on each other, they parted lips.

She heard the hoots and hollers around them, but she paid no attention. Dean's glazed eyes never left hers. Somehow, he mustered the strength to say, "Spend the weekend with me."

And she whispered back, "Okay."

Chapter Six

The lobby of Samantha's hotel bustled with activity. Dean planted himself beside a large ficus tree that afforded a view of every direction. He didn't want to miss her approach. Didn't want to miss a second of her.

He'd spent the night replaying their kiss in his mind. What little sleep he'd managed to get had led to dreams of Sam in various stages of undress. He couldn't stop thinking about her. She'd saturated every cell of his body.

And right about now that made him the world's biggest fool.

A root canal sounded less painful than spending more time with the woman who had starred in his every fantasy, been the source of his fondest memories, and invoked his current state of mental and physical arousal.

So why torture himself?

Because he couldn't help it.

Because he couldn't *not* be with her one more time.

After their mind-blowing kiss last night, she'd tried to practically bolt from the bar. But after he'd insisted on seeing her to her hotel, she'd relaxed and again agreed to spend the weekend with him. Her well-kissed lips had pressed gently to his cheek in good night, and he'd known he wasn't the only one affected.

Still, he was an idiot. Or, more accurately, a selfish bastard idiot. He'd left her once and he knew he'd have to leave her again. But he didn't want to regret not spending every possible moment with her that he could. Maybe after this time around, he'd get her out of his system.

Today he'd lined up just the thing to spark another memorable adventure.

Trying to calm his overeager nerves, he pulled his arms behind his back for a stretch. Every muscle in his body was tense, on alert, ready to sweep Samantha off her feet for a day she'd never forget.

When his phone vibrated in his pocket, he prayed it wasn't her canceling. He tugged it out and breathed a sigh of relief.

"Hey, Mom."

"Hey yourself. Guess where I am?" Her youthful voice always made him forget that she was twenty-five years older than he was.

"Mountain biking?" His mom rode every weekend.

"No. I'm sitting in Elmer's trying to decide between the French toast and Belgian waffle and wondering where the hell my son is."

Shit. "Damn. I forgot."

"So I guess that means you're not on your way?"

"You guess right. Sorry, Mom. I'll make it up to you at

dinner tomorrow night." He rubbed two fingers across his forehead.

"Really?" she said, a mixture of surprise and shock in her voice. "You must be up to something pretty important this morning to surrender to playing a game of Scrabble with *me*. That is what you're implying, is it not?"

Dean chuckled. "It's not *that* bad."

"Says the boy who told me he'd never play with me again."

"Consider it part of your birthday present." Dean glanced at the time on his phone. His mother might not be the only one stood up this morning.

"Deal. Have time to tell me what you're doing today?"

Dean's vision tracked a young couple with a toddler in a stroller, the young boy giggling at something his mother had said. After they turned a corner Dean swept back across the lobby to find Samantha, eyes focused on him, making her way over.

"I don't. I'll see you tomorrow. 'Bye." He might've pressed end before getting the 'bye out.

"Good morning," she said cheerily.

Good didn't begin to describe it. She wore a pair of knee-length beige pants and a red tank top over a white one, brand-spanking-new Nike tennis shoes, and a loose ponytail that carried her blond waves away from her face. Damn, she did more than send good vibrations through him.

"Morning," he managed to get out.

They gazed at each other like they couldn't believe they were together again.

"I hope you haven't been waiting long. I had a hard time waking up this morning. Lots of tossing and turning last night."

Dean wondered if her lack of sleep had anything to do with him. He reached out and put his arm around her waist, bringing her in close. Her feminine frame fell into his body and their mouths connected for a proper greeting. Temporarily satisfied, Dean let go long enough to grab her hand and pull her toward the exit.

"Let's get out of here. I've got something special planned for you."

"You do? What is it?"

"You'll see. We've got about an hour's drive. I'll fill you in along the way. But trust me, it's beyond your wildest dreams."

"Why, Dean Malloy, are you whisking me away on another adventure?" Her voice chimed with an excitement Dean recognized from their summer together, and his own anticipation shot up a notch.

As they reached his car, parked outside the lobby doors, he tossed a sideways glance at her, not worrying about the look of adoration he knew showed on his face. "You'll be over the moon about this one."

He'd wanted to do this for a while. Lucky for him, after a call last night to his pilot buddy, all systems were a go for today. Looking over at Samantha, sitting so picture perfect in his passenger seat, his stomach flip-flopped.

"We're going zero-g this afternoon," he said once they'd hit the highway that led far from town and toward the airport.

"Zero-g?" Samantha shifted in her seat and regarded him with interested eyes, like she had x-ray vision.

"Zero gravity. We'll experience what it feels like to be

weightless. It's you and me, babe, floating around like a pair of astronauts. And I for one am hoping to accomplish what no man has done before."

"What's that?" she asked.

"Getting frisky while floating." He pegged her with his most charming smile, raised eyebrows and all, hoping she wouldn't be opposed to his plans for more touching.

She broke eye contact to look out the windshield for a few moments before turning her head back to him, the naive expression on her face replaced by a look he couldn't read. He wondered if her reaction stemmed from the zero-g comment or the frisky comment.

"Is this simulation on the ground or up in a plane?" she asked, her tone giving him little hint to her disposition.

"Our weightless flight is on a seven-twenty-seven aircraft." He leaned over, lowered his voice. "It's too bad I think we have to wear jumpsuits."

He conjured up a vision of Samantha floating to him in nothing but a sheer black teddy, the material swaying around her body giving him glimpses here and there of her curves, and the flurry in his stomach moved south, causing his jeans to tighten. Damn.

I wonder if I can get a hard-on when weightless?

She smiled, and when she spoke a lighter tone fell from her luscious lips, like maybe she was on board with this adventure now. "You betcha."

"What?" he choked out. She hadn't just read his mind, had she?

"The jumpsuits. We have to wear them. I remember now, seeing a segment on *Good Morning America* or something, where they did this and everyone on board wore these thick gray jumpsuits."

"Maybe they have a suit built for two?"

"Mmm. You wish."

As if hearing the "mmm" come out of her sexy voice wasn't enough to send his cock directly to a ninety-degree angle, she included a smile that amped up the sexual desires surging through his body. Fun was a great aphrodisiac for him, and today was already more amusing than he'd antici-pated. By the time they got back to her hotel room tonight, he planned to take her every which way and remind her of just how potent her feminine wiles could be.

"I'm wishing for a lot of things," he replied.

She let out a breath. "You know, you've done it again."

"What?"

"You have this amazing way of making me feel like I'm freefalling even when my feet are on the ground. It's the same way I felt the first time you took me hang gliding or river rafting. For the past few years, I've missed that." She shifted her body so she faced him, one leg under her bottom. "Thanks for being the one to show me what it's like to lose my inhibitions and really feel alive."

"It's easy with someone like you." He lifted his arm and ran the back of his hand along her cheek. She was so soft, so lovely. When her head tilted to press against his skin he felt her reservations about him slip away. "You've got an adventurer's spirit hiding inside that beautiful body."

"You bring it out in me."

Her words reminded him of her willingness to do what-ever he'd suggested during their summer together. He re-membered how she'd trusted him completely with her safety and well being. She'd never doubted his strength or abilities;

she'd always looked at him with admiration and awe. Samantha gifted him with the utmost confidence, and he'd never forgotten that feeling. On days when work nearly got the best of him, his recollection of her faith in him restored his faith in himself.

"We should come up with a plan," he said.

"For what?"

"For how to defy the odds of gravity and keep our hands on each other."

She giggled. "What makes you so sure I want your hands on me?"

Dean felt a wide grin flank his face. "Just a hunch."

"Some hunches are good," she purred, straightening her back against the seat with a little shimmy that had his mind and other parts of him standing at attention.

Hell. Things were worse than he'd thought. When did he lose his mind and think time with her was a good idea? Because come forty-eight hours from now, he'd have the Route 66 contract and would be heading back to California, where he now realized a stint in rehab would be required to save himself from the pain of leaving Samantha again.

"Are you planning on getting me drunk up there?" Samantha eyed the bottle in his hand as they exited the car. She hoped he *was* up to something like that. Ever since their hallucinogenic kiss last night, she'd teetered on the edge of wishful thinking, ready to catapult herself into Dean's world and stick there whether he liked it or not. What a fool she was to think spending time together would remedy the hopeless devotion she felt for him.

Maybe getting drunk would help.

"It's only sparkling apple cider. I hear even liquid is weightless during our parabolas, so I thought it might be fun to make a toast and try to catch the floating bubbles on our tongues."

He picked up her hand and walked toward the large plane sitting on the runway. Once again, the contact made her forget her own name. She'd planned to keep things platonic today, but when Dean started flirting, she couldn't help but relax and dish out some of her own playfulness. She knew the risk he posed, knew she was tumbling back into a painful repeat of their last good-bye, but she didn't have the strength to stop herself.

Or the desire, if she were honest with herself. *Foolish girl.*

"What are parabolas?"

"They're the flight maneuvers that allow for weightlessness. It's kind of like a roller coaster. The plane pulls nose up then levels off for a bit, then goes nose down. I think we get to enjoy about fifteen parabolic arcs that each last around thirty seconds. That's when we'll experience zero gravity."

"And how long did you say your friend's been piloting these trips?"

"A while now. You're not nervous, are you?"

"No," she said, shaking her head.

He stopped in his tracks and turned to face her. Then he brought her flush against him and kissed her. Hard. "You've got nothing to worry about with me around."

"I know," she lied. She wanted to believe whatever happened between them was innocent. But what if Dean was simply trying to distract her? Make her forget about the Route 66 contract? After the way he left her five years ago, she'd be a fool to trust him again.

When ninety minutes later they were dressed in the requisite jumpsuits and laying on the padded floor of the wide-open airplane preparing for their first parabola, Samantha forgot about Dean's motivations.

They'd been instructed on what to expect. The position they were in now, on their backs, waiting for the parabola, would be required between each weightless timeframe. As Sam looked around, the emptiness inside the aircraft reminded her of a giant playroom. And she couldn't think of anyone else she'd rather be with. Despite the looming job decision and their personal issues, Dean filled her with more joy than she'd felt since…well, since their last adventure.

"Ten, nine, eight…" their coach (and expert at zero-g) said, ticking off the time until the first arc. He looked about fifty, was built like a tank, and had a kick-ass attitude.

Her stomach fluttered with anticipation. When the countdown got to one, she and Dean were airborne.

"Holy shi…" Samantha floated up, up, and away, weightlessness stealing her body and tossing her around the aircraft as if she were light as a feather. The feeling tickled her from the inside out. Giggles from deep in her gut spilled out of her mouth and she couldn't stop. She was part of the air, had little control over her movements. Just had to go with the flow. Dean hovered across the way on the…ceiling? She had difficulty telling which end was up.

Thirty seconds later, they were back on the padded floor.

"That was incredible! How many more of these do we get?" she asked.

"At least a dozen," the coach replied.

Dean beamed at her, his eyes twinkling brighter than the stars wishes were made on. A jolt of euphoria struck her. She had to feel the floor to be sure she wasn't still floating on air.

"You're amazing, and your excitement is so damn contagious. I can't imagine experiencing this with anyone else."

"Me neither." She'd like to wish upon his gaze—wish for things to be different, wish for something she swore she'd never think about again. Because she knew better than anyone that Dean's commitment lay with the environment, not with any woman.

Today was make-believe. A game of pretend: *Let's pretend we're a couple one more time; have a wild, crazy adventure that we'll never forget, but never tell anyone because there is no "we."*

Sam knew come Monday, everything would change. But lying next to Dean, she did want something. She wanted to push aside the fear of heartache and dance with him one more time.

Several tries and fits of laughter later, they'd only achieved parabolic pantomime, reaching and grasping for each other with swipes of contact to show for it. Though they moved in slow motion, the lack of contact was her fault. She couldn't keep still.

"No more zigging when I zag," he teased, seconds before they lifted off again.

"I thought I was zag and you were zig."

"Yank and spank," the coach said with an authoritative voice, like he'd had some experience navigating the sea of weightless interaction between opposite sexes.

Samantha and Dean exchanged glances and grinned. Without saying another word, they knew what they had to do. As their bodies floated up, Dean hauled Samantha toward him with both hands on her shoulders, sliding them down to her back and landing firmly on her butt until the space between them dwindled. Samantha wrapped her legs tightly around Dean's waist and crossed her ankles. Her arms slid around to his backside. She grabbed hold of his jumpsuit.

It worked. Chest to chest, pelvis to pelvis, they held on to each other until an attempt at lip contact resulted in bumped foreheads and loss of stronghold. They spiraled away from each other, laughing at the botched attempt, Samantha doing a backward somersault and some other acrobatic maneuver deserving of an Olympic gold medal. Weightless kiss or no kiss, though, Samantha was on cloud nine.

An hour later, Dean still couldn't stop smiling. "That was amazing," he said, walking back to his car. "It far outweighed my imagination."

"Mine, too. It's definitely something I'll never forget." Samantha walked with a spring in her step, like she'd just had the best day ever.

"Me neither." Opening the passenger door, he watched Samantha get comfortable before closing it and stepping around to his side.

He clicked his seatbelt into place and sat for a moment, committing everything to memory before fumbling to put the key in the ignition. "I'm sorry," he said.

"For what?"

"For hopping on a plane five years ago without telling you how I felt."

Sam sucked in a breath and turned her head to look out the passenger window. Seconds ticked by. She pressed her hands into her lap.

"I was a jerk. And then I lost your number when I was sailing and dropped my phone into Lake Cascade."

Sam met his gaze, and the skeptical look he saw in her glassy blue eyes hit him straight in the gut. "You were going to call me?" she asked.

He undid his seat belt and turned his body toward her. Could she see how furiously his heart was beating? "Honestly, I don't know. Our lives were going in different directions. But having the choice taken away from me sucked."

Her eyes moved to something over his shoulder.

"So I flew to Chicago. I had a friend at Northwestern who helped me track you down."

She flinched. "But—"

"But when I got there, you were with another guy, so I left." His pride had taken a big hit when he saw her with someone else so soon after they'd been together. Maybe that made him an ass, since he'd thought it was okay to leave her. But he'd changed his mind. He'd missed her. And she'd moved on.

She searched his face, shook her head. "That's impossible."

Was she saying there hadn't been anyone right after him? He pushed that thought aside, because if his eyes had been deceiving him that night...

"I wasn't with anybody during law school."

This completely derailed him. "Tall, black hair, big build,

wearing an old Cubs sweatshirt and had his arm around you in a very intimate way."

Sam pushed him in the arm. "You big idiot! That was my *cousin*. He was a year ahead of me and probably consoling me over a class. Or you. Those first few months are sort of a blur."

Dean rubbed a hand across his jaw. "Me?" Regret flooded him. He'd been too cocky to approach her that night. He'd wanted her to continue thinking she didn't matter to him, when the complete opposite was true. What an idiot he was.

She stared at him like he'd just asked if bears had fur.

"You didn't exactly tell me how you felt either, you know." Dean wondered deep down if she'd loved him. But wasn't that part of the reason he'd fled? He'd never been a coward until that day at the airport. Afraid of the depth to which they'd connected and how that might affect his future.

Rather than argue with him, she said, "I guess we both could have done things differently."

"Yeah."

Silence splintered the confessions between them. There was nothing else to say, really. They couldn't change the past. Dean slipped his seatbelt back on and turned the key in the ignition.

Samantha leaned over and kissed him on the cheek. "Thank you," she whispered. "Today was great."

He appreciated the way she focused on the present and let their misunderstanding from five years ago fall away. "You're welcome."

She leaned back in her seat and put her feet up on the dashboard. "Once again, Mr. Malloy, you've succeeded in expanding my horizons. We'd conquered the earth, and now the skies. What do you have in store for me next?"

Her words and posture were casual, but if he didn't say what was on his mind, he knew he'd regret it. "If it's okay with you, I'd like to see the inside of your hotel room."

Chapter Seven

The elevator door closed, trapping Samantha and Dean alone for the ride up to the fourteenth floor of her hotel. This was no parabola, but the air in the small confines of the space felt so charged, Samantha doubted her feet were touching the floor.

"Room service sounds good to me, too," she said.

"Good, because I'm hungry for much more than food." He pressed her back against the cold metal rail, his body cornering hers. Lifting one arm, he placed his palm on the wall just above the left side of her face. He leaned in close, her thigh now snug in the crux of his legs.

With his devilish smile, he made her pulse quicken. She felt her nipples tighten and tingles radiate out from their peaks. An unwonted flutter settled low in her belly and a craving for more blunted all thoughts of reason. When his warm breath touched her neck, dizziness overcame her.

Was she really about to do this? Despite his apology and

their misunderstanding from five years ago, Sam still wasn't sure she could trust that Dean had no ulterior motives to this seduction.

He steadied her with his other hand, gently cradling her lower back. The feel of his arm around her added to the surrender taking over her body. She let her head fall back, her neck becoming a pliable muscle she couldn't hold upright. With his eyes glued to hers, he came forward and nibbled on her bottom lip.

Ding. The chime of the elevator door stopped any further interaction. Dean pushed away from the wall and led her down the hallway—her walking rather clumsily behind his steadfast strides.

Samantha weighed her options on the short walk to her room. From a purely physical standpoint, she wanted to make love to Dean all night long. But from an emotional standpoint, she wasn't sure she could handle the ramifications.

Would she ever be rid of her attachment to him if she succumbed to what he offered? She didn't think so, but she felt like she couldn't stop herself. The pull to be with him was too great. She wanted Dean no matter his intentions and even if it meant trying to forget him all over again.

"You know we really shouldn't be doing this," she voiced, hoping that if she said the words out loud, some sense would come back to her.

"We shouldn't?" He paused, his relaxed shoulders stiffening.

"I want to…"

"But?"

But what? Should she put her feelings on the line? Confide her desire to have him for much longer than one night? Tell him how she'd never gotten over him? How she loathed and loved him?

God. She still loved him.

She hoped she meant more to him than just a quick hook-up, but he seemed unbothered by the short time they'd have together—and unaffected by the fact that they were after the same lucrative job opportunity. He'd simply asked her to spend a little more time with him.

And that's what she planned to do. If she didn't, she'd regret it. "But nothing. Forget I said anything."

Arriving at her door, Dean reached out his hand to stop her from sliding in the key card. "It's not nothing. If there's something on your mind, please tell me. I care more about you than you could possibly know."

What did that mean? Had he missed her as much as she'd missed him? Had he been heartbroken when he misinterpreted what he saw between her and her cousin? Emotions she had no business second-guessing assaulted her, and for one long beat she wanted to ask him exactly what he meant.

Fear held her back. "It's okay." She smiled, hoping it reached her eyes without revealing her true feelings.

"This has been one hell of a day," he whispered, "and I want to make your night just as memorable."

She had no worries he'd do just that. When she thought back, tried to remember happy times, it wasn't to childhood occasions like birthdays or other family celebrations. It was to her summer with him.

She pressed her lips to his, deciding to stop thinking so hard, then turned to open the door.

They tumbled inside, anxious to put an end to the foreplay that had taken place all day. Dean moved swiftly, his hands circling her waist as the front of his body embraced her backside, connecting them like dancers in perfect sync. His lips tickled the nape of her neck, distracting her from finding the light switch. They shuffled to the bed, where he let go, allowing Samantha to fall to the mattress.

Turning over, she looked up at him and found his hungry eyes darker than she'd ever seen them. This wasn't their first time, but it was new. When they'd first met, he was young, cocky, charming. Now he was more virile, more potent. And she couldn't wait to feel his body deep inside hers.

The setting sun allowed a hint of light to stream in through the uncovered window. The glow cast a halo around Dean's head and she wondered if Cupid had hid somewhere in the room—because she'd just been struck with a sharp point in her backside.

"Ouch!"

Oh, hell. It wasn't Cupid's arrow, but the damn umbrella she'd bought yesterday morning, and which now was lying on the hotel bed. She reached behind her and pulled it out.

"You okay?"

"Just removing the umbrella that decided to introduce itself to my ass."

Dean laughed. "It's never a dull moment with you."

"Yeah, I'm a regular one-woman show." She flung the umbrella to the side and flashed a look of embarrassment before bringing her head down.

He lifted her face and peered at her with lighter, more thoughtful eyes. "You're the most extraordinary woman I've ever met."

His thumb grazed her bottom lip, sending a rush of warmth from her cheeks, to her chest, to the spot between her legs. His stare ripped away any misgivings she had about herself and the situation. Desire, unconditional, passed between them.

"Scoot back a little."

Samantha did as told, sudden impatience building up. If they didn't get naked soon, she'd go crazy. An urgency to feel his heated flesh against hers stirred the sweetest sensation she'd ever felt.

Lifting her leg up, he slid off her shoe and let it drop to the floor. He handled her ankle with delicate pressure, branding it with a light kiss before lowering it. He gave the same attention to the other leg, the shoe dropping with a *thud*. Then, leaning over her, he undid her pants and pulled them down while dropping kisses along her thighs, her knees, her calves. When he reached her feet, he let the clothing fall, looking uninterested in anything but her body.

Damn. He'd decided to devour her slowly, just like he had all those times in their tent, when he'd seduced her so carefully she thought she'd burst.

"While I love the attention you're giving me, I'm not sure I can handle a slow seduction," she said.

"Feeling on edge?"

"Just a little." A moan escaped her lips as he danced his fingertips along the top of her foot while lifting her leg back in the air. He moved slowly down, caressing his way to the back of her knee.

"You've got the sexiest pair of legs."

Samantha arched her back. They weren't even near an X-rated body part, but he still had her raw with anticipation, wondering where he'd touch next.

"Take off your shirt." She needed to see some skin. Now.

"I will if you will."

Obliging, she maneuvered out of her tank top while Dean quickly pulled off his tee. Since her tank top had built-in support, she wasn't wearing a bra and sucked in a breath as she exposed herself to him.

Resting back down, she witnessed his eyes narrow in on hers before they did a slow rake over her body.

"God, you're perfect." His words warmed her, but his bare chest set her on fire.

Hello, Gladiator.

His broad shoulders and smooth chest were more defined than the last time she'd had the privilege of viewing them. The planes of his pecs were deeper, his stomach muscles more pronounced. She'd suspected he was buffer than before, given the way his shirt clung to his body, but seeing it for real far outweighed her imagination. She smiled up at him.

He pushed her back down with a nudge on the shoulder and lifted her leg again. "I'm not going to stop this time."

He resumed with kisses at the inside of her ankle, slowly, meticulously working his way up her limb. The feel of his lips and hands on her sent blissful pulses straight to her sex. The closer he got, the more she quivered.

She took her fingers and traced the outer curves of her breasts, then shifted her shoulders and drew her pointer fingers down her cleavage before returning to the outside slopes. Dean let out a moan at her display and reached for the button and zipper of his pants.

Dropping a kiss on her foot before lowering it to the bed, he removed the last stitch of his clothing, revealing an erection that brought to mind too many naughty positions to name. "Now, I said I wasn't going to stop."

"Okay," she said breathlessly.

His lips hit the inside of her thigh and massaged their way to her heated center. When he brushed his mouth across the satin of her panties, she reached out to cradle the back of his head, twirling her fingers in the soft waves of his hair.

He continued on up, his mouth giving affection to her stomach, hip bones, and rib cage before finally settling on her breasts. His tongue slinked its way out to circle her left nipple before grabbing it with both lips and firmly sucking and toying with it. While he tasted the one, his hand covered the other, his thumb rolling over the engorged nub. Then he switched, repeating the given pleasure.

Everything he did felt so right, she didn't want him to stop. Ever. Images of them making love five years ago flashed in her mind and her anticipation of having him inside her grew impossible to handle. He navigated her body like he knew exactly where to go, but this time he used a more mature, ripened hand.

Dean lifted his head and for a few moments they were lost in each other's intense gazes. He lifted his body up higher so that he was nestled in the satin between her legs. When Samantha reached down to stroke his thick, hard shaft, a moan escaped his lips and he dove in for a little mouth-to-mouth.

While their tongues intertwined, she gently groped him, sliding her hand up and down his length, rolling her thumb over its head until a drop of moisture slipped out. When he deepened the kiss and adjusted his pelvis against her, she lost her concentration. Her hand fell to the mattress.

With their bodies aligned, she finally felt the smooth,

hard planes of his chest on hers and nearly lost her breath. She broke the kiss to catch some air and he grinned at her, always able to have fun in the throes of passion. She couldn't help but smile back, sheer happiness rivaling the ecstasy her body experienced.

She still loved this man.

He didn't linger long, instead tobogganing down her body until he reached her panties. With a flick of his fingers, he had the satin moving down her legs, his body sliding off the bed in the process. Once they were removed, he flung them like a slingshot into the air, where they landed on the arm of the light fixture hanging from the ceiling.

And there was that damn irresistible grin again.

Then, like a panther, he preyed on her. She sucked in her surprise as his palms eased her legs apart, wider, and wider still, so he could access the glistening folds of her sex.

His breath touched her first, and she almost thrust into his chin. The tip of his tongue grazed over her swollen flesh. She spread her legs farther, arched her back enthusiastically, bit down on her bottom lip.

Samantha bucked against his mouth. Endless vibrations wove their way through her body. Her legs shook. She couldn't stifle her moans. Her heart throbbed so forcefully in her chest she thought it might rupture. Holy cow, this was better than she remembered.

"That feels soooo good."

She felt a smile cross his lips while he remained tight against her. Grabbing the back of his head, she ran her fingers through his hair, holding him snugly. The pressure hit just right, and a climax hit her so hard she grabbed the bed sheets to stop from lifting off the mattress.

Dean backed off slowly, lingering for a moment to kiss her thigh. He reached down to his pants, pulled a condom from the pocket, and sheathed himself.

He kissed his way up her body until he was positioned right where she wanted him most. He paused for a second, as if wanting to drive her mad with desire. It worked. She wrapped her hands around his waist and pulled.

The second he slipped inside her, she cried out. He moved slowly, then faster. Controlled, then carefree. She bit her bottom lip to keep herself from crying out further. His thrusts had delectable coils of pleasure bubbling in her womb. She linked her legs around his thighs and met his pelvic ride with her own give and take, creating friction that had her ready to explode again.

With his hands on the bed on either side of her head, he bent his arms and lowered his mouth to her ear. He nibbled on her lobe, then moved to nudge the corner of her jawbone with his nose. Pressing back up, he whispered sweet nothings before capturing her mouth with his.

While slow, steady thrusts stroked her, his mouth indulged hers with kisses that set her on fire. She lifted her eyelids and found him watching her.

He shifted his pelvis upward and pressed against her until she couldn't hold out any longer. A second wave of climactic bliss swept over her. This time she yelled out his name.

That was all it took to get him to unravel. Before she was through, he met her at the peak of ecstasy and they tumbled over together.

Lying with her in his arms, her back and bottom nestled against his front, Dean realized Samantha had raised the stakes. She was far beyond ordinary…far beyond him. He reminded himself they were together for tonight only. He'd be on a plane back to California on Monday with the Route 66 project in his pocket.

He'd been determined to take his time making love to her, wanting to treasure her, make it feel like the first time all over again. It took every ounce of his resolve not to drive inside her from the get go. Her sinful body had developed new, shapely curves. She'd grown into a sexy-as-hell woman.

But besides her outer splendor, her inner beauty impressed the hell out of him. He loved how she made him laugh and how she loved to tease. She was smart, outgoing, willing to try new things. He didn't think she feared anything. Save dropping a drink on her lap or tripping over something.

A chuckle escaped his lips.

"What's so funny?" she murmured. She turned to face him, her satiated eyes settling on his.

"Nothing."

She gave him a closed-mouth smile, accepting his answer without any further inquiry. "Be right back. I need to use the bathroom."

As she left the bed and walked away, he couldn't pull his gaze from the outlines of her naked body. Even in the dim light of the room, she stole his breath.

Dean sighed and sat up, leaning against the headboard of the bed. He let his eyes drift shut for a couple of minutes before he reached over and flipped on the lamp sitting on the bedside table. When he looked back in the direction of the bathroom, Samantha stood in the doorway, one hand on her hip, the other on the doorframe.

"So big guy, getting hungry now?"

His dick twitched and started to rise. Her suggestive stance had all his synapses firing—he wanted round two. "I think I need to have you one more time before I think about food."

"Oh, really?"

"Damn straight."

"Well, that's good, then, because I had the same thing in mind." She sauntered to the bed and climbed on—literally.

"God, what you do to me," Samantha purred. She raked a fingernail down his chest.

At that moment, Dean was speechless.

He still loved her.

But damned if he knew what to do about it.

Chapter Eight

"You'd better get out here fast or there isn't going to be anything left." Dean spoke with his mouth full, then washed down his final chews with a gulp of juice. He'd tried to pace himself, but he was too hungry. A night of wild, passionate sex did that to a guy.

They'd had room service last night, too. After feasting on each other a couple more times. Those late-night snacks hadn't been nearly enough, though.

"I mean it. You'd better hurry," he called, a little louder this time.

Ten minutes ago, the small room service table had full orders of French toast, scrambled eggs, bacon, bagels with cream cheese, strawberries, orange juice, and coffee. Now smaller portions of each remained.

Dean leaned back in his chair, willing himself to stop eating. He occupied his hands by running them down his bare stomach, then hooking his fingers around the arms of his seat. Looking in the direction of the window, he smiled. A bright, sunny day awaited *them*.

He'd every intention of keeping Samantha within arm's reach.

Her scent lingered on his skin. A mix of honeysuckle and gardenia driving him mad with desire this morning. Waiting for her to come out of the bathroom was pure torture. He wanted to jump her bones.

But he wouldn't. He'd decided there would be no body contact this morning. He couldn't think straight when she touched him. Even a simple brush by his arm sent do-me signals spiraling to his brain. He needed to put some distance between them, remind himself this was a weekend affair. Remember he didn't do attachments.

Too late, bucko.

They'd woken up around eleven, Dean having slept more soundly than he could remember. He'd awoken to her head on his chest, her leg draped over him, and the cadence of her heart beating along with his. He could still feel it against his side, and a cascade of peaceful warmth spread through him.

"I hope you saved me something."

She exited the bathroom wearing his T-shirt and a grin. A vision he could get used to. The curves of her body were evident, her long, lean legs painfully appealing. Golden locks fell around her shoulders like she'd simply run her fingers through the tousled strands. But her eyes. Oh, how they did him in. Her eyes sparkled like treasure in a shallow river flow.

Damn.

Taking the seat across from him, she studied the buffet left for her.

"I tried to leave you a little of everything."

"*Little* being the operative word," she teased, placing a napkin across her lap and picking up a fork.

"Hey, what can I say? I worked up an appetite. And it's not like I haven't been trying to get you out here."

She smiled. "It's the perfect amount. Thank you."

Dean watched her eat, mesmerized by the simple act of Sam putting food in her mouth. He hadn't spent the night with a woman and woken to have breakfast with her since, well…since Samantha.

The thought knocked around his head for a minute. He'd had plenty of dates over the years, but no one sparked enough interest to warrant his undivided attention. No one interested him more than the work he did, the travel he thrived on, or the projects he devoured with every ounce of energy he had.

Now, a little over a year into his own company, the Route 66 project on the horizon, he didn't think life could get any better.

Could it?

"So, do you have anything planned for today?" he asked.

Samantha eyed him while she finished chewing her food. Her jaw kept moving for much longer than necessary to make the eggs ready for swallowing. Was she stalling? Trying to decide if she wanted to spend any more time with him?

His gut tightened.

Her captivating lips looked ready to answer when the telephone rang. Holding up a finger, she stood to get it. Dean watched her, his shirt reaching just below the curve of her ass, and he wasn't sure how long he'd be able to keep his hands-off vow. Reaching for the receiver, she plopped down on the bed, exposing more skin for him to drool over.

I need bacon. With her occupied, he took the opportunity to sneak a piece. Anything to get his mind off her body. Like pork would do the trick? Only if he choked on it.

"Hello? Gretchen? Is everything okay?"

She glanced over at him, catching him in the bacon act. Titling her head, she gave him a look that said, *Paws off, buddy.*

"What? When? I can't believe he'd do that. I can't believe he'd stoop so low." She shifted uncomfortably on the bed and gave him her full back. "No, I haven't talked to him. Not since I left four months ago."

She'd lowered her voice, but Dean heard every word. Unease lanced through him. He noticed Sam's shoulders drop and knew whatever news she'd just received had something to do with her father. He seemed to recall Gretchen was the name of her sister.

"Thanks for letting me know. I think... No. No news on the account yet. I'll know tomorrow morning... Yeah, you too. 'Bye."

Dean watched Samantha slowly hang up the phone. What felt like minutes passed before she stood and returned to the room service table.

"Want to talk about it?" he asked, her guarded-yet-injured expression killing him. Despite doubts that anything he said would help Samantha, he had to try. *Wanted* to try.

"It's nothing," she said, sitting back down and scooping up a piece of bacon.

"Sorry, but you only get one of those."

Confusion clouded her weary eyes. "Excuse me?"

"You said 'It's nothing' to me last night. This morning,

it doesn't fly. Not after the last twenty-four hours we've had together. Maybe I can help."

Her expression softened before resolve replaced it. She didn't want to let her defenses down around him, and hell, he couldn't really blame her for that. Whatever transpired between them, it didn't go beyond tomorrow.

A deep breath that did really nice things to her chest preceded her answer. "My father decided to take back the present he'd given me for my last birthday. My sister stopped by my apartment yesterday to bring in my mail and found my *car* hitched to a tow truck. It seems he not only wants to leave me without any financial security, but without a means of personal transportation as well."

"At least you'll save money on gas."

She arched an eyebrow. "There is that."

"Sounds like he misses you. Wants you back at the company." Dean's dad had acted similarly when Dean told him about his plans to start his own business. His dad hadn't let Dean go without a few choice words and reminders of what he was leaving behind.

Now the opportunity to work with the company that had taught him everything he knew filled him with bone-tingling enthusiasm *and* comfort.

"More like he wants to be in control of me. I told him when I left that I wanted to make my own way, but he just doesn't get that. He likes to take care of people whether they want his help or not. I was miserable working for him, and he ignored it. All he could see was his own reputation, bringing in his daughter to lend more clout to his powerhouse firm."

"Maybe he didn't realize how unhappy you were?"

Sam's gaze shifted over his shoulder, a faraway look in

her unfocused eyes. After a few seconds she said, "He knew. He didn't care. Never has. And I guess this whole situation is my own fault. I wanted to be left to my own devices, and he's certainly making sure that I am.

"He told me when I left that I'd amount to nothing." She flinched, as if hearing those words directed at her again. "I thought he meant professionally, and I was more determined than ever to prove him wrong. Now I realize he meant personally, too. God forbid he should leave me with something to fall back on as I start out in a new profession. It's not like I didn't work my ass off for him."

Dean reached his hand out to take hers. The coldness of her palm burned him with the urge to keep her from feeling pain ever again. "I've no doubt you'll prove your father wrong. You're going to leave an extraordinary mark on the world of heritage conservation."

She pulled her hand back and reached for the last piece of bacon. "Yes, I am," she said with a firmness that erased the unhappiness and apprehension.

A smile settled over his lips as he watched her take a deep breath, like a weight had been lifted from her shoulders. He didn't think it possible to admire her more than he already did, but at the moment he held no one in higher regard.

"So how about we go shopping today? A buddy of mine just opened a new outdoor mall," he said.

For a split second, discomfort flashed over her face again. "You okay?"

"Never better." She held out the last bite of bacon. Dean leaned forward and took it from her with his mouth, his lips grazing her fingers.

"So what do you say?"

"I didn't think guys liked shopping. You mean for clothes? Or, I know. You want to buy a jet ski or a canoe or something."

"Actually, I need to buy a pair of nice pants and a shirt. It's my mom's birthday today, and I forgot to bring something to wear to dinner tonight."

"Oh…sure."

"Don't sound too excited. Maybe I'll buy you something, too."

"That's not necessary." She lifted her orange juice, took an unsteady sip.

He reached out to touch her arm, needing to feel her skin. "I know it's not. I want to. Something to remember me by."

Dean pulled into the parking lot of a very attractive outside promenade with shops and restaurants. A giant fountain stood in the middle, water dancing at different heights, and plenty of people milled about. Samantha wished she'd been strong enough to turn down Dean's invitation. She didn't want him to buy her anything; the last thing she needed was something tangible to remember him by. But once again, her heart won out over her head.

As they exited the car and made their way to the storefronts, she pushed away feelings of unease and tried to enjoy the cobblestone walkways and overgrown planters of ivy and brightly colored flowers. Tingles shot through her when Dean took her hand, wrapping his fingers comfortably around hers.

Window-shopping eventually led to the perfect shopping place.

"What do you think of this?" Dean asked a few minutes later in the dressing room area of Tommy Bahama.

"I think you could wear a paper bag and still look good." Samantha eased forward and adjusted the collar on the light blue button-down shirt. For a split second the scent of citrus mixed with something more musky flooded her senses. She bent her head into the spot between Dean's shoulder and jaw and sniffed. The seductive aroma had her picturing the two of them on a deserted tropical island.

"The store's signature scent," he said. "I put some on as I was coming back here. Like it?"

Samantha lifted her face to mere inches from his. "I'd like to be stranded on an island with you, drinking fruity cocktails and holding your hand."

"How about Maui?"

"I've never been." But she could picture it. With him.

"It's a date, then. We'll meet there sometime and conquer the sea. Snorkeling, scuba diving, whale watching. It's an incredible place."

Sometime? What the hell did that mean? How about right now? Throw caution to the wind, forget about Route 66, and just head to paradise.

She wanted to say regardless of who got the contract, they should get out a calendar and pen it in. Pen. It. In. But she didn't. She bit the inside of her cheek and stifled the urge to ask for an explanation, a rundown on the thoughts going through his mind. His nonchalance ate her up inside. She gave a silent curse.

He didn't owe her anything. And she had no right to ask anything more of him. They'd agreed to the weekend. But the pull on her heartstrings, the incurable desire to kiss him, the need to love him, pestered her every thought. The risk had been there from the beginning and she'd taken it. She had no one to blame but herself.

"So what's next"—her cell phone rang, momentarily interrupting her question—"to try on?" She backed away from Dean with a smile plastered on her face, hoping the expression would ease her anxiety. She pulled out the phone, then put up a finger and said, "I need to get this."

Her heart raced at the name on the caller ID.

"Hello. This is Sam."

"Sam. Bill Malloy. How are you?"

Confident she'd distanced herself enough from Dean, she said, "I'm good, Mr. Malloy. How are you?"

"Well, thank you. And please, call me Bill." His voice carried so much warmth over the phone line that Samantha relaxed her shoulders before sitting down on a bench just outside the clothing store.

"Okay. Bill."

"Listen. I've read over your proposal, and I need clarification on something."

"Sure." She crossed then quickly uncrossed her legs. Sat up taller, took a slow and silent deep breath. She watched the inside of the store for any indication Dean was on his way out.

"I like that you and Global Site have paid special attention to the architecture and amusements along the Route and that you see 66 as resurrecting the American road trip. Your site interpretations are cleverly detailed and you've done your research on local preservation organizations willing to lend a hand to such a large project."

"Like you, Global Site has personal relationships with community groups and government agencies across the country," Samantha said. "Our personal manpower only goes so far, given we have commitments to other sites across the world."

Bill chortled. "I've known Ben Thompson a long time. I think he's the only man busier than I am."

Samantha had met the head of Global Site only once. He ran the company from all over the world, preferring a mobile office to anything stationary. "Despite his assiduousness, I can assure you he's one hundred percent behind working with you on Route 66."

"I've no doubt. We've talked about partnering up in the past when the right project came along."

"I hope I don't sound too forward when I say this is the right project." Samantha closed her eyes. Spending time with Dean hadn't quelled her desire to get the partnership for her employer. In fact, reconnecting with him had made her more confident than ever. While she might not know where she stood with him personally, his compliments to her professionally sent her self-esteem soaring.

"Global Site's reputation and commitment to stem the loss of historic structures is hard to beat, but in your proposal you hold fast to the ideals the company has maintained for the past two decades. Do you see yourselves breaking tradition and exploring new and different preservation strategies in the near future?"

Dean popped into Samantha's line of vision. He looked around the store, and when he caught sight of her, the corners of his mouth lifted before he stepped out of sight.

Samantha hesitated, trying to decipher if Mr. Malloy was hoping she'd answer "yes." "Not likely," she finally said, deciding to hold true to her—and Global Site's—ideals. "To date we've helped save over a hundred endangered architectural and cultural sites with tried-and-true methods. Mr. Thompson likes to say if it isn't broken, don't fix it. When left to our own way of doing things, there's no one better, Mr.—Bill."

"That's what I wanted to hear," he said, his tone unreadable.

She couldn't decide if that meant she'd won the contract or if something else was going on that she didn't understand. Her newness to the industry suddenly had her shaking with uneasy tension.

"Thanks, Sam. And I'm sorry to bother you on a Sunday. I'll see you in the morning."

"My pleasure," she managed to squeak out before hearing the call disconnect.

A moment later an arm snaked around her waist. Lips grazed her neck. She quivered—whether from Dean's touch or from nervous energy, she wasn't sure.

"Hey, everything okay?" Dean asked, the sound of his voice signaling every synapse in her body to fire.

"Fine." Her body relaxed against him as if her mind had no control over her movements. "Just my sister checking up on me again." She had no intention of telling Dean who had been on the phone. It was her business, and she didn't think Dean would be happy about it. Plus, she didn't know if Mr. Malloy had given his son the same courtesy call, but she didn't think so. At least he hadn't in the last thirty hours she'd been with Dean.

Dean grabbed her hand and tugged her with him without another word.

Several stores and bags later, Dean had an outfit for dinner and plenty of other clothes for the Golden State, a place where he said he loved living. Samantha had a couple of bags, too, since Dean had insisted on buying her a few dresses he'd wanted to see her try on. Not wanting to hurt his feelings — and secretly thrilled that his eyes brightened with every dress she modeled — she'd agreed. But once she got home, she knew she'd hide them in the back of her closet so as not to be reminded of him.

Silence filled the first few minutes in the car on the drive back to her hotel, but the air crackled with enough electricity to muddle her thoughts. She'd grown so ultra aware of Dean that her body fed off his energy, sending pinpricks of desire scorching across every inch of her skin. She thought about going back to her hotel room. Forced herself *not* to think about going back to her hotel room. Wondered if Dean was thinking the same thing.

She took in a slow, deep breath to calm herself, and Dean's scent filled her, spiraling her back out of control. She hated his effect on her. Hated that she'd let herself tumble into something with him again. His nearness alone made her feel the kind of want she'd never experienced with anyone else.

She told herself when they got back to the hotel she'd kiss him good-bye, wish him the best, and hightail it back to her room — alone. Any more physical contact would plunge her over the cliff she'd promised herself never to stand on again.

When out of the blue Dean mentioned work, nausea punched her in the stomach. She pressed the button to lower her window and tried to focus on the breeze hitting her face. They'd successfully avoided the subject of Route 66, and Sam wanted to keep it that way. How could they mix what they were doing with work when one of them would win and one would lose?

They couldn't. And beyond what happened tomorrow morning, Dean's future plans still concerned the environment and nothing more. He'd given her no indication of a "you and me" going past today. Never said this weekend could lead to something more. She'd accepted that because she couldn't resist his invitation for one more fling. She couldn't give up taking what she could get from him and dealing with the rejection later.

"Hey, are you paying attention?"

"Yes, sorry," she answered, shaking away the thoughts ricocheting in her head. "You said the architect you've hired has an urge to combine lean places with benign suburban architecture." She felt her face give way to a hopeful expression, the words obviously rolling off her tongue without much thought.

Dean fell into full-fledged laughter. "Did you hear what you just said?"

She winced. "Um, not really. I'm sorry. I guess I did kind of zone out there for a second."

"You were close. I said he's the best in merging design and environment in urban green spaces. But I kind of like the way you said it better." He grinned, one more chuckle escaping his mouth. "We don't have to talk about work if you don't want to. I'm just curious to hear your thoughts on things, and I wanted to share my thoughts, too. I can't believe we're working in the same field. Still can't believe we've met again like this."

Samantha stared at Dean's profile. When he turned and cast his blue eyes on her, eyes she felt no amount of competition could turn ugly or bitter, she wondered what her reflection showed. There was no one else in the world she'd rather talk business with, but she couldn't remain indifferent when this contract meant everything to her. Dean's job wasn't at stake here. Hers was.

"Me neither." No other words came to her.

"How many sites is Global working on right now?"

"A dozen or so. We've got teams in Austria, Portugal, the UK. I'm hoping to head to Indonesia at the end of the month."

"Hoping?" He cast her a sideways look, his eyes gleaming like polished chrome. His confidence in her wiped away any misgivings she had about her upcoming job review.

"It all depends on when we start the Route 66 project." And if her freelance position became permanent.

He chuckled. Not with disrespect or a low opinion of her comment, but with genuine camaraderie, like he didn't discount her capabilities. Another admirable quality Samantha knew bettered her. Why did he seem to take their rivalry so lightly? Did he know something she didn't?

"Yeah, I guess we both can't plan too far in advance."

She wondered if he meant personally as well as professionally. She wanted it to be both. Wanted to believe that maybe this time he'd be open to making future plans with her. But that was unrealistic. She knew his love affair lay with the environment and always would. He'd never plan around that. And because of his integrity, he'd never put anyone in the position of second best.

"How many projects have you got?" she asked, giving in to her curiosity about his new company. There wasn't anyone she held in higher regard than Dean, and if their situation were different, she'd want to learn everything she could from him.

"Four, with two on the horizon. We're a small fish in a big sea right now, but that will change eventually. It took my dad almost twenty years to reach the notoriety he's got. With a staff of ten and a handful of field project managers, we plan to grow slowly. My dad taught me patience is a virtue. I'm taking that to heart."

Samantha threw a challenge at him, knowing he could handle it. "So you think you're capable of handling Route 66 better than Global?"

"I don't think. I know."

"Jumping in feet first can land you on your ass." She shifted in her seat, trying to mentally and physically put distance between them. If her company didn't get the contract, would it give her some comfort to know she'd lost to Dean? She wanted him to succeed. But was it despicable of her to wish he didn't this time?

"Darlin', I do some of my best work on my ass," he said, waggling his eyebrows at her.

She knew that to be true. But his words reminded her of memories she'd best not think about if she planned to make a quick getaway.

Chapter Nine

They pulled into the loop that led to the valet in front of the hotel. "Thanks again for everything, Dean. I've had a great time."

"I've got a couple of hours before I need to head to my parents' place. Why don't I see you to your room? Help you with all those bags?" The sound of his voice carried so much appeal and charm that she'd need earplugs of steel to remain immune.

"That's not necessary," she answered, mustering every ounce of strength she had left. It seemed to her she'd said that a lot this weekend.

"I know it's not *necessary*. I…I…oh, hell, I want to spend a little more time with you, Sam."

His vulnerability shot straight to her heart, upping the beats per minute. Would he have as much difficulty as she would when they parted?

"Dean—"

"Or I could come by after dinner?" He cast an optimistic glance her way, that sparkle in his eyes rendering her helpless. One more night with Dean was all she'd get. Foolish as it was, she wanted to take it.

"Okay."

"Great. It's all decided, then. I'll come on up and shower, and then be back later." He looked straight ahead, but she could see the irresistible smile in his profile.

What?

And why did she find herself agreeing? *Bad body.*

"Just what are you implying, Mr. Malloy?" Flutters took hold of her stomach and her breath caught thinking about what they were about to do. Acting on the fierce sexual pull between them was the only way to purge Dean from her every waking thought.

She hoped.

"I'm implying I need someone to wash my back." He laced his fingers through hers as they pulled to a stop in front of the hotel lobby. "And I seem to remember you were pretty good with a bar of soap."

"It would be my pleasure." Yes, she'd lost her mind.

"I'll see to that."

Ten minutes later they entered her hotel room. Samantha told herself not to get too caught up in Dean's tropical-island scent or the crazy thoughts running through her head. She wouldn't turn away from the dangerous consequences that being with him for a few more hours created.

She dropped her bags on the bed and twisted to find him studying her. For a long moment they drank each other in, as if they both knew there was nothing ordinary about the attraction between them but were afraid to make the first move or say the right thing to take it further.

Then he strode toward her, his intense and determined expression stealing her breath.

Something was different when he gently caressed her back and started to undress her. His defenses were down. Hers, too. His careful touch made her ache to have all of him and wiped away any lingering reservations she might have.

"Your skin is so soft," he said, sliding his hands down her bare arms.

Lazy circles on her palms followed, making her shiver in response.

Samantha swallowed. She wished Dean didn't affect her so much. His hands on her body, the words he said—and didn't say—were all a painful kind of good that she couldn't get enough of. He was a weakness she'd never be strong enough to refuse.

"God, you smell good, too," he whispered next, leaning in to feather his lips along the spot below her earlobe that turned her inside out.

When he pulled back and tugged his shirt over his head, she couldn't do anything but watch him. Once they were naked, he took her hand and led her to the shower.

They'd had sex under a waterfall during their summer affair all those years ago, but it didn't compare to the warm rivulets of water cascading down their bodies now.

Samantha's body quivered as Dean smoothed her wet hair back and held her cheeks in his hands. He looked at her lovingly, somehow reaching past the sentiment she knew her eyes held, plunging deeper into her psyche.

With the utmost care, he rubbed his thumbs across her cheekbones before bending for a kiss. The sensation of his mouth on hers while water streamed down her backside was extraordinary. Blissful vibrations took over. She wrapped her arms around his neck, deepening the kiss.

While his mouth devoured hers, his hands slid down to her waist and pulled her in tighter. Her breasts pressed against the smooth planes of his chest. She wiggled her shoulders side to side, teasing him with playful caresses.

The friction sent whirls of pleasure to every spot on her wet body. She wanted to feel him moving deep inside her so badly it hurt.

Dean slowly ended the kiss and put some space between them. He reached for the soap and rolled it in his hands to create lather. As he did so, he took in every inch of her body, examining her from top to bottom. Then with tender strokes, he washed her. Starting at her neck, he massaged down to her shoulders, spending some time loosening the muscles there. She felt herself relax. Her eyelids grew heavy. A deep breath escaped her mouth. His hands slid to her breasts next. He cupped them, rubbed, and kneaded them until she rolled her shoulders back and stared at him with tipsy eyes. Her stomach was next. Then lowering down to his knees, he glided up and down her legs with blissful strokes of his hands.

"I think you missed a spot," she teased.

"Don't worry." He stood and returned the soap to the dish. He took in the bubbles covering her and smiled. "I think that's enough."

"Enough?"

"To get me clean." Taking one step forward, he slipped and slided up and down the length of her body.

Pure euphoria shot through her system as Dean shimmied his way to cleanliness. From the shoulders down they connected in bits and pieces, the slick movement creating increased need for consummation.

Their soapy tango waned as water trickled its way between them. Dean steadied himself and put his hands on her shoulders before moving his mouth to her neck. His kisses were soft all the way up to her chin. He paused for a moment to shine a look in her eyes, and then he captured her mouth with strong, fluid sweeps of his tongue. Their lips mingled effortlessly, sending a pitter-patter feeling straight to her heart.

A rush of much more than sexual connection flooded her body. If she read him right, this was far more than just sex happening between them.

And from then on she was lost in how good it felt to be in his arms.

"So I'll be back around ten," Dean said, buttoning up his new shirt. His hair was still damp. A light shadow lined his jaw. Once again, Samantha couldn't help but watch his every move.

"Okay." Emotion welled up inside her, and she fought to keep her disposition in check. She'd never find anyone else who came close to hypnotizing her the way Dean did.

His cell phone rang, doing a vibrating dance on the coffee table where it lay. He picked it up on the second ring while sitting down on the couch next to her.

"Hey, Dad." The affection in Dean's voice made Samantha's heart lurch. Despite Dean's brief mention in the bar that he and his dad weren't on the best of terms, Dean still spoke to him with the warmth of a young boy.

Silence followed, though, as Dean held the phone to his ear. Dropping his chin, he ran a hand through his hair. Samantha noticed his jaw tighten. Watched his body shrink, the larger-than-life man of twenty minutes ago disappearing. Something was wrong.

"What hospital are you at?" he said finally.

Samantha put a hand on his leg and waited while he finished the conversation. She felt short of breath, like there wasn't enough oxygen in the room. Seeing Dean's body wither stripped away her own conflicting emotions.

He ended the call and fell back onto the couch. "My mom's been in a car accident."

"Oh my gosh. Is she okay?"

"Yes, thankfully. But my dad's a wreck. I need to head over there."

She moved her hand to take his and asked, "Is there anything I can do?"

"You can come with me."

Chapter Ten

Four years ago, Dean's aunt, his father's only sibling, died in a car accident. A drunk driver blindsided her and sent her small convertible spiraling into a tree. It had left an indelible mark on the family, especially his dad, who had doted on his younger sister since they were kids.

To this day his father still harbored deep-rooted fears about an accident claiming another family member. With all the traveling Dean did, he knew his dad worried about his safety. That was one of the reasons why his dad had been so against his starting a new company—Dean wouldn't be around for him to keep tabs on anymore. The thought scared the shit out of the old guy.

Dean swallowed down the bad taste that rose in his throat. Thank God his mom would be okay. From the sound of his dad's voice on the phone, the circumstances more than anything else would take time to forget. Hell, his dad might not let his mom get back behind the wheel of a car. Granted, the accident hadn't been her fault, but Dean knew his dad liked to have a say in things. It wouldn't surprise him in the least if he grounded his mom and told her she had to stay home.

Of course, her fiery personality wouldn't stand for it. She didn't sit still long, always dabbling in charitable causes, lunch dates with friends, and, oh yeah, extreme sports. Dean got every ounce of his adventuresome blood from his mother. She rock climbed, bungee jumped, sky dived, cross-country skied, and just for the heck of it, had recently taken up extreme unicycling with a group of teenagers in her mentoring program. She said it strengthened her core.

Dean thought it was amazing all the things his mom did, and they shared an incredible bond over it, while his dad often said she belonged in a circus act. The snide remarks hadn't fooled Dean, though. He knew his dad was still head over heels in love with her after thirty years of marriage. In fact, his mom had often told him it was her fearlessness that his dad found most attractive. And in equal fashion, it was his dad's play-it-safe attitude that she found most endearing.

At least they had each other.

Dean opened the passenger side door of his car and helped Samantha out. He appreciated her silence on the ride over to the hospital, her sense that he needed to sort things out in his mind. It had given him time to ruminate on what had happened. Now she cast him an easy smile, a smile that said, *I'm here for you.*

He found her hand and the feel of her palm in his settled the nerves skittering over his skin. He hadn't thought he could cherish her any more than he already did, but having her beside him while they made their way into the hospital, he thought his heart might burst.

And he realized he'd die for this woman.

As they entered through the sliding glass door, his thoughts strayed to where he was in his life. Who was in his life. He was lucky to have great parents, an abundance of cousins, work associates he'd bend over backward for, and friends who were never too far away.

But was there someone he could rely on, no matter what?

One person who would be there for him if he were lying in a hospital bed? Someone to sit with him all day and night and whisper loving sentiments into his ear?

He peeked at Samantha and a collision of love and admiration seeped through every pore of his body.

He'd never planned to rely on anyone. Until now.

She hadn't hesitated when he asked her to come with him, even though something uncomfortable had simmered in her eyes. He'd supposed it was the hospital. Most people found it an unpleasant place to visit. The last time he'd stepped foot in one he'd come to see his aunt. It had been too late.

A lump formed in his throat. He rubbed his brows to relieve the mental uneasiness sitting behind his eyes. If anything life-threatening had happened to his mother, he didn't know what he'd do.

They navigated the cold, sterile hallways that led to the elevator and took it to the third floor. Sam squeezed his hand tighter on the ride up and he squeezed right back.

"Thanks again for coming with me."

"Sure."

"I think I should warn you—my dad may seem overly

sensitive. My aunt died in a car accident so it's a real touchy subject. One that still holds a lot of pain for him."

"I'm so sorry." She paused. "But you said your mom's going to be okay, right?"

"Yeah. My dad said it's a few broken ribs and a fractured wrist. This is going to be horrible for her, though. She doesn't like to sit still."

"And there's nothing you can do about broken ribs but rest."

The elevator doors opened and he noted the direction of room 348 on the wall plaque. "I know. My poor mom. She's going to be miserable. And if I know my dad, he's going to keep her home for longer than necessary."

"That's sweet."

"Not to her it won't be. She doesn't like anyone telling her what to do."

"So that's where you get it from?"

A small smile crossed his face. He appreciated the attempt to lighten the mood.

Dean led her past gurneys and IV stands and nurses hustling about, then rounded the corner leading to the right place. He noticed every occupied room had a visitor in it. Someone sitting or standing, an arm stretched across the bed or hand clasped reassuringly. The faces were young and old, but all wore looks of deep caring and love. Acutely aware of Samantha's hand in his, a rush of emotion swept over him.

He loved Samantha. Had always loved her.

She triggered admiration and awe-inspiring hope in him. Hope that she'd share everything with him, would be there by his side on every adventure and ordinary day. She was his one in a million. The one to keep his feet firmly planted on the ground *and* to set him flying higher than he'd ever gone before.

He didn't want just memories anymore. He wanted the real thing.

She tugged on his arm, bringing them to a stop.

"What is it?" The thoughts of love swirling inside his head subsided when he looked at her solicitous face. She had something serious on her mind.

"I need to…need to…"

Worry shot through him. He'd never known her to be at a loss for words. "You need to what?"

"I know I came all this way with you, but I'm sorry. I need to go."

Searching her eyes, he saw fear and compassion, love and regret. Her gaze reached down inside him and plucked out his beating heart. She held it in her hands, the *thump, thump* at her disposal. His chest tightened. He wondered what she could possibly be talking about.

"Before we see my mom?"

"Before we see your dad."

"My dad? Shit. You're right, I'm sorry. I've been thinking so much about my mom that I completely forgot about business and the meeting in the morning. But look, it's okay. I'll give him a quick explanation."

She cleared her throat and straightened her shoulders, looking ready to pass on some top-secret information to him. Huh? The ache in his heart doubled as he noticed every little thing about her. Taking both his hands in hers, she seemed to gather strength from their contact, but a wistful expression crossed her beautiful face. Something else was going on.

"I thought I could do this. Be here for you. But…"

"Dean!" His dad's voice carried down the hallway on sound waves that easily rounded the corner.

Dean turned and took the few long strides necessary to greet his father. His dad wrapped his arms around his back and squeezed; the embrace lasted longer than any he'd received since that fateful day four years ago. A man of few words, Dean knew the gesture was his father's way of saying he loved him.

"How are you holding up?" Pulling away from his father, Dean kept his hands on the old man's shoulders, wanting to feel his answer as well as hear it.

"I'm doing okay. Thankfully, your mom's going to be fine."

"She's a tough cookie."

"You can say that again. She wants to go home already. Damn woman doesn't know when to take it easy."

Feeling the hunch in his father's shoulders subside, Dean dropped his arms. "They're not letting her go home, though, are they?"

"No. She'll be here a few days. They want to be sure there's no internal bleeding or injuries that haven't shown up yet. Of course she's spouting her mouth off about how strong she is and how well she knows her body, blah, blah, blah. Says there's no way she's got four broken ribs, only feels two."

Dean's mood couldn't help but improve. His feisty mom did what she did best: drive his dad to adore her more. The love in his dad's eyes when he talked about her was so evident that Dean smiled with pride. His parents' marriage was a love story he wanted to emulate.

His story, he realized, had started five years ago and

resumed with a kiss Friday night. Samantha was his happily ever after.

"Sam? What are you doing here?"

Side stepping him, his dad moved toward Samantha. Dean looked over his shoulder and watched his dad accept her outstretched hand. He couldn't see his father's expression, but Samantha's face radiated warmth and respect on top of the uncertainty Dean had noticed when she'd blinked a few extra times.

"Hello, Mr. Malloy. I'm sorry to hear about your wife."

"It's Bill, remember? And thank you. I thought after our phone call this afternoon I wouldn't see you until tomorrow morning."

Phone call? For some reason, those two little words hit Dean like a ton of bricks. He watched his father and Samantha speak to each other like they'd been acquaintances far longer than one meeting, and he didn't like it. He saw their lips moving but couldn't hear their words. Anger—irrational, he knew, but present nonetheless—drowned out their voices.

"You two talked this afternoon?" he managed to say. *That* must have been the call she'd received while they were shopping. The news made him want to punch a hole in the wall. Sam had lied to him.

Bewilderment flooded Dean and he felt his stomach twist. Questions stormed his mind, littering his head with rubbish he didn't know how to process. *Why didn't Sam tell me the truth? Has Dad told her she got the job? Is he offering her something more?*

His dad turned, Samantha at his side, an apologetic look on her face. Her eyes beckoned for him to understand, but he stood frozen. Confusion toiled with longing. He needed an explanation before he said or did anything more.

"We did," his father said. "I had to clear something up." He glanced back and forth from Samantha to Dean, scrutinizing them like he couldn't decide what to say next. Silence stilled the air between them and the hum of a medical machine droned in the background. "I didn't realize how well you two knew each other."

"Oh, we don't know each other *that* well," Sam said, her voice passing off their relationship as mere acquaintances.

"Well, I need to get back to your mother," his dad replied, stepping toward the room. He slapped Dean on the shoulder. "Come on in. She can't wait to see you. She's so upset dinner was ruined, and with your leaving tomorrow, we'll have to make due bedside." Pausing at the door, he looked over his shoulder. "Sam, why don't you join us?"

"Oh, thank you, but I was just leaving."

"I insist you come in and say hello first. If my wife finds out you stopped short in the hallway, she won't be happy."

Dean tried not to choke on his father's invitation. He wanted to settle things with Sam privately before he saw his mom.

His dad gestured for them to follow with a sideways nod of his head. *Shit.*

Samantha darted another apologetic glance at him. Her bottom lip trembled ever so slightly. "Just for a minute," she said, then stepped around him.

"Dean!" his mom said, her eyes less bright than normal. Seeing her in a hospital bed pierced Dean's heart with worry.

"Hey, Mom." He wrapped her in a gentle embrace. She felt whole, thank God, and she squeezed him back with the same fierceness she always did.

When he stepped away, his mom's eyes settled on Sam and Sam's settled on hers. Damn if Dean didn't think some weird female comprehension passed between them. Like an instant camaraderie that turned strangers into friends for life.

"This is Sam Bennett," his dad said. "She works for Global Site Preservation."

"It's nice to meet you, Mrs. Malloy. I'm so sorry about your accident."

"Thank you." She extended her left arm and squeezed Sam's hand. "It's nice of you to stop by. I've…" She glanced at Dean. "I've been hoping for more visitors."

Dean closed his eyes in silent thanks that his mom left it at that. She knew about Samantha. He'd told her about their relationship after he'd gotten home that summer, and no doubt his astute mom realized this was the same Sam.

"There's only so much Food Network television I can take," his mom added, lifting her chin toward the television hanging on the wall.

He and Samantha looked up. "Oh, I love *Cupcake Wars*," Samantha said.

"I do, too. But now I'm craving a chocolate cupcake with whipped cream frosting." His mom smiled at Sam.

Sam smiled back. "Maybe we can sneak one in for you?"

We? Dean clenched then unclenched his hands. If Sam's goal was to confuse him, it was working.

"I would love—"

"You can have a cupcake when you get out of here," his dad interrupted. "Inside a hospital, you eat hospital food." He put his hand on his wife's arm and looked at her tenderly.

"It's for the best."

Sam watched his parents. Then she looked up at him. The connection lasted a few seconds, until his mom cleared her throat and said, "Dean, please help me out here and tell your father I cannot survive on hospital food."

His mom's plea put his focus back on her. "I think Dad might be right on this one, Mom." Dean eyed the IV, then took in his mom's pale complexion. She'd just been through a big trauma and probably shouldn't be eating too much sugar.

She huffed. "Samantha, surely you can come to my rescue. I need someone on my side. I'm outnumbered with these two."

"Umm…" Samantha made a panicked face.

"We girls have to stick together, you know."

"True," Samantha agreed, a small closed-mouth smile spreading across her face. "I don't know what I'd do without my sister and mom. But maybe Bill can have a *box* of cupcakes waiting for you at home?"

"Done!" Dean's dad grinned at Samantha.

Dean's stomach knotted. It hurt to watch Sam's charm and friendliness when he wasn't sure if it was for his benefit or his dad's.

His mom winked at Samantha. "A girl after my own heart."

"Well, I really should be going now. I hope you feel better soon, Mrs. Malloy." Sam took slow steps backward. "Bill, I'll see you tomorrow."

"Thanks for stopping in," Dean's mom said. "It was delightful meeting you."

Dean followed Samantha out, the tension between his

shoulder blades only slightly lessening now that they stood back in the hallway.

"Your mom is really—"

"We don't know each other well, huh?" The words Samantha spoke before his father interrupted them still resonated.

"I'm sorry. But *you* didn't say anything, so I had to say *something*. I didn't want your father's decision clouded by a relationship he thinks we might have. That could hurt both of us. I came to Idaho to get the Route 66 account and nothing more, Dean. I represent Global Site Preservation and unfortunately, I think I lost sight of that this weekend. Your father's opinion of me matters whether I'm in his office or in a hospital room."

Or in bed with me. He hadn't really expected her to share how she felt about him with his father, but hearing her declaration out loud still stung. "And what about the phone call?"

"What about it?" Remorse passed over her face as she took a step toward him.

He took one back.

"Does anything matter more to you than the job?" he asked.

Her eyes widened. "You're asking *me* that?"

Maybe it was the stress of his mother's accident. Maybe it wasn't. But he didn't want to remain in the same air space with her any longer.

"I should go." He turned around.

"Dean, wait a minute." Samantha grabbed his arm. "Please."

Heat rushed through him at her touch, her fingertips

eliciting desire that came from both his head and his heart. He looked into her eyes and wanted to lose himself in the tangle of her hotel sheets, lock the two of them away and forget that anything else in the world mattered.

But with careful intent, he removed her hand from his arm. A shiver coursed through him and cold waves returned to his unnerved body. "You lied to me."

"What are you talking about?"

"You lied to me about the phone call. And now I don't know if I can trust anything you've said to me. Was it all part of a plan? Were you hoping maybe I'd slip some valuable World Heritage Fund information to you? Give you the leverage you'd need to retaliate in case you lost the account?"

"I never lied to you."

He shot her what he hoped was a *don't play me for a fool* look. "You sure as hell did."

"Okay. I lied about one silly phone call. But not about anything else." She pulled him into the vacant room beside his mother's and in a hushed tone added, "Dean, I've completely lost myself with you." A deep breath heaved her chest up and down, while an audible sigh blew out her mouth. "I came here this weekend for the meeting, never thinking I'd run into you, let alone that you'd be vying for the same job. And then there you were, and so many feelings came flooding back to me that I thought I'd drown in them. Don't think for a second that I didn't mean everything that happened between us."

He searched her eyes and saw the truth in her words. But dammit, he was pissed off. He hated, too, that he couldn't help but wonder what else might be lurking behind her careful expression.

Maybe what tore them apart five years ago resonated as too great an obstacle to overcome. She wasn't the same naive girl, but a woman with a purpose backed by determination he didn't think he could crack. Not with what he knew about her father.

"But," she continued, "the bottom line is I came here to get a job for my employer, and we both know that come tomorrow whatever this is between us will end."

He wondered if she truly believed that or if she was speaking out of self-preservation. "How do you know that?"

"I've got no delusions about you, Dean. Your aspirations and dreams are the same as they were five years ago."

Dean understood her words and they left a bitter taste in his mouth. Damned if he wouldn't hurt her again and she knew it. But things were different this time. *He* was different.

And yet, she didn't see it. That hurt just as much as her lie.

"Did my father give you any indication that you'd won the account when he spoke to you on the phone?"

"No."

"Well, I'm sorry, then. It looks like you've lost." Dean watched Samantha squirm and knew his declaration stung. He had no idea if he'd actually won the account, but he had to say something hurtful before he said something stupid. Something personal. He needed to take the focus off their relationship or he would crumble. His heart ached. His head throbbed. And when he swallowed, it hurt. As much as he wanted to wrap her in his arms and tell her everything was okay, it wasn't.

"That cockiness always work for you? Or are you holding out on me now?" She took a shaky breath. "I knew

I shouldn't trust you."

"Huh? You're throwing trust back at me? My methods are tried and true, sweetheart. You don't like them, get out of the fire."

A look of defeat crossed her face, like her lifeboat had just capsized. She stopped beside him and reached out to touch his arm before leaving the room. "Thanks for putting things in perspective for me."

He stepped away, not wanting her touch to dictate his feelings. Running a hand through his hair, his eyes on the cold gray floor, he said, "No problem."

Chapter Eleven

"Happy birthday, Mom," Dean said, bending to kiss her cheek good-bye.

"Thanks, honey. I'm sorry about the cafeteria food for dinner. If I can convince them to let me out of here in the morning, you'll stay an extra day and come over tomorrow night for Maurice's chicken parmesan. Okay?"

"You know I can't resist Maurice's cooking. Count me in."

Her face lit up at his agreement. "Hey, are you sure everything's all right?"

"Leave the boy alone, Mags. He's fine." Dean's dad stepped around the hospital bed and nudged him toward the door. "But because I know you won't get any rest unless I get some answers for you, I'll walk him out."

Dean gave his mom a smile over his shoulder and followed his dad out of the room.

"Thanks for spending a few hours with us. Not the ideal

place to celebrate a birthday, but she really misses you. Having you here meant the world to her."

"I wouldn't have been any place else."

As they moved down the hallway, most of the patient doors had closed and a heavy quietness filled the air space. Dean slowed his footsteps, as if something invisible wanted to postpone his exit. When he noticed a vacant waiting room behind a large glass window, he knew he wanted—no, needed—to talk to his dad before he left the hospital.

"Got a minute before I go?" Dean asked, nodding toward the room.

"Where do you think I'm headed? I can't go back to your mother without a report."

His father led the way and they sat on blue vinyl couches across from each other. The fluorescent lighting in the square room cast a yellowish tinge on everything.

"I don't know what's going to happen in the morning," Dean started, "but whatever does, I wanted to say a private thanks for the opportunity to partner on Route 66. I know I used Mom's birthday as a way to get the chance, but I would've flown here to meet with you any time."

"I appreciate you initiating things."

"Yeah. I didn't think you'd be calling."

His dad broke eye contact. "You're probably right. I was mad, Dean. I—"

"Was?" Dean interrupted.

A sigh sounded from his dad. "Truthfully, I haven't fully gotten over you leaving, but I understand it better now. I'm old. Stuck in my ways. You, on the other hand, are young and impulsive, and as long as you were working for me, you'd never be able to reach your potential. I'm proud of the man you've become and the environmentalist you're hoping to be." His eyes settled back on Dean.

Dean gulped down the emotion threatening to make his voice crack. "Thanks, Dad." He'd always craved his father's approval and after leaving World Heritage, he didn't think he'd ever have it again. "It wasn't—" He paused to steady himself. "It wasn't easy for me to leave, you know. But I had to break out on my own. I started to resent being here, and I didn't want my memories of this place to be anything but good."

"You never said a word."

"Would you have heard me if I did?" Dean rose to his feet, paced. "I love the company as much as you do, Dad, and if I'd stayed it would've suffered. *We* would've suffered. Not that we haven't anyway."

"I'm sorry, son." He sunk into the couch, deflated. "I saw you were restless. Noticed you holding your tongue, and I didn't do anything about it. I figured whatever was bothering you would pass. Because I'd molded you. I'd made you. It never occurred to me that you might leave. When you did, it was a slap in the face, and I behaved in a manner I'm not proud of."

Dean took the spot next to his dad, hoping his close proximity would pump some life back into the old guy. "I didn't act that great, either. But I'll tell you this. It's because of everything I learned from you that I'm a success."

"I'm not so sure about that, but thanks." He pressed up taller. "I think we've just made your mother's day."

"She's always been the one to stress the importance of good communication."

"That she has. Now tell me about Sam."

"Nothing to tell," Dean said—too quickly. Too dismissively. His dad wasn't a fool and Dean was sure he could read the lie on his face as if he'd just heard Dean claim dogs had wings.

Raising his eyebrows, the older, and some might say wiser, Malloy said, "Bullshit."

Dean laughed. From frustration or hurt or nervous tension, he didn't know, but his dad coaxing a laugh out of him made the pain in his chest slightly less sharp. "That transparent, am I?"

"You've never been a good liar, son."

"I think I should spare you the details until after our meeting tomorrow." Dean stood, ready to make an exit now. His feelings about Samantha were too raw, too private. He didn't want to say anything he'd regret later on.

"Good idea." His dad rose and they headed toward the elevator. "I've made my decision, though, so seeing the two of you together tonight has no bearing on the contract." He put a hand on Dean's shoulder. "I want you to know that."

Dean fought the urge to ask whom he'd chosen. Not that he'd get an answer. His dad had too much integrity to share something that important without Samantha present as well.

"Thanks. I'll see you at ten." Dean entered the elevator and pressed the lobby button.

"I always thought you'd take over for me one day," his dad added quickly as the chrome doors slid closed.

"Maybe I still will."

In the confines of the elevator, Dean couldn't stop thinking about Samantha. He'd made huge strides with his dad tonight, but he feared his gains would be Samantha's loss. If he'd won the contract because of family ties, then he'd be considered a jackass. If he'd won because his company was the best team for the job, then he'd be considered shrewd. Either way, Samantha would see him as ruthless. The thought unsettled him to his core.

He wanted the deal.

She needed it.

She hadn't said as much, but he could sense that losing the account might have a negative impact on her freelance job. No doubt a defeat would cost her headway with her overbearing, narrow-minded father.

Forget about it, Dean told himself. She'd told him where he stood.

He got to his car and sat motionless behind the wheel for several long minutes, stuck. Stuck in the floral scent that lingered there, its notes stirring something inside him he wanted to remember. The summer weeks they'd shared, and the past weekend, were permanently engraved in his being whether he liked it or not. A girl like Samantha Bennett came around only once in a lifetime, and fuck if she didn't make him want more.

Both his hands slammed down on the steering wheel, and he put the car in drive. The bar was only ten minutes away. Tonight he'd drink his way to forgetting.

"You look like shit," McCall said, entering the office and taking the chair across from the desk Dean rested on.

Dean lifted his arms from the glass top and leaned back into his seat. "Looks can be deceiving, pretty boy. I feel like a million."

"Hangover?"

"You bugging me for a reason this morning?"

McCall crossed his arms over his chest. "Your dad's running a little late. He's on his way from the hospital. I'm sorry about your mom."

Dean slanted a look at the clock. Nine fifty-five. "Thanks. She'll be good as new. It's my dad I'm concerned about; he already worries about my mom, but now he'll be tense every time she gets behind the wheel of a car."

"Rumor has it she isn't getting her car back."

"Let the Malloy games begin," Dean said, a smile spreading across his face.

He sort of wished he'd be around to witness it. The way his mom wrapped his dad around her finger was worth an expensive admission ticket. The first time she'd told his dad she wanted to bungee jump had elicited a reaction that bordered on—

"You going to answer that?"

McCall's question broke into Dean's thoughts. He hadn't heard the phone ring. Actually, he had, but he'd thought it was his head pounding. He glanced down and noticed the green light indicating the call came from the reception desk, so he pushed the speaker button.

"Hey, Gloria. What's up?"

"Is McCall with you?"

"I'm here, Gloria," McCall answered.

"I wanted to let you know Miss Bennett has arrived. Mr. Malloy just phoned and he's five minutes away."

"Thanks, Gloria," McCall said. "I'll come up and get her."

Dean ended the connection and got to his feet. "I'll go,"

he said.

"Sit your ass down, Dean. You don't work here anymore, remember?" McCall rose. "We'll meet you in your dad's office."

Unwelcome tension thrummed through Dean. He ran a hand through his hair. "Fine."

He followed McCall into the hallway and made a left. His head throbbed with each step, so he took a detour to the small kitchen and grabbed some aspirin. A minute later the feminine voice wafting to his ears as he crossed the threshold into his dad's office seeped into his pores and eased the alcoholic remains from last night.

Sam sat next to McCall at the conference table and didn't pay Dean any attention. When McCall leaned closer to her and whispered something, she giggled.

Every muscle in Dean's body went rigid. "Good morning," he said through clenched teeth.

"Morning," she said, looking up at him.

Her hair was pulled back to reveal radiant eyes that robbed him of the indifference he'd tried all morning to talk himself into. Her heart-shaped lips reminded him of every wicked thing she'd done with that mouth. He couldn't look away from her. She looked away from him.

"I was just telling Sam about fishing this weekend," McCall said as Dean took the seat next to Samantha. "The trout were practically jumping into the boat."

A slight tilt to Samantha's head was alluring enough to make breathing difficult for Dean. "I've never really been fishing," she said in that soft voice of hers. The same one she'd used to render him spellbound on Friday morning.

McCall looked more than interested. "I'd love to bring

you sometime."

"I just might take you up on that."

Dean wanted to take McCall and leave him dogpaddling in the middle of a mile-wide river. Instead, he fisted his hands underneath the table. The childish jealousy coursing through his blood had to stop. Immediately. Sam hadn't brought any personal feelings with her this morning, so he'd play right along.

We fished off the bank of Emerald Lake in Banff.

When McCall's phone rang, drawing his attention away from Sam, Dean gave silent thanks. He couldn't think of one goddamn interesting thing to add to the conversation.

McCall pulled the phone from his pocket. "Excuse me. I need to take this."

He and Samantha watched McCall leave. They both squirmed. The office door clicked shut, and they were alone.

The next several seconds ticked by in agonizing silence. She kept her gaze forward, studying the photographs on the far wall. Dean took in her stiff posture, her clasped hands, her business attire. Seconds felt like hours. Finally she turned her head.

"How's your mom this morning?"

"She's…she's good." All of a sudden Dean wanted to take back everything he'd said to her last night in the hospital.

"I'm glad."

"If she has her way, she'll be home today."

"My mom was in the hospital a few years ago. Her appendix burst. I remember they wanted to keep her for a couple extra days, but she insisted on going home. She said the best way to heal was in her own bed surrounded by the things she loved. It was one of the few times I remember my dad taking off work. To be with her."

Dean stared at Sam, not sure what to make of her friendly but casual disposition. Was this the moment he forgot about the past and moved forward? If he didn't let go, all those moments with Samantha would bog him down for the rest of his life. They'd bog her down, too. He could see it in her eyes no matter how hard she tried to disguise it.

"We're both adults, Dean. This doesn't have to be awkward," she said, breaking his train of thought.

"*Awkward* isn't the word I'd use."

"I'm sure our paths will cross again given our professions, so I think we should agree to be friends. I've no regrets. But I don't plan on looking back anymore."

His body burned with an ache he'd never felt before. Conflicting emotions—relief, refusal, fear, *love*—boomeranged around his insides. He thought he'd be satisfied after a weekend with Samantha, but the opposite was true. For the first time in his life, he hungered for more.

Dean had always gotten what he wanted. Had *earned* what he wanted. But that wasn't the case this time. He wished there were another way. Wished this beautiful, funny, generous woman sitting beside him hadn't become a priority he didn't know how to deal with.

"I've no regrets either."

The small smile that spread across her lips didn't calm the fervor inside him. It started a riot. Especially when he noticed, for a split second, her mask slipped.

He was about to do battle with her, make declarations, when his father walked through the door.

Samantha turned her attention to William Malloy, relieved to have the company. She'd thought she could handle seeing Dean, had rehearsed over and over again the words she would say to him, but the force of will it took to come off unfeeling had almost caused her to crumble.

Sleep had completely eluded her last night. Tears on her pillow hadn't wiped away Dean's lingering scent, and more than anything she'd wished he was with her. She also wished she'd told him about the phone call the moment it happened. Then taken a chance and declared her feelings for him right then and there. Fear had held her back.

"Good morning," she said, pushing aside the flash of affection she saw in Dean's eyes. Her lie had hurt him, but the words he'd spoken to her last night had stung right back. His ludicrous accusations had diminished their relationship to nothing but a passing fancy, and Samantha hated him for that.

"Morning," Bill said. "Sorry I'm late." He put down a stack of papers on his desk and then stepped to the chair at the head of the conference table.

Sam watched his every move. Every nuance. She had to focus on something besides the showered scent of Dean, the tired look on his face that hinted he hadn't slept much either, the way her nerves were about to fracture into a thousand pieces. She was a fool to think she'd lost Dean. She'd never *had* him. But the Route 66 contract was supposed to be a done deal. She'd poured everything into it these past few months and had been ready to accept a partnership over the telephone. Then something had changed. *Dean*.

"You get any sleep last night?" Dean asked his father, the concern in his voice chipping away at her manufactured coolness.

"Not much. It's damn uncomfortable sleeping in a hospital."

"I'm sure your company meant a world of difference to your wife," Sam said, her heart rate picking up.

Bill looked at her with emotion that far outweighed any her own father ever spared her. "Thank you. I hope it did." He exhaled and then split his attention between her and Dean. "Thank you both for coming in this morning. I appreciate the hard work you put into your presentations for the Route 66 project. They were well written and persuasive, and the decision on which company to partner with has not been easy."

Samantha nervously ground her teeth together. She put a hand on her knee to stop her leg from shaking.

"Sam, the enthusiasm you have for this job is contagious. You've far exceeded my expectations in regards to assessing a monument's integrity and significance. The desire for Global Site to reestablish Route 66 as a cultural legacy that can be sustained for generations is indicative of your company's long-term preservation successes."

"Thank you." God, Samantha hoped he couldn't see how hard her heart was beating.

"I've long agreed with the ideals and work strategies of Global Site. Hell, we've borrowed heritage approaches and procedures from each other for years. It makes sense to partner with a company I not only hold in high esteem, but one that also shares my thought processes."

Samantha took a shallow breath. "I couldn't agree more, Bill. We're dedicated to adapting and replicating methods from both companies to guarantee Route 66 prospers far beyond our days in the field."

He nodded and relaxed into his chair, seeming to gather his thoughts before continuing. Sam stayed glued to his body language. Tried to decide if his words meant she had the deal. She didn't want to get her hopes up, but it sounded like an offer was about to be made.

"But," he said, squashing Samantha's confidence, "Dean, you've created a rare partnership opportunity by proposing conservation solutions that will propel us into new hands-on techniques and philosophies bolstered by partnerships with individuals and groups eager to go beyond today's methods."

For the first time in the last couple of minutes, Samantha felt Dean stir. She'd been ultra aware of his stillness and now cast him a sideways glance.

"I'm eager to change things, yes," Dean said. "With new and improved technologies spilling into environmentalism and a new generation of artisans and preservation specialists enthusiastic about sites all over the world, it's time to work out of the box.

"However, change doesn't have to happen today. Global Site is extremely effective and far better known than my company. The global recognition of a partnership between you two would skyrocket advocacy efforts. And from what I know of Samantha, she'd be an amazing asset to any field operation."

Chills raced up Samantha's arms. She slowly turned her head and took in the man who'd just sung her praises, but at the same time made quite a convincing case for himself.

His diplomacy ripped at her heart. She'd never have acted the same way. As a silent pause filled the room, she looked down, and that's when pain flooded through her.

"Nicely said." Bill's voice had her quickly gathering her wits and looking back up. The admiration on his face as he regarded Dean stole any remaining hope she had. *I've lost.*

"This is a small field we work in," Dean added. "And the more we have one another's backs regardless of who works on what project, the more the field of heritage protection will prosper."

No one had ever had Samantha's back. No one but Dean.

Bill turned his attention to her. "Sam, I've no doubt your contributions to Global Site will better the company's already formidable reputation, and that they'll continue to remain a leader in cultural heritage preservation around the world. But the ideas that Dean and his company have set forth are what World Heritage needs to better position ourselves for a future that will only present greater challenges."

Samantha nodded.

"I'm sorry we'll have to wait for something else to partner on. Please give my sincere thanks to Global for taking the time and consideration to explore working with us."

"Thank you, Bill. I will." She rose and extended her arm. Bill stood and took her hand in both of his.

Dean got to his feet as well, and Samantha shook his hand. "Congratulations, Dean. Best of luck with this project and all your others."

"Thanks. Good luck to you, too." He looked ready to say something more, and he didn't release his grip right away. A hundred crazy thoughts raced through her head.

If she didn't turn and leave in the next second, though, she'd hyperventilate. She pulled her hand back, gave both men a tight-lipped smile, and walked as fast as she could out of the office.

As she made her way to the elevator, she fought the disorientation threatening to trip her. Concentrating on putting one foot in front of the other, she wished more than anything she could snap her fingers and be back home.

She wanted Dean to come after her. She wanted him to tell her he loved her and that they should keep seeing each other. When the elevator doors opened, she was thankful the space was empty. She turned to press the down button and slowly watched the empty lobby of World Heritage Fund disappear from view.

Chapter Twelve

Samantha marched into her father's office intent on telling him exactly where he stood in her life. She would no longer let his words hurt her. Her life was none of his business, and his manipulations and narrowed views ceased to hold any power over her.

He'd seemed so sure she would fail when she left his company that she'd allowed herself to believe it a possibility. But after three months with Global Site and her weekend with Dean, she'd let those doubts go. Her father might measure success in billable hours, but she measured it by doing what she loved. Dean had trusted she would leave her mark on the world of heritage conservation, *and she would*.

Her father looked up from his desk with a mixture of relief and smugness on his aging face. "Samantha."

"Dad."

"You got my e-mail?" His pompous tone of voice was a direct hit to her heart, but her walls were strong enough now to deflect any discomfort.

Samantha stood at the edge of his desk and looked down at him. "It's the only reason I'm here."

As apologies went, her father's impersonal message was abysmal, but she knew it was all she'd get.

"Have a seat."

"I can't. There's a cab waiting for me downstairs."

For probably the first time in her life, she watched her dad's eyes widen in surprise. He thought she was here to accept his job offer. She wasn't.

"I'm not coming back, Dad. Not today. Not tomorrow. I came here to tell you in person that it doesn't matter what you think of my chosen career path. I'm going to live my life the way I want, and if you want any part of that life, then you have to let me go without reprimand or criticism."

There. She'd said it. She'd only practiced in front of the mirror for half an hour this morning.

"Your mother and sister—"

"May have misled you a little. But that's only because they were cautiously optimistic you'd come to some conclusions on your own after they told you how much I love heritage protection. That it's where I want to belong."

Not a hint of emotion showed on her father's face at her declaration, so Samantha had no idea what he was thinking. For a few very long seconds they stared at each other. Then she turned and strode out of his office. He didn't say a thing to stop her.

And that was the best gift he could have given her.

She reached the first floor of her father's office building a few minutes behind schedule. Pushing open the lobby doors, she hurried to the waiting cab without consideration to where she stepped. Her three-inch heel lodged itself into a division in the concrete.

"Crap!" She avoided a face plant by falling into the arms of the yellow checker driver, but her ankle twisted and the heel of her shoe snapped.

The cabbie righted her and then stepped on his cigarette. She felt discomfort in her ankle, but the embarrassment at her clumsiness and now-mismatched shoe height was worse. So much for knock-off shoes. With no time to spare, she limped into the cab.

Once settled into the vinyl of the backseat, she redirected her anger over her heel to Dean. Everything was his fault nowadays.

Four weeks had passed since their good-bye. And for four weeks she'd tried with little success to hate him. So she blamed him instead: for forgetting to pay her cable bill, for her broken fingernail, for the milk spilling, for misplacing her keys. Blame eventually led to hate, didn't it?

"I can break the heel on your other shoe if you'd like," the cab driver said over his shoulder. "That way you'll at least be even."

She laughed, appreciating the cabbie's sense of humor and kindness. "That would be great. I'd hate for my first impression with a new company to include a fashion disaster."

New company.

Goose bumps popped up on her arms just thinking about it. Global Site hadn't extended her a full-time position or kept her on a freelance basis in the end. The dismissal had stung, but one call to a headhunter and she had a phone interview the next day with a heritage protection company just outside of San Francisco.

Several conversations and one video-conference later, they'd made her an offer. Today's trip was a quick in-person meet and greet before she signed her contract.

Sam let out a deep, contented sigh.

She'd jumped at the chance to leave Chicago and start a new job somewhere fresh. Despite their upsetting farewell, Dean had taught her the importance of sticking to her heart's desire.

Dean.

His image appeared everywhere. Behind her eyelids, in the puddles after a rain, in the corner of her eye when she tried to focus on reading the newspaper. She couldn't escape him. Would never be free of him. Would never forget him.

Samantha looked out the cab window and saw the airport in the distance. The Monday morning traffic had been light, and in a few minutes she'd climb aboard the private plane the company had sent for her.

Butterflies filled her stomach. She knew this job would take her to a place where her contributions reached into her professional and personal life and gave her the satisfaction and pride she craved.

The cabbie confirmed her departure spot and the next thing she knew, they'd pulled up beside the airplane. She slipped off her good shoe, and the cabbie broke the heel. "Perfect," she said, stepping around the cab. "Thank you."

Thirty minutes later, she pressed her nose against the airplane window and blinked away tears of joy.

It was a done deal.

Samantha's jaw hurt from smiling so much. She fingered the contract in her bag, her foot tapped the floor of the cab, and she stared at the passing San Francisco scenery with so much excitement bundled up inside her that if someone put a pin to her she'd pop.

She started her new job in two weeks.

The cab pulled up to a private plane. "This is a different plane from the one that brought me here," she said, leaning forward and peering out the windshield.

The cabbie shrugged. "This is where I was instructed to bring you."

"Would you mind waiting a minute until I confirm I'm in the right place?"

He nodded and Samantha got out of the car.

A man exited the plane and stepped down the movable stairs. She watched him approach, taking in his casual appearance. He wore a pressed white collared shirt tucked into khaki pants. There were no gold wings on his breast pocket, but the aviator sunglasses atop his head made her assume he was, indeed, her pilot.

"Miss Bennett?"

"Yes."

"I'm Thayer Collins, your pilot." He extended his hand and said, "Please follow me."

"This plane is going back to Chicago, right?" Even though Thayer Collins knew her name, she had to ask.

"Yes, ma'am."

She quickly thanked and paid the cab driver, then followed her pilot. She stepped up the temporary stairs, pausing at the top to breathe in the cool San Francisco air. Once inside the plane, Thayer instructed her to head to the back while he entered the cockpit.

Making her way down the aisle, she was completely knocked for a loop when a familiar laugh reached her ears. She stopped, stunned. She'd know that sound anywhere. He laughed again and then said "'bye," as if he'd just finished a phone conversation.

Her legs turning to noodles; she reached for the nearest seat to steady herself. Flutters invaded every pore, every nook and cranny, every cell of her body.

What was Dean doing in San Francisco? What was he doing on her plane? What was she going to say to him?

She still hadn't moved when the most handsome face she'd ever laid eyes on poked out from behind a seat. "Hey, beautiful."

Those two words alone nearly landed her on her ass, the tone in Dean's voice a ballad that reached to the deepest part of her.

Her heart pummeled the inside of her chest; nerves bunched and coiled low in her belly. She took careful steps toward him. When she was close enough, he sat back into an oversize window seat, looking at her with voracious eyes.

"What are you doing here?" She leaned against the side of a seat, trying to play it cool but needing the support to keep her upright. Confusion stormed her. Her entire body shook.

"Take a seat." His hand patted the cushioned spot next to him while a grin that had her legs feeling like spaghetti again crossed his sexy mouth.

"I think I'll stay standing," she said, getting a grip on the unwanted reactions he stirred. The air between them was hot. His gaze possessive. She tried to remain composed, but being in such close proximity to him made it difficult.

"Okay. I'm here for two reasons." He leaned forward, his elbows on his knees. "But before I get to that, congratulations."

"Huh?" He couldn't possibly know what she was doing in San Francisco.

"On your new job. Congratulations. HP is lucky to have you."

HP. Historic Preservation. My new employer. "How do you know about that?"

"Funny story." He shifted in his seat and stared at Samantha. "HP and I have been in negotiations to merge. We finalized our agreement today."

Samantha hoped Dean couldn't hear the way her heart pounded inside her chest like a jackhammer. "I'm working for you?"

Dean patted the seat beside him. "Will you sit down now?"

She didn't have a choice—her legs were about to give out. She collapsed into the seat beside him, shocked at what he'd just told her.

"You're working for HP, Sam." He reached into her lap and unclasped her hands. When he laced his fingers with hers, he annihilated any hope she had of staying immune to him. "You'll be working *with* me. I couldn't believe it when I saw you there today. I knew HP was bringing on a new person, but I didn't know it was you."

A knot lodged in her throat.

His hand squeezed hers. "Say something."

"I'm floored." She swallowed and lifted her gaze from

their hands to his eyes.

"Then you'll love the second reason I'm here."

Sam felt lightheaded. The way Dean looked at her with so much adoration in his eyes melted everything inside her.

"I'm here to escort you home."

"Why?" she whispered.

"Because wherever you are is where I want to be." He brought his other hand to her face and held her chin, his thumb gliding over her bottom lip. "These past few weeks without you have been hell, and I'm sorry about how we left things. I'm sorry for being such an ass, and I never want to be away from you again. I want to experience the rest of my life with you by my side.

"I never thought I'd say this to anyone, but you mean more to me than the environment, Sam."

The honesty in his eyes, the words she never thought she'd hear him say, collided like tiny pinpricks of fairy dust all around her. "Could you repeat that, please?"

He chuckled, a look of delight and relief crossing his face. "You're everything to me, Samantha. I love you."

Samantha stilled. She believed him, but she wondered what would have happened if they hadn't met up today. What if her new job had taken her to New York?

"I know what you're thinking," he said. "And I was coming to see you before today. Thayer can confirm it. He had me down for a flight to Chicago days ago."

That was all she needed to hear. She lunged at him. "I love you, too," she said before pressing her lips to his.

He kissed her back. Tender at first, but then so passionately that she knew nothing would ever come between them again.

Breaking the kiss, Dean pulled back to display a crooked smile and glint in his eyes—a mischievous expression that said he wasn't done with her yet. "So, I hear you don't start work for another two weeks."

She sucked in her bottom lip and nodded.

"I just hung up with my VP, and I'm taking some time off. We've got enough fuel for Maui. What do you say?"

Her stomach somersaulted. "I say I don't have any clothes with me."

He grinned. "Perfect."

"Dean!" She pushed his arm. "I at least need a bathing suit."

"We'll buy whatever you need." He raised his eyebrows. "Sound good?"

"Yes." She would have agreed to go anywhere with him. Happy feelings drugged her body, so much so that she thought she might lose consciousness.

He lifted her hands in his. "Good. But I want more than Maui, Sam. Now that we'll be working side-by-side, I've got to warn you that this partnership is permanent, without any possibility of termination. Can you handle that?"

"I can handle anything you toss my way, Dean Malloy."

"That's good, because I plan on loving you all over this great big world, Samantha Bennett."

Acknowledgments

Thank you to Adrien-Luc Sanders for offering me my very first contract. Your enthusiasm for my story and belief in me has meant more than words can say, and you've made a dream of mine come true. I will always be grateful to you for that. Thanks also to Stacy Abrams for your guidance, incredible support, and awesome feedback. I was so very lucky to get to work with two amazing editors like you guys!

A very special thanks to my family and friends. Your love, encouragement, and cheers have made this first release even sweeter!

Risky Surrender

Entangled Publishing, LLC
2614 South Timberline Road
Suite 109
Fort Collins, CO 80525
Visit our website at www.entangledpublishing.com.

Indulgence is an imprint of Entangled Publishing, LLC.

Edited by Wendy Chen

Manufactured in the United States of America

First Edition August 2013

To Colin.

Chapter One

It wasn't that the woman standing in front of him wasn't intelligent and beautiful. The problem was she spoke exactly like all the others that had tried to get his attention. And Keats McCall would rather throw himself over the side of the historical iron windjammer than make small talk with the well-rehearsed socialite seeking a wealthy husband.

"Excuse me, would you," he said, phrasing it as a statement and cutting her off mid-sentence.

The woman blinked in astonishment. He hadn't wanted to be rude, but he'd finished mentally ticking off what needed to get done this coming week, and in good conscience he couldn't keep nodding without listening.

He smiled and stepped away to search for a few minutes of peace and quiet on the century old, California Historical Landmark, *Star of Aesa*. When he'd agreed to attend the annual heritage protection fundraiser on the seaworthy museum ship, he'd forgotten how much he dreaded his bachelorhood being up for negotiation.

"McCall." His friend and work associate Connor Gibson called out before he could make his escape. "There's someone I want to introduce you to."

"Give me a minute." McCall lifted his chin and backed away. It never got easier mingling with the rich and famous even though he fell into the same category.

Letting out a deep breath he took two more steps back and then turned to round the bow mast. The late afternoon sun cut a nasty glare and for a moment he couldn't see where he was going.

He could feel, though. And hear.

A warm body brushed up against his. Something clattered as it hit the hull. And an irate but sexy-as-hell voice said, "Goddammit. Watch where you're going."

His arms instinctively went around the woman to stop her from falling after colliding with his much larger frame. Soft yet solid, her body made contact with his in all the right places and triggered a visceral response that surprised him. She smelled amazing. Like—like no other woman he'd been this close to. Soap. She smelled like good, old-fashioned soap and woman.

Before he was ready, she pushed his chest away.

He finally blinked away the sun's rays and his gaze locked on captivating green eyes. The woman stared back, her breath hitched.

Then she dropped to pick up the silver tray and chicken satay appetizers that had scattered around them.

"I'm sorry," he said, bending to help.

"I've got this." She practically shouldered him out of the way. "You can get back to the party."

"I'm right where I want to be." His hand grazed hers when they reached for the same skewer, sending a hot current through him.

She yanked her arm back and glanced at him. Flecks of brown in her green irises created an earthy and seductive combination that he imagined rendered many men incoherent of thought.

For example, he couldn't for the life of him remember what his name was so he could introduce himself.

"Well I don't want your help." She gathered the rest of the mess onto her tray and stood.

He rose as well, taking in every inch of her. Black pumps, black skirt that hit above the knee, tight white button down shirt. She was a waitress. And drop dead beautiful. "Not the usual language or disposition for the catering crew," he said.

But it wasn't just her looks that sucker punched him. It was her attitude. She could give a flying fuck about him.

Her full lips pressed into a tight line. "You're right. I apologize for my obscenity, sir."

Sir? His father and grandfather were *sir*. Not him. "Thanks, but uh—"

"Have a nice time tonight." She turned to go, cutting *him* off mid-sentence.

"Hang on." He lightly gripped her upper arm. He wanted to tell her to drop the formality. Hell, he wanted to tug her with him somewhere secluded. He needed to know more about her.

"Sir," she said with distaste in her voice, her attention on his hold.

"Could you please drop the sir?'"

"Could you please drop my arm?"

He did. And she made a quick getaway without further word or acknowledgement.

Damn, but he couldn't remember the last time a woman had turned her back on him. Probably not since high school when he was a sophomore and tried to look down the senior homecoming queen's dress.

"Dude, I need you now." Connor came up beside him, his hand loosening the stiff collar of his dress shirt. His friend hated business attire, preferring the T-shirts and shorts he wore out in the field while preserving historical sites. "I'm being bombarded with questions only World Heritage Fund's President of Field Operations can answer."

McCall followed Connor to the stern and a small circle of environmentalists keen on helping raise awareness for WHF. With a cool San Diego breeze at his back, the smell of salt in the air, and the Pacific Ocean surrounding them, McCall could be in a lot worse places.

A few minutes later, a flash of reddish brown hair caught his attention and his pulse sped up. His waitress flitted by, her hands empty, her eyes narrowed in concentration. She stopped at the entrance to the quarters below deck and looked over her shoulder.

Directly at him. McCall kept talking as his body came alive with the intensity of her stare. She bit the corner of her bottom lip. He had to look away before he did something foolish like follow her.

"Work on the Aztec village starts next month then?" the man to his left asked.

"Yes. I'll be overseeing the start-up before returning to several spots along our current project, Route 66. Then it's off to Greece and the First Cemetery of Athens." McCall glanced back in her direction. She was gone. He looked around, but only came across the interested glances of the women he wanted to avoid.

Without further distraction, he finished his conversation, securing support from the restoration ecology firm he'd been hoping to partner with on the Aztec village. The iconic Indian village might be in the middle of the dessert, but once revitalized the surrounding land needed attention, too.

"Gentlemen," he said, excusing himself to look for the woman he couldn't get out of his head. Another waitress passed by with a tray of stuffed mushrooms. Her nametag read *Stephanie*. Huh. His mystery woman hadn't worn any identification.

Now more curious than ever, he walked the circumference of the ship. When he didn't find her, he took the steep wooden steps below deck. Guests mingled around the dining room table in the mess hall and sat on the upholstered couches. The hanging lanterns and ornate wall sconces cast a pleasant glow over the area. Preserved in its original state, the living quarters were admirable. McCall sighed in appreciation.

He acknowledged acquaintances with a nod and smile and hurried to the kitchen. It bustled with activity, but no sign of his waitress.

Where the hell had she disappeared to? She'd interested him and usually that took some doing. The fact that she'd drawn him in like a magnet with just a few choice words and eye contact made her even more captivating.

And he had to see her again.

Lucy Davenport squeezed her eyes shut and took a slow, deep breath. She'd locked the door to the captain's quarters, but still didn't want to take longer than necessary. The quicker she got off the ship, the better off she'd be.

Especially since she'd drawn unwanted attention.

Attention that did things to her body she hadn't felt in a very long time.

She reached back into the bottom left opening of the eight-keyhole china cabinet and got back to work. The serving table at her waist held fine porcelain china and the tools she'd brought to excavate what she'd come for.

After a month laboring over the ship's design and history, Lucy knew that the antique emerald ring was somewhere in these walls. A quick pass over the aged wood planks with her hand-held metal detector and the gem was right at her fingertips.

Freedom was, too.

This was the last job for her employer, billionaire collector Malcolm Holmes. After she handed over the ring, estimated to have a value of over nine hundred thousand dollars, she would owe him nothing. She could sever all ties and start making her own choices.

One more cut and… bingo. She carefully pulled free the wooden square she'd chiseled out and put it down next to her hammer. At the turn of the century, the ship's heedful captain had hidden the ring from pirates who boarded the ship and killed him. The woman he'd planned to propose to had mourned his death until her own forty years later.

That kind of love and devotion took Lucy's breath away every time she thought about it. She'd loved and lost and it hurt. It hurt like hell.

Lucy shook her head to rid thoughts of Matt and her dad and reached into the hole. She lifted on tiptoes to reach further.

Behind her, someone jiggled the door handle. She didn't panic. She wiped the perspiration from her forehead and took quick inventory for a hiding spot in case the person had a key to enter.

A moment later the intrusion quieted.

Having learned from experience that she didn't get second chances, she quickly leaned her body against the serving piece and stretched her arm as far as she could back into the hole. It took some feeling around, but she finally found it—a two-carat round cut emerald with a cluster of small diamonds on each side of the gold band. It was the most exquisite ring she'd ever laid eyes on.

She put the cut wall piece back in place and gathered her tools into her small black pouch, looping its string to the thin utility belt around her thigh. She smoothed her skirt and pressed her shoulders back. Mission almost accomplished.

She strode down the empty hallway, completely focused on getting off the boat. She was so focused that when she turned a tight corner, the big, hard male body she bumped into took her by surprise.

For the second time.

"What are you doing down here?" she asked, hyperaware of his broad shoulders, incredible smell, and impossibly attractive smile.

"What are *you* doing down here?" he threw back, before glancing over her shoulder. "The kitchen's the other way."

Lucy had two ways to play this since she couldn't seem to avoid Mr. Blue Eyes. She could be the seasick waitress on her way back to the kitchen. Or she could be the flirty waitress who was hoping for a little adventure away from the job.

The guy had *hero* written all over his face so she went with the latter. It would be quicker to ditch him that way than risk him trying to help a supposed damsel in distress.

"I got bored and wanted to look around." She slid a finger down his arm. "I hear jewels are hidden somewhere on this ship."

He chuckled. It had been a long time since she'd made someone laugh and her heart perked up. But it wasn't her intention to amuse him. She wanted to entice him. So much for her womanly charms.

"The only jewels on this ship are on the guests." He leaned closer so that his very fine mouth hovered at her ear. "But you strike me as someone who could care less about wealth."

She didn't want his words to affect her, but they did. Growing up with thrift store clothes and just enough to keep her and her dad going, she'd learned her place in the world at an early age. If her father hadn't made her feel important and cared for, and loved her with all his heart, she would have believed the unkind words from the popular girls.

"You're right," she whispered back.

"I always am." He kept his close proximity, caging her against the wall.

His nearness started an amatory ache deep in her belly. She hadn't been this affected by a man since Matt. "Really?" she managed to say with disbelief in her tone and not like he'd just tilted her world.

"Need more convincing?" He lifted his arm and put his

hand on the wall just above her head. His lips hovered far too close to her neck.

"As a matter of fact, I do." She moved around him, careful to avoid any further contact. "Let's talk about it on deck." Where she could breathe easier and be closer to her escape.

"After you," he gestured for her to lead.

She felt his eyes on every inch of her backside and she had to fight the urge to flee. Butterflies filled her stomach. No one had paid her any attention for the past two years. That was how she liked it.

Above the stuffy lower quarters, the setting sun painted red and orange streaks across the cloudless sky. She always noticed the sky. Matt had spent an entire month's paycheck to skywrite his marriage proposal after their senior year of college.

Lucy made her way to the port side of the ship. She leaned against the railing and crossed her arms over her chest as the guy took the spot beside her. "So, Mr. Always Right, what am I thinking right now?"

His arm grazed hers and she took a step away. He cut her a sideways glance that screamed confidence. "That you'd like to get the hell off this ship."

She almost swallowed her tongue. "What makes you say that?" Did he know who she was? It wouldn't be the first time she'd had competition. She was part of a small group of archeologists who recovered important artifacts. And while she did her best to remain anonymous, her last find for Malcolm, a copper scroll dating back centuries, had garnered closer attention than usual from those in the know.

"The fact that you've abandoned your job, for one. And

two, you're tense."

"I am not." She didn't show weakness to anyone. Even under pressure. There was no way he could see that she was anxious to be done with this job. His scrutiny really got on her nerves.

"I make you nervous."

"Ha! Don't flatter yourself."

"If not me, then what?" He turned and looked at her with playful, interested turquoise eyes. She lost herself in them, just as she had when they'd first collided.

Time to go. "Fine. I'll tell you. But first I better see if I'm needed. The other waitress likes to flirt with the waiters rather than work."

"Wait." He caught her hand just after she'd inched by him. "What's your name?"

She tried to pull her arm back at the exact same time he looked at her hand. She wore the emerald on her left middle figure, turned so no one could see the stone, and he'd felt it on the inside of her palm.

He lifted her wrist. "What's this?" He twisted the ring around.

Lucy tried to wiggle free, but it was no use. His eyes widened when he saw the one-of-a-kind piece of jewelry.

Her heart rate kicked into double time. "It's my grand-mother's." She yanked free of his hold and stood confident-ly. If she made a quick getaway now, he'd definitely suspect something and follow her.

He eyed her cautiously. "You weren't wearing it before. When I helped you pick up the appetizers I knocked over."

He'd checked out her hand for a ring? "Sure I was."

"Did you steal it?" His voice was void of all tenderness

now and she gulped.

Not because she was afraid she'd be caught, but because he'd drawn that conclusion so quickly and easily. And while he was at it, she could see the attraction he'd felt for her vanish.

"I don't steal things." She took them within the confines of the law—she just needed to bypass the red tape and rules so that she could complete Malcolm's jobs as quickly as possible. Occasionally, a site protected under cultural heritage laws housed an artifact Malcolm wanted. Technically, no one was supposed to excavate for artifacts in those instances, but she always worked with care and tried to leave minimal disruption to every site.

She ignored the tight bundle of nerves at the base of her spine. *One more time, then I'm through.*

"McCall. Jesus, where have you been?" A good-looking guy with wavy hair and sunglasses hanging off his shirt collar approached them.

McCall took his attention off her for a split second and that was all the distraction she needed. She wove her way through the guests to make her way to the starboard side of the ship.

Once there, she got into one of the motorboats used to transport guests to and from the party and fired up the engine.

"Hey!"

She looked up. McCall had his hands braced on the railing, ready to jump overboard to catch her. With a tight grip on the steering wheel, Lucy gunned it. And she couldn't help it—she waved goodbye, twisting her hand at the wrist like they do on parade floats, so that he'd be sure to see the emerald ring on her finger.

Chapter Two

Lucy wiped the dust from her sunglasses with the hem of her T-shirt and stared at the centuries old sandstone Aztec village. She'd rather be anywhere else but the Arizona desert. Even with a tiring sun, heat stroked the back of her legs and neck. Dirt and rock and sand stretched for miles, baked into barren slopes that vanished into the horizon.

She gulped down a boulder-sized knot in her throat. This morning she'd been sure she could handle this. But casting a wide glance at her surroundings, she felt more alone than she had since Matt and her dad's death.

An unforgiving wind propelled her forward. Her hiking boots kicked up earth and grime. The closer she got to the hand plastered walls, the smaller she felt.

Finding the sixteenth century gold Tlaloc sculpture had taken over two years. She'd promised Matt and her dad she would continue the search, no matter how long it took to find.

After she'd delivered the ring to Malcolm, she'd packed up everything she owned and thrown it into her aged but trusty Land Cruiser. She'd driven across the country, taking a little time to see the spots she'd always wanted to visit: Graceland because her dad had been a big Elvis fan, Mount Rushmore, Yellowstone National Park, and the small town in Colorado where her grandmother had lived.

She played with the small opal gem around her neck—the one souvenir she'd allowed herself on the trip. She'd always loved her grandmother's birthstone and last week would have been her seventy-fifth birthday. The necklace didn't come close to replacing the family she'd lost, but it did give her the comfort that had been eluding her these past few weeks. Her grandmother had always been the one to lift her spirits and remind her to cherish every moment, no matter how small.

The roar of a car engine reminded her where she stood and drew her attention over her shoulder. She lifted a hand to cut the glare from the sinking sun. Two pick-up trucks stirred up dust as they climbed the road leading to her position.

Shit. She needed time to explore the village on her own. Minimal damage to historic landmarks always took top priority. She had to be certain about where the sculpture was hidden before she started excavating.

She ran to the main entrance, her army-green canvas knapsack bouncing against her side as she raced to avoid making an acquaintance.

Once shaded from the elements and unwelcome truck drivers, she marveled at the architecture within the walls of the village. She ran her sweaty palms down the sides of her shorts and swiped a hand over the cool, rough stone. The age and tradition of such a primitive site elicited a tingle through her fingertips. She never got tired of brushing up against history.

For a few minutes she let herself remember all the adventures she, Matt, and her dad had been on. They'd navigated jungles, oceans, temples, underground tunnels. She'd forget about Malcolm and his cold, ruthless way of caring for nothing but uncommon relics and how much they were worth, and instead enjoy the excitement of finding something rooted in history.

None of those searches mattered as much as this one though.

Footsteps brought her back to the present.

Only it was too late.

The hand on her shoulder was big, the male scent tickling her nose pleasant—and familiar. She spun around.

"You?" he scoffed, his voice the same deep timbre she remembered.

Lucy's heart stopped. The guy from the *Star of Aesa*—McCall—looked none too pleased to see her. She was pretty unhappy to see him, too. She'd seen enough of him in a few of her dreams lately.

"We meet again," she said, because she had no idea what else to say. Of all the times for fate to intervene, it couldn't have happened at a worse time.

"Yeah. Wow." He took a step back and his disposition softened some. He ran a hand through his messy, straight, dark brown hair.

"What, uh, are you doing here?" She briefly wondered if he'd been looking for her since that day on the boat before she mentally slapped herself. A man like him did not look for a girl like her.

He shook his head. "You don't get to ask the questions. Why are *you* here?"

Nope. Not looking for her. "I'm sightseeing."

"You're trespassing."

She dug the toe of her boot into the hard ground. "How do you figure?"

"Because you're standing in my preservation project. This is a protected site that's closed to the public."

"You're in heritage protection?" Crap. She'd assumed he was some rich guy on the *Star of Aesa*, there to invest his money in a worthy cause. She squeezed her thigh to stop her leg from shaking.

"Keats McCall." He extended his hand. "President of Field Operations, World Heritage Fund."

Lucy stared at his hand. *Shit. Shit. Shit.* He was *that* Mc-Call? Lucy had thought it his first name, not his last, when she'd heard it on the ship. "So you know." He'd no doubt read about the emerald ring's discovery in the newspaper. Malcolm always made sure to garner as much publicity as possible for himself. He never divulged who did his work for him, but McCall had seen the ring on her finger. For the first time, she'd been caught in the act.

"That you stole the Malta emerald. Yeah." He dropped his arm.

"I didn't steal it. I found it."

He knitted his brows. "You do all the finds for Malcolm Holmes? He's got quite a collection. And reputation."

"I used to. I don't anymore." And she'd only worked for him in the first place because of her father. Her dad had had an amicable relationship with Malcolm for years, offering his knowledge and expertise to authenticate artifacts. But after Malcolm had funded one of their hunts for the Tlaloc sculpture and they'd come back empty handed, they had to repay him by working for him.

"Why not?" He put his hand on the textured wall beside them and narrowed his eyes as if he knew what treasure lay within its structure.

Which was ridiculous. There was no way he knew why she was there. Most historians knew nothing about the Tlaloc sculpture. Those that did thought the god of rain, fertility, and water a hoax. Rumors dispelled it as a female deity. But she'd done extensive research on Aztec culture and *knew* the statue was real. And hidden in this village.

"I don't owe you an explanation." She dug her nails into her knapsack. If he pressed her, she would have to lie and for some reason—with this man—that didn't sit well a second time.

His fingers drummed the wall, drawing Lucy's attention away from his contemplative face. "I think you do."

"I'm currently unemployed and work is the farthest thing from my mind. I'm on vacation and the Aztec village was just one spot on my itinerary." The Tlaloc sculpture wasn't work. It was redemption.

He gave her a megawatt smile that made her knees weak.

"What?" she asked.

"You just gave me an explanation."

"Whatever. I've got to go." She turned and squeezed her eyes shut before walking away.

McCall followed her. The barren land wasn't a favorite of Lucy's, but she marveled at the desert sky painted with soft strokes of red and yellow.

"Is there something here I should know about?" He stopped her with a gentle hand on her shoulder. The contact sent a jolt of electricity all the way down to her toes.

But the anger in his tone nearly undid her. After their last encounter, he didn't trust her on his site. He could fish all he wanted, though. Lucy *had* to retrieve the last remaining sixteenth century gold Tlaloc sculpture. McCall's job might be to prevent any type of excavation, but there was no way she'd let him interfere with her plans.

She'd promised she'd find the sculpture. Keeping her promise was the only way she'd be able to move forward.

She looked right at McCall. "No."

"You know looting is against the law at historic sites. I'd hate to see you get arrested."

Anger flamed her cheeks. She put her hands on her hips "You did not just call me a looter."

"What if I did?"

He stood too close. The stubble on his chiseled jaw distracted her. The slow curve of his irritatingly seductive lips, too. He was baiting her, trying to get her to spill more details about herself. Well, he could try all he wanted, it wasn't going to work.

"I am not a looter." End of story. She spun around and walked down the dirt path leading to her car.

"I'll stop you," he said, falling in step beside her.

"No you won't."

His arm shot out in front of her, almost making her trip over her own feet. She twisted to face him at the same time he took her hands in his. "I will."

Lucy sucked in a breath. First off, his hands were big

and warm and callused just enough to make her wonder
what they'd feel like rubbing the kinks out of her neck. And
second, being eye level with his full mouth made her curious
about what he could do with it besides admonish her.

She stepped around him and leaned on the retaining
wall that lined the dirt walkway. They were perched on a
narrow edge of land, the drop drawing her eyes to rugged
terrain that looked like the surface of another planet. "I told
you, I'm here on vacation."

"Forgive me if I don't believe you."

"Believe what you want, McCall."

M cCall pressed two fingers to the spot between his neck
and shoulder blade. No amount of pressure, however,
curbed the throbbing that came when he was on edge.

The sexiest, most intriguing woman he'd ever met stood
beside him and fuck if he knew what to do with her. He was
furious with her for making him look like an ass on the *Sea
of Aesa*. But worse, he was pissed off that he was happy to
see her again.

She was a liar, but he sensed it was a means of self-
defense. Secrets hid behind eyes that reminded him of the
emerald ring. Caution, too.

No doubt due to Malcolm Holmes. He and Malcolm
had been friends at Princeton. Crusaders for history and the
preservation of important landmarks. Then Malcolm had
stumbled upon an ancient piece of pottery in Peru and decided collecting artifacts was better than fieldwork. Malcolm
abandoned his principles—and his friends—and screwed

over anyone who got in his way to becoming one of the world's biggest and wealthiest collectors.

McCall's attention dipped to her bag. He'd bet his Rolex she didn't carry the usual girl stuff in there.

"How about a deal? You tell me what you're looking for and I give you access to my village. Legally." If Malcolm was involved in this, McCall sure as hell wasn't going to let him win. And that meant keeping tabs on the beautiful thief beside him.

Really, he'd be wise to get her the hell off the property or call the authorities. But that idea sucked. Because what he stupidly wanted was to find out more about her.

She tossed him a sideways glare and turned to sit on the wall. "I don't do deals. And even if I did, I've no reason to make one."

No reason his ass. But if she wasn't going to be honest with him, then he'd have to think of another way to keep an eye on her.

It was highly unlikely that anything of significant value would be found at a protected site in the US, but that didn't mean it wasn't possible. First thing in the morning he'd have Connor do some research.

McCall lived and breathed heritage protection. He was passionate about the environment and keeping historic monuments intact. His job was to strengthen the Aztec village, not poke and prod it. *If* anything were in its walls, he'd leave it there.

Yet... He knew of finds where the integrity of the monuments had for the most part been left undamaged and therefore no legal action had been taken against the "treasure hunters."

"Your nose is growing," he teased, sitting next to her.

She absently touched the tip of her nose before her eyes and mouth narrowed in annoyance. The look did nothing less than tempt him further. *Shit*. It had been too long since he'd been with a woman. Too long since he'd let loose. And the fact that this woman had *trouble* written all over only made her more appealing. He hadn't been in trouble in a while.

"So when does work start?" she asked.

Bold move. He admired her nerve and didn't hesitate to answer. "Monday."

"That's four days from now. What brought you out here tonight?" Her voice had the kind of sweet but sexy sound that made it difficult not to tell her exactly what she wanted to know.

"I brought my security guy up." He nodded toward Clay standing beside his truck. "He's ex Navy SEAL. And by my best estimate, hasn't taken his eyes off us since we came out of the village."

"He have a crush on you or something?"

McCall laughed. He and Clay had been friends for a couple of years now and constantly gave each other shit about the opposite sex. "You jealous?"

It was her turn to laugh. And the dimple McCall discovered on her left cheek damn near killed him. He wondered if there was a matching one on the other side.

She dropped her knapsack between her calves. Her khaki shorts were frayed at the edge, her boots scuffed. He tried not to stare at her smooth, tanned thighs.

"So do I get to know your name?" McCall asked.

It took her a few seconds to answer. "Lucy." She looked

out past the horizon, nibbled on her bottom lip, and took a very deliberate deep breath. "Lucy Davenport."

"Well, Lucy Davenport, the guy over there that looks like a tank is Clay Doherty. He's on watch here starting tonight." He wanted her to know what she was up against if she decided to sneak back to his village.

"You had McDonald's French fries on the way over here, didn't you?" she said, completely changing the subject and confusing the hell out of him.

"Huh?"

"You smell like them." She swiped at a strand of hair that escaped her ponytail. Then her stomach growled loud enough for Clay to hear.

"You hungry? We can finish this conversation over dinner."

She jumped to her feet. Her eyes darted to the ground before settling on his. He saw a maze of intelligence there and wondered if he'd ever know what she was truly thinking.

"No thanks. I've got plans." She stepped away.

"Break them." An ice cold bath would probably feel better than getting tangled up with her, but he was easily seduced by her refusal. He liked a challenge.

He followed her to her car, the sway of her hips hypnotic. His lips curled into a smile. A fling. A few days of fun. That's all he wanted. He never committed to any more than that. Never lost control of his emotions. Besides, it made sense to stay in contact so he'd know what she was up to.

"No can do," she said over her shoulder.

"Where are you staying?" he asked when they reached her SUV with South Carolina license plates. He did a double take. "Did you drive across the country?"

Her spine stiffened. "Could you quit breathing down my neck?" She turned and pressed her hands to his chest to back him up a few paces.

His T-shirt was thin. Her hands were…on him. And he liked it. A lot.

He guessed she liked it, too, because she jerked her hands back and her cheeks reddened. "Please leave me alone."

"I'm finding that hard to do."

"Why?"

"You're on my site with intentions I'm not clear on yet."

She blinked repeatedly before turning to open the passenger door and tossing her bag on the floor.

Wrong answer, dumb ass. Jesus, put the kind of woman he wasn't used to in front of him and his charm plummeted. "Hang on." He wrapped his hand around the car door before she could close it.

"No, thanks." She rounded the hood.

McCall didn't force a woman do to things, but peeking inside Lucy's car, he'd use whatever force was necessary to keep her with him. He surveyed the contents with disbelief. Pillow and blanket. Clothes strewn about. Wrinkled fast food bags. Maps. "You've been sleeping in your car."

"Yeah. So what?" She climbed into the driver's seat.

"So that's not safe." His gut clenched in an unfamiliar tangle at the thought of her parking somewhere and spending the night without proper shelter.

"I've slept in worse conditions." She reached to put the key in the ignition. "Goodbye, McCall."

He jumped into the car.

"What are you doing?" The car keys clanked as they

slipped through her fingers and landed at her feet.

"I'm getting you a place to stay so I can keep an eye on you and then I'm taking you to dinner. Unless you'd rather my security team follow you."

Her eyes practically bugged out of her head. "You're not in charge of me. Now get out of my car."

Something poked him in the hip. He reached between the seat and the center console and pulled out a carving chisel. She grabbed it from him.

A horrible thought raced through his mind. Did she have it to protect herself while sleeping?

"Out!" She waved the tool, but what he couldn't tear his gaze from was the tug-of-war in her eyes.

He'd never before let himself get snared by a woman's belligerence, and now that he was, adrenaline shot through his system. They may be on opposing sides, but the sparks between them were undeniable.

"Or what?" he challenged.

She mumbled words that sounded like jackass and annoying and son-of-a-bitch all rolled into one. Finally she settled on a clear, "Seriously?"

"I'm always serious."

"Yeah. I can tell." She reached down for her keys before pushing back against her seat. Her eyes closed and she took a deep breath. "I'm not getting rid of you, am I?"

He detected a hint of gladness in her tone. "No."

Her head lolled to the side and she gave him a defeated look. "You'd be better off staying away from me."

"I'll be the judge of that."

"Fine." She turned the key in the ignition. The car didn't start. She tried again. Still no luck. "Dammit."

They got out and McCall looked under the hood. The scant amount of remaining daylight made it tough to get a good look. Clay sauntered over. "Problem?"

"You got jumper cables?" McCall asked.

"For the pretty lady, I've got whatever she needs." He smiled at Lucy.

The only reason McCall kept his cool at his friend's blatant attempt to one-up him was because Lucy didn't smile back.

Five minutes later, a jump hadn't worked. "I'll get a tow truck out here tomorrow," McCall said. "Grab whatever you need for tonight and we'll take my truck."

Lucy shook her head. She took her knapsack and another shoulder bag out of the car and clicked the alarm. "I don't need a tow truck, I need gas."

"You couldn't have mentioned that a few minutes ago?"

She shrugged, a mischievous grin lifted the corners of her mouth. "I thought I'd make it a few more miles. I'll walk to a gas station and get a lift back."

Clay laughed, no doubt amused that the last thing Lucy wanted was to get in a car with him.

"You do realize the nearest gas station is about four miles away?" McCall hadn't been around many women who didn't agree with whatever he said, but he knew putting his foot down with Lucy would only backfire. She needed space. And he'd give it to her—for a mile or two. Just long enough for her to get her thoughts in order.

"I went to college. I'm good with distances. But thanks for that." She waved over her shoulder and started down the dirt path leading to the highway.

McCall leaned against the car and watched her go. Sweat

trickled down his side.

"Wow," Clay said. "Never thought I'd see the day a woman walked *away* from you. And in the middle of the desert." He cracked up and pulled his cell phone from his pocket. "I'm definitely tweeting this."

"Shut the fuck up."

"Who is she?"

"Her name is Lucy. We met last month." McCall pressed away from the car but couldn't pull his gaze from her retreat.

"She blow you off then, too?"

McCall turned his head and glared at Clay. He should tell him about Lucy, but he held back. If Clay knew she was a thief and probably on the hunt for something at the village, he'd be all over McCall to stop helping her.

"I'll take that as a yes."

And he wanted to help her. At least for tonight. He glanced into her car for a clue that might help him draw a better picture of this complicated woman. Independent was all he came up with.

"There's something else going on," Clay said, his keen perception annoying as hell.

"Maybe. But I'll fill you in later." He'd *never* chased someone before, but Lucy made him forget himself. He strode to his truck. "You good, here?"

"When am I ever not?" Clay called back.

"I'll talk to you tomorrow."

"Won't I see you when you come back for Lucy's car?"

"We're not coming back tonight."

Chapter Three

An evening shade swallowed the scenery around Lucy as the desert slipped into sleep. She picked up her pace in hopes of getting to a gas station before complete darkness fell. Nocturnal creatures didn't bother her much, but coyotes preferred the night, didn't they? And ever since she was ten and a coyote had killed the stray dog she'd found, she'd been afraid of them.

A car pulled up and idled along beside her.

"Get in," floated out the passenger window.

She stopped and slowly turned. McCall's voice did things to her that no other sound had ever done before. The reaction hurt as much as it aroused. Even though Matt had been gone for over two years, she felt like she was betraying him.

For a few long seconds she just stared, not sure what she wanted to do. He'd stopped the car and was staring back, and his quiet patience snared her. Her heart skipped a beat. She'd meant it when she told him he'd be better off keeping his distance. She wasn't good for anybody. And especially not him. Because no matter what, she was taking the Tlaloc sculpture from his village.

"Come on, Lucy. Let me give you a ride."

The way he said her name, like he really liked it, lured her into his truck with relative ease. She shouldn't be doing this, but she was unable to stop herself.

The cool air circulating inside his truck was a welcome relief from the warm desert breeze. "Thank you," she said, only because she had good manners and not because sitting beside him made her feel safer than she'd been in a long time.

"No problem."

They drove in silence until they passed the gas station and her back went ramrod straight, the seatbelt cutting across her chest uncomfortably. "Where are we going?"

"I'm getting you a room and feeding you dinner."

"No, McCall."

He slid her a look out of the corner of his eye. "One day you're going to say 'Yes, McCall.'"

"One day?" she said. "There is only right now and if you don't pull over at the next gas station I'm going to scream out the window for help."

"Go ahead."

She pressed the button for the window, but realized no one would hear her plea. "Damn it, McCall. You can't do this."

"Why not?" He drove up the freeway onramp, further away from her car, further away from the vow she'd made.

"Because I'm not a charity case and I can take care of myself." Tension and excitement combined to put her head and body at odds with each other. The air crackled between them despite the fact that they came from different worlds.

His day job earned him a nice living, but he also came from a wealthy family that the media loved to cover. McCall's grandfather was an international businessman worth millions. McCall's father had followed suit, adding philanthropy to their family company. And from the expensive watch on his wrist to the light blue Polo shirt that did little to hide his broad, muscular chest, he seemed every inch the do-gooder playboy she'd read about.

"Getting help doesn't mean you're not capable," he said, his hands tightening around the steering wheel. "But not helping means I'm a jerk. And while I think I've figured out you'd rather be anywhere but in this car, I'm not giving you a choice tonight."

Lucy thought about her tight budget and bit the inside of her cheek. "Fine. But I don't need anything special."

McCall lifted her hand. "You can quit squeezing the life out of your bag. Tonight is on me."

She wanted to argue with him, but if she were really honest with herself, a free night's sleep in a bed sounded much better than her backseat. And if it made him feel better about himself then who was she to deny him?

A few minutes later they exited the freeway and arrived at the *El Cabazon Canyon Campground*. Luxury cabins and tents sat amidst natural surroundings. Tiny white lights twinkled in the trees. Lucy laughed.

"What's so funny?"

"This is your idea of roughing it, isn't it?" She'd heard about glamping, but never thought she'd experience it.

He parked and tossed her a glance as he slid out his door. "You have a problem with comfort?"

"No." Lucy put both her bags on her shoulder, refusing

to let him help when he reached to carry the larger one. She followed him along the cobblestone path to a large main cabin. "What's that smell?" Her stomach growled for the tenth time.

"Corn roasting in adobe fireplaces. I promise we'll eat just as soon as we get you a room."

While he made arrangements at the check-in desk, Lucy sat in a wicker rocking chair and picked up the *Outside* magazine lying on the cedar side table. She couldn't remember the last time she'd read anything other than history books and maps.

"I've got good news and bad news," McCall said a couple of minutes later.

Lucy got to her feet. Again, he lingered too close, his scent and size overwhelming her. She teetered back a step. "Okay."

"The bad news is there are no available rooms. The good news is my cabin is big enough for both of us. Let's go."

His words all ran together as if speaking fast would make that arrangement okay. She stood frozen to her spot for a second.

"Don't worry," he tossed out, as she hurried to keep up with him. "I promise to be a perfect gentleman."

As far as bad ideas went, this ranked at the top. Lucy already found it hard to breathe around him. Spending time under the same roof would only fuel the combustible air between them.

You can do this. He might push her beyond her comfort zone, but she'd been keeping her distance from people her whole life. No one got in unless she wanted them to, and Keats McCall was no exception.

She walked beside him as they took the path to his cabin. Pine trees and red Bird of Paradise shrubs flanked them on both sides, the campsite a far cry from the desert of an hour ago.

The path narrowed and his arm grazed hers. Every time he touched her the urge to touch him back swelled inside her. He nodded to the right. "That way."

A minute later McCall led her up wooden steps to a large deck and cabin. Two Adirondack chairs and a small oak table sat off to the side. He unlocked the sliding glass door and eased it open.

Lucy took a deep breath then followed him inside, confident she could handle one night and keep the upper hand. "Wow."

The king-sized canopy bed, plank flooring, Native American rugs, and high ceilings were cozy and inviting and put her right at ease. Off to one side, she noticed a footed tub in the bathroom and two sinks. On the other side was a wall made of side-by-side tree trunks with an open entryway. She stepped through and found a second bedroom with a queen-sized bed.

"This is for me?" she asked, startled to find he'd been watching her.

"Yep."

She dropped her bags and jumped onto the bed. It felt like heaven as she rolled onto her back and sank into the soft cotton comforter. After being stuck in her car for the past ten days, the bed was nothing short of amazing.

It wasn't that she couldn't afford a cheap motel room here or there. But after spending the last two years working for Malcolm for basically nothing because of the repayment her father owed him, she had to be careful with what little she'd managed to save. Until she got a job, she couldn't afford any luxuries. And she couldn't get a job until she kept her promise to recover the Tlaloc sculpture.

"Better than last night's sleeping arrangement, I'm guessing." McCall leaned against the doorway, his arms crossed over his chest. He didn't sound smug or pitying. He sounded...happy.

Lucy blinked away the warmth that ignited inside her. "I guess this will do." She rolled onto her side and propped her head up with her hand.

His smile upped her warm factor. "I thought I'd order us a pizza if that's okay with you."

"I like pizza." And she was quite happy he didn't want to go out somewhere. Now that she was lying down every muscle in her body asked to stay right where they were.

"Great. Any particular topping you want?"

"Pineapple and anchovies."

He made a face like he'd just eaten something sour and then chased it with Tabasco sauce.

"I'm kidding. I'll take it any way you like it."

"Promise?" McCall's eyes darkened and she had a feeling he wasn't thinking about pizza anymore.

She wasn't either, now that she realized what had just come out of her mouth. A mouth that now had the attention of his heated gaze. She rolled over onto her back and pretended she had no idea he was flirting with her.

Getting too chummy with the enemy wasn't part of the plan.

Lucy's position on the bed reminded him of making angels in the snow. But when she closed her eyes and took a deep breath, hell if that didn't make him think about crawling on top of her and making her scream his name before he flipped her over and took her a second time.

If she was trying to give him the biggest hard-on of his life, it was working.

She rolled onto her stomach, her chin in her palms, her legs bent at the knee. "You're still here."

"Uh, yeah." He needed to wait for a certain body part to settle down.

"I'm really hungry."

So the fuck was he. With wisps of hair around her face, her ponytail in complete disarray, and her full lips absent of a tastes-like-shit colored beauty product, she muddled every sane thought in his head.

He pushed off the wall and moved toward her.

"What are you doing?" She scrambled up onto her knees.

"It's time for a little question and answer." He sat on the edge of the bed.

"Are you trying to kill me? Because if I don't eat soon, I might die." She relaxed some on her haunches. "But maybe that's your plan. If I'm dead you don't have to worry about what I'm doing here."

"Just where to bury the body." He winked.

She bristled and it was damn cute. He picked up the phone on the nightstand and ordered a pepperoni pizza from the place down the road that boasted the best deep dish in the southwest. He included a Caesar salad, side of spaghetti and meatballs, and four bottles of water.

"Thank you," she said on a breathy sigh before moving

to sit back against the headboard. She reached down and undid her boots, then tossed them to the floor. Her socks were pink leopard print.

They made him wonder what her other undergarments might look like. He cleared his throat. "Should be here in forty-five minutes."

"Perfect. My expiration date was one hour. So you have questions?"

He moved beside her, his legs extending several inches beyond hers. "You're awfully agreeable all of a sudden."

"No. Just smart. I figure for every question you ask, I get one, too. Otherwise you can forget it."

McCall inwardly groaned. How had she turned *his* question and answer into *her* game? Time to take back control. "How long have you been a thief?"

"I'm..." She jutted her chin out and looked at him. Eyes far too beautiful and assessing studied him for several seconds. "I'm not a thief. I'm an archeologist."

"Honestly?" He searched for the truth in the swirls of green and brown still locked on him and found so much more—strength, perseverance, devotion. "Then I don't understand." And he wanted to. He wanted to know what drove Lucy more than he'd ever wanted to know about anyone else.

"I find objects of historic value. What's not to understand?"

"You steal them, for one. And your employer is an asshole, for two. The archeologists I know split their time between honest fieldwork and laboratory studies."

She brought her knees up and wrapped her arms around her legs. "I told you I don't work for Malcolm anymore and who are you to judge how I use my degree? You know nothing about me."

"Fill me in." He wondered if she'd go for it.

"What's being done at the Aztec village?"

He chuckled at his wishful thinking. "Stuff."

Lucy glared at him. "They give you that fancy president title for doing *stuff*?" She turned her head, slid her hands down her shins, and rubbed her feet.

"My stuff is better than anyone else's." He grabbed her ankles and pulled until she was on her back and her feet were in his lap.

"Hey!" She lifted, but the second he started to massage her foot, she leaned back on her elbows and her shoulders relaxed. Her eyelids fluttered shut, a tiny moan fell from her lips. She slapped her hand over her mouth and her eyebrows furrowed.

"Been awhile, huh?"

"Wha…What?" She stammered, moving her hand away.

"Since someone's taken care of you." He watched a flash of pain cloud her eyes and drain the color from her cheeks. *Shit.* Had she lost someone?

She tried to pull her feet back, but he held tight. He wanted to rub every bad thing that had happened to her away with each stroke of his hands.

"Where was the last place you visited just for fun?" he asked, hoping to steer the conversation to more pleasant memories.

"Here." She grabbed one of the bed pillows and put it behind her head.

"Lucy. You are not fooling me a second time."

The corners of her mouth split into the kind of smile you couldn't help but return. *Only the one dimple.* But the damage it did ruined him for other smiles.

"The look on your face when I waved from the motor-boat *was* priceless."

He dug his fingers a little harder into the pad of her foot before switching to the other one. "Why do you do it? It's obviously not for money."

"It's a long story."

"That involves someone else?" He'd keep prying until she told him. She couldn't be more than twenty-six or twenty-seven, which meant her story couldn't be that long.

She undid her ponytail and shook her head. The wavy auburn strands fanned across the pillow when she lowered her head back down.

McCall gulped. His eyes roamed over her face, down to her chest, and followed the smooth skin of her tanned legs until he reached his hands. In his grasp, her small foot almost disappeared from view.

"I told you I'm on my own."

"But you weren't always."

"Guess my superpower and I'll tell you everything you want to know." She wiggled her shoulders from side to side and burrowed a little deeper into the comforter.

"Sorry?" What the hell was she talking about?

"You know, if you could have any superpower, what would it be? Guess mine. I already know yours."

"Ah. And what's mine?"

"Oh my God. Don't stop. That feels so good right there." She closed her eyes again as he pressed his thumb into the bottom of her heel.

His superpower at the moment? Restraint. It took everything he had not to move his hands up her legs and touch her *everywhere.*

"You," she continued, "would like the power of invisibility."

"What makes you say that?" He had no idea what superpower he'd want. He'd never thought about it.

Very slowly, her eyelids lifted. "You come from a wealthy family, but do quite well on your own. You live for your job and have a great deal of notoriety, but you'd rather blend in with the crowd than be put in the spotlight. Your looks, job title, and background make that difficult."

Every muscle in McCall's body pinched. She *saw* him.

"So if you could, I'm betting you'd like to make yourself invisible sometimes. That's why you were talking to a waitress on the *Sea of Aesa* rather than one of the socialites."

"You're wrong." He fought the urge to press his fingers to the throb on the side of his neck.

"Don't think so." She pulled back her legs and sat up. A smile tugged at the corner of her mouth.

Despite his ill at ease over her assessment, he wanted to wipe that smirk off her face. Not with further denial, but with his mouth securely attached to hers.

"You can think what you want," he said.

"I will."

He wasn't half as close to figuring her out. "I'm guessing your superpower would be to fly." He did imagine she'd like to have her feet off the ground, her head in the clouds, and feel unencumbered. To be far from the lingering pain he saw in her eyes.

She shook her head. "Nope."

"What then?" He shouldn't care. He should get the hell off the bed and leave her alone for tonight. Every word out of her mouth drew him closer, made him more interested, when what he should be focused on was whatever stake she — or Malcolm — had in his village.

"You didn't guess right so I don't have to tell you." She pulled the pillow that was behind her head into her lap.

"Chicken."

"No."

"Then tell me." Why this stupid game mattered to him he had no idea. But he couldn't deny when the topic of conversation was her, he was helpless to stop it.

Lucy squeezed the pillow. Several seconds ticked by in silence.

"My superpower would be whistling," she said, her voice serious and quiet.

Her tone stopped him from calling her bluff and joking that such a basic skill was not on the list of superpowers. "You can't whistle?"

She blew through her lips and nothing but air slipped out. Her pucker, though, spiraled his self-control into dangerous territory. He thought about having her breath all over him. *Get off the fucking bed.*

"But it's not that kind I'm talking about. I want to be able to do the one where you put your fingers in the corners of your mouth and whistle sharp and loud. The kind of high pitch sound that people could hear from miles away."

"Why?"

Lucy tilted her head. "If I told you I'd be giving away top secret information."

McCall stayed silent. She hadn't meant it as a challenge, but he took it as one.

Chapter Four

Lucy woke Friday morning in a panic and scrambled out of bed cursing the time. She'd never slept until eleven in her life. Damn comfortable bed. After stuffing herself with Italian food last night, she'd sunk into the soft mattress, pulled the down comforter around her, and passed out.

"Why didn't you wake me?" she said, slipping through the cabin's open sliding glass door. She perched herself on the edge of the Adirondack chair next to McCall's and stretched her arms wide.

"I didn't know I was your alarm clock," he said to her chest. Lucy glanced down and without a bra underneath her tank top McCall had quite the view.

She quickly dropped her arms. "Whatever. I need to get to my car. Can you be ready in ten?"

He smirked. "Not necessary. Your car is here."

"*What?*" She fisted her hands. If anyone had snooped through the things in her car they might discover what she was doing in Arizona.

"It's not the gas tank, by the way. But I didn't think you'd appreciate me taking your car to a mechanic without your permission." He folded the newspaper in his hands and tossed it onto the small, slatted wood table.

"Back up a minute. How did my car get here then?"

"I had it towed. Clay tried the gas route first. Didn't work."

Lucy ground her teeth together. "How did Clay do that without a key?"

McCall ran a hand through his dark brown hair. Eyes the color of blueberries—her favorite fruit—gleamed with misdoing. "Before the military he worked in the automobile industry."

"Yeah, obviously under questionable circumstances." Lucy picked up McCall's coffee mug and took a sip. She couldn't resist the rich Kona smell. McCall watched her, his lips curled in amusement.

"Finish it," he said.

"Thanks. So any idea what's wrong with my car?" Her stomach knotted at the word "wrong." She couldn't afford to have anything wrong that cost more than a few dollars.

"Clay said best case scenario it's the starter or ignition switch."

"And the worst?" Lucy tried not to show unease by keeping her voice calm. Whatever needed to be done, she'd find a way. On her own.

"Could be something with the engine."

She put down the coffee and crossed her arms. A cloud blocked the sun and a chill swept through her. Engine trouble would mean an expensive fix.

"I can help," McCall said, as if he could read her mind.

"I don't want your help." Lucy stood. "I'll get my stuff and if you could arrange for another tow, my car and I will be on our way." McCall had already complicated things enough. She needed to put distance between them—the sooner, the better. She'd come to Arizona for the Tlaloc sculpture and nothing more.

McCall put his hand on her wrist. Sparks skittered up her arm. "Hear me out. I need a favor from you, too."

"I don't do favors." Especially not for sexy heritage preservationists who had already helped more than she was comfortable with.

His grip tightened ever so slightly. "Give me one minute."

"Could you please drop my hand?"

He did. "Could you please drop the attitude?"

She stared down at him and reminded herself she got better results with sugar than vinegar. It wouldn't hurt to hear what he had to say. As long as she didn't focus on his very fine mouth or bluer than blue eyes or broad shoulders or annoyingly appealing stubble, she'd be okay. She sat and looked at his knees.

"What is it?" she asked.

"I know money is tight for you." He leaned forward with his elbows on his thighs and laced his fingers together. "I'd like to pay to have your car fixed, but I also know you won't accept it. So I'm proposing a deal. I've got an event to attend on Sunday night and I'd like you to be my date."

Lucy's jaw dropped. Her gaze snapped back to his. "You're asking me out on a date?" Tiny trembles sped through her.

"No. I'm asking you to be my date. There's a difference."

Of course there was. Mr. Calm, Cool, and Gorgeous was only proposing a business transaction.

"I go with you and you pay to fix my car." Not a bad idea, actually. She didn't have extra money. He hated mingling with wealthy single women looking for a husband.

He unclasped his hands and leaned back. "Exactly."

The chances of her car being fixed in half a day were slim so she'd probably need to wait until Monday to get it back anyway. A slight problem for her plans, but she could work around it.

"Does this deal include continued room accommodations?" Keep your friends close and your enemies closer and all that.

His nod and smile worked together so damn nicely that she regretted her inquiry. She should have just said no thank you. She'd scraped by for years and managed just fine. "You in?" he asked.

She nodded. *Dammit*. Why did she feel like she'd just walked into a trap?

She ran her hands down her bare legs. "Wait. What kind of event is this?"

His gaze followed her movement. "Black tie."

She turned her attention to the grooves between the wood planks of the deck. The way he watched her triggered whirls of pleasure low in her stomach that made it difficult to think straight.

Black tie? Her wits returned.

"Can't do it. I don't have a dress." She got up, grateful for the excuse to decline the deal. "I'll be ready to go in a few minutes." Besides not having the proper attire, she'd never been to a formal affair and had no desire to start now.

McCall followed her into the cabin. "Look in your closet."

"Why?" She didn't bother turning around. Then silently scolded herself. The fewer questions she asked, the quicker she'd be on her way to sneak back into the Aztec village.

"Please." The sincerity in his voice jabbed her in the heart, nudging her toward the closet.

"Fine." Lucy opened the closet door and gasped. Three dresses hung inside. No, not dresses. Gowns. Beautiful, floor length gowns. She spun around.

McCall leaned against the large open doorway, his arms crossed, a smile on his face. He raised his eyebrows.

She marched right over to him and poked his chest, knocking him off balance. Anger ran through her veins. "I am not some bimbo you can buy and dress up to suit your needs. How the hell did you do this? And how dare you presume I'd go along with it." She pushed him again, with both hands this time.

He caught her by the wrists and brought her right up against his royal blue T-shirt. The soft cotton and his shower fresh scent took some wind out of her irritation.

"That isn't at all what I think, Lucy."

God, she barely knew him, but she knew his intentions weren't as she'd accused. She'd pushed him away as if that could make him take back his kindness. Lucy didn't know how to handle herself on his playing field.

"I thought to make things easier for you," he said.

Easy? Nothing about McCall was easy. "You thought wrong." She told herself to step back, only she didn't. Because once again she stood eye level with the kind of mouth that put all other mouths to shame.

"Look, we both need something and we can give it to

each other. Dress up for one night and save me from having to make small talk and fend off unwanted advances."

Somehow he made cocky sound endearing. Lucy had seen the women on the *Star of Aesa* eye him like a winning lottery ticket and that had to get old.

"If I do this, it has nothing to do with saving your ass." And everything to do with getting information about his site that would help her find her sculpture.

"Of course not."

Let him think it was to save her own ass, which was the truth. She was incapable of saving anyone else. Otherwise Matt and her dad would still be here.

Memories of their accident bombarded her and she stumbled away from McCall. *Shit.* Tears stung the back of her eyes. Breathing suddenly required effort.

She didn't do this in front of strangers. She didn't do it in front of anyone.

"Hey, you okay?"

"Fine." She gave him her back. "Let's set this plan in motion."

"You sure?" His warm breath caressed the back of her neck, telling her he'd stepped closer.

One foot in front of the other. She'd repeated that dozens of times over the past two years. "Positive." She stepped away from him, back to her own room.

A couple hours later, Lucy sat in McCall's truck, her body a tight knot of tension, her gaze unfocused as they drove away from the mechanic's shop. She'd gotten everything of importance out of her car before it was towed, but she still hated the idea of leaving her belongings with a stranger for the weekend.

When they reached the highway Lucy realized she had no idea where they were headed.

"Where are we going?" she asked.

"I've got an appointment and thought I'd take you along."

Her head snapped to the left. McCall's easy tone of voice lit a fuse inside her. "Just because you're in the driver's seat does not mean you're in charge of me. I don't plan on being attached to your hip all weekend. I've got things to do, too."

He slid her a carefree, crooked smile. "I think you'll enjoy this."

"And why is that?"

"Because you're good at finding things."

Lucy sat up taller. "I'm great at finding things."

"So what is it you hope to find in my village?" His eyes were on the road, one hand wrapped casually around the steering wheel.

His question got a smile out of her. He could keep trying, but she'd never tell him about the Tlaloc sculpture. "What do you need help finding today?"

"I don't need help. I'm taking a group of kids geocaching." He exited the freeway and headed towards the mountains.

"What's that?" she asked.

"It's a treasure hunting game that uses GPS coordinates to lead us to a hidden cache. There's over a million caches buried all over the world. Quadruple that amount and you've got your participants. A big percentage of that is kids." He turned his head. Lines etched the corner of his eyes, undoubtedly from long hours in the sun and smiling too much. He had a killer smile. "Whenever I'm at a project site and there's a geocache nearby, I round up some local kids and take them on a hunt. It's amazing to see the look on their faces when we locate the cache and open it up."

Every muscle in Lucy's body went languid, yet her body stirred with the kind of tension that came from one thing: desire. Hearing that McCall did his own version of finding objects of value *and* did it with children, stirred up long buried feelings.

One of the last arguments she'd had with Matt had been over settling down and starting a family. Lucy wanted children, but Matt didn't. He was content with the way things were. It hurt like hell, but made perfect sense. Matt's free spirit and insatiable desire for adventure were why she'd fallen for him in the first place. That and her father had adored him. She'd met Matt in their freshman archeology class, brought him home to meet her dad, and that was that.

"What have you found so far?" she asked, a happier memory edging out thoughts of Matt. When she was a child her dad had made it a birthday tradition to draw a treasure map for her to follow around their small house. The maps got a little harder every year, but the treasure was always the same—a Pez dispenser.

"Coins, buttons, small toys, books." He parked the car in a patch of dirt at the base of a mountain. A wood sign said *Riverback Trail.*

"I wonder what we'll find today." Lucy slipped out of the truck and met McCall at the rear bumper. "What?"

McCall slid on his sunglasses, but not before Lucy caught a glimpse of something in his sea blue eyes. Something like interest or fascination maybe. "You sound excited about it."

"Maybe I am." If she was stuck with McCall she might as well make the best of it. Not that being with him was any real hardship. She was glad he couldn't see her eyes through her Ray Bans because his T-shirt clung to his chest and abs in a way that made her stomach hot. His cargo shorts hung just right on his narrow hips. Add in the afternoon sun and cloudless sky as a backdrop and her body might catch fire if she paid him any more attention. *Pump him for information on the Aztec site, nothing else.*

"Good. Come on. I see our group from the Boys & Girls Club. For some of them, it's their first time hiking."

He picked up her hand like it was the most natural thing in the world and led her to the kids. Flutters hovered near the pit of her stomach.

But she could not let this adventure mean more than it should.

McCall led Lucy and the six pre-teen boys and girls up the winding mountain trail with one eye on the kids and one eye on her. Christ, he could look at her all day. Right now her pillowy lips were slightly parted, and fuck if he didn't want to part them further and explore her mouth with his.

He wasn't sure if her car trouble was a blessing or curse. Either way, it allowed him to keep an eye on her for the next few days. He didn't trust her motives where his village was concerned, but then his motives weren't completely innocent either.

By keeping her close, he hoped to figure out her interest

in the Aztec village and do whatever necessary to protect it. He didn't believe her claim that she wasn't working for Malcolm. There's no way Malcolm would let someone like her go.

McCall had talked to Connor this morning hoping to get an update on the research he'd asked him to do. His VP hadn't come up with much of anything regarding historical artifacts being buried in the southwest. He had mentioned a statue found back in the sixties in New Mexico that scholars believed was a Tlaloc sculpture—the god of rain, fertility, and water. The statue turned out to be a female deity, but since then there had been rumors of a gold Tlaloc object somewhere in the western US.

If that's what Lucy was looking for and it was in his village, he'd do whatever he had to, to preserve his site.

"We almost there?" Lucy asked, disrupting his thoughts. She lifted her sunglasses off her nose and ran a few fingers across her glistening cheekbones.

McCall paused to wipe the sweaty sting from one eye and glance at his phone. The kids' cheeks were red, their hair matted around their foreheads. "Looks like it. You guys doing okay? Let's take a water break."

The kids nodded and guzzled from their water bottles. There were several levels of difficulty when geocaching and this was one of the easiest. From McCall's estimate, they'd stumble upon the treasure in five to ten minutes.

"So who here thinks I should take over the lead?" Lucy asked, the bait in her voice appealing on a level McCall had never experienced before. No one took control from him.

Every hand went up but his. "I do," times six sounded. It was no surprise. Lucy had charmed his group from the second she'd introduced herself. She'd led them in song, complimented their stamina, and related to their adolescence with ease.

"Go for it," he said, surprised at how easy he handed her the reins. He gave her his cell with the coordinates.

A smile enticing enough to lure a cat to water spread across her beautiful face. "Let's go, then."

For the next few minutes they walked in easy silence. Even Mother Nature was quiet, the warm March day still and almost dormant on the trail. McCall took up the rear and thought about what he wanted to do next with Lucy. Her obvious love for the outdoors warranted further exploration. Keeping her occupied was a bonus and allowed him time to figure out what she was after.

"What do you think? Is this it?" She stopped and lifted the phone in the air for the kids' agreement.

They gathered around for a peek at the screen and one of the boys said, "I bet it's in that hollowed out tree trunk." He pointed to a large splintered section of wood off the beaten path.

"Let's find out." Lucy cast an appreciative sideways glance at McCall as she let the kids take the lead.

McCall scratched the itch on the back of his neck, blaming the dry heat and brittle brush. Not the woman whose every move enchanted him.

Every time her green golden eyes flashed his way, he wanted more. More of her history. More of what made her so independent. More of her secrets.

"Look!" One of the girls said, pulling out a large plastic container from inside the trunk. She opened it and took out a plastic bag that held a bracelet made from seashells. The boys groaned in apparent disappointment while the girls squealed with delight.

"You should have it," the girls said in unison, handing the bag to Lucy.

"Me?" The sheer surprise and joy in Lucy's voice told McCall she wasn't usually on the receiving end of things.

"Allow me," he said, taking the bag.

He removed the bracelet carefully. The tiny shell treasure didn't come close to filling his palm, but the workmanship brought a smile to his face. He reached for Lucy's arm.

The moment his fingers skated along her wrist sparks skittered up his arm. She shivered as he turned her wrist up. Her pulse throbbed beneath his touch.

McCall never thought of a wrist as sexy, but Lucy's was. The creases, the one freckle, the graceful way she held it out to him. He wanted to kiss his way around it.

He dropped one end of the bracelet.

Lucy caught it. She put it back in his grasp and cleared her throat. "You always get nervous in front of an audience?"

Shit. That's right. "Stay still." He slid the tiny shells along her skin until the ends met.

"It's beautiful." Lucy turned away and held up her arm. "Thank you for giving me the honor of wearing it." She wrapped the three girls in a hug.

"The rules of geocaching say if you take something, you have to leave something of equal or greater value in return," McCall said. He pulled the small silver amulet he'd brought with him out of his pocket. "You boys want the honor?"

McCall placed it in one of the young men's hands.

"Is that a Brazilian token?" Lucy asked. She cradled the boy's hand to get a better look. "It is." She stared at the medallion as if it contained some magical power.

"It's supposed to bring—"

"Good fortune," she finished for him.

If he'd had any doubt to the truth in her archeology background, he didn't any longer. "I thought it would be a nice thing to leave for the next person."

"It is." A tremor in her bottom lip lodged an ache in the deepest part of his heart.

"Hey," he said, fighting the urge to run the pad of his thumb over her lip's fullness. If they'd been alone, he would have. "I didn't mean for it to upset you."

She shook her head. "It didn't. It goes in the bag?"

"Yes, but first we need to sign the logbook." He took the small leather bound journal and pen out of the bag and let the kids have the honor first. While they signed, Lucy sat on the tree trunk. He took the spot next to her and waited. Once the kids were through they gave him the book and wandered off, staying close enough to keep an eye on.

Lucy's shoulder brushed his arm as she leaned over to see the logbook. He flipped the pages, she edged a little closer. After a few moments she relaxed against him, her knee touched his. It was as if with each turn of the page, they got more comfortable with each other, until they got to a fresh unmarked sheet. The past behind them. Something new in front of them.

"You sign for both of us," she said.

The pen shook in his hand. He couldn't remember why he'd doubted Lucy's honesty. Why he'd needed to keep an eye on her. All he knew in that moment was that he wanted to wrap himself around the woman beside him and pretend nothing else but the two of them existed. Then he signed the book, *McCall and Lucy.*

Chapter Five

"Your lips are like sin and I want to be bad."

Lucy harrumphed with disbelief. "That has got to be the worst line ever," she said, her feet curled under a pillow on the couch in McCall's room. Some reality show played on the television and she couldn't stop watching.

McCall closed his laptop and leaned forward on the chair next to her. "Guys will say most anything to get into a girl's pants."

She twisted and narrowed her eyes at him. "What's your best line?"

"Not telling."

"Because you're afraid I'll laugh."

"I'm not afraid of anything, least of all you." He swallowed and held her gaze.

She swallowed, too. This afternoon when he'd put the silver Brazilian token into the geocache and signed their names in the logbook like they belonged next to each other, she'd been afraid. Afraid that her plan to use McCall for information about his site and then leave might be harder than she'd thought. Because despite wishing otherwise, she liked him. A lot.

Good fortune hadn't been hers in such a long time and her heart shimmied in anticipation of what spending time with McCall might bring. She wanted to believe in good luck charms again, and today a sliver of hope had blossomed inside of her. Maybe he was the key to her finding the sculpture and putting the past behind her.

"You look pretty deep in thought over there," McCall said.

Before she could answer, a knock sounded on the sliding glass door.

"Perfect timing," McCall said. "Dinner's here. Come on."

She padded behind him in her bare feet, happy and unhappy about the interruption. She was hungry, but again, he'd taken liberties without asking.

McCall slid the door wide and Lucy sighed with pleasure. Then she slapped her hand over her mouth. She could not make sounds like that. She could not take this for any sort of special gesture.

"What is all this?"

"Dinner."

"McCall, this is not dinner."

"What is it then?"

A large square blanket sat spread on the deck. Three tall candlesticks were in the middle and flickered big, romantic flames. The smell of beef and garlic and—she inhaled—sweet potato fries wafted to her nose. "This cannot be your usual set-up."

He let her sit first and took the spot opposite. "It's a nice night and I wanted to eat outside."

"Yeah, right. A nice night to charm me so I don't think about sneaking away to somewhere you don't want me to be."

"You have somewhere special in mind?" He poured some wine and lifted his glass. "To a truce."

Lucy gulped. She couldn't. "To agreeing to disagree." She clinked his glass and took two large sips to calm her overactive nerves.

"If you're up to something, I will find out what it is."

"I told you, I'm here on vacation." She cut into her steak and reminded herself not to let the romantic atmosphere tarnish her resolve.

"Then let me help you make it a memorable one." McCall's sexy as sin voice disarmed her completely, and her hand shook as she lifted her fork.

Matt had never spoken sexy things in her ear or made ordinary phrases sound hot and dirty. He enjoyed her body and she enjoyed his. And not a day passed that he didn't tell her he loved her. But romance never played a big part in his actions.

She and McCall stared at each other, lost in tangled threads of obligation, conflict, and desire. Lucy had been attracted to McCall from the second she'd laid eyes on him, and she was pretty sure he felt the same way. Nothing would come of it, though. She didn't belong in his privileged world. Not when she intended to take something from the kind of place he'd dedicated his life to protecting.

He popped a fry into his mouth and Lucy had the unwanted urge to follow it. Not unwanted. Unfamiliar.

Suddenly food and McCall had her mind racing to ways of eating that required cooperation and someone else's hands.

"How do you suggest we start?" she asked, curious about his intentions.

"I'm going to teach you to whistle."

The piece of filet she put in her mouth lodged itself in her throat. That was the last thing she expected him to say. It was also the most dangerous. She wanted to whistle almost as much as she wanted the sculpture. A shiver slid down her back like a water snake and she tried not to squirm.

"How?" she whispered. She'd tried and tried during the past two years and couldn't do it.

McCall smiled. "Form an A shape with your index and middle fingers like this." Using both hands he extended his middle and index fingers while his thumbs held down his ring and pinky fingers. Then he placed his two middle fingers together to form an A.

"Good," he said, his eyes on her hands. "Now we move to the mouth. Lip placement is very important."

Lucy's gaze landed on his lips. She could think of a few places on her body she'd like to have those lips.

"Tuck them back over your teeth." He demonstrated.

"Like I did when I was younger and pretended to be an old woman without any teeth. It always got a laugh out of my grandmother." She demonstrated.

He laughed.

"Hey!" She leaned over and pushed him in the arm. "You aren't allowed to laugh."

"I can see why your grandmother did." He dodged right to avoid another push. "Now comes the more difficult part. You have to push your tongue back into your mouth. Get your hand ready." He made the A. "Then you're going to put the tip of your fingers under your tongue, push it back with your fingers so the tip folds back on itself, and push until your first knuckle reaches your bottom lip."

Lucy tried it. She had no idea if she was doing it right, but with McCall as her teacher it was fun to try.

"Now with your fingers in your mouth, keep the tip of your tongue folded and your lips tucked over your teeth, close your mouth around your fingers, and blow through the hole between your two index fingers."

The tips of her ears tingled as he whistled. The sharp, attention-getting sound threw her emotions into the back of her throat and clamped it shut.

If she'd been able to whistle like that, she might have been able to save Matt and her dad.

McCall must have sensed her distress because he withdrew his hands and looked at her with tenderness she didn't deserve. "You probably won't get a sound right off the bat. It takes practice. You'll know you're getting close when a sound like blowing over a beer bottle comes out."

Her fingers found her mouth, and she concentrated on everything McCall had told her. Nothing happened on the first try. Or the second. Or the third. But McCall's steady gaze, the faith she could read in his eyes, had an interesting side effect. She had no intention of giving up trying this time.

"Let's eat before dinner gets any colder," Lucy said. "I'll keep practicing later. Thanks for the lesson."

"I've no doubt you'll have your super power."

She didn't know how to respond to his kindness so they ate in amicable silence. Several minutes later, she said, "Tell me about working for World Heritage Fund." The largest non-profit international organization that worked to preserve historical sites garnered unparalleled respect and notoriety.

McCall leaned back against an Adirondack chair and extended his jean-clad legs. "It's fantastic. I took over presidency of field operations a year and a half ago and have been travelling nonstop, getting up close and personal with iconic sites that make you catch your breath. Our biggest efforts right now are on Route 66 and I'm seeing parts of the US I've never seen before."

"That's a huge project."

"We're working on it with another preservation company."

"How long are you in Arizona?"

His head slanted to the side.

"Not that I'm anticipating your departure or anything," she added before she pressed her lips together and grinned.

"Now what fun would it be if you knew how long I was in town? Unless you're planning on leaving at the same time?"

Lucy sighed and reached for her last two sweet potato fries. The truth was, after she got the Tlaloc sculpture she had no plans. Thinking ahead wasn't her strong suit and for the first time in her life that neglect left her on edge. She'd dreamed of teaching, though, and after spending today treasure hunting with the kids, wanted to pursue that possibility. "Is that an invitation?" Her regard crashed into his.

"Do you want it to be?"

She bit her bottom lip. And wow. His gaze fell to her mouth and he watched it with such keen interest that everything inside her fluttered. She had a feeling if she moved left or right, he'd track right along with her. She'd swear everything between them stilled, even the air molecules.

"McCall."

"Yeah?"

"I need you to tell me." She inched closer to him, unable to stop the pull.

"Tell you what?" He leaned a fraction closer, his interest steady on her mouth.

"What exactly is going on here. I'm having trouble thinking clearly." The space between them dwindled further.

"I'm not sure, but it's been my experience that thinking is highly overrated." He extended his arm until his big, warm hand cupped her cheek.

Her breath caught at the contact. "It's been a long time since—"

"Shit!" He yanked his arm back and jumped to his feet. His shirt was on fire.

It took Lucy half a second to stand, leap over the offensive candles, and tackle him to the ground. She'd smothered more than one clothing fire and knew what to do. Heat licked at her stomach, but as quick as it ignited, she'd extinguished it.

McCall moaned, apparently having hit the deck pretty hard. She ignored him and wiggled, guaranteeing that every last ember died. Once satisfied, she pressed up and looked down at him.

He wore a grin that stretched from ear to ear.

"I think you missed a spot," he said, "better keep wiggling."

Lucy didn't move at first. "Like this?" she finally said, deciding to rock her hips against his in a slow, steady rhythm that had a certain part of his anatomy standing at attention.

McCall knew the second she felt him because panic wrinkled the corners of her eyes and forehead and she rolled off him.

He rolled right along with her so that he pinned her beneath his weight.

"What are you doing? The flames are gone and you smell terrible. I probably do, too. I need to go change."

He wanted to shut her up with a kiss that would make her forget every other kiss, but he stopped himself. If he wanted her to kiss him back, he had a feeling she needed to be the one in control.

Her continued struggle against him dragged him to his feet. He offered a hand to help her up.

"Thank you," she said, relief—and disappointment?—in her voice.

"You know, if you're looking to do something new, I hear the Panthers are scouting for an offensive tackle."

She pushed him in the chest. "I can't believe you reached over the candles like that."

"Not the last stupid thing I'll do." No. He suspected before the weekend ended he'd commit a couple dumb things where Lucy was concerned.

"Are you okay? You didn't get burned, did you?" She lifted his charred shirt. "Oh, McCall, you did."

"I'm fine." He tried to push his shirt down. His body still hummed from their hip action and the gentle touch of her hand near his stomach tested his willpower.

"Come with me." She tugged him into the cabin and

with a firm grip on his shoulders forced him to sit on the couch. "Don't move."

"Where are you going?"

"To get something." She disappeared into her room and reappeared seconds later, holding what looked to be a container of honey in her hand.

He had no idea what Lucy was up to, but his mind immediately raced to X-rated scenarios.

"Take your shirt off," she commanded, dropping to her knees in front of him.

Holy shit. "Uh, Lucy?"

Her long eyelashes lifted and innocence sexy as hell shone in her eyes. "Don't worry. This won't hurt."

Looking at her hurt. Being this close to her and feeling sensations zing around his lower region hurt. He was an idiot to think he could ignore the power she had over him.

"How do you know?"

"I've done it before." She helped him out of his shirt.

When she traced her finger along one of the ridges of his abdomen, he couldn't stop the unrestrained groan. He gripped the edge of the couch cushion. "What exactly is *it*?"

She rolled her eyes and opened the honey. "Honey is a natural antiseptic. It heals and prevents infection." She poured the golden remedy onto her palm.

"You are not rubbing honey on me."

"Don't be a baby. I promise it will feel good."

"That's what I'm afraid of."

That got him the sexiest and sweetest gasp he'd ever heard. She blushed, but rather than stop the stream of honey, she squeezed the bottle tighter.

"I recall Keats McCall saying he wasn't afraid of

anything."

"You, Lucy. I'm afraid of you." His heart hammered inside his chest. He'd never been more honest in his life.

"Afraid I'll ruin your Aztec village," she mumbled. Her honeyed hand moved toward his burn.

He grabbed her wrist. "Don't start something unless you plan on finishing."

"I always finish." Her eyes blazed so clear and beautiful that he had no doubt she'd devour, drain, and exhaust him if he let her. But he wasn't sure they were talking about the same thing.

"Now hold still." She used two fingers to scoop up the honey onto her palm and then smoothed the sticky stuff onto his stomach.

Her gentle technique—dip into the honey, slide it on his skin, dip into the honey, slide it on his skin—would have been less painful had she used sandpaper. Trying not to squirm, not to take some honey and swipe it on her, grew more difficult by the second.

"This cure is amazing," she said. "By tomorrow morning your burn will be completely gone. The tricky part is letting it absorb into the wound for a couple of hours. There. *Finished*." She sat back on her haunches and studied her work, avoiding eye contact.

McCall noted the generous layer of honey before scooting to the edge of the couch and pulling Lucy up onto her feet. No way were they done.

"What are you doing?" Her startled reaction was exactly what he expected.

His hands held the hem of her T-shirt. "Checking you for burns. Maybe I need to put some honey on you?"

She squirmed and stepped back. "I'm fine."

"Show me."

"This is not show me yours, I'll show you mine. I barely felt a thing when I dropped you to the floor."

"Liar." He'd bet his village she felt his growing arousal while she wiggled against him.

"I'm not lying. See?" She lifted her shirt for exactly two beats and then let it fall back down.

"I see." The quick peek proved two things. She hadn't lied about getting burned. And her tanned, trim middle was sexy as hell. "But I wasn't talking about a burn."

She rolled her eyes again. "Whatever you think I felt during our brief body slam has completely escaped my mind. Which can only mean one thing. It didn't leave a big impression."

He laughed. "Clearly the barriers between us are at fault." He reached down and unbuttoned his jeans. To mess with her, to see if he could redden her cheeks further.

"Don't even."

It worked.

"I'm going to my room. Alone." She tripped in her haste to escape.

"You know this isn't the end of anything," he called after her. She'd seemed more than willing before the candle fiasco, but he wouldn't push. Hell, if he were smart, he'd forget the whole thing.

She tossed a flirty look over her shoulder. "I know."

Chapter Six

A full moon drew the kind of shadows over the campsite that kept most people tucked safely in bed. The spooky kind of shadows that Lucy loved because they offered protection from curious eyes.

She zipped up her jacket and leaned against the fencing at the camp entrance. Her boot tapped the ground. Her finger flicked her flashlight on and off. Where the hell was he?

Headlights finally appeared out of the corner of her eye, sending a rush of emotion through her. She blinked repeatedly to stop the tears pricking the back of her eyes. When the car stopped and Owen McAllister stepped out, Lucy thought she might collapse from sheer delight. He rounded the hood and wrapped her in his arms. His hugs always settled down the tension at the base of her neck.

"I'm so happy to see you," she said, squeezing him back and holding tight to the man who was like a father to her.

"I've missed you, too," he whispered before pulling

"I'm fine."

"And still prettier than any girl has a right to be."

Lucy gave him another hug. "Thanks for making the drive from California." She hadn't seen him since the funeral and hadn't realized until this moment how much she missed him.

"You know I'd do anything for you." Owen had been her father's closest friend and confidant. He never worked for Malcolm, but he was an engineer slash gadget genius and had helped them in their recovery efforts numerous times. "Now why am I here and not at the Aztec village?"

The original plan had been for Owen to meet her at the village and use the camera he'd invented.

The "magic snake," as she liked to call the camera, looked like a hose with a tiny five-pronged head. The prongs drilled through any material, a small lens followed it, and four feet of camera cable with an LED light and zoom feature came next. It was an amazing device that could see over, into, and around anything. It would help her find the Tlaloc sculpture inside the sandstone walls without causing too much damage.

Lucy explained the entire situation with McCall, her car, and Clay's surveillance on the village.

Owen ran a hand through his graying hair. Even with only a scrap of moonlight across his face, Lucy saw the disapproval in his eyes. "You need to back off, Lucy. The site is protected and that means it's off limits."

"You know I can't."

"I know you're blaming yourself for something that

wasn't your fault. Let it go."

"I can't." Every muscle in her body went taut, as if they'd snap in two if she moved too quickly. "I promised I'd find the sculpture."

"And you have. Now leave it alone."

"You know that's not what I mean."

"Lucy." Owen put his hands on her shoulders. "Your dad would not want you putting yourself in jeopardy like this. If you get caught, you're going to jail. There's over a dozen federal and state laws protecting national monuments from any loss of integrity."

"I won't get caught."

"Goddammit." He twisted away. His shoulders were more rounded since the last time she saw him.

It was her fault Matt and her dad were dead and she'd do whatever it took to fulfill her last promise to them. She owed them that much. Once she did, she'd finally be free to forget the horrible things in her memory.

She thought she'd done the right thing, separating from them in the Guatemalan cave.

The tunnels had been dark and dank, until the pentagonal opening that took her into another world. Monolithic columns and a cathedral-like cavern looked like a set from a science fiction movie. The earth beneath her feet was spongy, false floors prevalent. No one was supposed to get close to the ancient Mayan crystalline artifact that helped explain the Mayan's beliefs about the underworld

Lucy had navigated the wide perimeter and gotten to the ancient rock formation believed to house the crystal with careful, precise steps. Her heart had pounded inside her chest. When she looked over her shoulder to find her dad and Matt across the cavern and on their way, relief and worry washed over her.

Their footsteps weren't as light or cautious as hers. She wanted to yell to them to watch out, but she'd been sick with laryngitis and could barely whisper. A whistle would get their attention, but she couldn't do that either.

They fell into a disguised pit fifty feet deep and had only survived for minutes before their injuries took them from her.

The recollection knocked the wind out of her. The risk of letting someone get close again and then losing him or her reminded Lucy why she kept her distance. She struggled every day to see why she'd survived and the two people who meant the most to her had not.

Retrieving the Tlaloc sculpture was the only way to atone for what she'd done.

She leaned against the fence. "We just need to adjust our plan."

"Because there's a goddamn Navy SEAL keeping night watch. Yeah, I'd say so." Owen paced around his car.

"I can use the camera on my own. If you distract him, I can sneak inside the village, do what I need to do, and be out in under twenty minutes."

Owen let out a resigned sigh. "This is dangerous, Lucy."

"When has that ever stopped me? I'm going to do this with or without your help, so what do you say?" She could get the sculpture without the camera. It would just take longer.

"How do you feel about this McCall fellow?"

Lucy picked up her knapsack, anxious to get going. "What does that matter?"

"It matters a lot. It's his site and if I'm reading you right, you like him. You've never taken an artifact away from *someone* and that's what you'll be doing."

"I don't *like* him. I'm stuck with him."

"Okay," Owen said, stretching his arms behind his back. "How about staying close to him. Volunteering at the site and working with his crew. You could gain access to the village legitimately that way."

Lucy hadn't thought of using that approach. But McCall had said he'd stop her. He didn't care about making a "find." His priority was to preserve the site. Period.

Besides that, staying close to McCall for longer than necessary might lead her to act on the impulses he'd awakened.

"I don't want to stick around here longer than necessary. Let's do this thing tonight and then you can go home and I'll take care of the rest." She reached for the passenger door handle.

"Just like that?" His annoyed tone almost cut through Lucy's resolve. She hated arguing with him.

"Just like that."

He got in the car. "If I didn't know how goddamn stubborn you are, I'd take you to California with me right now. But that would only delay you. What's the plan?"

She slid on her seatbelt. "Thanks, Owen. We'll drive up to the village and you'll tell Clay that you're a professor and you heard the Aztec village was haunted and wanted to check it out. You'll lure him away from the car first, and then to the south side of the village. Toss out some necromantic shit and keep him entertained while I sneak into the north side."

"Necromancy is not shit."

Lucy laughed and put a hand on his arm. "I know."

They got to the settlement and under a full moon, Lucy tiptoed in one direction while Owen worked his magic in another. Inside the walls of the village, the air felt stagnant, as if the inner chamber wanted to squeeze the breath out of her before she upset the stillness.

That's what happened in the dead of night. Treasure sites imbued a mysterious force field that daylight somehow countered. All those stories told around campfires and bedtimes about being afraid of the dark caused these crazy thoughts.

She shook her head and found what she thought to be the right spot. Religion was a staple with the Aztecs and they worshipped hundreds of gods. Ceremonies were important and according to reliable scripture she'd read, she was positive she was at least close to the sculpture's position.

With a gentle hand, she slipped the camera and other equipment out of her knapsack and did what she'd come to do.

The fact that Lucy came back meant something, right? McCall feigned sleep when she eased open the sliding glass door and tiptoed back to her room. Despite the clench of every muscle in his body, he was relieved to see her. The digital clock on the nightstand read five thirty-two. He'd noted her absence at three forty-five when for some reason he needed to check on her. And wipe the damn honey off.

When she padded by him in pajama shorts and a tank top to use the bathroom, his damn libido forgave her before he even blinked. Her long legs, perfect ass, and sculpted arms teased him into dismissing her agenda.

No doubt she'd been up to no good.

He pushed himself up.

A minute later she crept by him again, her attention on the floor. Which made the jutting out of his arm that much sweeter.

Something sounding like *oomph* spilled from her mouth. He couldn't be sure because he'd stood, brought her into his arms, and her mint breath short-circuited his brain.

"McCall!"

That he understood. "Yeah?"

"Let me go." She squirmed against him.

He flipped on the bedside lamp. He could get used to this wiggling of hers. "So you can sneak back out?"

Her body stilled. Seconds of silence dragged between them. In the dim light of the room her eyes twinkled with excitement. "I told you I had things to do."

Being so close to her, the last thing he wanted to do was talk. But until he knew for sure what the glow on her face was about he'd keep his distance.

"Okay." He sat back on the bed, willing to let her win this round. She couldn't have gone far without a car, could she?

She wrapped her arms around herself. "Quit looking at me like that."

"How am I looking at you?"

"Like I've been dipped in a caramel chocolate swirl." She stared at him in fascination. Her chest rose and fell. Heat entered her eyes, no mistake about it.

He stood. "My favorite."

She took a big step back and put her hand up. "That wasn't an invitation."

"What was it then?" He stopped just shy of her palm.

"I don't know. I'm half asleep and can't be held responsible for the idiotic words coming out of my mouth."

He couldn't help it. His gaze dipped to his favorite part of her anatomy—her mouth. One kiss. One kiss and he could stop fantasizing about what she'd taste like.

Then reality clocked him upside the head. She didn't know what she was saying because she'd been awake all night figuring out a way to get what she wanted in his village. He sat back on the edge of the bed. "Right. Why don't you get some more sleep then? We're heading out at ten."

She frowned. "*We* aren't going anywhere."

"*We* are. I think we should get to know each other better before our date Sunday night." He'd keep Lucy close and try to get her to confide in him. She intrigued him far more than he cared to admit and discovering what she was all about while safeguarding his village was a priority.

"You have something against *asking*? Do this. Do that. I'd be less surly if you asked me to join you."

"Meaning you'll agree with my plans?" He expected her to laugh or at the very least harrumph. Instead her shoulders relaxed and a soft sigh gave away her acquiescence.

"Sure."

"You're going to blame this conversation on sleep walk-ing aren't you?" Ten seconds ago she'd seemed ready for battle.

"No. But I am exhausted. So hurry up and ask before I fall asleep on my feet." A tiny tremor shook her body.

Maybe he'd overestimated her stamina. He almost

scooped her up and carried her to bed. But then he'd be tempted to fall into it with her. "Would you like to go climbing with me later today?"

"Okay. Goodnight." She turned and wobbled to her room.

McCall tried to draw in a deep breath, but shallow was all he got. *Hell*. Tired or not, that had been way too easy. She was up to something, and he was up to the challenge of unraveling her cagey side.

Her bed creaked. She exhaled into slumber. He fought the lust those sounds stirred inside him by whipping the bed sheets over his aching-for-her hot body. Lucy curled up in bed, all the tension finally drained from her shoulders, turned him on.

Little did she know, though, the surprise was on her.

Chapter Seven

McCall craned his neck to glimpse the tops of the giant five-hundred-year-old Douglas fir trees. Since the day he'd climbed his first tree in second grade to escape the girls who wanted to kiss him, he'd sought the solitude of heights. Time spent far off the ground meant freedom. Control.

Lucy's fist jabbed him in the upper arm. "Who's ever heard of climbing trees like this? I thought you meant rock climbing." Her chin tipped up to the cerulean sky visible behind the tree canopies over a hundred feet high.

"I promise you'll enjoy it."

"You have no idea what I'll enjoy."

"Oh, I think I do." Even though they weren't touching, he felt Lucy shiver.

She bit that damn corner of her lip. "I think I'll stay down here."

"McCall, how are you?" Pete Anders' booming voice arrived a couple of seconds before the man himself.

McCall extended a hand to his friend in greeting. "Lucy, this is Pete Anders, our guide. Pete, this is my friend, Lucy Davenport."

Pete raised his eyebrows and gave Lucy a once over that almost wrenched a predatory growl from the back of McCall's throat.

"Hi," Lucy said, her tone sweet and sexy. She shook Pete's hand and McCall watched as Pete puffed out his chest and ran his free hand through his hair.

"Very nice to meet you, Lucy."

She smiled. Pete smiled. McCall clenched his jaw and just in case Pete got any crazy ideas, put his arm around Lucy.

When she tried to wriggle free, he brought her tighter against him. That got her to stop squirming. He gave Pete a victory grin.

Pete gave a slight nod and wink that probably had steam coming out of Lucy's ears, but McCall didn't give a shit. Lucy was his—at least for the next couple of days—whether she liked it or not.

"You guys ready to get outfitted?"

"Let's do it," McCall said.

Lucy listened as Pete explained how tree climbing worked and then she pulled the harness up and over her legs and khaki shorts, cinching it around her waist. She double knotted her boots before slipping on the bright yellow helmet and gloves.

Before Pete could step in, McCall double-checked her equipment. Without comment, but a scowl on her face, she dropped her arms to her sides to let him test the give on her straps.

His fingers skated along the curve of her hips, the hollow

of her back. Her clothing didn't stop a surge of electricity from shooting up his arms. Once satisfied, he stepped back and looked at her. Tomboy sexy, it took every ounce of control he had not to haul her against him and kiss her into smiling.

"I'll be right beside you as you ascend into the canopy," Pete said. "If you need to rest, just let me know and we'll take a break. After we spend some time in the trees, we'll descend down and eat dinner. When night falls, we'll head back up and settle into the hammocks for the evening."

"Wait. What?" Lucy said, her voice incredulous.

Oh yeah, he'd *forgotten* to mention they'd be spending the night in the treetops.

Pete darted a glance at McCall. "I'll leave you two alone for a few minutes before we get started."

Lucy tore off her helmet. Her eyes clouded with fury. But the helmet shook in her hand like she was more nervous than angry.

"What's wrong?" he asked.

"Besides the fact that you've kidnapped me?"

"I believe the term is 'whisked away' since I had your consent." McCall had no intention of letting Lucy slip away from him a second night.

"For a climb, not a sleepover."

"Did you have somewhere else to be tonight?" Damn she looked hot when he asked a question that pissed her off.

The pulse in her neck throbbed to life. Her eyelids drifted shut, like she needed a second to regroup. Her lips parted, but no sound came out. She shook her head.

"So what's the problem?" McCall sensed an unease around her that had nothing to do with his Aztec village. It gripped the muscles in his upper back and squeezed.

She looked away.

"Lucy?" He put his hands on her shoulders. A slight tremor thrummed under his fingertips. *Hell.* "Talk to me."

"I'm not fond of heights."

He turned her chin so he could look into her eyes. Was this her way out? "Since when?"

"Since always."

"You're telling me in your line of *fieldwork,* you've avoided heights?"

"I tolerated certain situations because I had to." She shrugged out of his reach. "And because they didn't last long. You're asking me to sleep *in a tree.* For hours."

Damn. It killed him to think Lucy pained, but he didn't want her out of his sight.

"With me." Two words that held far more weight behind them than he cared to acknowledge.

"Huh?"

"You'll be sleeping in a tree with me. The hammock can hold both of us, no problem. I won't let anything happen to you up there."

Her stubborn expression softened. His Tarzan mentality soared. Something simmered between them and adventure fueled it. He could see it in the depths of her eyes.

"Look, I know something is troubling you. If you go up there, I promise you'll experience the sweet bliss of *nothing.* Your mind won't be able to do anything but take in the sounds, smells, and views of the forest."

"What if my hammock mate is the trouble?"

He smiled. "Then you can punish him. Tomorrow."

She tilted her head up slowly. McCall followed her contemplation and took in the tangles of branches and greenery that allowed only shards of sunlight to reach the forest floor. He reached out and took Lucy's hand.

"I never back down from a challenge," she said, keeping her hand tucked inside his.

"Neither do I."

"You two have things worked out?" Pete's voice brought their gazes back to ground level.

Lucy put her helmet back on. "How many times have you done this, Pete?"

"Every weekend for the past six years." He saluted another guide walking past with two climbers.

"I'd say I'm good to go then."

McCall followed Lucy and Pete to the base of a two hundred and fifty foot fir tree. McCall had climbed it a couple of years ago. This time, though, a thrill rushed through him that had everything to do with the beautiful woman standing beside him.

Not once in all his outdoor escapades had he needed company. Sure, he'd joined groups, depending on the activity. Followed a guide when mandated. But he took the greatest delight in doing things alone because his job left little time to himself. Glancing at Lucy, all those other adventures paled. He wanted to experience this through her eyes.

She made everything better.

Pete clipped Lucy into the rope attached to the crown of the tree and tugged on all the connections to verify safety. He did the same with McCall and then himself. "Lucy, you'll set our pace. If you need to rest on a limb, we can do that. There's no rush."

A precocious smile spread across her sinful lips. "You boys better catch your breath now."

Catching Lucy would be his pleasure.

Lucy felt McCall's eyes on her. The awareness made it difficult to climb without squirming. She liked the attention. But the insatiable look she saw glittering in the depths of his clear blue eyes had her wanting to climb *him*.

"You okay?" he called out, a smirk on his face, as if he sensed the impact his gaze had on her.

"You asking because you need a break?"

He chuckled. "I'm asking because you've stopped moving."

"Oh." She put her gloved hands back in motion and pulled herself up. "Dammit," slipped out in a whisper. She had to stop thinking about McCall and how being with him discombobulated her.

A branch scratched behind her knee. A fern tickled the side of her neck. She peeked down, surprised by how high they'd already climbed. The view stole her breath—and made her a little nauseous. The air cooled the deeper they moved into the canopy, and goose bumps sprang up on her arms. Birds chattered. A robust musk scent filled her nose. Tiny bright red berries thrived among the greenery like confetti.

A smile bloomed across her face and stayed.

"We're here," Pete said a little while later, lifting his arm to check his watch. "And in record time."

"What now?" Lucy asked.

"Now we enjoy the scenery for awhile before we descend."

She took in McCall's muscled calves, broad shoulders, and locks of brown hair that spilled out of his helmet. The scenery was damn perfect from where she sat suspended in midair.

Once they'd scaled down and their feet were back on the ground, they ate an early dinner with others daring enough to spend the night as a tree dweller. The second climb went slower. Lucy's nerves twitched. She tried not to think about being stuck so damn high off the ground for ten long hours. But the setting sun, quieting of the birds, and unfamiliar surroundings sent her heart skittering into panic mode.

By the time they reached the hammock, Lucy wanted to strangle McCall for talking her into this. Not that he'd had to do much talking. His promise of peace and safety—the two things her troubled mind had difficulty feeling—were all it took to convince her.

He crawled onto their canvas sleeping surface first, moving with confidence and skill, his muscles pulling his shirt tight across his back. He clipped his harness to the hammock, allowing for plenty of room to move around. Then he placed a backpack and blanket off to the side and put his hands on his thighs.

"Ready," he said.

One word. That was all it took to weave sensations of need through her body and put out the fire of doubt flickering in the back of her mind. Caught in the warm masculine tone of his voice, Lucy moved forward.

Pete helped with her transfer before saying goodnight and leaving them alone.

McCall got comfortable on his back, put his hands behind his head, and lifted his eyebrows.

Lucy sat still on her knees and tried to gain her balance. "How would you feel if I tossed up dinner?"

"Come here," he said, ignoring her discomfort and

patting the spot beside him.

God, everything out of his mouth lit her up like the Fourth of July. What had she been thinking when she agreed to this? Worse than the height, a night wrapped in the warmth and safety of McCall's arms would make her wish for everything to be different.

"I don't bite, Lucy."

She wanted him to. She wanted him to bite and suck and nibble and have his wicked way with her. She had a feeling he did things to a girl that made her body so turned on it took hours to turn off.

"Do I need to come get you?"

Shaking her head, she crawled to him. The hammock didn't rock, its sturdiness calming her sensitive nerves. She'd slept in far more dangerous conditions before and pushed her fear aside.

He tucked her into his side like she meant something special. She almost couldn't breathe.

Her head on his shoulder, she curled closer, her leg moved over his, and she put her arm across his chest. A contented sigh sounded.

From both of them.

"I know," McCall said after a few minutes of comfortable silence.

"Know what?"

"Know what you're hoping to find in my village."

Lucy didn't move a muscle. But her blood ran cold, pumping lethargically through her system. "I told you—"

"I had an associate look into the possibility that something of historical value was on site. The call I got at dinner was confirmation." He took a slow, deep breath, as if giving

Lucy a chance to refute his claim. "He said there's a few archeologists who believe in the existence of a gold Tlaloc sculpture. Is that what you're looking for?"

Stunned that he'd so easily figured things out, she rolled away. It pissed her off that it hadn't occurred to her he'd do some digging. It frightened her that his tone wasn't accusatory, but hopeful. He wanted her to tell him the truth. To let him in.

His hand touched her shoulder. "Level with me and we can figure this out together."

"There's nothing to figure out. I *know* the Tlaloc sculpture is in the village and I'm going to take it." She stared into blackness, the silhouette of branches and leaves barely visible under a night sky scattered with clouds.

"You can't do that."

"I'm not asking for your permission." After her surveillance last night with Owen's camera, she knew exactly where the sculpture was. It lay deeper in the walls than she'd hoped, but that wouldn't stop her.

"I thought you didn't work for Malcolm Holmes any more."

"I don't."

"Then why are you here?" The hammock dipped.

Lucy twisted back around. Her pulse pounded in her ears. She found McCall on his side looking down at her with his head propped in his hand.

"I'm not going anywhere," he said.

She covered her face with her hands, hoping to hide the panic he'd surely read.

He gently moved her hands aside. When his focus was on her, *right* on her with concentration that outdistanced anyone else's, she thought maybe it wasn't his village that motivated him. Maybe he cared about her as much as he did his job.

"I made a promise to get the sculpture, and I always keep my promises." Her dad had sought the Tlaloc god for as long as she could remember. He'd believed the charitable god who gave life and sustenance would protect them. Keep them well nourished and finally change the course of their fortune. When Lucy's mom had died, her father had lost more than a wife, he'd lost his faith.

Hard times didn't help. Declan Davenport lived by the seat of his pants as a sometime archeologist, sometime treasure hunter, and he never gave up his search. He'd told Lucy if they found the sculpture, they'd be set for life. Not just financially, but spiritually, too.

"Who did you promise?" McCall twisted a strand of her hair around his finger.

Lucy blinked away her recollection and pulled in a lungful of air. "My dad and... my husband. Matt."

McCall froze. "You're married?"

"I was. They both died a little over two years ago." Her heart ached saying it out loud.

"I'm sorry." He eased her clenched hands apart and held one warmly in his. Soft, but a little bit rough too, his touch quelled the turmoil in the pit of her stomach.

She looked away, needing a break from his intensity. "Thank you. We were in Guatemala on a job for Malcolm and there was an accident." She sucked in another breath and then the words tumbled out. She told McCall everything and how not a day went by that she didn't blame herself. "You have no idea what this kind of loss feels like, and I have to get the sculpture."

McCall rolled to his back. "I know exactly what if feels like, Lucy."

The canopy swayed with a breeze, revealing and obscuring the stars in the sky. The smell of earth and bark and clean air filled her nose. Birds went to sleep. Night insects woke up. There was a timeless sense to their spot in the treetops and Lucy wanted to know everything that McCall kept tucked inside him.

She turned and pressed up onto her elbow. "Tell me." She'd never imagined someone else understanding the feelings that chipped away at her soul.

"Four years ago I was in charge of a chapel's conservation in Brazil. The monument was built against a mountain. We'd been warned of landslides, so I had engineers come in and we determined the area safe. But our work changed the stability of the slope and I lost eight men in a slide. My decisions took the lives of fathers, husbands, sons." He swallowed. "I know what it's like to feel responsible."

Lucy settled back against his side and wrapped her arm around him. "I'm sorry."

He told her more and then he was quiet while they stayed like that, their bodies touching one another for comfort, until McCall twisted so they were face-to-face. "I have an idea." His hand found the curve of her waist before moving to her ass and bringing their hips closer.

Heat burned a path across her cheeks. "You do?"

His fingers ran through her hair and settled on the back of her head. She shivered with desire so great her body tingled with sensations no other time or place matched. Her body's surrender confirmed what her mind had been telling her. She wanted McCall.

"I'm going to kiss you."

"Nice of you to warn me." She looked at his mouth. Since the first time she saw him she'd thought about it touching hers.

"I'm all about fair play." His eyes darkened and Lucy wasn't fool enough to believe he meant that about his site, too.

But whatever this game was between them, Lucy did want to play. She wanted to *feel* again. Matt's signature had long since vanished from anywhere on her body. She couldn't remember his taste, struggled to hold on to his scent.

McCall's nose touched hers and he let his warm breath tickle the corners of her mouth. He teased her mercilessly by hovering just out of reach. Anticipation welled up inside her so much that she thought she'd burst if he didn't kiss her in the next second.

"McCall," she moaned, pressing against him, seeking *more.*

"Is that a yes?" There was a low growl in his tone, attitude in the smile that played at his impossibly frustrating lips.

"Yes, McCall." She gave him the words he'd told her she'd say one day.

Finally, his lips moved against hers in a gentle glide that liquefied her insides before her eyes drifted shut. His careful caress made her humble and hot at the same time. McCall wasn't in a hurry, and his slow seduction of her mouth was better than anything she'd imagined. She wiggled closer, wrapped her arm around his neck. He had to feel the pounding of her heart against his chest.

He slid his tongue between the seams of her lips and

groaned when she opened for him. Their tempo accelerated. He thrust his tongue deep into her mouth and explored everywhere. His fingers massaged the back of her head while his leg hooked around hers and brought her tighter against him.

She sank into him, sensations spiraling out of her control.

His stubble rasped against her skin in the most exquisite way. Not rough, not smooth, but with the kind of friction that begged to be continued.

But what really got her? He kissed her like nothing else mattered. And that notion made everything around her disappear. For the first time in her life she lost all track of time and place and purpose. She existed only for this man and this moment.

"God, Lucy. You taste better than I imagined."

"You, too," she murmured.

He plunged his tongue inside her mouth again, but with skill and tenderness and earth shattering care, like he couldn't get enough but wanted to give her everything he had. She wanted to kiss him for hours.

His hand moved around her shoulder to the outside swell of her breast. She tried to twist to give him better access, but his harness got in her way.

"Ow," she said, pulling back. "Something on your harness pinched me."

McCall's dazed eyes looked at her with concern. "I forgot I was wearing one."

That made her smile. He'd been affected by their kiss as much as she was. "Good to know."

"Doubting your abilities?"

"No. It's just been—"

He cut her off by reclaiming her mouth with hungry urgency, his body above hers, his devastating caresses so intense she didn't care if their harnesses left permanent imprints. She pulled him closer.

Nibbling and teasing, McCall's full lips played with hers, his tongue danced with hers. Insane bursts of pleasure wove a web of desire that made her desperate to feel him *everywhere*. She imagined writhing beneath him, arching in wild response, answering his thrusts until she climaxed like never before. She wanted—needed—a McCall induced orgasm.

And if he kept kissing her like she was the sexiest thing in the world, she might have one in the next half a minute.

Lucky for her, he saved her from embarrassment when he gently eased off with a ragged sigh. "If we weren't two hundred and fifty feet off the ground I'd keep going." He traced his finger down her neck and chest to the tiny buttons of her long-sleeved cotton shirt. "Although, maybe if I undo a couple of these I can taste at least two other parts of you tonight."

How she found the strength to grab his wrist she had no idea. "No. Not like this, Keats."

His breath caught, and the look in his eyes wasn't one she recognized. Like she'd said something far more substantial than his first name. She'd spoken it to let him know this wasn't something casual for her. As much as she wanted to make this only about physical release, she couldn't.

He dropped delicate kisses to her forehead, the corner of her eye, the spot just beneath her ear lobe. "Say that again," he whispered.

His warm breath tickled her neck in the most delicious way.

"Keats." She didn't recognize the soft, sultry tone of her voice. She moved a hand to his chest then lower to feel how hard he was for her. "Keats," she said again, this time more breathy.

He pressed into her hand. "God, Lucy. Tell me why not like this."

"Because, because..." His lips found that place on her neck that made her quiver with pleasure. "We're up in a tree, remember? And you said yourself that's a bad idea." She couldn't bring herself to say she wanted to be someplace they could do it over and over and over again. "Plus," she continued, "I'm—"

"Afraid you'll wake the nightlife when I make you scream?" He lifted up and the corner of his mouth quirked into a devilish grin.

"What? No! I don't scream." Her nipples tightened thinking about it.

"We'll see about that."

Meaning he wasn't through with her. Meaning this wasn't just a fleeting moment. He wanted her when they were back on solid ground. She struggled to keep her delight guarded.

Through a gap in the canopy, a piece of the moon drew her attention. When something scurried across a branch above McCall's head, she buried her face in his shirt.

He laughed. "I'm sure you've been in far more dangerous sleep spots than this. What gives?"

"The height, you jerk." She pushed him away. "On the ground I can run away. Up here, I can't."

"Then think of me as your personal bodyguard." He tucked her back against his side and reached over his head for the blanket.

"Hang on." Lucy sat up and pulled the backpack into her lap. She took out some tissue and tore it into strips.

McCall watched her with interest, and a jolt of contentment she'd never felt before rushed through her. She rolled one strip of the tissue into a loose ball and placed it in McCall's ear. She turned his chin and did the same with his other ear. Then she plugged her own.

"To keep the bugs out," she said in response to the confusion etched in lines across his forehead. "You don't want anything taking up residence that doesn't belong there."

"Thanks." He poked at the tissue to make sure it stayed in place. "No one's ever been worried about my ears before."

"You're welcome." It felt nice to take care of him, to look out for him. She squeezed her eyes shut. She'd best forget that if she planned to get her gold statue.

Lucy fanned open the blanket, covered them, and lay down. The hoot of an owl sounded in the distance. The braches around her reached out with wrinkled arms twisted in uncomfortable poses. She bit back a chuckle. Even the trees McCall liked were ancient.

She wasn't too upset anymore that he'd planned this overnight trip. Adventure swept her away. And tonight, even though the dust around them was unsettled, McCall had felt the same way.

Her thoughts reached back to days with Matt. She'd made a choice and then life took her somewhere she hadn't wanted to go. Love and hope had muddled her judgment. Recovering the Tlaloc sculpture would be her goodbye gift. Once she did that, she'd be free.

A tight, dull ache made a pilgrimage to the pit of her stomach. She hoped McCall would forgive her for that.

Chapter Eight

Lucy wore the green sequined gown.

McCall wore a hard-on that made his tuxedo pants damn uncomfortable.

The dress hugged every curve of her lean body. The plunging backside undid him—her smooth, bronze skin beckoning him to touch. The front molded to her breasts with perfection, the V-neck straps left her toned arms bare.

Her reddish brown hair fell in soft, loose waves just past her shoulders. An opal necklace adorned her neck. The seashell bracelet they'd found geocaching hung on her wrist, testament that she'd meant what she said about being out of her element.

Still, one word best described her—breathtaking.

McCall stopped outside the entrance to the El Tovar Lodge and took her hands. "You don't need to be nervous. You will by far be the most gorgeous woman in the room tonight."

"Not true," she said, her gaze darting to the ground. "We both know *you* will be garnishing the most attention tonight."

"The most envy." The beauty and expanse of the Grand Canyon over Lucy's shoulder caught his attention for a moment. He stared in wonder as twilight cast an otherworldly glow over the burnished amber rock.

"Stop that."

"What?" He traced a finger down her arm. She shivered. They'd been tap dancing around each other all day, and McCall didn't know how much more he could take. After their mind blowing kisses last night, Lucy had run hot and cold and he figured she needed some space. But distance made him crave her more.

"Being charming." She leaned closer, honest words out of his mouth a seemingly magnetic pull he was grateful for.

"Can't help it." His mouth hovered at her temple. If he hadn't promised Dean and Sam he'd show up tonight, he would have dragged her away to an intimate dinner for two.

They hadn't talked about the sculpture again, but last night had changed things, hadn't it? He wanted to believe she'd let her quest go and instead decided to explore the undeniable chemistry between them.

"I'm not used to any of this. Please don't make it worse."

He framed her face with his hands. Her eyes sparkled with warning. "I'll try. But I'm not making any promises. You're mine and if anyone even looks at you the wrong way, I might burst a blood vessel."

She grabbed his wrists and brought his hands around to her backside. "I thought I was only a date. Not *your* date." She shimmied against his lower region, causing more goddamn discomfort.

Before the night was over, he was going to have her.

"Changed my mind." His stomach knotted. He meant it. This thing with Lucy was more than he anticipated. It wasn't an attempt to divert her anymore.

"But you haven't changed mine," she teased and moved around him. "Let's go, preservation boy."

McCall breathed in the crisp, invigorating air and marched up the steps of the hotel beside her. In his mind, her easy dismissal meant one thing—he was under her skin as much as she was under his.

Inside the landmark establishment, the dark brown log posts and patterned carpets gave the lobby rotunda a cozy Southwestern feel. They took a moment to look around and then McCall put his hand on Lucy's back to guide her toward the dining room for the annual gala for the National Register of Historic Places.

Lucy trembled under McCall's touch as they checked in at the entrance. "How about we make a beeline for the bar?" he whispered, guiding her inside.

"You read my mind."

They wove through the crowd, McCall nodding and smiling at friends and business associates. "I'm not the most comfortable at these events either, you know."

"Really? All the women staring at you is bothersome?"

He turned her chin. "The only woman I see is you."

She *pfft* and put her elbows on the bar. "I'll have a Malibu and pineapple please."

"Coming right up," the bartender said, his eyes zeroing in on Lucy like he wanted to undress her.

McCall bristled. He caged Lucy from behind, his hands

spread on the bar, his chin in the crook of her neck. With her ass nestled against him, he was painfully reminded of his aroused state. "You are the sexiest thing I have ever laid eyes on," he whispered, just before a large hand landed on his shoulder and yanked him around.

"You having a drink without me?" Dean Malloy said, giving McCall one of his cocky smiles.

McCall shook Dean's hand. "Absolutely."

"It's good to see you." Dean added a pat to McCall's upper arm. Despite working on the Route 66 project together, they concentrated their efforts in different regions. Tonight's meeting resulted from a rare close proximity.

"You, too. Even better to see you, Sam." McCall grinned at the woman to Dean's left before kissing her cheek. "Lucy Davenport, this is Dean Malloy and Sam Bennett. They work in heritage protection."

"Nice to meet you," Lucy said. "Your dress is beautiful, Sam."

"I tried to take it off her on the way—"

Sam elbowed Dean in the side. "Please ignore my fiancé. He thinks he's being cute."

"Fiancé?" McCall darted a glance between them.

"As of two days ago." Sam's entire face lit up as she waggled her fingers and flashed a diamond ring large enough to blind him.

"Congratulations," he and Lucy said at the same time.

Dean slung an arm around Sam and the two exchanged a look that left no doubt to how much they loved each other. McCall couldn't help but peek at Lucy. She definitely drugged him with her looks, intelligence, and passion. Could there be more to it than that?

"We're thinking about saying 'I do' from the top of the Golden Gate Bridge," Dean said.

"You're thinking that. My vote is for Vernal Falls in Yosemite." Sam tore her gaze from Dean and looked at Lucy. "It's where we first kissed."

At mention of the word kiss, McCall thought back to last night with Lucy. He'd never imagined a kiss could be so hot. So damn good that he ran his tongue over his bottom lip and still tasted her.

He slyly took Lucy's hand, lacing their fingers together and bringing them next to his thigh.

She darted a glance down before composing herself and saying, "Either one sounds romantic and adventurous. I'm guessing you'd have more guests in Yosemite, though."

They laughed. "We've been debating the big wedding, small wedding thing all weekend. I offered up a nude beach idea thinking that would eliminate most everyone, but Sam won't go for it." Dean winked at his bride-to-be.

"Enough wedding talk," Sam said. "McCall and Lucy don't need to hear about our conversations. So, Lucy, what do you do?"

"I'm an archeologist."

A line started to form for the bar so McCall edged them away. The restaurant hummed with quiet conversations, the native stone and pine décor bouncing sound waves with a feather-light touch. A waiter stopped and offered them an appetizer.

"Are you in the field?" Sam asked.

"Mostly. Yes." Lucy let go of McCall's hand and took a beef skewer. She angled herself slightly behind him, as if she wanted to slink away from any more attention to herself.

"Have you started on the Aztec village yet, McCall? Is that what brought you two together?" Sam asked.

"We begin tomorrow," he said.

Lucy took a small step away from his side. Her stance reminded him that even though they stood only inches from each other, there was an iconic village between them.

That notion tangled the thoughts in his head for a minute. He needed to talk to her. Because if she tried to get the Tlaloc sculpture, he would stop her.

"No. I'm not working with McCall at the village." Lucy's voice, but more importantly her words, flung McCall back into the conversation.

"Actually she is," he said with conviction.

"What?" Her empty cocktail glass shook in her hand.

He took the glass and put it on the passing waiter's tray. "Lucy is incredibly knowledgeable about historic sites. She's got an amazing eye for architecture and no one can match her skill at sizing up infrastructures and giving damage assessment."

"McCall." There was alarm in her voice, but she didn't need to worry. The Tlaloc sculpture wasn't his secret to tell.

He gazed into her surprised and suspicious eyes. "I've never known anyone with more guts and dedication to her philosophy on significant cultural landscapes and buildings than Lucy. She's traveled the world and knows how to work endangered sites, take what she wants, and stem the loss of integrity."

Her eyes softened, her full lips parted slightly. McCall wanted to stop talking and possess her mouth—and every other inch of her.

"I'm planning on her teaching me a thing or two over

the next few days." He meant every word he said. He wished he'd thought of inviting her to work with him sooner. Once he introduced her to his plight, she'd forget about gold sculptures.

"Take what she wants?" Dean asked.

McCall watched Lucy gulp. "She is an archeologist. They do find things."

Lucy smiled. "No one's better."

McCall couldn't keep his eyes off Lucy. "I agree."

"You two want to get a room?" Dean asked.

"We already have one," Lucy answered. "I mean, McCall does and he's been gracious enough to let me stay with him."

A two-legged desert bighorn sheep could have walked by him and he wouldn't notice. He was transfixed on Lucy.

Sam cleared her throat. "How did you say you two know each other?"

"We didn't." McCall wrenched his gaze away. Women looked at him all the time with dollar signs and penthouse dreams and he blinked away their superficiality with ease.

Lucy didn't give a shit about what he had in his bank account or who his family was. She looked at him like the only thing that mattered was *him*. He wanted to wake up every morning to that look.

Before falling asleep last night, he'd shared more of himself than he'd shared with anyone else. No one knew how deeply the avalanche had affected him. How he'd doubted himself for months after. Lucy had let her guard down, too, and the goodness and down to earth passion that lay behind it pulled him in deep.

"But it's a funny story," McCall said with no intention of sharing the total truth. He just needed to get his mind off how much Lucy affected him.

Something drew Lucy's attention and she looked across the room. He tried to follow her line of sight, but then she angled her chin up and seemed to take in the view of the canyon out the restaurant's window.

"Would you excuse me for a moment? I need to use the ladies room." Lucy moved around him without waiting for a reply.

Naturally, his gaze followed her until she vanished around a corner.

"You are in deep, man" Dean said, "and I'm glad I was here to see it."

"What the hell are you talking about?" McCall lifted a pork chop from a passing tray. It pissed him off that his wayward thoughts showed on his face.

"Someone has finally cracked that control-freak, fling-only mentality of yours. And I'm glad it's not your usual upper cruster."

"She seems really great," Sam piped in.

McCall was saved from further discussion about his personal life when Connor made his way over with the president of the NRHP and talk turned to business. Others joined them, including a few wealthy single women, intent on charity and *him*. He cringed every time one lightly touched his arm.

Several minutes later, Lucy's vibrant green gown caught his attention. Among the flower arrangements of orange roses, violet hydrangeas and red orchids, she stood out like the most beautiful feature of a Matisse painting. She stood in conversation with a man who had his back to McCall.

Her eyes met McCall's across the crowded room and his

knees weakened. Christ, he hated being this far away from her. He was about to excuse himself when the Director of the National Park Service joined them.

Finally, when it was just him with Sam and Dean, Sam said, "So who do you think is going to win *The Amazing Race* this season?"

McCall appreciated that she lightened the conversation and brought up their favorite TV show.

"Hey," Lucy said, snaking her arm around his and leaning against his side. "Sorry I was gone so long. I got cornered by a gentleman whose son is thinking about being an archeologist."

"My vote is for Jared and Raquel," McCall said, his body relaxing now that Lucy had returned.

"I have to agree," Dean said. "If Sam and I were contestants, we'd wipe the pavement with everyone. Nothing scares my fiancé."

Sam pressed into Dean's side and looked at him like she'd go to the ends of the earth and back if he wanted. "As long as there isn't a river infested with spiders that I have to swim through like they had in season nine, I'm good."

"No way would you beat us," Lucy said, surprising the hell out of him. "Put McCall and I together and nothing can stop us." She paused for a moment, a moment that took his feelings for her and magnified them times a thousand. *Put McCall and I together and nothing can stop us.* That's what he wanted. A woman to stand by him and conquer whatever they set their mind to.

"Fear has nothing to do with it," she continued. "There's a quote from Eleanor Roosevelt, 'you gain strength, courage, and confidence by each experience in which you really stop to look fear in the face. You are able to say to yourself, I have lived through this horror. I can take the next thing that comes along. You must do the thing you think you cannot do.'"

"You are seriously sexy when you quote," McCall whispered in her ear. Her soft hair tickled the corner of his mouth. Her soapy fresh scent stimulated other parts of his anatomy.

Dean shook his head. "'Do the thing we fear, and the death of fear is certain.' Ralph Waldo Emerson." He flashed that cocksure smirk of his. "Sam's great, great, great uncle."

"Once removed," Sam said.

"Suffice it to say, we'd both make it to the finals." McCall nodded toward the dining tables. "Looks like they want us to sit. How about I buy a bottle of champagne so we can toast your engagement while we eat?"

"Sounds perfect. Thank you," Sam said.

Lucy brushed her mouth along his jaw line until it was angled away from their companions and whispered, "You are seriously sexy when you're considerate."

Yeah, he was also seriously horny.

The second after they finished their dessert, McCall said goodnight to their table and helped Lucy up with a hand on the small of her back. Touching her made his pulse quicken, but not touching her was impossible. "It was great meeting you all," Lucy added, then shook hands with Dean and Sam. "Best of luck with your wedding plans."

Goodbyes on the way out with several other work associates followed, then McCall rushed Lucy to the car. The night air carried the last remains of winter's bite and he didn't want her getting too cold. He opened the passenger door for her and then nearly leaped across the hood to get to his side. Not because he was cold. Because he was *hot*.

Safely tucked away in the confines of his truck, he wanted to take Lucy right there. Touch her. Learn every pleasure point on her body. His choppy breathing must have given him away because she said, "We are not doing it in a car. At least not the first time."

It turned him on even further knowing that the sexual tension he'd felt coming off her during dinner wasn't just his imagination.

"First time?"

The mind-boggling smile she gave him burned with a sweet sensation.

Tonight he'd put an end to the teasing between them. They hadn't known each other for very long, but he knew. Knew he'd never find anyone else he wanted to be with more. If she'd let him in all the way, he could prove to her she could trust him. There was much more to the undeniable chemistry that sparked to life whenever they were near each other. He'd admired her from afar. Tonight he'd show her up close how much she meant to him.

Chapter Nine

Lucy had never been more nervous.

Or more aroused.

Each step toward the cabin sent throbbing tingles straight to the tips of her breasts and inflamed the endless ache of desire low in her stomach. The control she'd tried so hard to hang on to had vanished about an hour ago when McCall took one hand off the steering wheel and toyed with her seashell bracelet. Then he'd drawn delicate circles on her palm, lazy lines between her fingers, like a fortuneteller playing a one-of-a-kind instrument.

Her fortune? *You will soon gain your heart's desire.*

No. Really. That's what the fortune she'd refused to show McCall after their Chinese food lunch had said.

She'd tried all day to convince herself it meant the Tlaloc sculpture, but hearing the click of the sliding glass door behind her and feeling McCall's big, strong hands on her waist, she knew that wasn't it.

She was falling in love with McCall.

If she could keep this just about sex, do the casual thing, then it wouldn't matter that McCall would never love her back. That he wanted tonight and maybe the next few days, but beyond that, she didn't fit in his world.

When she took the Tlaloc sculpture, she'd be the last person he'd ever want to see again. She really had no choice now. Malcolm's surprise appearance at the gala, and his threat to McCall if she didn't get the statue for him, increased the stakes immeasurably.

"You make it hard to breathe, Lucy. And I've been thinking about this all night," he said in her ear, the husky sound of his smooth voice teasing her in the most delicious way.

"I have, too." God, how she'd thought about it.

He drove her to the edge of his bed, his body steering her hips with expert guidance. After his lips performed a bone-melting caress to her neck, he turned her around.

She blinked away thoughts of the job she had to do and concentrated on the right now. It wasn't too difficult. The heat in McCall's eyes burned a path straight to her core.

Being with him filled the empty spaces inside her. She hadn't thought that possible.

She put her arms around his neck and kissed him. Hard. She wanted him to know he made it difficult for her to breathe, too. She wanted him to feel everything she did.

The devastating touch of his full lips made her toes curl. She rocked against him, pressed her mouth tighter. His hands were everywhere. And she couldn't ever remember feeling this much *need*.

A groan—his? Hers? She wasn't sure—wrenched the

kiss from her control to his. He explored her mouth like a man desperate to brand her. His hands cupped her ass and he brought her tight against his arousal. Knowing she was responsible for that sent a thrill through her bones and she couldn't wait to feel him deep inside her.

He pulled back to catch his breath. To slide her gown straps off her shoulders. She pushed his tuxedo jacket off his body and undid the buttons of his crisp, white shirt, dying to run her fingers over his skin.

When she'd finished, again his mouth crashed into hers. One hand cradled her head while the other slid through her hair. She palmed his chest, moved lower. His skin was hot, muscled, smooth. A tiny bit raw where he'd been burned by the candles. He grabbed her wrist before she reached below the belt.

"Not yet, sweetheart," he said.

"Afraid I'll cause you trouble?"

"Oh, you're already trouble. But I'm too far gone to care." He raked a gaze over her from head to toe that bloody could have caused her clothes to go up in flames. "And intent on following through with my promise to you before my own needs are met."

"Promise?" She raked a finger down the middle of his chest. She didn't remember any promise. She couldn't recall what they ate for dinner.

He tilted her chin so she met his clear blue eyes. "The one where I make you scream."

Oh. *That one.* She tried to laugh off his confidence, but instead a high-pitched rasp she'd never heard before slipped out between her lips. "I guess you could try that."

"I will." His clever hands unzipped her gown in seconds.

It fell to the floor, leaving her in nothing. His gaze caressed her all over, and her body responded with raging tingles that wove a brand new path through her.

When he sucked in an unsteady breath as she swayed back onto the bed, her heart did a back flip.

"See something you like?"

"Every fucking thing." He crawled over her body, straddled her hips, and lifted her arms over her head. "Keep those there."

She arched her back and pressed her shoulders into the bed, surprised at her brazenness, but happy to give him unhindered access.

He didn't waste a second. He kissed under her earlobe, along her neck, across her collarbone. His slow seduction drove her wild. She wanted him lower. When he finally got to her breast and licked and played with her nipple between his teeth, she moaned.

"You taste so damn good," he murmured against her skin. "Sugarcoated." His lips moved to her other breast to give it equal attention.

Then holding her gaze, his ministrations moved south until he cupped her mound, his hand stroking her in the perfect spot to tear a ragged sigh from the back of her throat.

"That's a start," he said, before claiming her mouth again.

"I need to touch you, McCall."

"Where?" His mouth slid down the small valley between her breasts.

"Here for starters." She lowered her arms and ran her hands through his hair.

"And after that?"

She moved her hands over his shoulders, down his back. "Here." Firm, hot, sleek muscle vibrated beneath her fingers.

He slipped further, licked her hipbone. "And after that?"

"Here." She lifted up to reach his ass and tugged, bringing the hard bulge in his tuxedo pants right where she wanted it—between her legs.

McCall groaned at the contact. He pushed up and looked down at her. The corners of his mouth lifted into a smile.

Gorgeous didn't begin to describe the look on his face. Staring up at him, she couldn't ever remember looking at anyone more handsome. The whole "when God made him he broke the mold" totally applied.

"You are the most breathtaking creature I've ever laid eyes on," he said.

She believed him. Because once again he kissed her like she was the most precious thing in the world.

Then his mouth moved all over her body. Her hands undid his pants and pushed them down. He tugged his boxer briefs off with them.

He stood and she swallowed. His hard, muscled body was perfect. And the hardest part of him wanted *her*. She gathered fistfuls of bedding, her body waiting in torment. She needed his skin against hers so bad she clenched her legs together, worried she'd come apart with only his gaze. Watching him slide on a condom, she bit her lip to keep from begging him to hurry.

The second he positioned himself at her entrance, a raw surge of arousal she'd never experienced before made her tipsy.

The possessive look in his eyes made her feel loved.

He moved inside her slow at first, as if he wanted to

savor every stroke. She wrapped her legs around the back of his thighs, wanting him to bury himself all the way. His thrusts turned more demanding, his strength and skill taking her to the edge. She arched to meet his next powerful push.

She cried out when he drove his body into hers with intensity that far surpassed a simple physical connection. Her heart thudded inside her chest. Her nails dug into his back.

"Oh, God, Keats. Just like that!" The incredible sensations taking over as their bodies worked in tandem destroyed any lingering doubt about her choice tonight. She hated what she had to do to him, but she'd been left with no choice. He'd hate her, but his reputation and integrity, not to mention his well-being, would be left intact. Lucy had never hated Malcolm more than she had tonight at the gala.

She'd thought she was rid of him, but Malcolm wasn't quite ready to let her go.

"Lucy." McCall's husky voice drew her eyes open. "Don't drift away from me now. Let me hear you. *Feel* you."

Looking up at him, her breath caught in her throat. He couldn't fake the worship in his eyes. The passion. Could he? Desperate to believe his intoxication matched hers, she crashed her mouth against his.

She rocked against him in unconscious harmony. He found that pleasure spot again and moved hard against her, pressing her into the bed.

When he lifted his head to catch a breath, she had only a second to catch her own before a noise sounding suspiciously like a scream ripped from deep inside her chest and she climaxed.

Keats followed right behind. His groans of pleasure

swept her up in joy that verged on torment. He collapsed on top of her, buried his nose in her hair. "That was amazing."

"Yes, it was."

He rolled over and pulled her with him so she could cradle her head on his shoulder, burrow into his side.

"What are you thinking?" he asked.

"I'm not. I think you wiped out all my brain cells." Not exactly true, but if she told him about Malcolm he'd push her away.

"Want to know what I'm thinking?"

"No."

"No?" He shifted to try and get a peek of her face.

She lowered her chin and wrapped her arm around his chest. Knowing McCall's thoughts was a danger she didn't have the strength for at the moment. "No. But I do have a question." He stayed silent so she continued. "Did you mean all those things you said tonight? You want me to come to the village with you?"

"Absolutely. I think you could offer some insight I don't normally receive. We rarely work with archeologists, and I think if you see the work we're doing you'll gain some appreciation for it." His chest rose and fell. "The invitation is there if you want it."

Confusion collided with attachment. He respected her. He valued her. Even after she'd made it perfectly clear that she wanted only one thing from the Aztec village.

"Okay."

He squeezed her tight. "You won't regret it."

Yes. She would.

McCall woke up most mornings with a hard-on. But for the first time in years, it was pressed against an ass of epic perfection. Soft, round, warm. Lucy's body gave new meaning to "getting up."

He swallowed the moan that would lead to more feel-good friction and scooted back a few inches. Full rays of sunlight washed over them, meaning he'd already slept later than intended.

"Morning, sleepy head." He placed a kiss in the spot in the crux of her neck that he knew drove her wild.

He knew every single spot on her body now. His favorite? The tiny freckle on the outside slope of her left breast, just under her arm, because every time he licked there she shivered.

Her shoulder shrugged. She murmured something.

"Lucy, we need to get up." He inwardly laughed, his lips curling into a smile. He couldn't get any more *up*.

"Hmmm?" She rolled over, her tousled hair, her pink cheeks, her well-loved lips more breathtaking than anything imaginable.

It thrilled him that she wanted to come to the village, but he wasn't completely convinced her motives were pure. Last night he'd made love to her over and over again and he was sure he hadn't imagined the deep admiration between them. But he knew how to read a woman, and Lucy was holding something back.

She hadn't made him any promises, but he'd damn well hoped she'd leave the sculpture alone. Not only was the integrity of the village at stake, but possibly the reputation of his entire organization if she duped him again.

"It's time to wake up." He gently shook her.

She bolted upright. The sheet fell to her waist and exposed golden velvet skin. "I told you not to let me fall asleep here!"

"Good morning to you, too."

Her head whipped around the room like she expected an ambush. When her gaze settled back on him, his smile must have reminded her of her manners because she said, "Morning." And yanked the sheet up to her neck.

"Aren't we past modesty?"

"What time is it?" She looked around him to view the digital clock on the nightstand.

He followed her line of sight. Eight o'clock.

She let out a breath and leaned back against the pillows and headboard. "I asked you to kick me out of your bed."

"Just one more minute, Keats, then I'm going to my bed," he said in his best Lucy imitation. After they'd spent hours exploring each other, she'd huddled against him to "rest."

He laughed at the glare she shot him.

"Hey, it's not my fault I fell asleep first." He may have made sure his arm was fastened securely around her before he'd allowed himself to doze off.

Her head fell into her hands.

Suspicion made his stomach clench. Two nights in a row she hadn't been happy about spending the night with him. Guess his plans to keep her mind off the Aztec village had worked. Why that suddenly hurt like hell he wasn't sure.

His intentions had been honorable. Never once did his actions mean anything less than a desire to be with her unconditionally. But somehow with her agitation this morning, he doubted Lucy would see it that way.

"How about some coffee and blueberry pancakes before

we head out?" He slipped out of bed and headed straight for the bathroom. He returned with a towel around his waist and picked up the phone to dial room service.

"You need to put some clothes on," she grumbled when he ambled back to the bed.

"Why?"

"Because you're distracting otherwise."

"I like that I distract you." He tiptoed his fingers across the sheets towards her.

She squashed his hand with a knee-jerk. "I don't."

"Your loss. I can do very talented things with these fingers."

She tried really hard not to smile, but she lost the battle. Her lips twisted, one edge of her mouth quirking higher than the other. Creases etched the corners of her sleepy eyes. "Yeah. Whatever. You want the first shower?"

"Depends," he said.

"On what?"

"On whether or not you're taking the first one. I'm all about conservation, you know."

Lucy moved her mouth from side to side, implying without words she was considering his offer and picturing the shared shower space like he was. Sexiest morning look ever.

She slid out of the sheets, smoothed her hand across the rumples as she rounded the bed, and strutted her naked body into the bathroom. "I'm all yours," she said over her shoulder.

For the moment, yes, she was.

Chapter Ten

"You're slacking."

"I'm watching." McCall wiped the perspiration off his forehead. From his position on the retaining wall of the Aztec village he had a damn fantastic view.

"The dirt bake?" Lucy asked, taking the spot next to him.

"You." He couldn't take his eyes off her perfect legs, her bare shoulders, her friendly disposition. She moved in a way that made people gravitate toward her.

For the past four days she'd worked tirelessly with his staff and local Native American Indians wherever needed. She didn't care about getting dirty. She didn't care about doing the grunt work. And when his preservation philosophies and knowledge of conservation science went over the heads of the people he wanted to help, she explained things with amiable charm and familiar words.

Everyone loved her.

He loved her.

"You need to stop that." She bent her neck from side to side.

"Why?"

"You might see me do something you don't like."

Ahh. So they were finally going to talk about it. He took a swig from his water bottle. "So this has all been surveillance? Reconnaissance to find your Tlaloc sculpture?"

She shuddered. From his accusation or the breeze that blew by cooling off their overheated bodies, he didn't know.

Then she chuckled. "I meant sweat like a pig or flirt with Connor since he seems determined to get your goat and I can't help but play along. But good to know what you really think of me."

If she knew what he really thought—that he loved her—what would she think? They'd spent every night this week naked underneath the bed sheets. She'd given her body so willingly he got hard just thinking about it. When they talked about their pasts and families, she drew him in further with her guts and attitude. His family wouldn't be thrilled with her upbringing and status, but no other woman turned him inside out like Lucy did, and he wanted more from her.

The truth, for starters. Because there was still something about being here that she wasn't telling him.

He turned to face her. "I think you're complicated and keeping something from me. I also think I'd do anything for you, so how about putting it all on the line, right here, right now."

She kept her gaze on the dirt underneath her boots. "It's not…" She paused and cleared her throat. "It's complicated. I told you you'd be better off without me and that's even truer now. I think it's time for me to go."

His hands fisted. "Just like that? You're willing to walk away because you're afraid it's complicated?"

"We come from two totally different worlds, McCall. And… And I'm afraid you'll get hurt." She stood.

He got to his feet. "Look at me, Lucy."

Fuck if her green eyes didn't trap him in a web of concern and fortitude. "Stop looking at me like that," she said.

"Like what?"

"Like… I don't know! I told you I was here for the Tlaloc sculpture and that hasn't changed."

"A lot has changed." He wanted to help put her painful past to rest. Wanted to protect her and fight for her, no matter what. And when a guy had those kinds of feelings and impulses, he acted on them despite what it might cost.

"You don't understand." She toyed with the hem of her shorts.

"Explain it to me." He wished she'd toss aside the self-isolation she clung to. He hated feeling like he was stumbling in the dark. "Please."

She looked away.

"We don't have to take opposite sides on this." From their work together, McCall could see Lucy cared about the village. She might be surveying it, but she was also admiring it. "Do you know where the sculpture is? We could come up with a plan together. Bring attention to the site and the sculpture. If you think you can get it with minimal structural damage, we'll figure out a story to tell."

"No." Lucy shook her head. "We can't do this together." She fanned her loose, sleeveless top away from her stomach. "I won't have you compromise your integrity because of me.

And I don't want your help."

"That's very noble of you, but I can make my own decisions."

"Not this time." She started back toward the north side of the village where the impact of high temperatures, little rainfall, and high winds had damaged the hand-plastered walls the most.

He fell in step along side her. "Tell me why," he insisted.

"I can't."

He grabbed her arm, bringing her to a halt. "At the very least, you owe me an explanation."

"I don't owe you anything. Now let me go." She tried to pull her arm back, but he held on.

"You've never violated a protected site before and I've seen the care you've taken this week. I know you think you owe this to your dad and Matt, but you don't. Don't risk it."

She froze. Her eyes fell shut. He stared at her long, dusky eyelashes wanting to kiss them, but refrained. When her lips quivered, it was like being slammed in the chest with a bowling ball.

"You don't know everything about me McCall. And you've no idea if I've violated a protected site before. I'm sorry."

He cradled her face in his hands. "Their deaths weren't your fault, Lucy. I know you think you need to redeem yourself, but you don't. They wouldn't want you to do this. If you try, we're going to have to call the authorities." Even if McCall looked the other way, there was Connor and Clay. Both men were devoted to their jobs and McCall would never ask them to compromise their positions.

"I promised, McCall. It was the last thing I said to them

and I can't move on until I keep that promise."

McCall knew the importance of promises and looking at the pain marring Lucy's sun-kissed complexion, he wanted to promise her anything. "I'll help you, then."

She took a giant step back. "No."

"I want you with me, Lucy. And if the only way to make that happen is to find the sculpture, then I'm in."

"No!" She turned on her heels and ran away.

Why the hell not? He couldn't understand why she wouldn't accept his help. Why she'd want to do things illegally when he offered an alternative.

The sun beat down on him like he stood under a heat lamp. His heart beat hard and fast. The eyes of all nearby workers fell on him. Lucy disappeared into the village and he steeled himself for a showdown before going after her.

L ucy leaned against the spot where the Tlaloc sculpture lay. Focus on this area of the village was weeks away, proving to relieve and antagonize her. The urgency to extract the sculpture increased every time Malcolm's words came back to haunt her. *Rumor has it you've found the Tlaloc sculpture. My employees don't leave and work against me. I want the sculpture or I'll ruin McCall. Or worse. I'd be only too happy to see Keats McCall gone. Do I make myself clear?*

Two things about his threat had overwhelmed her with dizziness that night at the gala. The first was his intimation that he knew McCall. Had they met before? McCall's tone had been bitter when he'd mentioned Malcolm a couple of times, but she'd chalked it up to the general consensus in their field that Malcolm was a jackass.

The second thing that bothered her and set off warning bells concerned Owen. If rumor had spread about her, had it started with him? Had someone been keeping tabs on Owen? His association with her and her father wasn't a secret. Malcolm had eyes and ears everywhere.

Her chest tightened now, squeezing hard enough to make her breath catch. She could not let McCall get involved. It would kill her if something happened to him. She'd made a choice when she married Matt to live his and her father's life, and that had taken her somewhere she hadn't wanted to go.

She was making a choice now to keep her world as far away from McCall as possible. It was time to get the Tlaloc sculpture and leave.

Footsteps sounded to her left so she took off in the opposite direction. And smacked right into the hard body she was trying to avoid.

McCall didn't give her a chance to right herself or to tell him to back off. His hands found her shoulders and his mouth connected with hers in a fierce kiss that instantly made her legs wobble. Against her better judgment, she leaned into him, her mind losing all control over her body. He moved his lips over hers with the kind of passion that made her want to back down. When his tongue made sweeping, swirling motions inside her mouth, a harsh groan of masculine satisfaction sounded. She answered with her own ragged sigh.

She ran her fingers through his hair. He slid his hands to her lower back, bringing her closer. His kiss flooded her with elation she wanted to live off of forever.

The hot intensity of their kiss slowed in tempo, but the

magnitude built. McCall tasted her like she was his lifeline, his salvation. Lucy needed to pull away, but she couldn't. She knew a different life existed and for this brief moment with McCall, she'd get to live it.

I want you with me, he'd said.

A week ago she hadn't known she could feel like she was right where she belonged. McCall made her feel so much more than she ever had before. She'd loved Matt, but *this* pull and admiration and awe with McCall immersed her in a different kind of love—unconditional.

This had to stop. She had to break free. If McCall were hurt because of her, she would never forgive herself.

She pushed him in the chest, fighting the urge to grip his shirt. Her fingertips touched her swollen lips. She willed her revving pulse to slow down.

"Did you feel that?" he asked. She must have looked as dazed as his kiss made her feel because he added, "I'm willing to risk everything for you."

Shielded from the desert sun, from the fresh air that carried history and hopes around everyone working on the village, and trapped in close quarters with a man she wanted to fight for, Lucy faltered for a moment. No one had ever felt that way about her before.

"Don't," she managed to say. "You need to stay away from me. I need to do this on my own."

He ran a hand across the stubble on his jaw. "Goddammit, Lucy. Why?"

"I just do." She'd lost everyone she'd ever loved. Her mom, her grandmother, Matt, her dad. Icy, sharp-tipped prongs battered her heart at the thought of causing McCall harm and she'd keep her silence to protect him.

Because she loved him.

"And if I don't let you?"

If he thought he held all the power here, he was mistaken. "I don't need or want your permission. I've done just fine without you."

He winced. "No doubt. But you're on my turf and if it's an ultimatum you want, then fine. Tell me what's going on in that head of yours or I'll stop you."

She flinched. "Fine."

"Fine what?" He crossed his arms over his broad chest.

"Just fine. I'm not explaining myself further and you can do whatever you want." She stepped around him. "I'm tired and filthy and think I'll head out."

"Lucy?" His calm, quiet voice made her turn around without hesitation. "I protect what's mine." He didn't make any move to stop her from leaving and for that she was grateful.

"I know you do." And she wished more than anything she fell under that category, too.

When she got back to the cabin, every muscle in her body groaned with fatigue. A splitting headache made it hurt to blink. She went into the bathroom, popped two pain relievers, and started a bath.

She eyed their toothbrushes on the counter. His was navy, hers pink. His toothpaste was neatly rolled up halfway. Hers was kinked and twisted and had gel toothpaste around the cap.

Even something as mundane as his oral hygiene products turned her on. She looked in the mirror. The person staring back had loved and lost and she didn't have the strength to go through it a second time.

Her cell phone chirped, alerting her to a voice message from a private number.

Lucy padded to the coffee table and picked it up. The moment she heard Malcolm's voice, her heart lurched.

"Time's up, Lucy," he said. "A source tells me someone else could be after the sculpture and I don't want to lose it. You need to move quickly or I will make good on my threat against McCall. Once you have the Tlaloc god in your possession, let me know and I'll make arrangements for you."

Click.

Tension built in the back of her neck and she put the phone down. She went to the bathroom, turned off the water, and gathered her things on the counter. She moved around the cabin picking up her clothes and piled them on the bed in her room. A knot lodged in her throat as she stuffed everything into her bags.

Leaving without saying goodbye speared her chest with a gritty, sharp pain. But McCall threatened her resolve. He almost had her convinced they could do this together. Malcolm was ruthless and vindictive, though, with friends in powerful places, and he wouldn't accept McCall's participation even if McCall did let her hand over the sculpture to him.

The crushing realization that the Tlaloc sculpture could hurt the man that she loved if she didn't get it quickly turned her stomach into a pit of vile aches. She'd thought keeping her word and following through would set her free, but she was even more trapped than before.

She grabbed her bags and rushed to her car. Her hands trembled when she put the key in the ignition. It shouldn't matter that she was back to being on her own. She'd never wanted anyone getting close to her again. Her attraction to McCall was too risky.

Once she had the sculpture, her past and present would collide and she could forget about it all.

Chapter Eleven

"You need a drink."

McCall closed the back door of his truck and turned around. Clay stood behind him blocking out the sun straddling the horizon. "A stiff one," Clay added.

"You think?" McCall moved around him to grab the extra drop cloths and throw them into the truck bed.

"You've been barking orders ever since Lucy left. And don't think I didn't notice her exit."

"What's that supposed to mean?"

"You did something to piss her off."

McCall leaned against the side of his truck. "I thought I told you to keep your eyes to yourself."

Clay laughed. "Watching is what I do best. And you, my friend, have got it bad."

"You've no idea." Since Lucy stormed away, he could barely think straight. He missed her smile. He missed how she pushed her sunglasses up when they slid down her nose.

He missed the dirt on her knees.

"So what did you do?" Clay phrased it as a question, but most of his questions weren't requests. Clay interrogated with a professional military nicety that McCall found damn annoying.

"Nothing." McCall glared at his friend. "Yet."

Clay stared at him with sharp, steel eyes and waited.

"Jesus, what is it with you? You could fucking get a mime to talk." He blew out an irritated breath. He and Clay had worked many sites together. During the day, Clay worked out safety precautions and kept an eye on personnel. At night, he stayed onsite to keep out unwanted trespassers.

Would Lucy try to sneak past him? It was the only possibility McCall could think of.

He'd introduced Lucy as a friend and archeologist, never mentioning her private sector work. The second she opened her warm, satiny voice and shared stories about her travels, everyone onsite admired her. Leaving out the details about the objects of historic value she'd found for Malcolm Holmes had seemed easy for her, leading him to wonder what else she found easy to omit.

"She thinks she's better at architectural assessment than I am, and I told her she was wrong," McCall said, some seed of truth there.

"Was she?" Clay's tone indicated he didn't think so.

"Do you fucking read between every line?"

McCall didn't know right from wrong anymore. His head told him to stop Lucy from trying to get the sculpture. His heart ached to do it for her. His site. His rules. No one need be the wiser. If she'd only confide in him.

"You're not telling me everything."

"No shit. The less you know, the better." The last thing McCall wanted was to bring any of his team members into something that might violate historical preservation policies if not handled the right way. An item found unintentionally, under preservation tactics—that would be a different story with no legal ramifications.

Clay crossed his arms over his massive chest. "If it's a security issue, I need to know."

"Shit." McCall pressed away from the truck and ran a hand through his hair. He didn't know what the right thing to do here was. He'd protect Lucy at any cost, but having his security guy aware of the situation might not be a bad idea. Especially if she was keeping Malcolm's involvement to herself. "This doesn't go beyond us."

"Got it."

McCall paced back and forth, kicking up dust with each heavy step. "Lucy believes there's a rare sculpture of historic value here and she plans to take it."

"Define *take*. This is a protected site. It's against the law—"

"I know." McCall stopped and leveled Clay with a do-you-think-I'm-stupid look. "The thing is she needs it and I'm inclined to let her have it."

"So what's the problem?"

"Exactly."

"Ah, I see." Clay unfolded his arms and put a hand on McCall's shoulder. "She doesn't want your help. I could have told you that thirty seconds after meeting her. Give her some space."

"But something isn't right and I'm afraid if I back off I might never see her again." He swallowed that truth down with growing anxiety. Too much time had already passed since he'd seen her. If he didn't get to touch her soon, he'd go insane.

Every time he looked at her or thought about her, he couldn't imagine letting her go. She captivated him, challenged him, fulfilled him.

"That's your problem. You're in love with her."

McCall stopped pacing and glared at Clay. Was his judgment clouded by the fact that yes, he loved Lucy? His job as president of field operations was to protect sites. If it was anyone else after the Tlaloc sculpture he wouldn't think twice about having him or her arrested.

"You're not thinking with the right head," Clay added.

"Fuck you."

Clay leaned against McCall's truck. Only a few wisps of sunlight remained, and cooler air finally circulated around them, carrying the scent of musk and wildflowers. "I'm not knocking it. Hell, this is the first time I've seen you fall for someone. But you take your job pretty seriously and there could be repercussions if you're not careful."

"There's never been a find of any historic value on a pro-tected US site, you know." McCall rubbed the side of his face. "It could garner the company and heritage protection some nice publicity."

"What are Lucy's plans for the sculpture?"

McCall lifted his chin and studied the mountains in the distance. "I don't know. I never asked." He should have, he realized now. He didn't want it to, but her plans for the Tlaloc god mattered. He wanted to believe she was donating it to a museum or foundation—something respectable. But given that she currently lived out of her car, he wondered if she was simply selling it to the highest bidder.

Malcolm.

That notion confirmed what he first thought of her—she was a thief. Maybe she wasn't working for Malcolm anymore, but she was stealing it to sell to him.

"Do me a favor," McCall said, "keep an eye out for her, but if she shows up don't…" He clenched his jaw, not sure what to ask of Clay. "Don't engage until you call me."

"Easy enough." He slapped McCall on the back. "Now get the hell out of here and tell her how you feel before it's too late."

McCall made his way around the truck. "Since when are you doling out relationship advice?" Clay's reputation with women reached territories McCall had yet to visit.

Clay laughed. "Since your sorry ass met the right woman and I'd hate for you to screw it up." A flash of uncommon pain wrinkled his forehead and the corners of his eyes.

"You speaking from experience?"

He shrugged and waved McCall off. "See you later."

"Yeah," McCall said half-aloud as he climbed into his truck.

Fueled by promises he wanted to voice to Lucy, McCall sped back to the campsite. Traffic kept him under the speed limit on the freeway. Nerves kept his fingers thrumming the steering wheel.

His thoughts raced back to the *Sea of Aesa* and the first time he'd laid eyes on her. He'd been immediately smitten, intrigued beyond measure, bursting with desire. He'd wanted to flee the ship with her over his shoulder. Damn the consequences.

Her scent, her full lips, eyes that told a story she'd only share with the right person, were the hat trick to his heart. After ten goddamn minutes, she'd stolen a piece of it.

His foot slammed on the brake, shaking him from his memories. He cursed the sea of slow moving cars in front of him. A knot twisted between his shoulder blades. When he got back to the campsite he'd tell Lucy he loved her. Three words he'd never spoken to anyone before.

He parked haphazardly ten minutes later, taking up two spots. He rushed to the cabin, his feet barely touching the ground.

"Lucy?" he called out. His heart sank the moment he slid the glass door wider. The room was dark. Motionless.

Empty.

Once again, Lucy had left him wanting.

"I can't believe you stuck around," Lucy said, staring at Owen's weary face and falling back against the red vinyl seat of the diner.

"You texted me you were having trouble viewing the camera footage you took." He dotted the corners of his mouth with his napkin. His tired eyes told her he'd been worried and she wished she'd never told him that. What she could see inside the Aztec village's walls when she'd downloaded the footage onto her laptop was grainy, but good enough.

"So?" She lifted her coffee cup to catch the waitress's

attention. It was close to midnight and Lucy needed to be alert.

"So, I couldn't leave. Besides," he covered his cup with his hand when the waitress tipped her carafe, "I had a feeling you'd need me."

Lucy sighed, feeling a little guilty, but thankful his uncanny senses had brought them back together. She poked a piece of crust from his apple pie with her fork. "Lucky for me you have feelings."

"You do too, you know. That's why we're sitting in a diner in the middle of nowhere drinking coffee that tastes like tar and raising our cholesterol with pie."

"I didn't mean those kinds of feelings."

He winked. "I know you didn't."

Headlights bisected their position in the tiny booth. She flinched and glanced out the window, careful to cover half her face with her hand.

It wasn't a truck. Wasn't McCall.

"He sneak a tracking device on you?"

"What? No!" Lucy slouched down in the seat. At least she didn't think so. She fought the urge to check her pockets, the grooves in the soles of her boots. She eyed her knapsack. He wouldn't, would he?

Owen put a hand on her arm. "I was teasing. McCall's expertise is heritage protection, not witness protection. But from what you've told me, I doubt he's going to let you get away with this."

She grappled with Owen's troubled gaze. " It's not just McCall. Malcolm wants the sculpture."

He raised his eyebrows and sat back against his seat, his posture stiff. "I thought you'd settled everything with that sonofabitch."

"I had. But I think you staying in town tipped him off to my being here and he somehow figured things out. The two of us in the same place usually means one thing."

"Shit, Lucy. I'm sorry."

"He told me if I don't get the sculpture for him he's going to ruin McCall. Or worse."

"You have to fill McCall in. For both your sakes. You need protection and if you love McCall like I think you do, then I'm sure he loves you back. Let him help you deal with the situation. Whether you like it or not, he's part of the equation."

Was it possible McCall loved her? If that were true, she had an even stronger reason for keeping him at bay. "You don't understand. I can't get McCall involved. I can't risk his job and honor and principles. I can't risk his *life*. I don't want him doing something for me that can jeopardize his safety. I won't allow it."

Owen clasped his hands together atop the table and smiled.

"Why are you smiling?"

"Because it's nice to know you're nothing like your father or Matt." He reached for her hand. "You don't just care about objects, Lucy. You care about people. McCall is a lucky man."

Lucy looked at his hand around hers. Warmth seeped into her chilled fingers. Owen was right. For her dad and Matt it was always about the job. Even with their last breath, the final words they'd spoken to her had been about the Tlaloc sculpture, not concern for her. They hadn't said what she most wanted to hear: *I love you.*

Pain stabbed her in the chest. She'd always put them first, but they hadn't reciprocated. She knew they loved her. But they were driven by the thrill of the chase more than anything else.

"I hate being confused like this." She looked around the diner. An older couple sat at the counter talking with a waitress. A guy with a Diamondbacks hat relaxed at a table. The only other occupied booth seated a family of four, the kids' heads held in their hands, the parents sifting through maps.

"They've got problems, too," Owen said, following her gaze. "We all do. It's how you deal with them that matter."

"You're watching too many daytime talk shows."

He shrugged and scratched at the hairline on his forehead. "Maybe."

She moved aside her crumb-filled plate and coffee cup and leaned forward with her elbows on the table.

"I've never told you what to do, and I'm not going to start now, but you've got my suggestion." He crossed his arms over his chest and a tiny smirk played across his lips, reminding Lucy of her favorite geology professor in college. He liked to give advice too.

She thought about her discussion with Owen over the last ten minutes. If she really wanted to change her life and make a fresh start, there was only thing to do.

Malcolm had said someone else might be after the sculpture. That meant she had to find it first for two reasons — to guarantee minimal damage to the village and to make sure no one got hurt.

"I'm going to talk to McCall."

Owen's smirk blossomed into a grin. "That's my girl."

Her playful banter with McCall, all their touches and caresses, and all the pieces of herself she'd happily lost to him this week flitted through her mind as she stood. Owen looked up at her with approval in his gray eyes and the weight on her shoulders lightened.

"Thank you." She bent and kissed him on the cheek.

"Thank me after you've got the sculpture."

"I will."

Chapter Twelve

Time stood still.

McCall swore the digits on the bedside clock read one-two: three-four every time he looked at it. Which happened to be every five minutes.

His mind wouldn't stop reeling, the pressure in the back of his head wouldn't let up.

He threw the bed covers off and paced around the cabin as if that would bring him the answers he needed.

Where was Lucy? Was she safe? She hadn't answered his phone calls or texts and it killed him. It hurt like he'd been cut open and sewn back up with chicken wire.

Five times he'd grabbed his keys, ready to drive to hell and back to find her.

Ready to drive to his village in case she'd gotten past Clay.

And five times he put his keys down.

Because the half of him that believed she'd be at the

site tonight didn't want to find her there. He wanted her to get away free and clear. The complex emotions that stirred sucked the air out of his lungs. Duty stung like a son of a bitch. But picturing her victory soothed the sting like nothing else.

McCall knew she'd be careful. She'd leave as little evidence as possible she'd been there. He smiled. Thinking about her with a hammer and chisel as she meticulously worked to free the gold Tlaloc sculpture sent goose bumps up his arms. She wove a pretty powerful charm when she touched things.

He slid open the sliding glass door of the cabin and stepped onto the deck. Normally, the after-midnight air unchained him from troublesome thoughts keeping him awake. But the unusual humidity and silence from night creatures only fractured the insanity.

Something in the air seemed off, and his mind raced to another scenario. Lucy hitting the highway back to Charleston because she couldn't go through with taking the sculpture.

But that would also mean she didn't care enough about him to see how far they could take this thing between them.

The whole distance. That's what McCall had wanted. He'd found a woman he'd give up everything for and whom he knew would accept him with nothing but the shirt on his back.

He flexed his fingers to relieve the stiffness in his hands. He looked out into the dull, indistinct woods and conjured a vision of Lucy stepping through the darkness, walking towards him with slow determination until she got close enough to touch. He blinked and reached his arm out. The image seemed so real. Had she come back to him?

His hand went through nothing but air.

"McCall?"

Lucy stood just out of reach, not a figment of his imagination, but a gorgeous, living, breathing woman.

"Lucy." He didn't move a muscle, afraid to siphon the moment.

"Can we talk?" Her breathy, sexy voice sent ripples of relief and gratitude through him. Her eyes took in his bare chest and the closer she got, the easier it was to relax.

When she stood in front of him and lifted her chin to meet his gaze, he said, "Right after this." And then he kissed her.

Not quick, but slow. Not hard, but sensual. He moved his lips across hers with delicate pressure that he hoped said *stay with me forever*, because Lucy was the kind of woman where actions spoke louder than words.

Her arms went around his neck and her body melted against his. He cupped the back of her head and wrapped an arm around her waist. When he slid his tongue inside her mouth and deepened the kiss, she moaned her approval.

For several minutes they stood there, enraptured in the kiss, hearts beating together as one. When it dawned on McCall that this was possibly a good-bye kiss, he pulled away.

"Tell me this isn't good-bye," McCall said, taking her hand and bringing her down to sit beside him on the top step of the deck.

Lucy's satiated but weary eyes answered with *maybe*.

He leaned back on his elbows, hoping to look casual and hide the worry hammering behind his ribcage.

"I don't think so."

"Okay. What is it?"

"Confession." She looked out into the darkness. "You've been nothing but honest with me and I want to give you the same courtesy before I do what I've come here to do."

"I'm listening."

Hugging her knees to her chest, she said, "It's about more than my promise now. Malcolm found out what I was doing here and he wants the Tlaloc sculpture. If I don't get it for him…" She looked at McCall out of the corner of her eye for a long time. "If I don't get it for him, he's going to come after you."

McCall drew up, his back straight. "That's why you pushed me away?"

"Yes."

"You're worried about me?" He twisted to face her.

"Maybe. I know Malcolm is capable of—"

He cut her off with another kiss. Pressed her back, covered her torso with his, and fed from the sweetness of her mouth until he had to come up for air. "Malcolm Holmes doesn't scare me," he said, looking down at her. "But you do, Lucy. I've never felt—"

This time she cut him off, pulling him down and claiming his mouth with a long, drugging kiss. When she'd apparently had enough, she nudged him in the chest. "I have a plan."

So did he. Big plans, but he had a feeling she wasn't quite ready for that. He took a deep breath. He hated not being the one in control, but Lucy's comfort mattered more than his. Whatever happened with the Tlaloc sculpture, he'd make sure Malcolm got what he deserved. Clay's ties with the military extended to some very powerful people.

"I'm listening." He angled away from Lucy's warm body to cool his overwhelming urge to carry her to his bed and forget about everything but the two of them.

"Hire me for real."

"Excuse me?"

"Hire me on as a consultant. If I'm on your site in an official capacity, I can get the Tlaloc sculpture and like you said, bring attention to the find *and* your village. Retrieving an elusive sixteenth century gold artifact from the Aztec village while at the same time preserving the village's heritage would bring notoriety to World Heritage Fund and protect you, me, and the sculpture."

"A similar thought occurred to me."

Her eyes twinkled. "If we can get some national press and use your family connections to garner publicity, too, then Malcolm wouldn't dare come after us. At least, I don't think he would."

"When do you see this happening?"

"This weekend." She put her palm on his chest, over his heart, like she needed to feel he was okay with this.

He covered her hand with his and their eyes connected. Held. For several long beats they stared, electric feelings of friendship and adoration and *love* filling McCall's soul. If he'd had any doubt about Lucy's devotion, he didn't any longer.

"You know where the sculpture is." A statement, not a question. The last of her secrets, he hoped.

"Yes."

"Do I want to know how you found it?"

"Do you?" A slow smile spread across her irresistible lips at the same time she withdrew her hand.

"Over margaritas after we get it."

Her smile slipped. "After I get it, that's when I'll say

goodbye."

Everyone Lucy had ever loved died. Her mother when she five. Her grandmother when she was twenty. Matt and her father two years ago.

She was worried that the next person she loved would leave before she was ready, too.

So she was scared. Scared because she loved McCall's kisses with soft caresses one minute and white-hot urgency the next. Loved when he journeyed from her mouth to every slope and curve of her body with his tongue like he wanted to memorize each pathway. And loved when he moved inside her without the control he prided himself possessing, groaning without restraint.

"I see," he said, the joy on his face vanishing.

"What do you see?"

"An even bigger thief than I thought you were." He stood. His sweatpants hung low on his hips, accentuating his trim waist and broad shoulders.

Lucy forced herself to look elsewhere and jumped to her feet. "What's that supposed to mean?"

He didn't answer, just strode back into the cabin and flipped on a light. Lucy leaned against the glass door and watched him. He changed into jeans and threw on a T-shirt, ran a hand through his soft, brown hair. She could watch him all day and night.

"McCall?"

He forced his feet into his shoes. "You're never going to trust yourself around me, are you? You've stolen something from me, Lucy. Something I've held tight to but was power-less to keep the minute I met you."

She frowned. What was he talking about?

"My heart." He took two strides and stood right in front of her. "When I called you a thief," he whispered, "I meant you'd stolen my heart." He cupped her cheek and his glori-ous blue eyes gave her hope for a future she'd been pushing away because of fear. "And I was hoping you might like me along with it."

Her breath caught and she leaned into his palm. "I'm sorry. It's just… It's just I've lost everyone I've loved and I don't want to lose you, too."

A grin that reminded her he was worth the risk spread across his face. "Did you hear what you just said?"

"Umm…"

"You said you love me."

"I didn't say that exactly. What I was trying to say… what I meant to say…" He'd totally flustered her!

He touched his forehead to hers and sucked in a deep breath. "I love you, too."

She melted against him, powerless. Wrapping her arms around his waist and nuzzling his neck she said, "Even if things don't go the way we've planned?"

"Even then." He pulled away. "There's one question I need to ask you, though, before I throw you onto the bed behind me."

"Okay. But make it quick. I'm really in need of a bed."

"Before Malcolm's threat, what were your plans for the sculpture?" A flash of concern passed over his handsome features and for a moment she wanted to take back the last five minutes. But then he took her hand and his touch was warm, tender. "It doesn't matter," he said, maybe realizing his mistake. "I promise you it doesn't matter."

"I have a friend at the National Museum of American History. I'm donating it to them in my father and Matt's names."

The worry in his eyes dissipated. "That's... You're a good, honorable person, Lucy. I'm sorry if my question made you doubt I thought that."

"Thank you."

He tugged her with him toward the bed. "Now about this need of yours. I think I should take care of it. Slowly. Very, very slowly."

McCall's phone rang, breaking their momentum and giving her a moment to absorb his words. "Dammit," he said. "That can't be good." He pulled the phone out of his pocket. "Hello?"

His eyes never left hers as he listened to whoever had called. "Call the authorities and I'll be there in twenty minutes." He lowered the phone from his ear. "Clay caught someone trespassing at the village."

"I'll go with you," Lucy said.

"Damn right you will." He took her hand and led her out of the cabin. "As my newest team member, you've got a job to do. If anyone is going to get the Tlaloc sculpture, it's going to be you. You ready to do this?"

"Very." For all the *this* he threw her way.

An hour later a quiet so eerie filled the hallway of the Aztec village that Lucy froze and held her breath.

Nerves skittered across her shoulder blades until she sighed and shook her head to rid the unsettling stillness. In the hour or two before dawn things sometimes just stopped for a second. Especially in centuries old sacred dwellings where Owen would say sprits lingered. She wiped a bead of sweat from her brow and returned to work.

She shifted a little on her stool, accidentally tapping the light stand with her elbow. Light bounced around for a moment then settled down. She hated the nervous feeling gripping her. She'd worked with a hammer and chisel dozens of times. The slow work guaranteed the artifact protection. The last thing she wanted was the wall crashing in and damaging the gold statue.

Her arms dropped from fatigue and she took a break before her unsteady hands got back to task. She glanced constantly at her laptop and the footage from Owen's camera to be sure she worked in the right direction. Minutes ticked by too quickly. Serious doubts she'd get to the sculpture before sunrise and before someone else showed up for it plagued her. Whoever had buried the Tlaloc god didn't want anyone to find it.

A high-pitched ping echoed off the walls each time the hammer connected with the chisel. Lucy focused on moving the sharp-edged tool a fraction this way or that, edging deeper into the wall, getting closer to the alcove where the sculpture lay.

A metallic taste tickled the back of her dry throat. Sweat trickled down her side. Her hand slipped, and the hammer took a small chunk out of the sandstone.

"Shit." She brought her hands to her lap.

"Not what the president of field operations wants to

hear." McCall's amused voice calmed her overactive nerves. He laid his chin on her shoulder.

She tilted her head back, which gave him access to her neck. He took it and with a soft touch his mouth grazed.

"Everything okay out there?"

"Yeah. The guy's in custody. Clay's making a few calls to friends about Malcolm. I missed your beautiful face."

A shiver raced through her. She'd missed his. "I'm close."

"I can see that." He nodded toward the monitor at the same time the ground shook and a large rumble sounded. "What the hell?" He raced into the darkness. "Stay here," he called over his shoulder.

Lucy recognized the noise and quickly got back to work. Archeologists sometimes used small excavation devices that bulldozed through brick and mortar and sounded like a tiny explosion. Someone else was in the village. Someone who most likely worked for Malcolm and who must have used the trespasser and his arrest as a decoy. Lucky for her, the new trespasser was in the wrong area of the village.

Panic lanced through Lucy. McCall and Clay would be on whoever it was, but what if they were outnumbered. Out-weaponed? The Tlaloc sculpture was worth an estimated two million dollars.

Plus, McCall and Malcolm *knew* each other. When Mc-Call had told her about their one-time friendship on the drive over, she'd been floored. And more worried than ever. Ill feelings were like lighting a match to gasoline—explosive and dangerous.

It explained Malcolm's threats, and quadrupled the reasons he'd send someone else to look for the sculpture, too.

She picked up her hammer and swung it at the wall without care. The quicker she got the sculpture, the quicker she'd have a bargaining chip if necessary.

Three swings and she'd found it. She dug to get close enough to pull it out. Dirt caked underneath her nails, the skin on her knuckles cracked. Once in her hands, she made a run for fresh air.

The first glow of a new day greeted her. Across the dusty floor of the village, near the entrance to the south side of the buildings, Lucy caught sight of a man who worked for Malcolm. She recognized him from a job they'd done together in Turkey. He didn't play nice and he had a gun in the waistband of his pants. She scanned the area. McCall stood at his truck, phone at his ear. With his back to the intruder, the guy pulled the gun out and stepped toward McCall.

Her throat still parched, she couldn't find her voice to yell loud enough to warn McCall.

Lucy put the sculpture between her legs, brought her hands to her mouth, and…

Only a low hum sounded when she tried to whistle. Cold tendrils of fear whipped through her as painful memories swallowed the newfound luster around her heart and her legs almost buckled. She inhaled deeply to stop the stutter in her breathing and tried again. Something low-pitched squeaked out.

The guy cocked his gun.

She squeezed her eyes shut for a split second. A second to gather her determination. Her tenacity. McCall loved her. More than his village. More than any artifact. For the first time, she meant more than anything else to someone.

And he meant more to her.

Fingers in perfect placement, she tried again. A clear high-pitched sound traveled the distance and both McCall and the man turned. She lifted the sculpture in the air, hoping to lure the man toward her and away from McCall.

The guy obliged and Lucy walked to meet him. Recognition crossed his face and he lowered the gun.

That's when McCall tackled him from behind. Clay came out of nowhere to help. Lucy's heart raced with sickening speed. The next few moments passed in a flurry of fists and punches until Malcolm's man went down and stayed down. Clay handcuffed him and dragged him toward his truck.

She'd done it. She'd kept McCall safe and gotten the sculpture.

In an instant, McCall had her wrapped in his arms and was planting kisses along her hairline. "Are you okay? What the hell were you doing?"

Swallowing hard, she sniffed back tears and took a moment to get her voice back. "Distracting him so I could save the man I love."

He pulled back to look at her. "You could have been hurt. Or worse. Jesus, Lucy, don't ever do that again."

"Okay."

Like they'd done so many times before, they looked into each other's eyes, saying without words what Lucy knew to be true: they belonged together.

"Nice whistle, by the way."

"Thanks. Some heritage protection guy taught it to me."

"I want to teach you a lot of other things, too." He cradled her face in his hands. "I want to spend the rest of my days with you by his side. I'm on this earth to breathe your air. There's no one else I want to surrender to, fight for, be with. No one has ever made me feel the way you do." He paused. "You scare the shit out of me at the same time you make me feel invincible. You are the love of my life."

She put the sculpture back between her legs, cupped his jaw, and kissed him. The kind of kiss that said she couldn't take her next breath without him either. The kind that said she was his forever. She might be reckless and impulsive sometimes, but for the first time in her life, her heart was all in.

"I want to teach you things, too. I want to build a new life with you and laugh with you and have adventures with you. I didn't know what true love was until now. I've found the best treasure… You." She pulled back and lifted the sculpture. Pride and relief coursed through her.

McCall glanced at it. "It's smaller than I imagined."

"Yeah."

"So we have ourselves a deal?"

Lucy looked up, her forehead creasing in confusion. "I don't know, do we?"

He took her hands and said, "I love you and want to spend the rest of my days showing you how much."

"I'd say we have a deal."

Epilogue

Lucy licked her way up McCall's smooth, muscled chest. She'd never tire of tasting him. Never tire of being skin-to-skin with him. Her hands pressed into his shoulders, keeping him in place on the giant, five-star hotel bed, and her very hard nipples slid along his abs.

She traced her tongue along his collarbone and up and around his neck until she reached his earlobe and nibbled.

He shifted restlessly beneath her attention. His hands cupped her bare ass and brought her very ready center snug against his very ready arousal. One more inch up and he'd slip inside her.

But she wanted to prolong this a bit longer. Savor the hot, potent pulses zinging around her every body part. She slowly rotated her hips against him, each stroke taking another piece of his self control. He let out a harsh breath.

"You're killing me, you know that?" His husky voice brought a smile to her face.

With a little more pressure, she kissed his jawline, his chin, the corner of his full lips. He turned his head and caught her mouth with his. He had the art of kissing down pat. He nibbled, teased, and took pleasure from her mouth with each caress of their lips and tongues, his every moan telling her how much he loved it.

She slid one hand to the soft cotton sheet while the other cupped the side of his face. Their tongues circled, twined, danced with wild abandon until she couldn't stand it any longer. She pulled back and he knew. He just knew. With one quick move, he flipped her onto her back and positioned himself at her entrance. The smirk that turned her insides to mush and felt like a meteor of love had crash-landed in her heart, took hold of his sexy and talented mouth.

"Now. I need you inside me now," she said breathlessly.

"I thought you'd never ask." He joined their bodies slowly at first, sinking himself into her just enough to drive her mad and then pulling out to drive her even madder. The whole time, the smirk stayed. His eyes twinkled.

She thrust her hips up, begging him to fill her completely. "You were amazing today," he said. And then he guided himself unhurriedly, inch by magnificent inch, inside.

A cry of pleasure tore from the back of her throat as she finally took all of him in. They moved together in perfect harmony. Everything inside her flooded with so much love for this man that it took only seconds for her to reach a blinding, pulsing release that stretched into long, drawn out moments of satisfaction.

Keats's harsh groan of masculine satisfaction followed

close behind.

He rolled off her, taking her with him so he could tuck her against his side. She put her hand over his heart and closed her eyes.

"Thanks for standing beside me," she whispered. She'd been so nervous during the presentation at the Museum of American History, but then McCall had taken her hand and all the tension with it.

"There's no place else I'd rather be." His fingertips grazed her side, the curve of her hip. "Thanks for sharing the recognition with World Heritage Fund. I think my boss wants to hire you."

Lucy pressed up and looked down at the most gorgeous face on any continent. They'd kept the news about the Tlaloc sculpture to themselves for a while, waiting until Malcolm was held under investigation and there were no ties to her. She'd spent every day with McCall since that awful night when he could have been shot and every day she shared another piece of herself.

They also talked about the future. She wanted to teach. He wanted to cut back on his workload. She wanted babies. He wanted at least four.

Starting now.

Owen had let it slip that McCall had asked for his blessing to ask Lucy to marry him. The old fashioned gesture made her grin every time she thought about it.

"We've talked about what's next," Lucy said. Now would be a great time for him to pop the question, but she'd wait until he was ready.

"You've got that mischievous look in your eye again. What's up?"

"Nothing. I just have no plans to work for WHF."

"I know." He tugged her back down. "That's why I've decided to take on more of a consulting role so I don't have to be away from you. Once the house is finished I'll be able to work from home and cut way back on travel. Connor's more than willing to take on a larger workload."

The house. He was building them a house in Colorado. Tears pricked the back of her eyes, she was so happy.

"Wait. What?" She lifted her head and put her chin on his chest. "Are you sure that's what you want?"

"I'm sure I can't be away from you for longer than necessary." He smiled. Her heart melted. "Which reminds me. There's something I want to—"

"Yes!"

Lines creased his forehead and his mouth twisted into an adorable curve. "Ask you."

"My answer is yes, Keats." She said it with tenderness. Devotion. Love.

"You haven't heard the question."

"A little birdy might have let slip some confidential info."

"Oh, he did, did he?"

She sucked in her bottom lip and nodded. Owen had been at the museum this morning, too. When he'd said good-bye before heading to the airport to catch a plane back to Los Angeles, he'd told her he'd be there to walk her down the aisle. Whenever. Wherever.

McCall slid out of bed and in all his glorious nakedness got down on one knee. Her breath caught in her throat. She pushed up onto her elbows. He stared into her eyes and she was caught. Forever.

"I love you," she said. "I love you so much."

A wide smile touched the corner of his eyes. "Lucy Davenport, you would make me the happiest man on earth if you agreed to spend the rest of your life with me. I love you with all my heart. All my soul. Will you marry me?" He lifted his hand and the most brilliant diamond ring she'd ever seen sparkled between his fingers. She had no idea where he'd been hiding it, but it didn't matter.

"Yes, Keats. I'll marry you."

"Say that again, would you?"

"Yes, Keats."

Acknowledgments

To my husband, whose support and love is always unwavering even when I'm attached to my laptop and we're eating cereal for dinner. Again. You're the best. My hero. My everything.

To my editor, Wendy Chen, who made this story better with her amazing input. I am so lucky and grateful to have you on my side and appreciate more than I can say your guidance and love of my work. Thank you!

To Morgan Maulden and the gang at Entangled - you all rock!

To my family and friends whose kind words and enthusiasm for my writing mean the world to me. I love you all.

And last, but not least, to my readers. From the bottom of my heart, thank you for reading my stories!

His Million Dollar Risk

Entangled Publishing, LLC
2614 South Timberline Road
Suite 109
Fort Collins, CO 80525
Visit our website at www.entangledpublishing.com.

Indulgence is an imprint of Entangled Publishing, LLC.

Edited by Wendy Chen

Manufactured in the United States of America

First Edition February 2015

To Duncan.

Chapter One

Connor Gibson didn't mind being the center of attention—when that appreciation came from a woman's deliberate eyes and soft, kissable lips in the close confines of a bedroom. Scratch that, he didn't care where they were as long as it was just the two of them.

Sitting poolside at the trendy Sunset Hotel in Scottsdale, Arizona, he could do without the constant awareness. He'd politely refused several drink offers from Spring Break coeds and declined pickup lines that might have worked if he'd been in a better mood. He'd only sat in the late-afternoon sunshine because he'd gotten to the hotel earlier than planned.

A lounge chair, cold drink, and rare nap had sounded like a good plan. Once he hit the road tomorrow morning he'd have very little down time.

Or peace of mind.

For the umpteenth time he thought about "accidentally"

forgetting he was supposed to pick up a reporter from Natu-
ralWorld.com and have her accompany him for a weeklong
interview on his stops along Route 66. He hated reporters.
He hated liars.

His muscles tensed and he squeezed his hands around
the edge of the lounge chair. Okay, so he probably shouldn't
label all reporters as liars and hate the whole lot of them. If
the article were for any other magazine, he would have been
okay with it. But no way in hell could he forgive what Natural World had done to his mom. If not for the fact that Route
66 was his baby, that no one knew the project as well as he
did, Connor would have assigned the exclusive interview to
one of his VPs. But this was a chance to bring national recognition to the Route as World Heritage Fund's preservation
efforts were coming to a close, and Connor had the most at
stake. He'd worked nonstop for two years and wanted the
country to take notice.

He unclenched his hands and laced them behind his
head. House music streamed out of speakers disguised as
large rocks at the base of several palm trees. A game of
Chicken took over the shallow end of the pool. He lifted
his Oakley sunglasses away from his face and wiped the
perspiration under his eyes.

"Is that chair taken?"

Plenty of lounge chairs remained vacant around the
pool, including the one between him and a woman asleep
on her stomach to his right. He eyed the sleeping beauty
with her fair skin, blond hair, and shapely curves. She hadn't
moved a muscle since he sat down an hour ago.

"Yes," he said, turning his head to address the woman
who'd asked the question. He liked his view and didn't want

to disturb it.

"Oh. Okay." She batted her eyelashes anyway, but he didn't take the bait.

His friend and work colleague Clay had told him numerous times his indifference only made women more interested. Made them look at him as a challenge. Apparently, his I'm-unavailable vibe flashed like a beacon today.

"Cannonball!" some guy shouted before he leaped into the air and landed with a splash in the deep end of the swimming pool.

The jump sent drops of water into Connor's lap. The spray must have also hit his neighbor because she stirred.

Then bent her legs and wiggled her feet in the air as if to shake them dry. After a few moments she straightened her long, toned legs and slipped her hands to her sides to retrieve the ends of the bikini top she'd unhooked. With her head canted down and away from him, blond hair that had been loosely piled behind her neck fell over her shoulder.

Connor watched as she lifted up slightly to reach behind her back and connect the ends of her top. She tried unsuccessfully for several seconds before letting out a sigh and releasing the straps to relax her arms.

Offering to help crossed his mind, but the way his body had suddenly perked up told him that was a bad idea. A very *good* bad idea, the devil on his shoulder said.

That devil had gotten him into trouble before. Just because he found it nice that this girl was the one woman yet to lay eyes on him didn't mean he should lend a hand.

Her back rose and fell, and she went to grab the ends of her bikini top again. It looked like the clasp on one end had gotten stuck to her towel because she shimmied her hand against her side while her other arm stretched across her back.

A muffled "dammit" reached his ears as she laid her chin on the front edge of the chair. He really was a jackass for not volunteering to lend a hand, especially since she'd probably decline assistance from a total stranger.

She tried again. This time she raised enough to give him a peek at the outside swell of her breast as she wrestled with the uncooperative bathing suit.

His gaze traveled down the slope of her back to the curve of her ass. Her angles and edges looked soft and inviting. Not too small and not too large. She looked just right.

Goldilocks in the flesh.

He zoned out for a second, lost in the smooth texture of her skin, so he had zero time to react when the bikini top flying through the air hit him in the chest.

"Oh my God!" she said.

Connor blinked and watched as Goldilocks sat up, one arm covering her chest, followed quickly by the other for double protection. He reached down and picked up the red top, a hell-yeah smirk on his face.

"I can't believe that just happened," she said. "I'm so sorry. The hook got stuck on my towel and then I guess I pulled too hard." Her hair fell in waves down her back, sleep lines creased her cheek, blue eyes bright with embarrassment stared at him.

"I'm not," he said, swinging his legs off the lounge chair so he sat facing her.

She narrowed her eyes. "You're not what?"

"Sorry it happened." Elbows on his knees, he toyed with the bikini top, but kept his attention on her.

"Do you mind?" she asked, eyebrows raised, her tone flustered.

It had been a while since he'd flustered a woman.

"Mind what?" Yes, he was messing with her, but her cheeks had reddened and he suspected it wasn't from the warm temperature. "A beautiful woman loses a piece of clothing, it's no bother whatsoever."

His gaze slid down the pretty column of her neck, down to her chest. He knew she couldn't see his eyes behind his sunglasses, so he didn't feel the least bit insolent checking her out. Her arms did a nice job of covering her breasts, but didn't detract in the least from the sexiness of her pose.

She contemplated the ground for a second. "I'd like my top back, please."

"I don't know," he teased. "It could be construed as a deadly weapon."

"Excuse me?" Her lips parted in charming confusion.

"I think I've got a knick right here." He glanced down and pressed a few fingers to his abdomen.

"Shut up." By the sound of her voice, she got that he was poking fun. Still, she studied his body—for a little too long.

"Injury aside, there's also the fact that there's not a lot of material here." He examined the strapless top like he hoped to figure out a tough mathematical problem.

"So?" She dropped her chin and looked around her chair. Probably searching for her shirt or cover-up. He appreciated that besides her embarrassment and impatience, she'd taken the situation lightly. The girl had spunk.

"So. Are you trying to cause an accident? Because this could make a guy forget to watch where he's walking."

Her attention shot back to him. She gulped, and he got

the feeling she didn't receive many flirtatious compliments. Hell, he didn't usually give them. Women sought *him* out. His position as president of field operations for World Heritage Fund, the largest and most influential nonprofit organization dedicated to heritage protection, garnered him plenty of notice. But it was his family and the wealth that came with his name that really had women clamoring to get close to him.

When he had a few moments of free time.

"Umm…"

He smiled. A genuine, feel-good grin he hadn't had the pleasure of in a long time.

She broke eye contact and bent forward to retrieve a pale yellow T-shirt under her chair, careful to keep one arm firmly locked across her chest. A sketch pad sat underneath where the shirt had been.

Once she had the garment and sat back up, though, Connor could tell she had no idea how to get it on without using two hands. A second later she lifted her bottom and pulled the towel out from under her. Goldilocks paid him no mind as she managed to get the towel underneath one arm, then the other, before letting out a deep sigh. She tossed her shirt into a bright pink bag and finally her sapphire-blue eyes registered on him again.

"Could I have my top back now? I, uh, need to get going."

"So soon?"

A tiny smile pulled at the corners of her seductive mouth. "I think it's for the best."

"I hate to see the best thing to happen to me all day walk away." This girl intrigued him and he wouldn't mind spending more time with her.

She laughed, the sound easy on his ears. "That's nice of you to say, but I'm not here alone."

Damn. "Boyfriend?" She wasn't wearing a ring so he didn't think she had a husband.

"Girlfriend."

Double damn. "Oh. Well, she's a lucky girl." And his luck sucked. Goldilocks equaled the perfect distraction for tonight. Maybe too perfect. His bet with Clay flashed through his mind and the million dollars he had on the line. He gave himself a mental shake. Better for her to leave.

She grabbed her sketch pad and bag and stood, wrapping the towel all the way around herself. "It's not like that," she said before smirking. "But it was cute of you to think so."

He got to his feet, too. "You think I'm cute?"

Goldilocks rolled her eyes. She put out her hand, palm up. Connor really didn't want to give up the bikini top since it was the only thing keeping her there, but he did. With his elbow at his side, he dangled it in front of his chest.

Pursing her lips, she reached out and snagged it.

"Well, it's been a pleasure..." He trailed off, hoping she'd fill in her name.

"Charlie," she said before she took off like a pack of wild dogs were on her ass.

Charlie leaned against the elevator wall as the doors slid shut. Her legs were still shaking and her heart was still under attack, the beats pounding in her chest and ears.

That guy, whoever he was, had been too gorgeous. Too

charming. Too intimidating. Guys like him didn't normally notice her.

She pressed the button for the eighteenth floor and took a deep breath.

Somehow, she'd kept her composure while he teased her about her bikini top. How humiliating to fling it at him! Talk about mortifying. He'd stayed cool the entire time, amusement playing in those very fine lips of his. She couldn't fault him that. The situation *was* ridiculous. Add it to her long list of mishaps.

Add being half-naked in public to a reputation that lately seemed to focus only on her failings. She needed to go from accident-prone to flawless sophisticate pronto if she had any hope of getting her father to take her more seriously.

Pool guy's half-nakedness had been quite all right, though. Men didn't really have abs like that. Or shoulders. Or arms. Or smiles that showed off perfect white teeth and said, *Hi, yes I'm beautiful, but I'm friendly too*. Only this one did. He was hotness on a stick and no doubt every girl who looked at him wanted a taste. Good thing she hadn't been able to see his eyes or she might not have been able to walk away. She had a thing for eyes and no doubt his matched the rest of his unbelievable self.

The elevator doors opened, and she headed down the hallway. "Hey, I'm back," she called out as she entered the hotel room. "Are you feeling any better?"

Charlie and her best friend, Ashley Morgan, had taken a little road trip from California so Ash could do some research on Route 66 in preparation for her big interview for Natural World, the largest online magazine focused on anything and everything outdoors. Charlie wrote for the company, too. Only her pieces were all fluff, never substance.

The owner and publisher, Thomas Beckett, didn't think she was ready for more. Just like he hadn't thought her ready to get her ears pierced until she turned thirteen and date until she was seventeen, and…

"Charlize Beckett, where have you been? I think I'm dying." Ashley lay curled up in a ball on the bed with her hair matted to her forehead and all the color gone from her face.

"I'm so sorry." Charlie rushed to her side. "I fell asleep. And then… It doesn't matter. You're feeling worse?" She put the back of her hand on Ash's forehead. She hadn't wanted to go lay out by the pool, but Ashley had insisted, saying it silly for both of them to be cooped up. "You feel warm."

"I think the chicken I ate last night has zombified and decided it would be fun to tear the lining of my stomach to pieces."

"We should get you to an emergency room. It could be serious, like your appendix." Charlie jumped to her feet. She dropped the towel and found some clothes to put on. "Which by the way has nothing to do with your dinner so don't think you have to stop eating chicken." Picky didn't begin to describe how Ash felt about food.

"Why were you topless?"

"I'll tell you on the way. Come on." Charlie helped ease Ash into a sitting position. "You can do this, right?"

"As long as you get me to a doctor and not lost, yes."

"Hey, I'm not that bad at directions. We'll ask the concierge and be on our way." She grabbed their bags and waited for her friend to slide her feet into flip-flops.

"You can never even find where you parked." Ashley

clutched her stomach and stepped slowly out the door.

"Well it's a good thing we valeted the car then."

Ashley gave a small chuckle. "Yeah. And whatever this illness is, it has to be gone by tomorrow morning. I've got to be ready to hit the road at nine."

Charlie put a hand on Ash's arm. "You'll be fine."

Only she wasn't. While sitting in the waiting area of the emergency room Ash's appendix ruptured. Emergency surgery followed and the doctor wanted to keep her for at least another twenty-four hours to guard against infection.

"You can," Ashley said in a groggy voice from her hospital bed a couple of hours after surgery.

"I can't," Charlie answered, shaking her head. She sat in a vinyl chair next to Ash. She wanted to say she could, but if she messed up, it wouldn't be just her head. It would be Ashley's, too.

"This is the opportunity you've been waiting for. An assignment like this doesn't come around very often. Read through my notes and you'll be good to go."

"The guy is expecting Ashley Morgan. You've written dozens of stories on important people and events. My pieces are on gear and getaways."

"And they're most excellent," Ash said on a yawn.

Charlie glanced at the wall clock. Almost midnight. "Why don't you just call the guy in the morning, tell him what happened, and join up with him in a couple of days?"

"Or you can meet him, introduce yourself, and write a kick ass story that gets your father's notice."

"My dad will be furious."

"He'll get over it. Look, I really think this is the only way to handle it. Schedules are tight, and you know how I hate when things start off on the wrong foot. It's not like you don't work for Natural World. Just explain the situation and the guy won't mind one bit."

"What if he does?"

"He won't." Ashley's eyes drifted shut.

"If I screw up—which you know is a possibility given my track record with things—then I'm putting Natural World's reputation at risk." Charlie shook her head even though Ash couldn't see her. "No, I think this is a bad idea."

"All you have to do is be a passenger, ask a bunch of questions, take really good notes, and be your naturally wonderful self. We can write the story together if you want." Ash opened her eyes. "How's that sound?"

A mixture of excitement and nervous energy raced through Charlie. This *was* exactly what she wanted, wasn't it? To prove herself as a journalist and gain greater respect from her father and peers.

"I'll feel bad leaving you."

Ash waved a weak hand. "I'm perfectly capable of taking care of myself. Just like you're perfectly capable of writing this story."

"Okay."

"You'll do it?"

"Yes." Charlie rose and gave her best friend a hug. "Nine o'clock in the lobby, right?"

"Right. He said he'd have on a shirt with a World Heritage logo, and his name is Connor Gibson. I don't know much more about him, but there's a bio in my notes."

"Hey, I'm the queen of winging it, aren't I?"

"Spontaneous is your middle name." Ash gave a feeble smile. "You've got this."

Charlie had something all right. She just hoped it was enough to make those she cared about proud.

Chapter Two

Charlie sat in the hotel lobby and crossed and uncrossed her legs for the tenth time. She rubbed her hands down her linen pants. Pressed down on her thighs to stop their shaking. Nothing had ever made her this jittery. But then she'd never had so much riding on this next week.

The pep talk on the phone this morning with Ashley relieved the worry about her friend. She'd sounded happy and comfortable. But nothing made the unfamiliar nerves traipsing along her skin settle down. Just last week while getting on the elevator at NW's offices, she'd accidentally bumped into and spilled her blackberry Naked juice on Bear Grylls. The adventurer and TV show star hadn't minded—too much—but her father had shit a brick when he'd heard about her mishap. *Don't think about your slipups, Charlie. Stay focused.* She covered a yawn with the crux of her arm. After reading through Ash's notes and doing some research on WHF and the preservation efforts for Route 66, she'd only gotten a few hours sleep. The small in-room coffee she'd sipped while getting ready had yet to provide the kick she needed.

Several people circulated around the rotunda, including a couple with two small children at the concierge desk. Charlie watched the young boys drive their tiny toy cars up and down the front of the desk, then get on their knees to push them along the marbled floor near their parents' feet. She smiled and her fingers itched to grab her sketchbook, but she didn't have enough time.

A minute later, the energy in the lobby changed. Charlie lifted her gaze to find men and women alike taking notice of someone who must have walked in. She tracked their attention until her eyes landed on a tall man with broad shoulders, a familiar jawline, and wavy dark brown hair.

Oh crap.

The last person she wanted to run into this morning when she had to be super-professional was Hot Pool Guy. Before she had a chance to hide behind a plant or something, his gaze connected with hers and held her hostage.

He flashed a smile and headed her way. *Shit*. She got to her feet thinking she'd say a quick hello before telling him she was meeting someone and excuse herself. *Look away from those amazing dark eyes before you get yourself in trouble*. She forced her attention down.

And found a logo on the breast pocket of his white polo shirt.

World.

Heritage.

Fund.

Kill her now.

She'd thought her quota for coincidences full, but

obviously fate had other ideas. This was all that fortuneteller's fault. Charlie and Ashley had stopped for lunch at some tiny town two days ago and right next door had been a palm reader. The peculiar woman had thrown "tall handsome stranger" out into the universe and it had evidently stuck.

Charlie's mind raced. She couldn't possibly go through with the interview now. No way could she spend a week alone with him on a road trip and keep a proper disposition. The guy walked into a room and *everyone* noticed. Across the lobby she could *feel* his hotness like it was tattooed on her skin. Imagine what would happen if they accidentally touched?

And while his amusement and flirtation yesterday might have been nice, how could he take her seriously? If she had any hope of gaining his respect, it couldn't be as Charlie, the girl who had flung her bikini top at him…and who'd yet to write a real story.

"Connor Gibson," she said, her voice humorless and sensible as she extended her hand before he had a chance to speak. "I'm Ashley Morgan from Natural World."

What in the world was she doing? Not letting NW down, that was what. This interview was important to everyone involved.

He frowned, which did nothing to detract from his appeal, but did introduce new twinges of unease in her chest. What the? She'd never seen a smile disappear so quickly. "You're my reporter?" The sharp tone of his voice hinted at dislike and his brief handshake held zero friendliness.

Didn't stop a dash of tingles from shooting up her arm. "Yes."

A chill settled around him. "Yesterday you said your

name was Charlie."

Crap. She'd forgotten that.

In less time than it took to blink, the man before her had morphed into someone much more uptight than sexy and charming Pool Guy.

"It's a nickname." Not quite a lie. The tension in her shoulders relaxed a tiny bit. The name "Ashley Morgan" had come out of her mouth without thought. Somehow pretending to be her successful, talented best friend seemed better. Smarter than having to explain why she stood there instead of Ash.

"Did you know who I was yesterday?" He crossed his arms and studied her face like he could tell if she was lying. *His* expression remained guarded.

"No. I didn't know until I saw the logo." She nodded to his shirt. Another truth. Name thing aside, so far so good.

He picked up her leather duffel bag. "Let's go."

She grabbed the rest of her stuff and hurried to keep pace behind him. Something had flipped Connor's switch and while he might be beyond easy on the eyes, his sparkling personality had taken a nosedive. Maybe it wouldn't be too difficult to stay professional after all.

Sunshine and warm, dry air greeted them as they stepped through the sliding-glass entryway. The valet hurried over to a white convertible Audi parked in front and opened the trunk. Connor tossed her bag in and looked like he was about to step around the car—to open her door?— but a second valet beat him to it. Charlie nodded her appreciation to the valet and climbed in.

"Thanks, Riley," Connor said, putting a tip in the valet's hand and getting into the driver's seat. Without a word or glance her way, he put on his sunglasses, turned the key in the ignition, and sped away from the hotel.

The roomy, plush leather interior meant a comfortable ride. The man next to her seemed anything but. Tension rolled off him, sucking the fresh air right out of the car. She took a deep breath and let it out slowly before rummaging in her messenger bag for an elastic band to pull her hair into a ponytail with.

From the little she'd read about Connor Gibson he was twenty-eight, dedicated to preservation, and had taken over as president of field operations last year.

Since he seemed inclined to skip any small talk, she decided to get the interview going. She pulled a pen, Ash's small tape recorder, and a notepad out of her bag. "Mind if I start asking you a few questions?"

"Fine." He kept his eyes on the road and his tone magnified her doubts by a thousand. It was one thing to be a novice reporter with someone receptive and open. Quite another to have to chip away at a cold shoulder. She cleared her throat. "You've traveled all over the world on behalf of heritage protection, and now your focus is on Route 66. Does the highway's US landmark distinction make it more meaningful?"

"Saving the world's architectural masterpieces, wherever they are, is equally important," he answered in a gruff tone. "The highway defined a particular period in US history and World Heritage Fund is hoping to help bring back a historic American experience."

"The original route was over two thousand miles. That's a huge undertaking."

"We're working with another preservation company to

cover as much ground as possible, but yes, given the length of road, we've chosen to support about three dozen projects."
Any of them igloos? she wanted to ask, his voice still cold.

Instead she said, "Where are we headed first?" She probably should have asked Ash about the itinerary for the week, but she'd never minded jumping into things with both feet and little thought.

Life stayed more interesting that way.

"A gas station."

"I meant which monument? That's what you call each site, right?"

He shot her a quick glance. "Right. And the station is one."

Oh. Rookie mistake. She licked her bottom lip, her mouth suddenly dry. "I guess gas stations are pretty important along a highway, huh?" Jeez. Could she sound any more amateurish? Ashley would never "guess." Ashley asked intelligent questions and put interviewees at ease. Charlie wished she knew how to get friendly Connor back.

"You could say that." A tiny bit of amusement reminded her of the deep, alluring voice he'd teased her with yesterday. His left hand slid off the steering wheel and he extended his arm out the open window. He turned his wrist in a circular motion, his palm flat, and seemed to enjoy the sensation of the wind against his arm.

They hit the open highway and he sped up. The sheets in her notepad ruffled so she closed the pad and tucked it between her legs.

"Have you driven the entire route? I mean is that still possible?" she asked out of her own curiosity. She didn't know where the flirty guy from yesterday had gone, but maybe if she got him to lighten up, she could squash her uncertainty and enjoy the adventure more. She'd never driven across several states before.

"I've traveled it many times. Parts of the original highway are gone, replaced with new road and a national scenic byway distinction, but you can still go from LA to Chicago."

Charlie put her things back in her bag and twisted to face him better. "Did you drive it for pleasure or work?"

Silence filled the space between them and she was about to repeat her question when he said, "Both."

"Were you alone? I mean as president of field operations, do you usually travel with a posse?"

The corner of his mouth lifted. He brought his arm back into the car and rested his elbow on the door ledge.

"A posse?" He sounded a little more like the Connor from yesterday now, but he still kept his attention straight ahead. "No, I don't travel with one of those."

"Hmm…"

"Hmm, what?"

"It must get lonely. I go crazy if I don't have someone to talk to."

He ran a hand across his jaw and glanced at her. She wished she could see his eyes behind his sunglasses because he seemed put off by her statement. "I get plenty of interaction with the teams on each site. The only time I get to be alone is while traveling."

"Except this week," Charlie said.

He turned his head and she saw herself reflected in his shades. "True. And you're not at all what I expected."

Not that Connor had had any idea what to expect. But he would've preferred if she hadn't been the beautiful blonde who wore skimpy red bikini tops and starred in his dreams last night. When he'd approached her in the lobby, his feet had carried him there without thought. Now he wished he'd canceled the interview. He might have liked Goldilocks yesterday, but he didn't today.

She unsettled him in more ways than one. He liked to be alone. Privacy had eluded him for much of his life—what with three older sisters and well-known parents. Having Goldilock's floral scent, lush mouth, and seemingly carefree disposition along for the ride now, clobbered his steadfast mentality. Out of nowhere, he felt like something was…off. And not in an altogether bad way.

With a reporter no less.

His jaw clenched. He didn't like feeling his control slip. Being attracted to Goldilocks was one thing. Dropping his guard with a reporter something dangerous.

"I get that a lot," she said, breaking into his thoughts.

Did her voice have to be so damn sexy?

"But don't worry. I can guarantee you I speak for both myself and Natural World when I say it's an honor to have this opportunity and we look forward to bringing awareness to the route and World Heritage Fund."

He gripped the steering wheel tighter. She probably had no idea what the online magazine had done to his mother. Given his mom used her maiden name in public, people didn't usually make the connection. And Connor did his best to stay out of the limelight. Just as his parents had always done their best to shield him from the scrutiny that came with being born to someone famous.

"Connor?"

One word. His name on her lips, and he was screwed. He liked the sound of it. He needed to get his head back in the car and carry on with the interview.

"Sorry. Just thinking about the week ahead."

She wiggled in her seat. "That's good. Better than thinking about... Never mind."

"Yesterday?" He eyed her more closely. Her sleeveless gray collared shirt and white linen pants were professional, but she still came off as accessible. Open.

Dammit. He couldn't wipe his first impression of her from his mind. He'd learned looks could be deceiving from numerous women who seemed genuine, but were only after his status or money. This situation might be different, but given his disrespect for Natural World, he had to tread carefully. He needed to keep the focus of the article on the sites to be sure it served WHF's best interest.

"Yes, okay? Let's just forget that ever happened."

"Can't." He tried to hold back a smile. Failed. Which pissed him off. He didn't want her to think he'd given much thought to their first meeting.

Her shoulders sagged. "It isn't going to affect our interview is it?" She swiped at some hair that had slipped free of her ponytail.

The sincerity—and uncertainty?—in her tone hit him square in the gut. Natural World had a big audience and being a jerk to the reporter doing the piece wouldn't score him any points. "That depends. Can we talk off the record?" She might think he was letting his guard down, but he wasn't.

Goldilocks frowned. "What do you mean exactly?"

"A week is a long time. I'd like to know not everything I

say is for Natural World."

She ran her fingers across the seam of her lips, drawing his attention to their ripe form. He mentally kicked himself and swore to keep his eyes on the road. "Reporters are never off the record," she said.

He scowled. "Then I want final approval on the article before you turn it in."

"I can't promise you that either."

"Then this interview is over." He switched lanes and slowed so he could get off the highway at the next exit and turn around.

"What bug crawled up your ass?" she demanded, taking him by total surprise. "You obviously aren't happy about this interview, but is the extra charm for my benefit because I flung my bikini top at you? Maybe you don't need this interview, but I do. I've been nothing but professional. You on the other hand—"

"Why do you need this?"

"Excuse me?"

"I asked why you need this. Was this interview assigned to you, or did you ask for it?" A mixture of admiration and irritation thrummed through his veins at her outburst. Goldilocks had guts, but he needed to know where that feistiness came from.

Didn't mean he'd trust her. She had a job to do, just like he did.

She closed her eyes for a moment and let out a shaky breath. "I didn't choose this story," she said in a quiet, steady tone. "But now that I'm here I want to do the best I can. For both our companies."

He steered the car back toward the fast lane. *She doesn't*

know, he thought. She had no idea how his connection to Natural World made this interview damn hard.

The sun warmed the back of his neck as they sped east down the highway. They had about nine hundred miles to go until they reached Oklahoma City. His scheduled stops added another one, one-fifty. He'd be a lot better off getting along with his companion for the next six days than not.

"Okay," she added, as if conceding something.

"Okay?"

"A week is a long time so not everything needs to be on the record."

That twisting in his gut cinched tighter. She wanted to make this work. "Good."

She leaned the side of her head against the back of her seat and kept her pretty blue eyes on him. "So will you tell me what's bothering you about this interview?"

Some of his best memories were of the two trips he'd made along the route with his parents and sisters as a boy, and WHF's goal was to revive that magic. Bring back the charm and attraction of the American road trip. He didn't want any part of the story connecting him to his family, though, and the fact that she knew something was up should've had red flags waving. Instead he found himself wanting to get the damn thing off his chest.

"Off the record?"

She nodded her agreement before saying, "Yes."

Compassion shone in her eyes and the soft set of her lips, prodding him to share the reason behind his unease.

"A couple of months ago Natural World did a piece on a private excursion to a little-traveled mountain hideaway in Morocco where…" He swallowed the thickness in the back of his throat.

"Where one of the travelers died," she said softly. "I remember. Sandra Swanson was the tour guide."

"Your magazine said it was her fault, but it wasn't. The reporter had his facts up his ass and posted incorrect information. He crucified her and then made sure other news media picked up the story. She was already devastated by the accident, but then to be blamed for it and to have her reputation discredited was too much."

"You know Sandra," Charlie half whispered.

"She's my mother."

Goldilocks straightened, her jaw dropped. "No way."

He got that reaction a lot from women. What followed next usually included a hand to his arm, some eyelash batting, and a voice with an even more obvious kittenish quality.

This time, though, the woman next to him pursed her lips and lines creased her forehead. "I can see why you're not fond of Natural World, but every reporter at the e-zine works with the highest integrity."

Connor wasn't sure what to make of her defensive, yet... pensive tone. "Not so," he said. "And the biggest liar and piece of shit is your owner and publisher. He refused to print a retraction even when my mother brought him evidence that proved the reporter had taken her words out of context. If not for WHF, I never would've agreed to this interview. And nothing you can say is going to convince me that Thomas Beckett is anything but a bastard."

Chapter Three

He hated her father.

There was no way Charlie could come clean about who she really was now. She swallowed the shame sitting in the back of her throat and stayed quiet.

It wasn't the first time she'd heard negativity directed at her dad. Thomas Beckett had a reputation as ruthless, smart, commanding, powerful. He hadn't amassed his fortune and status being nice.

As an only child, though, in his own way, he'd doted on her. Told her he loved her. He'd also kept a tight leash on her.

She absently rubbed her neck.

Had her father made mistakes? Of course he had. But his seeing them was about as likely as the car she rode in spreading wings and flying. Had he — or more precisely Natural World — wronged Connor's mom?

And *hello?* Sandra Swanson was his mom? She was an

American icon. Miss USA at eighteen, she turned her win into amazing philanthropic work and found herself invited to White House dinners. Then she married Amory Gibson, a British entrepreneur and environmentalist worth billions. And *then* she became a television star with her Travel Channel show, *Globe-Trotting with Sandy*. She took viewers on trips they might never get to experience otherwise.

"I've left you speechless," Connor said, breaking into her thoughts.

"I'm processing." Knowing it wasn't *her* that had him out of sorts relieved some of the anxiety in the pit of her stomach, but his dislike for Natural World and her father meant she had to be especially careful. She didn't want to screw up the interview and hand him more reasons to doubt the virtue of Natural World.

A lump the size of a boulder lodged in her throat. She'd read the article about his mom and the accident and knew the reporter who'd written it. Jed had a reputation as a self-centered, hardline journalist. Had he lied for a more sensational story? Maybe. Her heart had ached for everyone involved when she'd learned what had happened, but she couldn't let her feelings get involved while she had an assignment to do.

"I appreciate it." He switched lanes, a big green overhead sign alerting drivers to a freeway change. "And by the way, in one mile, we'll officially be on the Route."

Charlie smiled. With the wind in her face, a blue, blemish-free sky, and arguably the sexiest man on the planet next to her, she chose to stay quiet and enjoy the ride.

An hour later they got to United Oil Station. "This is the cutest gas station I have ever seen," she said as Connor parked off to the side and they got out of the car. Nothing else surrounded them but desert and mountains, a bit of the Old West meets the new and improved.

"We restored it to its former glory." He leaned against the driver's side door and admired the station. The slight jutting of his chin and the crossing of his arms told her pride welled inside him. "Kept the house-with-canopy style to give customers a relaxed feeling they could associate with home."

A warm breeze swayed the tin sign hanging from the roof. Charlie stood next to Connor. "It definitely feels comfortable. And I love the old-fashioned gas pump."

"You hungry?" He pushed away from the car. "There's a small café inside that serves the best homemade cinnamon rolls you've ever had."

Right on cue her stomach growled. "I could eat."

They went inside and Connor insisted on paying. He was right about the rolls and while they ate she asked him about the station and the efforts to revive it. The owner stopped by their table and she asked him a few questions, too. Thankfully she'd remembered to bring the tape recorder.

But she wanted to capture *her* impressions of the place, and since she hadn't remembered the notebook, she jotted some notes down on a napkin.

When she looked up, Connor's breathtaking gaze sat focused on her. She'd never met anyone with eyes so intoxicating, like shiny gray-brown pebbles sparkling in a shallow clear blue riverbank. Then he smiled, and she was tempted to walk around the table, straddle his lap, and see how that smile felt pressed against her own.

"Tell me I'm your first interviewee," he said.

Napkin note taking. Rookie mistake number two. Dammit. She blinked away her wayward thoughts and gave herself a mental slap. Followed by a silent promise to pay as little attention to his face as possible. Not that looking at this body would cure her attraction. She had seen him without a shirt and maybe dreamed about finding all his ticklish spots with her tongue during the brief sleep she'd gotten last night.

"You're not." Half lie. She'd interviewed her dad for a project in middle school and did talk to people for the pieces she'd written for NW. Just usually via email.

He glanced at her scribbles. "Apple pie?"

She slid the napkin off the table and slipped it into her bag. "The smell here reminds me of my grandmother's apple pie."

Something flashed in his eyes, but Charlie wasn't sure if it was surprise or kinship. "Well, you're my first interviewer," he said, sounding like she'd also be his last.

"Really?" She licked a bit of cream cheese glaze off her finger. He watched, and warmth made a lazy crawl up the back of her neck. "I promise not to make it too painful."

"Yeah, well, I'll settle for making it honest." He lifted his arms off the table and sat back in his chair. "How long have you worked for Natural World?"

"Two years. How long have you been with World Heritage Fund?" she shot back, not liking his innuendo. She ground her teeth. He'd already decided she couldn't be trusted. Which made her want to shake him. She was absolutely trustworthy. *You've already told him a big fat lie, though.*

"Five years."

"I'm guessing your love for the environment comes from your parents. They must be proud of you." She took a sip of her coffee, feeling very little pride in herself at the moment.

"When did you know you wanted to be a reporter?"

When she realized that was the best way to stay close to her dad. She hadn't exactly picked the job. It picked her. She rubbed at the hollow ache in her chest and wished away the discontent that kept creeping up on her. She wanted to be a writer, just not this kind.

This week was a chance to prove to herself that reporting could make her happy. "Since I was young."

"First love?"

"Bobby Galecki."

Connor grinned and she almost toppled right off her seat at the sheer magnitude of it. "I meant was reporting your first love. But lucky Bobby."

Every wire in her brain apparently crossed in this man's presence. "Right. Uh…" It wasn't her first love. What she loved… "Bobby wasn't so lucky. He liked someone else. How about you? You've obviously spent an insane amount of time outdoors. Any other loves?"

"Professionally or personally?"

"Which would you prefer?" Not that it should matter. Connor was her assignment, nothing more. Correction. He was Ash's assignment, and she could not screw this up for her. And she couldn't make Natural World look even worse in his eyes.

"I think you're proving to be a distraction I didn't count on this week." He stood. "Come on. Let's go."

She got to her feet. "What does that—" Her cell phone belted out the Beatles song Ash had programmed as her special ringtone. "I need to take this," she said, pulling the phone from her bag.

Connor nodded. Charlie stared at the very nice way his jeans fit as he walked away. "Hey, Ash. Is everything okay?"

"It could be better, but tell me how things are with you first."

Charlie's heart squeezed. "*You* go first."

"I have a slight infection. The doctor assures me it's nothing to worry about, but I'll be staying here until it's cleared up. My mom's flying in."

"I'm sorry."

Ash chuckled. "Yeah, I'm not sure which is worse. I'm really glad you took over for me this week. How's everything going so far? Connor wasn't upset with the change was he?"

"Not at all." She walked out of the small dining area and strolled around the quaint interior of the station that served as a welcome center, too.

"Charrrleee. What aren't you telling me?"

Nothing got by her best friend, even over the phone. "Connor is the guy from the pool yesterday."

"No shit."

"Shit." Charlie went on to explain their introduction, listen to Ash scold her, and then discuss word for word what had happened so far. By the end Ashley agreed Charlie had done the right thing.

"Wow. Okay, so he pretty much hates our publication, but the big question is, can you stay professional around him?" Ash said.

"Of course I can. This is the week I take charge of my life and make this story the first step in getting my father to notice what I'm capable of." And then maybe he'd listen if she told him what she really dreamed of doing.

"You go, girl."

"Thanks. And you take care. I'll call you tonight." She said good-bye and started toward the double glass front door when out of the corner of her eye she spotted a penny-stamping machine. Excitement shot through her. The souvenir she'd always wanted as a kid stood five feet away.

The one and only time she'd seen one was a trip to the zoo when she was nine—and the Press-A-Penny had been out of order. She'd been so disappointed that her dad bought her not one, not two, but three stuffed animals to make up for it.

She hurried to the machine, a big, goofy grin on her face, and bought one for her and one for Connor. They were smaller than she thought they'd be, but holding the souvenir pennies in her hand bloomed happiness she hadn't felt in a long time. The impression on the shiny metal read Route 66.

She strode back into the warm sunshine and found Connor inside the car, head resting against his seat, sunglasses on, his face lifted to the sky.

Her gait faltered like she had clown shoes on. She stopped and spent a minute just watching him. He looked more relaxed than he had all morning and with that peacefulness came a great deal of appeal.

As if sensing her stare, he dropped his chin and turned. He didn't exactly smile, but at least his sexy mouth wasn't set in a grim line anymore. She smiled in return because... because she couldn't help herself. She even waved before she remembered to get her feet moving again and to stop gawking at him.

"Hey, sorry about taking so long," she said getting into the car. "Here, I got you something."

"I've got a schedule to keep, so I'd appreciate it if you

didn't take calls on my time."

She ignored his reprimand and hovered her fist above the center console until he finally put his palm up. She placed one of the pennies in his hand, her fingertips touching his warm skin. Her pulse spiked.

For a few seconds he didn't move or say anything.

"You were expecting one of those spicy cinnamon jaw-breakers weren't you?" she teased. "Those things set your mouth on fire. This is much better."

He held the small souvenir between two fingers and the corners of his lips lifted. "I haven't seen one of these since I was a kid."

Charlie eyed hers more closely. "It's my first time."

"This is your first stamped penny?" He dropped his into his shirt pocket, which made all sorts of happy flutters jump to life in her chest. He liked it well enough not to toss it into some compartment in the car.

"Yep. I've wanted one forever."

"Forever, huh? You're what twenty-four, twenty-five?"

"Twenty-six." She tucked a strand of hair behind her ear. "And my family never did the road-trip or amusement-park thing, so I missed out on these lucky little babies."

She slipped the penny into her pants pocket. She'd keep it on her for good luck.

"Looks like this week is about more than an interview." He turned the key in the ignition and put the car in gear.

"What do you mean?"

"I'm your first road trip." He flashed that devilishly handsome smile at her, the penny obviously helping lower his defenses.

Even sitting, her legs turned to mush. And despite the

warm spring air, a shiver stole its way down her back. One way or another, Connor Gibson just might ruin her.

They'd made two more stops along the route, and Charlie drove him bat-shit crazy the entire time. He had a timetable to stick to, an agenda to keep, a *reputation* to uphold, and rather than follow along like a good little reporter, she'd charmed the crew finishing up work at the Roadrunner Diner and talked *forever* about nothing. The woman could make eating a turkey sandwich sound interesting.

The visit to Shake & Soda Shack, a tiny café that had finished restoration last month, should have taken a half hour. He'd sat down with the owner and given the older man the plans for continued preservation and support, wished him good luck, and then been ready to go. But not only did Charlie need to have a coffee-Oreo cookie shake to "get the full experience," she had to take enough pictures to make up for forgetting to take shots at the gas station and diner.

Not her first interview, his ass.

Which only made her that much more dangerous.

She wasn't the cocky, know-it-all reporter he'd expected for such a high-profile piece. She had amateur written all over her and he wondered why Natural World had sent someone so green.

He'd liked Goldilocks yesterday, and hell if he didn't like her today despite his mind's protests. He glanced over at the gentle rise and fall of her chest as the sun bid its final farewell. If he kept thinking of making this trip memorable for her, then he needed a stiff drink. This was business. And likeability and sexiness aside, she worked for a company that had nearly destroyed his mom.

Plus, he liked things predictable and she'd proven about as predictable as an earthquake.

She mumbled something in her sleep. Shook her head.

Connor turned off the low hum of the radio and tried not to break into a smile. The woman couldn't even keep quiet in slumber.

"Dad, no." She fidgeted in her seat. "I wanted to... please listen." A small whimper fell from her lips and Connor's mouth formed a tight line. His heart squeezed.

"Charlie." He put a hand on her shoulder and a far too pleasing current shot up his arm. He left his palm there, not wanting the sensation to end, but more importantly wanting to offer comfort. His body warmed just being close to her and apparently touching only heightened the sensation. "Charlie?" he said again.

She turned her head at the same time she lifted her shoulder so she could rub her cheek along the back of his hand. "Mmm...yes?"

The sensations coursing through his arm moved south. "I think you were having a bad dream." Hell if she didn't chip away at his distrust and bring out a protective side he hadn't felt in a very long time. He pulled his arm back, not happy with the unexpected detour his feelings had taken.

Her eyes flew open, and she jolted away from him. "Uh, sorry about that." A swallow worked its way down her throat. "Please tell me I wasn't talking in my sleep."

"You were."

"What did I say?"

"Something about your dad." Connor pulled off the

highway, the hotel he'd made a reservation at only a few miles away.

"Oh. Okay." She sounded relieved as she reached into her bag and pulled out a thin, black sweater. "Wait. What about my dad?" She pushed her arms through the sweater so she wore it backward.

His gut tightened. That one small move to make herself comfortable was cute as hell. *Shit.* "You wanted him to listen to you."

She studied him out of the corner of her eye. "Don't look so worried. Typical father-daughter stuff, that's all."

"Try me," he said, not sure where this sudden desire to play shrink had come from.

"*Try you?* Connor Gibson, I'm not sure how I should take that."

He grinned, unable to fight the pull she had on him. She wanted to flirt and damn if he didn't want to talk like they had at the pool yesterday. *Bad idea, bud.* "I've got three sisters. I watched a lot of father-daughter stuff go down. Maybe I can offer an outsider's opinion?"

"Thanks, but I'll skip the analysis. That our destination?" She looked out the windshield toward the Desert Oasis Inn. There wasn't much else in the tiny town.

"Yeah." He parked the car, they grabbed their luggage, and headed into the Spanish-style lobby decorated with smooth, brick flooring and colorful tiles on the walls. Connor checked them in and gave Charlie her room key as they headed up to the third floor in the elevator.

"I've never been able to figure out if adjoining rooms means we'll be next door to each other but not share a door to go back and forth, or if connecting rooms means we'll be next door to each other and share a door between rooms. I think it depends on the hotel. For us it doesn't really matter, but when families travel that's a pretty important distinction. I know I would want my kids to be able to wake me up if they needed something. And—"

"Got it," he interrupted. He had the feeling her prattling meant she was nervous. Another facet to this beautiful reporter that made him wonder about her experience. He held the elevator door and fantasized about what else she could do with that pretty mouth of hers besides talk. *Not cool.*

"By the way, thanks for making all the arrangements this week."

"Not a problem. I wouldn't have it any other way." He didn't like surprises and being in charge meant he kept a knowing finger on things.

She got to her room and he got to his. He slipped his key card into the door and toed it open. Goldilocks seemed to be having trouble, and he wasn't about to leave her out in the hallway so he waited. Contemplated inviting her into his room for the tenth time in the last two minutes.

But if he did that, no way could he trust himself to be a gentleman. And while he'd thought about doing all sorts of uncivilized things with her since watching her try to tie her bikini top, he had to kick those ideas out of his head. No way would he risk losing his million-dollar bet to Clay over her irresistible sweet-and-sexy temperament. Not to mention she was a reporter on assignment and getting up close and personal wasn't part of the deal. He only needed to keep his hands off for a week. After that, he'd never see her again.

Her door lock finally unclicked. She pushed it open and peeked inside. "Looks like we're connected."

"Don't even think about barging in on me," he said, unable to keep the hint of mirth out of his voice, and then he slipped into his room before he connected them in all sorts of ways.

Chapter Four

Charlie sighed. The words "painted desert" made perfect sense now. The stretch of Route 66 highway she and Connor were traveling on looked like something out of an Ansel Adams painting. And it looked even more picturesque the second time.

She peeked at her none too happy driver. The tense muscles of his neck stood out and the tight set of his jaw put her a little on edge. Only a little because he still looked irritatingly gorgeous with his wavy hair, defined cheekbones, and blue cotton polo shirt. Not rumpled in the least given all the time they'd spent in the car. The silent treatment, however, killed her. Pretty soon she'd start belting out, "Get your kicks on Route 66" to see if that might get him to lighten up.

Yes, she'd accidentally left Ash's—her—camera at the Shake & Soda Shack and they'd had to drive back there this morning to pick it up, but she'd apologized. Twice. Once on the way there and once on the way back. Give a girl a break.

This was her first big assignment and she'd gotten a little flustered.

Only he didn't know that.

The *first* part anyway. He'd definitely seen her flustered yesterday and had smiled at her several times when no one was looking. It was as if he found her something of an anomaly and it had put her at ease for some strange reason. Maybe he did know about the *first* part and had decided to play along.

But mess up his schedule and *jeez*, he turned back into Captain Sourpuss.

She ran her fingers over the stamped penny in her pocket. So far luck had yet to make an appearance.

"Tell me why Route 66," she said in her serious-reporter voice to break the silence. The roof shielded them from the sun today, and she turned her air vent to the side for a little less cold draft. "There are monuments all over the world. What made this project a must?"

"Two main reasons." He tossed a quick peek at her. "The surviving businesses along the highway were struggling and the roadside architecture was deteriorating. If we can restore what is arguably one of the biggest tapestries of twentieth century Americana, then we help revitalize the communities whose economies have declined."

"History is important to you." She stared at his profile. He also hadn't shaved this morning and the stubble made him look even sexier—if that were possible.

"Yeah, it is."

"I can barely remember what happened last week."

He turned his head and though she couldn't see his eyes behind his sunglasses, she did notice his brows inch up. "I think we've established you have a memory problem."

"Oh come on. Like you've never forgotten something."

"Nope." His shoulders relaxed, and his voice took on a playful tone.

"Never?"

"Never."

"Then you're just weird."

He tried to hide it, but Charlie caught a teensy, tiny smile. He probably didn't get called weird very often. If ever. "More like mindful," he said. "With three older sisters who constantly acted like a Mother Hen, they drilled responsibility into me."

What little hair she had on her arms stood on end in annoyance. "Are you saying I'm not responsible?"

"I'm saying you might have a blithe disregard for organization."

Twisting to face him better, she brought one leg up under her bottom. Her insides itched to get into it with him. *It* having more than one meaning, but she'd focus on his flippant remark right now. "I didn't know nature boys knew words like blithe."

His smile widened. "My Stanford professors would be appalled to hear you talk like that. And my sisters would kick your ass."

Stanford? She'd graduated from there, too, but she'd rather talk about his family. "Sounds like you're close to them. What do they do?" Sandra Swanson and Amory Gibson had done a great job of keeping their kids out of the limelight. Charlie supposed her parents had as well.

"They're all married with small children. They do the mom thing and a lot of charity work."

"Do you see them very often?" Charlie had always wanted a sister. Someone she could confide in, who wouldn't judge or dismiss her.

Connor scratched behind his neck. "Not as often as they'd like. But they call and text and send me videos of my nieces and nephews."

Charlie closed her eyes and slid her leg out from under her. She settled back against her seat and looked out the windshield at the vast desert landscape. "Sounds nice."

"What about you?"

"It's just me," she said, letting a little too much wistfulness creep into her voice. Which was silly. She'd never been lonely. Her parents paid her plenty of attention—a blessing and a curse—and she never had a shortage of friends.

"Sounds nice." He gifted her with that full-wattage smile of his.

She appreciated it, sensing he knew she hadn't loved being an only child. "So your sisters tortured you with accountability. Did they paint your nails and put flowers in your hair, too?"

He laughed and the rich, happy sound was like a burst of sunshine inside her chest. God, when he relaxed, he could do serious damage to a girl.

"They did. That's strictly off the record by the way."

"Of course."

"I'm guessing you gave your parents a run for their money all on your own."

Her turn to grin. "Most definitely. They were overprotective, which meant I rebelled as best I could. Hey, what's that?" She squinted, trying to make out some activity up ahead in the sweep of barren land.

"Looks like—"

"It's a carnival. That's a Ferris wheel." Beyond the fair, a small town came into view as the highway started a slow descent. She leaned forward in excitement. "Let's check it out."

"No time."

Charlie shot him a pleading look. "Twenty minutes. Just one quick ride and one game if they have them."

He shook his head. "We're running late, and I don't plan to waste any more time."

"Okay, first off, stopping to do something fun is not a waste of time. And second, you really need to chill on the schedule, dude. I've got nowhere to be after our interview so don't think you have to keep to six days for my benefit. I'm flexible."

"I'm not."

She rolled her eyes.

"I've got somewhere to be," he added. "A buddy of mine is getting married and after we finish in Oklahoma City, I need to get to Denver."

"When's the wedding?"

"The twenty-third."

"That's the following weekend. I may not be the best at directions, but I don't think it takes a week to get there."

"True, but—"

"Please, Connor. I promise to be quick." They were almost upon it now, and she thought about reaching over and taking hold of the steering wheel to veer them off the highway.

His chest slowly rose and fell, the light blue shirt stretching across his very fine muscles. A peek inside his head would probably reveal a scroll of theories in bold font. Like, *stopping + carnival ride = 15.4 minutes* and *parking + ride and game = 22.7 minutes*.

"You've never been to a carnival before, have you?" Tenderness replaced firmness in his tone.

She shook her head, too choked up to answer. She'd traveled to a great many places with her parents, but her father only stayed in five-star hotels and considered the slides at the swimming pools amusement enough.

Connor let out a resigned sigh and took the exit. He got in line behind about a dozen cars to pay the parking fee before entering the festival grounds.

"Thank you," she whispered, reaching out to squeeze his arm. Touching him sparked feel-good prickles in her fingertips.

"You should probably use the bathroom while we're here, too."

Charlie laughed. "Yes, sir, Mr. Time Police." Could she help that she had a bladder the size of a walnut?

They parked and headed toward the red-and-white-striped awning at the entrance. Connor refused to let her pay for their entry, and when the girl in the small booth asked if they'd like to purchase ride tickets too, he bought them each the best deal: twenty-five tickets for twenty bucks. She wasn't sure if he only had twenties in his wallet or if he wanted her to enjoy more than one ride.

It didn't matter. She grabbed his hand, wanting to feel those warm sensations again, and headed straight for the Ferris wheel. "Come on!"

His grip tightened and she glanced back at his gorgeous eyes, sculpted cheeks, and mouth she was pretty sure could make a straw moan. Her heart pounded. She hadn't meant to turn this into something that felt a thousand miles away from professional, but from the attentive look on his face, she got the feeling deep down, he thought so, too.

The woman unnerved him. Confused him. And the only thing he knew for certain was one minute he wanted to throttle her and the next he wanted to get her naked and writhing beneath him. He'd never met anyone like Charlie before—strong but vulnerable. Impulsive, but considerate.

Her interest in the carnival had been palpable, filling the space in the car with enthusiasm that reminded him of his first time to a fair. But the eye-rolling was what had done it. Rather than find the expression irritating, he found himself turned on by her sass, and suddenly stopping to prove he had a fun side, too, was all he wanted to do.

He glanced down at their hands. No one else's grip had ever felt this good. The squeeze he'd given her fingers had been an involuntary reaction. When they touched, he forgot about everything else but being in the moment.

"Hurry!" she said, tugging him along faster. "I think we can catch the next ride."

He kept up with her, wondering if her excitement for the ride or his worry about time motivated her quick pace. Probably the former.

They were the last couple loaded onto the ride. "You ready for this?" he asked.

"So ready." She bumped his knee with hers and scooted a little closer. Her comfort with him made his pulse race.

The little touches were spontaneous, tiny gifts that whet his appetite for more.

The wheel kicked into gear, lifting them up, up and away. Charlie squirmed a little, giggled, and smiled so broadly no doubt the people on the ground could see it.

"This is awesome," she said when they reached the highest point.

Sitting beside her, it *was* awesome. The sun shined in a bright blue sky, a warm breeze ruffled her blond hair, and she smelled like a botanical garden.

"I'm glad you like it."

"Think the ticket guy will let us stay on for a second ride?"

The wheel rounded the bottom, their passenger car swinging slightly on the rise. "I'll see that he does." He couldn't explain why he'd grown more at ease with her, too, but he thought it had something to do with the penny she'd given him yesterday. That one small act of kindness and he knew she was the kind of girl a guy made promises to. The kind of girl a guy lost bets for.

She smiled and he found he couldn't take his eyes off her full lips, pert nose, and slightly rounded cheeks. "Thanks," she said, sparing him a quick glance before returning to take in the scenery.

They made another rotation. And another. Just about to the top of the next revolution, the ride jerked and the wheel abruptly stopped, leaving them in the twelve-o'clock position.

Charlie grabbed the edge of her seat but didn't say anything.

"This happens sometimes," he said to calm any fears she

might have about being stuck. "Especially with rides like this that travel to different locations. It'll start up again in a minute."

"I'm not worried." She looked sideways at him, but a little over his head so their eyes didn't meet, and the most adorable smile lifted the corners of her mouth. The grin spilled out playful and secretive.

"Did you know the world's tallest Ferris wheel is in Las Vegas?" she asked. "At five hundred and fifty feet, it's nine feet taller than the second tallest wheel. That one is in Singapore. The very first Ferris wheel was something like two hundred and sixty feet tall, so more than half the size of those. It was built in the late 1800s in Chicago."

Did Goldilocks ever stop talking? "I knew about the one in Vegas. So you're an expert on Ferris wheels? Did you do a piece on them?"

"No. I just happened to hear a segment on national public radio and useless knowledge tends to stick in my head."

"And useful knowledge?"

Finally her gaze settled on him. "Funny."

"Hang tight a few more minutes everyone," the ride operator shouted. "We apologize for the delay."

"This must be killing you," she said. "Wasting time up here."

Oddly, he didn't mind at all. "It's not too bad." He narrowed his eyes. "But I get the feeling you're not too happy about it."

"Oh, I'm fine." She looked away.

"What's up?"

"Nothing's up."

"Liar."

That got her attention. Her pulse leaped at the base of her neck. She wore a sleeveless light green blouse today and all of a sudden he wanted to put his mouth on her shoulder. Work his way up the smooth column of her neck to her earlobe, her cheek, her lips.

She twisted to face him better. "You really want to know what I'm thinking?"

"Yes."

"I've always…" She sucked in a breath when he kept his eyes on her midnight blues. "I've always had this fantasy of being at the top of a Ferris wheel with a gorgeous guy and having him kiss me."

"*Really?* That's your fantasy?"

"One of them." She narrowed her eyes, but it didn't diminish their light.

"And I fit the bill?" he said, unable to stop himself from moving his stare to her mouth. Christ, he wasn't expecting her to say any of that, but now that she had, he had the urge to fulfill *all* her fantasies.

"You asked." She shrugged and started to turn away.

He caught her jaw and tilted it up to his. "Do you want me to kiss you?"

Long, dark eyelashes reached the arch of her brows. "We shouldn't."

"That's not what I asked."

She squirmed, her breath caught. "Yes," she whispered.

There were a lot of reasons whey they shouldn't, but not one of them registered more important than fulfilling her fantasy.

"Good." He brushed his lips softly over hers, thinking he'd keep it light, quick, PG-rated. But the second he tasted her, the rules changed. Because she put a hand on his chest, moved closer, and kissed him back.

Her mouth crushed his, hard and hot. Hellish good sensations blazed trails up his arms, over his shoulders, down his sides, and lower.

He slid his hand up her back, then down, until it rested at the base of her spine. She tasted like coffee and mint and if she let him, he'd kiss her till Sunday.

In only two days, Goldilocks had gotten to him. Captured something he didn't think was up for grabs for longer than a night—his attention. And his admiration.

He slowed the kiss so it became more about learning and savoring instead of fast and furious. She moved her hand up his chest, snaked it around his neck, and ran her fingers through his hair. She let out a moan and Jesus, combined with her supple lips, he answered with some deep, guttural sound he'd never made before.

Chemistry.

They'd had it since the second he caught her bikini top.

And while he'd been trying to convince himself he preferred silence to her runaway mouth, she could talk all she wanted if it meant an uninhibited response like this when they kissed.

"Mmm," she murmured against his mouth as she brought her other arm up and around his neck. The move lifted her shirt and exposed her warm, soft skin to his palm. He splayed his fingers around her waist.

His other hand cupped the back of her head, and he touched her lower lip with his tongue. Her mouth opened in response and that's all it took for him to deepen the kiss. To give with mindless strokes and sweet invasion. Intense desire wove through him, marked him. Goldilocks knew how to kiss.

She pressed closer, the tips of her breasts brushing against the thin material of his shirt. His cock grew even harder. If they weren't five hundred and fifty feet up in the air inside a two-by-four box he would've had her naked by now. Moved his mouth down her body and let his tongue delve between her legs. He wanted to taste every inch of her. See how loud his name could be shouted.

A ragged sigh met his ears—hers? His? With their mouths fused together it was hard to tell whose rush of breath was whose.

Without warning, the Ferris wheel jolted back into service. Charlie pulled away. Her long lashes swept down and then up. She locked her electric-blue gaze on his and something in the atmosphere shifted. His heart thudded heavily and more than the all-consuming lust heating his blood was the urgent desire to make Goldilocks happy. Maybe it wouldn't kill him to let her spend as much time as she wanted at the carnival.

"Not bad, Mr. Gibson," she said, scooting back.

"Not bad?"

She gave him a simple shrug. "Some fantasies just don't live up to the reality."

Was she shitting him? No way had he been the only one to feel that kiss. "Just like some expectations are poorly fulfilled."

Her eyes widened as the ride swept by the ground and rose again. "Is that supposed to be some comment on my kissing?"

"It wasn't *bad*."

Connor watched her fight a smile, but she couldn't do it. And Christ, even a small, happy turn of her lips knotted his stomach. "Good to know," she said good-naturedly.

He fought his own grin. The woman could take as easily as she gave.

The ride took two more laps before stopping to let off riders. When it got to be their turn to exit, Connor said, "Go again?"

Charlie shook her head. "I think I'm okay."

She was better than okay, but he kept that to himself. He glanced at his watch as they walked down the rickety wooden ramp. Dirt kicked up under their shoes when they got to the bottom and Charlie headed toward the game booths.

"If you're going to keep looking at the time, then go do something else while I play my game. I'll meet you at the car after I've won something."

"What do you want to win?"

"*That.*" She pointed to a young girl holding a jumbo stuffed brown teddy bear bigger than she was.

He scanned the area and found the prize at the balloon-and-dart game. Goldilocks must have seen it too because she hurried in that direction.

"You good with darts?" he asked, handing over five bucks to the attendant before she could dig any money out of her bag.

"Thank you," she said quietly.

The guy handed her three darts. According to the rules posted on a painted red sign, she had to go three for three to win the grand prize.

"How hard can it be?" She took one of the small arrows

in her hand and bent her wrist back and forth in apparent warm up.

Connor bit back a grin. He'd bet money she had no idea how to throw a dart.

And was proven correct when she not only missed on all three tries, but on the last one, somehow managed to sail the dart into the next booth.

"Okay, so maybe it's a little harder than it looks," she said.

She tried again. And again. His foot started tapping. It took her forever in between throws and she'd yet to hit one balloon.

After a few more unsuccessful attempts, he pulled out one last five. "Let me help this time."

Without giving her a chance to veto his assistance, which he felt pretty sure sat on the tip of her mind-blowing tongue, he moved behind her. She tensed for a minute before letting out a breath and relaxing. He put his left hand on her hip and guided her right arm with his into the throwing position.

"Keep the dart stable and parallel to the ground," he said, slipping the dart into her hand and waiting for her to get steady. His hand cupped hers, her soft, warm skin a nice fit. "Now try to keep a light grip, letting only the tips of your fingers touch the dart. Yeah, like that."

God, her hair smelled good. He took a long, silent inhale. "Connor?"

Shit. He lifted his chin. "Throw the dart in one smooth, fluid motion. Don't flick it at the balloon. And you don't need to hurl it with much force to make it stick to the board."

"Okay."

"Also, follow through with your hand. That way the dart

won't fly left or right."

"Got it." Her whispery, sexy voice had him wanting to give it to her all right.

Pop.

Pop.

Pop.

She spun around and flung her arms around his neck. "We did it!" After a quick kiss to his cheek, she twisted to point at one of the bears hanging on the wall of the booth. "I'd like that one please."

He'd like the small tug on his heart to stop. Goldilocks might be captivating and appeal to every one of his urges, but he didn't really know all that much about her. And, he reminded himself, being a reporter meant she couldn't be trusted. She'd made no promises about the article and goddammit, he'd gotten way more personal than he'd planned. There was always the possibility she'd take his words out of context or share something private. Especially when she worked for a man as loathsome as Thomas Beckett.

Chapter Five

Sometimes the truth sucked. And so sometimes it was better to lie than face the brutal reality that the guy who had offered to help with a little fantasy kissed waaaayyyy better than the faceless man in a girl's dreams. Charlie had kissed a lot of guys. And Connor's kiss had been the best ever. Ever, ever, ever.

Pulling away from him had been painful. Looking into those incredible eyes of his, tingles had covered every inch of her skin, spending extra time between her thighs, and if they'd gone for a second ride, she might have begged him to touch her there to put her out of her misery.

Not very respectable of her.

It was bad enough her father wouldn't be happy with her once he found out she'd done the interview this week. But if he also found out that she'd engaged in anything un-professional, Charlie could kiss any regard she might get from him good-bye.

And now she was back to The Kiss.

Thinking of it as an event really didn't do her any good.

She glanced over at Connor asleep in the passenger seat. Last night they'd stayed at a little motel and the shower in his room had had a leak. The dripping kept him up all night and he'd looked so tired this morning that Charlie volunteered to drive for a while.

Skepticism had crossed his handsome face for a minute and she knew her taking the wheel didn't fit with his plans. So she rock-paper-scissored him—winner drove. No one beat her at the hand job—game! Oh my God, she'd meant to think "hand game." Not recall the wicked dreams about Connor that had kept *her* up for half the night.

This morning when she'd asked why he hadn't just switched rooms, he said he hadn't wanted her caught unaware of a room change if she'd woken and unexpectedly needed him for something.

She let out a happy sigh and glanced in the rearview mirror at the giant teddy bear sitting in the backseat. Connor Gibson was difficult to figure out. One minute he seemed wary of her and the next more at ease. She got the impression he wanted to relax but didn't know how.

His rattling off everything that stayed off the record when they'd said good night contrasted with the consideration in his words this morning.

They'd been driving for a couple of hours, the highway quiet between stretches of barren land that changed to rugged scenery when they drove through mountain areas.

In the distance, her eye kept wandering to a field. As they got closer, she slowed, trying to figure out what the massive, symmetrical landscape could be. It looked like some sort of white flower. Whatever it was, it called to her, and since Connor had his eyes closed she decided to pull off the freeway to investigate.

"Where are we?" he asked the second she slowed at the bottom of the off-ramp, his voice a little sleepy, a lot tempting.

"Just wanted to check something out really quick."

He straightened and looked out the passenger window. She eyed the stubble along his jawline.

"Charlie." He turned his head. "Did you stay on the highway like I told you to?"

"Um... I think so." She sucked in her bottom lip before making a right turn and then another down a small street. The field stood just up ahead on the left.

"You *think* so?"

"Well, there was one freeway interchange that I noticed after I'd passed through."

"And you didn't think to check with me?" His tone stayed even but that sexy jaw of his clenched.

"I didn't want to wake you." She drew her brows into regret even though she wasn't at all sorry. "You think I went the wrong way?"

"I *know* you went the wrong way." His head fell back against the seat, chin raised, eyelashes sweeping down to close his eyes.

"Well, if I hadn't, we wouldn't get to see this." She made a U-turn and parked in a patch of dirt on the side of the road. "It's a giant field of...dandelions! Come on."

She hopped out of the car and rounded the hood. Thousands, millions of the tiny Make-A-Wish flowers stood at attention just waiting for someone to traipse through their florets. Charlie slipped out of her shoes and took a tentative step into the fluffy white carpet.

Connor put a hand on her arm. "There's a path right there." He nodded to a narrow walkway.

"Oh. Thanks."

He shook his head. No doubt he thought her oblivious as well as forgetful. She grinned at him and the weirdest thing happened. Any hint of annoyance vanished, and his face lighted with dare she guess, pleasure?

The pit of her stomach whirled like a windmill. She twisted and skipped over to the path. When he let down his defenses and looked at her like that, it took everything she had not to hurl herself at him.

"I've never seen anything like this," she said, stepping between the dandelions.

"I haven't either." He followed behind her, close enough that his warm breath fanned the back of her neck. She wiggled her shoulders and pulled the clip out of her hair so it covered her exposed skin. The tiny defense would have to do for now.

They walked in pleasant silence, sunshine and blue sky painted at the edge of the field that appeared to stretch for miles. She stopped and bent down to pick a dandelion.

Connor's tall frame cast a shadow over her.

She glanced up. "You need to get down here."

"I *need* to?" He stayed put.

Her eye rolls were becoming habit with him—especially since she'd noticed it got a little rise out of him. She got comfortable on her knees, then took his hand and tugged.

He obliged her request with a grunt that had her picturing him as a little boy and doing something he didn't want to do.

"Now pick a flower."

"Someone woke up on the bossy side of the bed this morning." He put his hands on his knees.

Her mind went to waking up beside him, *his* side of the bed where she wanted to be. Hands, mouth, body, on his, no space between them. Skin to skin. Her cheeks heated. She canted her head down. "Just don't want you to miss out." She pointed to a large stem. "That looks like a good one."

"It's been a long time since I've blown on one of these." He picked the one she suggested. "My sister, Amanda, used to tell me if I didn't get all the florets in one breath then my wish wouldn't come true."

Charlie brought her dandelion to her mouth. "I've heard that, too. But this happens to be something I've done a lot and it's easy. Just take a deep breath, put your lips together, and blow." She closed her eyes and blew. When she lifted her lids, she found him watching her.

Or rather, watching her mouth. She let go of the flower stem and swallowed.

"I'm thinking those lips of yours could make any man's wish come true." His gaze hopped up and they stared at each other for a long beat. "So…" He held the dandelion in between them. "You blow and I'll make a wish."

"O-okay." She leaned forward and angled her head to the side so she didn't blow straight into his face. "On the count of three. One. Two. Three."

Connor didn't believe in making wishes. He believed in hard work. Determination. Having a plan and sticking with it until he got the results he wanted. But Goldilocks had him remembering how a dream could go a long way toward influencing purpose. His mom told him all the time while growing up that if he kept hope alive and well in the back of his mind, all his accomplishments would be worth something.

Seeing Charlie, so beautiful and carefree, he pictured her with a dandelion stem between her teeth and a hand between her thighs and he wanted to lay her back and ruin her for any other man. He'd never met anyone more genuine. More present. And one smile from her had him forgiving how far off course they were.

"Did you make a wish?" she asked, breaking into his musings.

"Uh, yeah." Her naked. Soon. He'd been helpless to stop the thought.

"Want to make another? There's no limit, you know." She plucked another dandelion.

"I'm good. And we need to get moving." Before he stripped her bare and gave the dandelions a show they'd never forget. "I'm supposed to be at Las Mundas..." He glanced at his watch. "Now, actually."

Charlie scrunched up her nose. "Sorry."

"Hey, like you said, if we'd gone in the right direction, we wouldn't have seen this." He stood. "Dandelion fields are hard to come by. This is the first one I've come across."

"Thanks to me." Goldilocks blew on the flower in her hand and got to her feet. She wiped at the dirt on her knees like it was no big deal.

A girl who didn't mind getting dirty. Despite a high-profile gig for Natural World, she didn't take herself too seriously.

"I truly am sorry, though. Sometimes I'm a little too spur-of-the-moment and this really isn't the right time."

Unthinking, he brushed a strand of hair off her face. "Don't sweat it. Keys?" he said, putting out his palm.

"Oh crap." She patted her hips. Her teeth sank into her bottom lip.

He closed his eyes and took a deep breath. If she'd locked the keys in the car, they'd waste more time waiting for a locksmith. And in the middle of nowhere who knew how long it would take. "I guess we'll..." he started to say, but stopped after he'd opened his eyes and found the keys dangling from Charlie's hand.

She wore a grin almost as big as the one she'd blessed him with when she won the giant teddy bear. "Just kidding."

"You are so going down for that." He grabbed the keys and headed back to the road. "When you least expect it," he added over his shoulder.

"I'm shaking in my shoes," she called out.

"You're not wearing any."

"Exactly."

Damn, he liked this girl.

They got back into the car, and it took Connor a minute to figure out they were about sixty miles off track. He silently cursed, but it was only a small curse. The detour had been worth it to see the joy on Charlie's face. She filled *him* with joy.

"Will we see any giant dinosaurs today?" she asked once they'd hit the highway.

He chuckled. "As opposed to miniature dinosaurs?"

She pushed him in the arm. "I mean those roadside dinosaurs with cheesy gift shops. There's a couple on the way to Palm Springs and I've stopped on every weekend trip I've taken there. It's sort of a tradition."

"Well, we wouldn't want to mess with tradition, but no, there aren't any on this stretch."

"But there are some on the Route?"

"Yes." And damn if he didn't want to take another detour and show them to her. What was wrong with him? "You're from California?"

"Yes." She pulled out her notepad and tape recorder. "Tell me about Las Mundas."

"I'd rather you be surprised." The unique garden filled with surrealist sculptures was best viewed without any preconceived notions.

"Okay, how about some facts about the route that people might not know."

"In the 1950s it became known as America's 'Mother Road.'"

"What else?"

He shared more interesting facts and watched as she jotted down notes. He also noticed her sketch some doodles. A cartoon drawing of a car. Dandelions. The iconic Route 66 road sign. As he talked, her pencil didn't stop moving.

"Do you have a favorite spot on the Route?" She closed her notebook, turned off the recorder, and stowed them back in the bag at her feet.

"Yes, and we're almost there."

"I'm glad I'll get to see it." She smiled in the direction of her knees and gathered her hair haphazardly into a clip.

Connor wanted his lips on the sprinkling of freckles at the curve of her collarbone.

"Besides Palm Springs, did you do much traveling growing up?"

She fidgeted in her seat. "Some. But not to anywhere that made a lasting impression. No favorite places I have to go back to."

"You live in LA?"

"Yep."

"Favorite place there?"

Goldilocks gave another coy, closed-mouth smile. She moved her attention out the windshield. "It's sort of personal."

"I'll keep it off the record then." So much about her intrigued him. He wanted to know more.

Her gaze slid his way. He beamed at her. Two could play the reporter game.

"My favorite place is this children's bookstore and art gallery not far from where I live. I visit at least once a week and once a month I volunteer for story-time readings. I'll often end up there on Friday nights." She rubbed a finger across her bottom lip and shook her head. "I can't believe I just told you that. Only my closest friends know I hang out there."

"Why?" He didn't see the big deal in hanging out in a bookstore. His pretty reporter liked kids and probably grew up with her nose in a book. He found it sexy.

"I'm actually a pretty private person."

"I'm easy to talk to."

"You think?" Sarcasm laced her words.

So he hadn't been the easiest person to get along with the past few days. He planned to change that. She'd peeled away his apprehension about the article and the only concern busting into his thoughts now was going further than a kiss.

In truth, most women put on such a show with him that he'd learned to tune them out. Conversation always centered on superficial crap and lies by the mouthful to get close to his family and bank account. The one time in college he thought he'd met a girl who really cared about him had been a big mistake. She'd lied about her past and her hometown because she thought he wanted someone with a background like his. She'd wanted to sound more country club than trailer park.

"My sisters used me all the time to go over the speeches in their heads for their boyfriends."

Goldilocks laughed. "Did you offer any words of wisdom?"

"Never. I was only supposed to listen. But…"

She turned in her seat to face him. "But what?"

"I might have made a few bucks telling their boyfriends a few things so they knew what to expect."

"You didn't."

He shrugged. "I was saving for a telescope and I saw an opportunity to help my fellow man. No guy should be caught unaware."

"You were interested in the solar system?"

Interesting that she chose the sky over his selling information to call him on. "I was into Heaven Brooks and *she* was all about the stars. Thought I'd impress her with the size of my viewfinder." He exited the highway and turned toward the mountains.

Charlie smirked. "Was she?"

Connor thought about lying, but only for a second. "No. She decided some other guy was more her type."

"Silly girl." Charlie got comfortable with her back against the seat again. "Pretty name, though."

"How'd you get the nickname Charlie? It's a big stretch from Ashley."

She waved her hand in the air. "It's a long, story and oh, look, the sign for Las Mundas."

All of a sudden Loose Lips Charlie didn't want to talk? If they weren't pulling into the entrance for Las Mundas, he would have pressed her more.

"Conner," she said, awe in her voice already. "What is this place?"

"It's the best garden you'll ever visit." They pulled into a spot in the busy parking lot. "Back in the 40s a wealthy artist and writer named Jonathan Mundas bought the land." Connor got out of the car and hurried around the hood to open Charlie's door. "He spent the next thirty years designing and building a surrealistic landscape with canals, sculptures, trees, and plants. I'll give you the tour."

She put her bag over her shoulder, slipping the camera out at the same time. "World Heritage Fund helped with preservation?"

"We restored several of the concrete structures, installed an interpretive display to teach visitors about the site, and support conservation research by local college students. Environmental factors have proven the biggest threat so we've brought in landscape architects to help teach the stewardship running the site that the fantastical creations can coexist with a natural landscape."

"You're talking tree roots."

"Among other things, yes. Marrying the natural world with man-made structures took talent and vision and we want to help protect it. The grounds get thousands of visitors taking a detour off the Route every year."

"I can see why." Charlie tilted her head back as they walked under the bamboo arch entrance, whimsical concrete columns lending support, colorful vines with waxy red flowers bundled in interesting shapes. "It's like a Roald Dahl sanctuary."

Connor let her words sink in. She looked at the world through lighthearted, inventive eyes that reminded him life shouldn't be taken too seriously. "That's exactly what it's like."

The impish crinkle in the corner of her bright blue eyes had him smiling in return.

"Connor, you made it," a male voice said, drawing his attention away from Goldilocks.

"Esteban, it's good to see you." Connor shook the older man's hand. "Sorry, I'm late."

"It's my fault, Esteban. Hi, I'm Char—Ashley Morgan with Natural World. Would it be okay if I took some pictures while I looked around?"

"Of course," Esteban said.

"Great. Thanks." She took off, obviously not interested in his tour-guide skills. Normally he preferred to let others have the task, but today he'd wanted to.

For the next hour he and Esteban drove a cart around the property and went over how the preservation techniques were working. The abnormally wet winter had allowed plant growth to go unchecked in some areas and Connor met with the group of landscapers, advising them on how to maintain as much wildlife as possible while safeguarding several concrete structures.

He and Esteban stopped at the wood-and-bamboo cabin that housed Mundas's writings on the walls last. The small, whimsical house had suffered damage that took Connor some time to assess. So lost in detailing the long-term steps to protect the building, he hadn't noticed Charlie standing just outside the open window frame. With her head tilted to the side and her eyes focused right on him, she looked as if she were hanging on his every word. Pride swelled inside him.

She nodded. A gesture, he guessed, that meant she wanted him to continue, so he did. When he and Esteban stepped out of the cabin, she was gone.

Hurrying back to the main area of the gardens, he thanked Esteban for the time and expertise he and local organizations were dedicating to the garden. He'd be back, he said, with a small crew at the end of the month to help revive the cabin. Then he went in quick search of Charlie.

Sunlight bounced off the land, brilliant in spots, subtle in others. Young and old alike strolled through the grounds as he made his way toward his favorite sculpture—the Stairway To The Sky. He never tired of seeing the winding stairs wrapped around a concrete pillar that reached toward the clouds.

A young boy stood at the foot of the architectural folly with his head craned back, chin jutting up. A woman held his hand. "Momma, are these the steps to Grandpa?"

The woman looked down at her son. "They lead to whoever you want them to. It's different for everyone."

Connor gulped. He'd been about the same age when his grandfather passed away and his mom had taken it hard. Maybe if she'd had a place like this to visit, it would've eased her mind. He'd never taken the time to realize it before, but many of the monuments he worked to preserve were about more than heritage. They were about hope.

His eyes were drawn away from the stairway to a small concrete bench. Goldilocks tucked a notepad away in her bag. He went and sat beside her, so drawn to her natural beauty that his heart pounded like it never had before.

They touched from their arms down to their knees, and it felt amazing to be connected that way.

"This place is magical," she acknowledged with admiration and respect, her focus straight ahead. "I could spend *hours* here."

"That a hint?"

"It wouldn't kill you to ease up on the time frame a little. Here, give me your watch." She put her hand out and waggled her fingers. "I'll keep time for a while."

"You want to wear my watch?"

"Uh-huh."

For some reason having something of his on her body sounded hot and worth being tardy for. He took off his Omega, a birthday gift from his parents last year, and slipped it on her wrist. It hung like a bracelet, but his gut tightened at the sight. "Now what are you going to give me?"

She twirled the watch. "I just gave it to you."

"What was it?" He looked around them.

"Free rein." She jumped to her feet. "Take me somewhere the public doesn't get to see and tell me more about heritage protection. Teach me everything."

He stood. Bossy Goldilocks jacked up his pulse and he wanted to be mad about it, but everything that came out of her mouth put a ridiculous smile on his face instead.

Chapter Six

Charlie slowly pried opened her right eye to see where they were on the highway. She'd feigned sleep for the last couple of hours to avoid talking. After asking a boatload of questions—professional and personal—at Las Mundas, she figured she owed it to Connor to be quiet for a while.

She gave a little stretch and fake yawn and took a better look out the windshield. Tiny white spots danced in front of her as the sun set, making it difficult to focus. "Where are we?"

"A small town just outside Albuquerque near the Sandia Mountains. We'll be here for a couple of days while I oversee a few things at the Hotel Buena Vista. It officially reopens next week."

"The area is beautiful," Charlie said, now that her eyes had adjusted to the sun's eye-level light.

Connor nodded.

"What makes this hotel special?"

"For almost ninety years it's been a popular place to stay for transcontinental travelers. It has a history of hosting thousands of interesting people, from bank robbers to celebrities, which makes it appealing to locals *and* vacationers. We've preserved the exterior and kept as much of the old look as possible, but brought the rooms up to date."

Charlie loved it already. She couldn't recall ever staying anywhere historic, let alone a hotel with a colorful history.

And she wasn't disappointed when they arrived. The quaint, four-story hotel with white shingles and red flowers blooming in windowsills charmed at first sight. Inside, the antique furnishings and dark, warm colors made her want to curl up in one of the high-back chairs with her sketchpad.

"Mr. Gibson," the white-haired man behind the desk bellowed. "We've been expecting you."

"Hello, Mac." Connor extended his hand in greeting. "And I keep telling you to call me Connor."

"Connor." Mac's full cheeks rounded further as he smiled.

"This is Ashley Morgan, a reporter tagging along with me this week. Please let everyone know to answer her questions and share any special insight into the hotel."

"It's a pleasure to meet you, Ashley," Mac said.

Charlie tried to swallow the guilt lodged in her throat like tar. It took her a second to reply. "Please call me Charlie."

"Mr. Punctual finally shows up," a deep, masculine voice said over Charlie's shoulder. "I was starting to worry."

She turned, grazing Connor's arm as he did the same, and electricity tap-danced across her skin. He cut her a quick glance like maybe he felt it, too.

"Worried my ass," Connor said to the man approaching.

They shared a one-armed hug with pats on the back. "Clay, this is Ashley, the reporter I texted you about. Ashley, Clay Doherty, head of security for World Heritage Fund."

Clay's assessing green eyes put her a little on edge. Not to mention he was all brawn and burliness and could probably knock her over with a tiny push from his pinkie.

"I, uh, usually go by Charlie. Nice to meet you." She smiled.

"I always go by Clay and the pleasure is all mine." Instead of smiling at her, he grinned at Connor and Charlie wasn't sure what to make of it. "I need to catch Gibson up on a few things. Why don't you look around?"

"Sure."

Connor picked up her duffel bag and then his own. "I'll have Mac hang on to these until we check into our rooms."

"Thanks. I'll catch up with you later."

She watched them walk away—okay, she watched Connor's very nice butt and broad shoulders walk away—before she strolled around the lobby, checked out the restaurant and lounge, and made her way outside along a brick pathway lined with sweet-smelling foliage and more red flowers. The sun slid into slumber as she reached the end of the walkway so she returned indoors and got comfortable on one of the high-back chairs. She started sketching and every muscle in her body relaxed.

"That's really good."

Charlie startled at Connor's sexy voice and kind words. She hadn't realized how much time had passed or noticed him approach, so lost in her drawings she'd tuned everything else out. He knelt beside her for a closer look. "Seriously good," he said.

"Thank you," she whispered and quickly closed her pad.

"Hang on." He stopped her hand and leafed through a few of the other pages. "You're incredibly talented, Charlie."

She sucked in a breath. His compliment made her light-headed, but his nearness put her heart into a wonderful flutter.

"This is a picture book?" Connor stood.

"Yes." She took her time meeting his gaze, her eyes tracking up his body. He had a beautiful body. Plus, she needed a few seconds to get used to the idea of him discovering her secret passion.

Her dream.

What she really wanted to do with her life.

Her father had thought it foolish when she'd broached the subject with him after college. "You don't go to Stanford and then draw pictures and write for children," he'd said.

"Charlie?"

She blinked away thoughts of her dad. "Sorry. What?"

"I asked if you were an illustrator as well as a writer."

Her chest tightened. She got to her feet and shook her head, slipped her sketchpad back into her shoulder bag. "No."

Lines creased his forehead before he said, "I've read to my nieces and nephews and what I just saw is right up there with the best of them."

Tears threatened the backs of her eyes. She looked down at the floor to study the floral pattern in the carpeting.

"Hey." He lifted her chin with the slightly roughened pads of his fingers. "What's going on?"

"Nothing."

"The look on your face says otherwise."

God, did he have to have a look on his that said *let me*

help you? Because at the moment all she wanted to do was kiss him and lose herself to his incredible mouth and honeyed eyes and bone-melting touch.

"My dad thinks being a children's author and illustrator is silly."

"So?"

"So end of discussion."

"I'm pretty sure you're old enough to make your own decisions."

"Not if I want to continue to have a relationship with my dad." She took a step away from him. "Let's just check in now, okay?"

He studied her for a beat before moving toward the registration desk. "It's a good name," he said.

"What?"

"Finley Quay. Kids would really like it."

She smiled to herself. She loved the name of her basset hound and main character.

"Mac, we're ready to head up," Connor said, leaning on the desk.

"Absolutely. Rooms 310 and 312." He handed Connor the key cards. "Things have been quiet on three."

"Great, thanks. Bags there already?"

"Yes, sir." Mac gave a nod and turned his attention to Charlie. "Enjoy your stay Miss Morgan."

"Oh, uh, thank you. I'm sure I will." Crap. She'd wasted an hour drawing instead of asking the staff questions and taking pictures. "And what did you mean 'things have been quiet on three'?"

"I'll explain on the way." Connor strode to the elevator where they joined two other couples. "Evening," he said, drawing nods from the men and flirty smiles from the women.

"So," Charlie said, as they got off on three and walked down the hallway. "What did Mac mean?"

"The hotel is supposedly haunted."

Charlie stumbled before coming to a halt. "*What?*"

Connor looked over his shoulder. "You okay?"

"No, I'm not okay. How could you bring me"—she gulped—"to a haunted hotel?"

Laughter danced in his gorgeous eyes, but a second later concern replaced the amusement. No doubt due to the panic in hers. He took her hand and rubbed his thumb across her knuckles. "There's no such thing as ghosts."

"Yes there is."

"You've seen one?" he asked honestly, and she wanted to kiss him again.

And God, her hand felt good where his thumb massaged. She wanted his fingers in other places. Which only proved how enamored she was with him because how could she possibly relax with spirits around?

"I'm not crazy."

One corner of his sexy mouth tugged up. "I didn't say you were."

"Something weird happened once to make me believe."

He laced his fingers with hers and tugged her toward room 310. "Let's get inside and you can tell me about it."

"I can't."

"Go in the room?" He pulled the key card out of the door and turned his head.

"Talk about it." She freaked herself out just thinking about it. The weekend away with her college boyfriend to a swanky hotel and being awakened in the middle of the night by the feeling someone was watching her. And then her boyfriend bolting up out of bed because he swore he felt someone place a hand over his mouth and he couldn't breathe. They'd later found out a woman had been killed in the room and thrown from the window by her husband. Similar reports had happened for over thirty years. Charlie told the concierge the room needed to come with a warning.

"Then we'll have to keep your mind on something else." Heat flared in his eyes and he opened the door.

Charlie forgot how to breathe. She already knew that mouth of his could kiss like nobody's business, but combined with flirtatious words like that?

The big yellow yield sign she'd been seeing in the back of her mind turned to dust.

"We definitely will."

The need to comfort Goldilocks almost matched the need to have her. Better yet, he could comfort her while burying himself deep inside her. That ought to make her forget about anything but him.

He pushed open the door and held it for her to enter first. Her teeth bit into her bottom lip as she brushed by him and he wanted to toss her onto the bed, strip off her clothes, lift her arms above her head, and slowly sink into her warm, welcome flesh.

Clay's smug smile and irritating words from earlier flashed in his mind. "You're going down, Gibson." Meaning the drunken bet they'd made last month over which one of them had sex *with* strings attached first, owed the other a

Porsche 918 Spyder. How the hell Clay knew he felt something for Charlie, he had no idea. Their friend and work associate McCall had often said Clay could see things in a person no one else could. And get them to share all their secrets. That was one of the things that had made him a top Navy SEAL before getting into security.

The Porsche's price tag? A million dollars.

"We're connected," Goldilocks said.

Connor's gaze jumped from the sweet curve of her ass in tight jeans to her beautiful face. "Sorry?" He sure as hell wanted them connected. Naked bodies pressed together until the scent on her skin covered and lingered on his.

She turned and nodded at a door. "Our rooms are connected. Which makes me a little more comfortable."

You're sleeping with me, he almost demanded. Instead he took a casual deep breath and stepped around her. Housekeeping had made sure all the lamps were aglow and the bed had been turned down. "If it helps, in all the times I've been here, nothing strange has happened."

"What's the story?"

"Stories."

"Shit."

He spun around in time to see her plop down on the edge of the bed. The view out the floor-to-ceiling window would have to wait. He sat beside her. "It's not anything bad."

"Okay." She pressed her hands into her lap.

"You really want to know?"

"Yes. Otherwise my imagination is going to lean toward bad."

"Over the years hotel guests have reported a knock

on their door and a muffled voice announcing room service. When they open the door, no one is there, but some guests have seen the figure of a bellboy in the hallways. A few famous visitors have claimed to see the ghost, too, which makes it more of a story, but everyone says the ghost seemed friendly."

The white of her knuckles lessened. "Go on."

"There's also a young boy who supposedly wanders the halls. Female guests have seen his image and some say the ghost touched their hand. The theory is he's trying to reach his mother."

"Anything else?" She peered at him under long dark brown eyelashes.

"On several occasions staff and guests have witnessed a transparent couple dancing in the cocktail lounge, smiling and laughing."

"So no murdered ghosts."

Ah, there was the crux of her fear. He took her hand. "No."

"Not the little boy?"

"There was a boy who died here, but it was due to a rare heart condition."

"That's a relief. I mean, it's really sad that he passed away but..." She gave him a weak smile just before the lights flickered and plunged them into darkness.

Chapter Seven

Charlie shrieked and landed in Connor's lap, her arms around his neck, her legs wrapped around his waist, her face buried in the crux of his neck, two seconds later. This vulnerable side of her spiked a desire he hadn't ever felt before. *Mine,* flashed in the back of his mind like the single most important word in the English language. He wanted to keep her safe. Be the only man to watch over her and erase her fears.

"Hey," he whispered, rubbing her back. "It's just a power failure. There've been a few electrical issues. I'm sure the lights will be back on in a minute."

She nodded against his throat but continued to hold on with a grip worthy of a championship fighter. Having her so close, her breasts pressed against his chest, the juncture between her thighs at his zipper, generated a hell of a lot of electricity in his bloodstream. He sucked in a breath.

And ran his schedule through his head to get his thoughts

off their compromising position. He had work to do here and one more planned Route stop before he dropped Goldilocks off in Oklahoma City and headed to Colorado to be a groomsman in McCall's wedding.

Thinking about how in love McCall was with his fiancé Lucy, though, had Connor's thoughts spiraling right back to the soft, warm body in his arms.

His cell phone rang in his pocket.

"Do not let go of me," Charlie said.

"I won't, but if you could lift your hips so I can grab—"

He toppled backward as she lifted at the waist and threw him off balance. Great; now he was lying on the bed with her sprawled on top of him and the last thing he wanted to do was answer his phone.

"Sorry." Yet she didn't budge.

He pulled out his phone and brought it to his ear. "Hey," he said, with no idea who'd answer on the other end.

"Five more minutes," Clay said. "One of the staff ran over the junction box on the street."

"He okay?"

"Fine. Feels terrible about it, though. I had him drop and give me fifty."

Connor laughed. "Only fifty?"

"One-armed."

A chuckle sounded against his neck. He guessed Goldilocks could hear the conversation. "Thanks for keeping me posted," Connor said.

"You coming down for dinner?"

Charlie shook her head, her hair tickling the side of his face. If she wasn't leaving the room, he wasn't either. "Think I'll put room service to the test."

"That the only thing you're testing out?"

"Hanging up." He tossed the phone to the side.

For a long time now, Connor had lived and breathed work. Given his heart and soul to the environment and dedicated his days to preserving important historical monuments and landmarks. He lived his life moving from one place to another. But with every hour that passed in Charlie's company, a growing ache for more, for moments like this, holding her close and letting her fill the space around his heart, had him wondering if he could take a chance on something more than a quick fling.

He stroked her back and wound his fingers around the soft, silky strands of her blond hair. Any last remains of tension seemed to leave her body as she grew heavier against him. Her warm breath tickled the underside of his chin. He inhaled her delicate floral scent and knew no matter what happened between them, he'd always remember it. Remember the way her fragrance made him…happy.

The lights flickered back on. Charlie let out a breath and pressed up just enough to leave a whisper of space between their noses. Grateful blue eyes he'd need hours, days, years to explore looked down at him. She hovered there, her lips near enough to kiss and continue what they'd started on the Ferris wheel.

Desire was stamped in the blush of her cheeks, the parting of that lush mouth.

She shifted her hips, a subtle movement, but he was so in tune to her that he had to stifle a groan. This unexpected woman lanced intense need and want that reached beyond basic arousal. The spark that had ignited poolside in Arizona had grown hundredfold with her smart motor mouth, enthusiasm, and sincerity. Today at Las Mundas had been something special.

Another little wiggle, followed by a smile, and he couldn't keep that arousal from growing. By the way her gaze flared with hunger, he knew she felt it. Was ready for it.

"Thank you," she whispered.

"My pleasure."

"I think I'm over my stupid anxiety."

"It wasn't stupid." He tucked a stray strand of hair behind her ear. "Certain situations can leave us with apprehension that sticks around. No shame in that."

"Has anything ever scared you?" Her fingertips danced along the back of his neck. The gentle touch aroused as much as it soothed.

He trailed his hands down her sides to her waist. She shivered. "A couple of years ago I was on site at a temple in Japan when a fire broke out. A few us were trapped and…" *Fuck*. He could feel the heat licking at him like it was yesterday. He gulped back his unease. *Man up, bud.* "And we were lucky to get out. I still can't be near any sort of fire without sweating and thinking back to that day."

She brushed the hair off his forehead. Her eyes searched his, looking for what, he didn't know. He'd never shared what happened in Japan with anyone outside of WHF.

And Christ, he'd just told it to a reporter. He wished he knew how she got him to open up.

"I guess a campfire is out of the question, then."

That was how.

He laughed, happy Goldilocks had a sense of humor to go with her scorching-hot body. A body that obliterated his misgivings and needed some thorough exploration.

It was time to see this attraction through.

"Yeah, but…" He flipped her onto her back. Took her wrists and lifted her arms above her head. He slipped his watch over her hand, brought his mouth near hers. "I'm hoping this isn't."

A sexy little catch in her breath fanned his jawline. He stayed still to give her time to say no. To push him off. But all she did was look up at him with eyes more beautiful than the bluest water on Earth.

"I don't make a habit of going on test runs," she said. "Just so you know."

"I don't do much testing."

"I'd say we're good then."

He lowered until his mouth grazed hers. "You're anything but a trial run."

Her lips stretched into a smile for a split second before he fused their mouths together.

They exchanged fierce, devouring kisses. He released her wrists, one hand slipping to the back of her head while the other found the outside swell of her breast. He skimmed his hand sideways and took her fullness into his palm.

She let out a breathy sigh and arched into his touch.

Connor slowed and softened the kiss. His thumb rubbed over her nipple, tight as a pebble through her clothing. At the contact she opened her mouth to welcome his tongue and slow returned to hungry.

Her fingers ran through his hair, and their bodies rocked together. She took his bottom lip between her teeth as her hands moved down and tugged his shirt up. He raised his head so she could pull it off.

"God, you're beautiful," she said, her palms roaming

over his chest. "I've never wanted to lick something so badly in my life."

He sat back, his legs straddling her hips. "Have at it."

She pressed up, her arms extended behind her, and swiped her tongue across his skin. "Mmm. If you taste this good here, I wonder how good you'll taste elsewhere."

Jesus. His erection strained against his fly with painful tension, ready to give her a mouthful.

But Connor did the pleasing first, and he planned to draw his name from Goldilock's lips before she had her way with him.

"My turn," he said, lifting her shirt and tossing it to the floor. She fell back and his gaze latched onto the velvety-smooth globes spilling out of her pale pink lace bra. Her nipples pressed against the fabric. "*You* are breathtaking."

The sweet bashful smile she gave reminded him of the girl he'd first met at the pool. He dipped his head for a taste of one perfect breast, tugging on her nipple through the thin material of her lingerie. She moaned in pleasure and stretched her shoulders back.

While his mouth played with one nipple, his hand played with the other. It was then that he noticed the front clasp. With one flick he had the bra open and her bare flesh exposed. She drew the straps off her arms and flung the bra across the room.

His mouth and hands took equal advantage, kneading, fondling, sucking. Sexy pants fell from her lips. Her nails raked over his shoulders and down his back sending a hot shudder through him. He moved south, his lips traveling over the flat expanse of her stomach.

Kisses tickled her waist—damn her giggle was hot—as

he undid her jeans and pushed them down.

Air rushed out of his lungs when he stared down at her in nothing but a tiny pair of panties that he could tell had nothing but a string in back.

Connor had never been so fiercely attracted to a woman before. The simplest of touches hurtled his nerve endings into the best kind of chaos. Her uninhibited responses told him she felt the same intensity he did. Whatever zinged between them was in a whole other orbit from his normal encounters. Goldilocks had messed with his orderliness from the second he'd laid eyes on her.

And he wanted to trust her enough to embrace it.

Connor's gaze whipped pleasure through her almost as hotly as his hands and mouth did. Flecks of silver sparkled in those gorgeous eyes of his and their attention traced over every inch of her with desire.

She pressed up, scooted her bottom to the edge of the bed, and went for the button of his jeans. "These need to come off."

One of his hands covered hers while the other lifted her chin. Their eyes locked and then he bent and kissed her. The slow, deliberate kind of kiss. The kind that made her heart beat out of her chest because there was feeling behind it. Care.

He let out a groan and stood, made fast work of his zipper and shucked out of his pants and boxer briefs. His shoes and socks somehow came off in the process, too.

Charlie swallowed. He was gloriously sexy. The hottest

man she'd ever seen with his sculpted chest and abs, narrow waist, long muscular legs dusted with dark brown hair. Her gaze roamed over every inch of him before settling on his erection. It was big, thick, and hard for *her*. Her mouth watered in anticipation.

She reached out to touch him but his hands moved to her waist and with quick speed and strength, he lifted her up and planted her farther back on the bed.

"You don't mind if I taste first, do you?" With eyes trained on her, he kissed the inside of her ankle, slipped his lips and tongue up higher.

"Not at..." Oh God, his mouth grazed the inside of her thigh and his fingers made contact with the curls between her legs. She tingled and tightened with excruciating pleasure and need. "All," she managed to get out on a breathy sigh.

His gaze burned with voracity. She felt his lips curve into a smile against her flesh.

"There's one spot I've been especially hoping to try." He hovered just above her mound, his nearness alone making her wet.

"My spots are all yours."

That drew an impossibly perfect flash of white teeth and crinkles in the corners of his eyes that reminded her this man had it all.

He skipped right over her needy, achy center—the big tease—but did cover her body with his. Sparks skittered over her skin. "You're sexy everywhere," he murmured. "But I've been thinking about the curve right here ever since the Ferris wheel."

Connor both thrilled and frightened her. From the moment he'd kissed her atop the Ferris wheel a piece of her had belonged to him. And with every touch and kiss and kind word, more pieces fell.

He doesn't even know your real name.

But that wayward thought fled the second he rained kisses along her collar bone. His open mouth sent delicious quivers to the tips of her breasts. Lower.

"So good." He nipped her shoulder. Kissed her neck next, skimmed his lips down her chest, teased her sensitive nipples, and finally closed his lips over one.

She pressed her palms into the bed covers and arched her back. He nibbled and licked, and everything inside her grew tighter. She moaned.

Then his mouth and hands traveled down until he had her panties in his fingers and slid them off. His warm breath fanned her core as he spread her legs apart.

"Please, Connor." She couldn't take any more. Her release hovered so close, his every touch bringing her higher.

"Please what?" He blew over her swollen flesh, the bastard.

"Please make me come."

His thumb rubbed over the magic spot and she thrust into his hand. "Nothing would make me happier."

After a few more seconds of stroking, he lowered his head and closed his mouth over her. His amazing tongue circled and skimmed and exquisite pressure built. She spread her legs wider and put her hands on the back of his head to keep him close. Every caress made her gasp in pleasure until one especially nice lash of his tongue sent her blazing over the edge.

She might have screamed his name loud enough for the next floor to hear.

He continued to suck and taste until he'd wrung every

last bit of her orgasm out of her. Only then did he stand at the foot of the bed and bless her with a gaze that put a whole new set of flutters inside her.

"I know just what you need next," he said, his voice husky.

"If it's not you inside me, then you guessed wrong." She pushed up onto her elbows. "And please hurry."

That wicked, sexy grin of his took hold but a second later it vanished. He glanced behind him. "Shit. My bag's in the other room. I don't have a—"

"Don't move," Charlie said, dropping a quick kiss to his abdomen and gliding a finger over the tip of his penis. "I do."

She grabbed all three condoms she had tucked away in her bag and jumped back onto the bed. Lying against the pillows, she dropped them down onto her stomach one at a time.

Just to make sure he got the message.

The happy bend of his lips made her legs weak. Good thing she was off her feet.

His hands and mouth worked their way from her ankles to the foil packets. Unbelievably, her body responded with pulses and trembles that spiraled her back to the verge of orgasm again. He positioned himself at her opening, the tip of him touching her swollen flesh.

Their eyes locked. He slipped inside her slowly until his restraint broke and he thrust deep, filling her completely.

Perfectly.

He laced their fingers together and brought their arms above her head. With delicious slow motion he moved in and out. Tingles rushed and curled inside her, heightening her senses. She smelled the scent of soap on his skin. Felt his possessive hold from the tips of her fingers to deep in her core, relished the husky sound of his voice when he said, "You feel so fucking good."

Saw the blazing sincerity in his eyes when she said, "So do you."

His strokes increased. She writhed and arched her hips as her pleasure surged higher and higher. Her eyes drifted shut, ragged sighs escaped her lips.

And then he kissed her. He captured her excited sounds and breathed new life into her. Rough, greedy. She felt impossibly sensitive to every brush of his lips and tongue. Her nails dug into his hands.

He left her mouth to kiss her cheek, her jaw, her ear. "This is what I call connected," he whispered.

A dizzying explosion of feeling overcame her and she shattered in release. He sank himself deeper and groaned in blissful agony right behind her.

Room service and lots more connections followed until sometime after midnight she fell asleep with her head on his chest, a leg swung over his, and one thought in her head.

You have to tell him the truth.

Chapter Eight

Goldilocks mumbled in her sleep again. Something about a name. Her soft whispers were hard to decipher, and Connor contemplated waking her, but he wanted to stare at her a while longer. Early morning sunlight streamed in through the window and he'd never woken to anything or anyone more beautiful.

He'd slept soundly. Peacefully. He'd gone too far and crossed the line between business and pleasure, but he wasn't sorry. Charlie had him actually *feeling*, craving an honest connection with someone. He wanted to know all of the things she'd seen, done, and overcome; all her mistakes and the chances she'd taken. Because her past made her the person she was today. And right now, after a night of making love to her and listening to her laugh, and staring at the warmth in her blue eyes, his heart was wide open and raw.

Not smart, given he had no idea if he could fully trust her. Charlie wasn't the prick that had misrepresented his mom, but that didn't mean she wouldn't do whatever was necessary to make her story stand out. If she dragged his personal life into the interview, even unintentionally, he'd never forgive that.

"You're thinking awfully hard this morning," Charlie whispered, catching him unaware, his unfocused attention having dropped to her bare shoulder. With a gentle touch, she brushed the hair off his forehead. "I was sort of hoping you'd be a little more relaxed today."

He took her hand and kissed it.

"I'm very relaxed."

"Really?" She raised her eyebrows and snuggled closer. "You feel a little stiff."

And getting stiffer by the second. He had zero control around this woman. "We should probably do something about that."

"Probably." Her soft morning gaze moved to his mouth.

He let go of her hand and cupped her cheek, slid his thumb across her lower lip. "But I'm already late. I need to get downstairs to help with some of the last-minute work."

"Duty calls?"

"It does." His team had worked hard the past eighteen months to maintain the hotel's authenticity and architectural integrity, to keep its sense of place among a historic American landscape. It was no secret that Connor was a history nerd and he hoped the Buena Vista, with its tales of ghost stories, celebrities, and scandal, would once again entertain and appeal to young and old alike.

Getting back to task also meant a chance to get his thoughts in order. Charlie had given him no reason not to trust her, and the more time they spent together, the more attached he grew. "Feel free to check out the hotel and talk to the staff," he said slipping out of bed. "And I'm happy to give you an up-close look at what we're doing."

When she didn't answer, he glanced over his shoulder. Then cleared his throat.

Her attention jumped from his ass to his face. "Sorry, what did you say?"

"I said—"

She sat up, letting the sheet fall to her waist. And damn if she wasn't the most gorgeous thing with her creamy skin, pert breasts, and mussed hair.

He moaned like a guy totally whipped and stalked back to the bed where he climbed on top of her.

"*Connor.*" She giggled and wiggled beneath him. Her arms went around his neck. "What are you doing?"

"Forgetting the time." He kissed her and didn't leave until they'd both had their fill.

"Hands in the ten and two position, eyes on the road," Goldilocks said and Connor's dick jumped to the up position. He hadn't thought she could get him any harder than he'd been the past two nights, her body fused with his in every position they could think of. But offering this on the desolate two-lane road off the main highway, the Hotel Buena Vista behind them, had him stiffer than steel.

Leaning over the center console, she undid his jeans and his erection sprang free. *This* was why she'd asked him to go commando today. His sexy, spunky reporter had actually planned something in advance. He grinned.

Then he groaned.

Her tongue licked his tip, and her hand gripped him at the base. She stroked him slow and gentle, her mouth following her hand, and Jesus Christ he was about to go off like a virgin. He grabbed a fistful of her hair and eased her head back.

"Problem?" she asked, looking up at him with the sultry sparkle in her eyes he'd come to learn meant she was just as turned on as he was.

"Just slowing things down, sweetheart."

"Ready now?"

He put his hand back in the number two position. She put hers back on his throbbing cock and with a firm, confident hold, slid up and down. The small, sexy circles she blessed him with had him gripping the steering wheel.

When she added her mouth, murmured "mmm," and pulled back to admire him before eagerly gobbling him up again, his ass lifted off the seat.

He slowed and took a turnoff. Charlie looked up.

"Something wrong?" She pushed back into her seat.

Mountains rose in the distance, fields of Big Bluestem— grass that grew to six feet tall with blue-green leaves—lay on either side of the uneven road. Connor dropped to five miles per hour and in a move that surprised him, drove onto the field.

"Uh, Connor, I didn't know Audi's could go off-road."

He parked the car, pressed the button for the roof to fold back, and undid his seat belt. "It's an emergency."

Goldilocks giggled. She unfastened her belt and hopped onto her knees. "Yes, I can see"—she glanced down at his crotch—"that we're in danger of a detonation. What's the protocol in a situation like this, Mr. Environmentalist?"

"I'm afraid I have no choice but to advocate for release. Climb into the backseat and lift your dress, Miss Morgan."

A moment of hesitation crossed her features and Connor wondered if maybe he'd overestimated Charlie's boldness. She hadn't been at all shy about her body and a quick glance of the area told him they had total privacy, but they were still outside and out in the open.

She climbed into the back next to the giant teddy bear.

He watched her lift the hem of her blue cotton T-shirt dress and gather it around her waist. She stayed on her knees and shared a coy smile over her shoulder. "Ready and oh so willing to receive."

It took him one point seven seconds to have his hands on her hips, his mouth at her ear. "A bow? Are you trying to make these cheeks of yours even sweeter?" The tiny pink bow at the center of her G-string hit with a sexy, wholesome one-two punch.

"I only thought to make you crack a smile."

He laughed. God, the best things came out of her mouth. He brushed his upturned lips against her neck. "Mission accomplished."

"Connor," she said breathlessly.

"Yeah, baby?" He kissed her shoulder while one hand slid down to the tiny scrap of material covering her and the other hand moved inside her dress to cup her breast.

"I am *really* turned on."

Yes she was, her nipple tight and hard, the spot between her legs wet as he slipped his fingers underneath the cotton. "What should we do about that?"

She wiggled her ass against his erection and moaned

when he pushed down the material of her bra to palm her bare flesh. When he slowly pressed one, then two fingers inside her she moaned and said, "That's a good start."

He'd never experienced responses like hers before. It had him so hot to be inside her he pushed down his pants, moved aside her panties, and thrust into her warm, welcome channel.

"Yes!" she cried, one hand gripping the back of the seat.

He groaned and plunged deeper. His hands molded to the curve of her waist as he pushed into her in a slow, thorough rhythm. She had his cock in such a tight hold he was already about to go off. "I want to hear you come," he whispered.

She exhaled unsteadily. "Keep doing what...oh God!"

In response he thrust harder, done with slow and steady. She met every drive, shifting restlessly with each stroke. He reached down and rubbed his thumb over her clit.

"Oh, Connor," she shouted. Then, "*Ohhhhh,* Connor!"

Never, he thought. He'd never get tired of feeling her unravel. Of hearing her pleasure as she rode the waves of an orgasm. His body went taut; his heart hammered. Heat burned through him. He cradled her against him, her slickness so unbelievably sweet that he couldn't hang on a second longer. With a low groan, he spilled himself inside her.

Oh, shit.

She let go of her dress and leaned her head back onto his shoulder once he'd stilled. "That was..."

Amazing.

"Amazing."

What this woman did to him had him losing his mind. He kissed the side of her head. "I was so caught up, though, that I..." He'd never in his life forgotten protection before. "I forgot a condom."

Her eyes found his. "It's okay, I'm on the pill. And I'm healthy."

"Me, too," he said in relief. He wrapped his arms tighter around her, unwilling to let her go just yet.

The Beatles sang out from the front seat breaking into their blissful silence. He'd heard the ringtone a few times now and she always took the call privately.

"Guess we'd better hit the road." He gently pulled out of her. They only had one more scheduled stop on the route before they reached Oklahoma City tomorrow.

"Probably a good idea."

They fixed their clothes and crawled into the front seat. Before Connor turned the key in the ignition, Charlie leaned over and took his face in her hands. Her lips met his in a tender kiss that whipped his heart into frenzy again. Only this time the wild excitement had more to do with emotions than lust. She let go, gave a contented sigh, and put her seat belt on.

When they reached the main road, her cell rang the familiar tune again.

"You're not going to answer it?" he asked.

"I'll just text a reply that I'll call back later." She pulled the phone out of her bag.

"So how did a girl who wants to write children's books end up working for an online outdoor magazine run by a dishonest prick?"

She flinched at his question, and he regretted asking it. He hadn't meant to sound condescending.

"Sorry. It just doesn't make sense to me. You're smart,

personable, easygoing, and Thomas Beckett is a relentless ass who refuses to admit when he's wrong. Why not work for a children's publication like *Highlights*?" His sisters all subscribed to the magazine and he'd had to read it cover to cover with his oldest niece.

Charlie let the phone sit in her lap and looked out the passenger window.

"Hey," he put his hand on the back of her neck, "Ashley Morgan, queen of talking cannot clam up on me now."

Slowly, she rolled her head so he could look her in the eye. She blinked as he pulled his arm back. The high they'd just shared a few minutes ago had vanished, her gaze flat.

Something he'd said had definitely struck the wrong note.

"A shley Morgan's not..." *My real name.*
She needed to blurt the truth out right this very instant, but she couldn't get her voice to cooperate. The back of her throat itched. Her stomach cramped. Ashamed for waiting so long to tell him, especially given everything they'd shared the past several days, she worried he wouldn't forgive her little fib.

"Not...?" he prodded.

"In a talkative mood for a change." This was so stupid. *Just tell him!* But she knew in her gut that if he found out she'd lied to him, he'd immediately end things both personally and professionally. *Thomas Beckett is a relentless ass...*

So she chose the selfish route and chewed the inside of her cheek rather than come clean. He'd been nothing but honest with her, sharing more than what she needed for the story. Stuff about his family, his adventures, his plans. And even though a name was a little thing, the more time that passed, the more significant it seemed. Because, she realized, Connor didn't do anything lightly.

What would he think when she told him she'd taken Ashley's place? That her friend was the star reporter and she was just a stand-in? What would he think when he discovered who her father was?

She wanted Connor to like her. She wanted him to *really* like her because she was falling for him. And with only twenty-four hours left until their time together ended, she wanted to enjoy them. The thought of never seeing him again made her heart pinch in the worst kind of way.

"Must be the awesome outdoor sex," he said, giving her a wink.

The adorable and sexy tone of his voice screamed for her selfish self to get her lie off her chest.

"Must be. And, uh, I've got a little confession to make. I'm not..." *Tell him the truth!* She swallowed her guilt and cleared her throat. "To answer your question, I sort of fell into the job." *By birth.*

Later. She'd tell him later—tomorrow when the interview officially ended.

"I take it your father approves?"

"He does," she managed to get out. This assignment meant proving she had what it took to be a good reporter. And if she could convince her dad of that, she could convince him about other things, too. Mainly that she'd succeed in doing what she loved if given the chance.

"Has he seen your drawings?"

She squirmed in her seat. "He hasn't actually. Has your dad seen any of the monuments you've worked on?"

Connor cut her a quick glance that lasted all of two seconds, but made her feel like crap for sounding so defensive and throwing an undeserved question back at him.

"I think that's my cue to change the subject. You hungry?"

"I'm always hungry."

"Yeah, I kind of noticed that." He reached over, opened the glove box, and pulled out a Violet Crumble. "To tie you over."

"No way. These are my favorite." She accepted the candy bar and ripped right into the purple wrapper. "And I don't eat them nearly enough given they're hard to find. *Mmm.* Whoever invented honeycomb was a genius."

"It's the way it shatters that matters."

"You did not just slogan me."

"I did." He grinned and she seriously thought she could stare at that face of his for eternity. "My buddy's dad came up with it. Plus it's written on the wrapper."

"Wanna bite?" She extended her arm.

He wrapped his hand around hers and took one. "Thanks."

"I don't give bites to just anyone." She settled back in her seat, the chocolate and morning sunshine that spilled into the car drawing her own smile while she chewed.

"You saying I'm special, Goldilocks?"

She whipped her head to the side. "What did you just call me?"

His mouth made an *O* and his eyes cinched shut for a second. "Goldilocks?" He asked, as if posing it as a question would make it okay.

It totally did. Besides "Charlie," no one had ever given

her another nickname and her parents rarely used any term of endearment.

"And how long have you been thinking of me as Goldilocks?"

"Since we met at the pool."

"So before you knew my name?" She handed him the last bite of chocolate goodness.

He waved off the offer. "Before we even spoke."

Her insides did a few cartwheels. He'd been checking her out while she slept on the lounge chair. And the fact that he had a "name" for her that had nothing to do with Ashley Morgan made her feel better about her lie. In his mind she *was* Charlie.

"I guess this means I'm special too." The last bit of honeycomb slid down her throat. A delicious fullness stole over her that wasn't entirely due to the chocolate.

"Let's just say I haven't nicknamed any of my other... friends."

They merged onto the main highway, a black-and-white Route 66 sign catching the corner of her eye as they sped by it.

"Is that what we are? Friends?" The twirls low in her belly slowed, a twinge of disappointment settling there. He didn't owe her more than that. She'd gotten physical with him because he made her feel safe. Treasured. Two things missing from the brief relationships she'd had lately. And two things, she realized, Connor might give without thought given his occupation. Protection was what he did.

"We are." He picked up her hand and laced their fingers. "I don't have a lot of close friends. People I trust."

Her stomach turned into the pit of doom. *Tell him the*

truth. Now.

"I had my doubts about doing this interview, but maybe not *all* reporters for Natural World deserve to be hung upside down over a pit of poisonous snakes."

A shiver reached all the way down to his fingertips. She instinctively squeezed his hand. "Are you afraid of snakes?"

"Define afraid."

Charlie held back the girlish simper threatening to expose how cute she thought he was. Connor exuded confidence and authority and don't-mess-with-me charm. So the thought of him frightened by a long, limbless reptile made him even more irresistible. "You feel the same about snakes that I feel about ghosts?"

"The next time you see a ghost are you running in the opposite direction as fast as you can?" he asked candidly.

"Oh yeah."

"Then we feel the same way."

"My own Indiana Jones," spilled from her mouth before she could stop it. "I mean, just like Indiana Jones. Which really isn't too far off, given what you do. Have you had to perform this run and hide very often?"

"It's been a while." He glanced down at their hands, still entwined.

"I guess you haven't watched *Snakes On A Plane*?" She bit her bottom lip to keep from cracking herself up.

"Well, would you look at that." He nodded to something up ahead, ignoring her.

She noted the billboard and then brought his hand to her mouth and kissed his knuckle. "That is *so* where we're eating."

His fathomless dark gray eyes sparkled. "It's always

something with you."

"A good something," she said, happy he held onto her hand as he exited the freeway.

Five minutes later they sat side by side in a booth at the Slippery Snake Diner and she couldn't stop giggling. On the back of the menu were snake jokes. "What is the best thing about deadly snakes?" she asked.

Connor smiled at the waitress dropping off their drinks. "Thanks," he said and the poor enamored woman almost spilled his orange juice right into his lap before spinning around and rushing back toward the kitchen.

"They've got poisonality," Charlie said.

He rested his arm along the back of the booth without so much as cracking a smile, but did play with a strand of her hair. "Okay, Joke Girl, one more."

She scanned the listing. "Why did the two boa constrictors get married?"

"Because they had a crush on each other."

"You peeked!" She elbowed him in the side.

He gave a one-shoulder shrug. "Not too hard to figure out."

"Or you peeked."

"There are much better things for me to peek at." He stuck out his chin and angled for a glimpse down her dress.

Not one to deny this particular Peeping Tom, she pressed her arms against her sides to increase the cleavage. He groaned in her ear and said, "We might have to find another field."

She scooted closer to his warm, inviting body. "Won't that make you late to the bridge?" Abandoned for decades, he'd told her about the vintage covered bridge almost ready to carry travelers again.

"Some things are worth being late for."

Her toes curled at the sound of his quiet, flirtatious voice. And her heart skipped a beat at his answer.

When was the last time someone had put her first?

Never.

Chapter Nine

"My dad knows?" Charlie put the lid down on the toilet seat and sat on the cold, hard surface. Elbow on knee, forehead in the palm of her hand, she barely noticed the opulent bathroom in the suite at the Four Seasons.

"I'm sorry," Ashley said into the phone. "I popped into the office for one quick minute *after business hours* and he caught me at my desk. Scared the life out of me. Your father moves like a ninja."

"He's furious."

She heard Ash take a breath before answering. "Yes, but I calmed him down."

"Not according to the numerous missed calls and texts I've received in the last hour demanding I get in touch with him. What am I going to say to make this okay?"

"Wait until you get home, when the story's done, so he can see the pride on your face. William Malloy, the head honcho at World Heritage Fund called your dad yesterday to say how pleased Connor Gibson was with the interview and that the reporter knew her stuff."

"My dad thought he was talking about *you.*"

"Yes, but as soon as I explained what happened, he got very quiet and sort of introspective. It was rather nice."

Charlie closed her eyes. "That's the look he gives when he's madder than hell and deciding what punishment to dish out."

"Oh. Damn. Still, he's got to give you credit for what you've done, and if he's too blind to see it, then you should—"

"Quit."

"I was going to say tell him to take you more seriously."

"Did he even ask how you were?"

"He…" Charlie pictured Ash pacing around their townhouse in thought. "He did not."

"That's shitty. You're one of his reporters not to mention my best friend."

"Your dad has never been the sentimental type. I didn't take offense."

Charlie dragged in a breath. "I do. He's selfish and it makes me so mad. I'm done, Ash. I'm tired of trying to please him. This week *has* been incredible. I proved to myself I could do this, but more importantly I discovered that my dreams are worth pursuing."

"I'm glad you finally see that." Quiet filled the phone line for a few seconds. "Did they put something special in the Route 66 water because you've got gumption, girl. Well, more than normal."

Not in the water, in her life. She'd shown Connor more of her drawings, shared her dreams, and he'd said he believed in her.

"Let's hope it sees me through telling Connor the truth."

"How is Mr. Hottie Environmentalist? I finally googled him and I may have licked my computer screen."

Charlie laughed, happy to lighten the conversation. "You really are feeling better." She stood and stretched her legs. A long soak in the whirlpool tub would fix her achy muscles.

"How can I not be when my mom is plying me with chicken noodle soup and babying me like I'm six years old. Did I tell you she bought me one of those activity books that has connect the dots and mazes in it?"

"No."

"There's a Disney princess on the cover," Ashley dead-panned.

"Oh, which one?"

"I. Don't. Know. But thank God you'll be home tomorrow."

Charlie glanced in the mirror and smiled at the ice-cream stain on her dress. She'd wanted a bite from Connor's spoon and caught him by surprise when grabbing his hand. They'd gotten into a mini food fight after that, fingers, mouths, and noses all part of the action until the very serious shop owner cleared his throat and raised his thick eyebrows.

"I'll pick you up from the airport and we'll go Dumpster diving for dinner."

"Sounds good."

"Charlize Beckett!" Ash shouted.

"Ow." She put some space between her ear and the phone. "What are you yelling about?"

"You zoned out on me."

Charlie turned and leaned against the marble vanity. "For a second," she relented. "I'm sorry."

"You've fallen for him, haven't you?" *Ding dong.* "Dammit, the doorbell just rang. Which means my mom is here with more soup. I'm going to drown in my sleep from all this liquid."

"Hang in there, and I'll bake you some banana bread tomorrow night."

"This conversation isn't over. Please call me later if you need to talk about Connor."

"I will. Thanks, Ash. Bye."

"Banana bread!" Ashley shouted before hanging up.

If only all the world's problems could be solved with a loaf of baked bread. Charlie opened the bathroom door and walked into the living area. "Hey."

"Hey. Everything okay?" Connor rose from the couch. His feet were bare, his hair in sexy disarray. The gleaming crystal chandelier above his head cast a soft glow as the sun set outside the floor-to-ceiling window behind him.

"Yeah." She slipped out of her shoes and padded over to the sofa across from him.

"Liar." He sat back down, a knowing glint in those too beautiful eyes. He'd heard her phone ring and texts sound numerous times in the car. "Get over here."

"Sorry?"

"Get that cute ass of yours over here." He patted the spot beside him.

Without thought—she was so tired of thinking—she plopped her butt next to his. "I should tell you—"

He shifted so his hands were on her shoulders, his thumbs pressing into her tension spots. "How about I work out some of this stress for you?"

Her head fell forward. "If you must."

He rubbed and kneaded, and her neck and upper back rejoiced. Relaxed. If he even thought about stopping, she'd have to…do something. She couldn't come up with anything at the moment. Not when even the muscles in her head went slack.

"You know, this hotel really wasn't necessary," she murmured. "I'm happy to stay anywhere with you."

"I know. That's what makes it even better."

The suite was gorgeous with its hardwood floors, mahogany furnishings, and botanical art. There was also a work area, a dining room, and a full kitchen. "Connor, there's something I need to tell—ooohhh that feels good right there." His hands massaged a little lower. She'd be a puddle on the floor after this.

"Back rubs don't work if your mind is racing. Relax. Tell me later."

She stayed quiet for a minute. "Thanks for calling your boss and mentioning me."

"Doing a little undercover work, huh?" He kissed the side of her neck. "Bill knew about my hesitation and I wanted to let him know what a great week it's been."

"It's been incredible. Your passion for your work is inspiring. And seeing what you've done, I can only imagine the amazing sites all around the world that are restored because of you."

"Thanks for helping me slow down to enjoy it more," he whispered and she inwardly smiled, happy that the guy she'd gotten into a car with five days ago had changed some, too.

His hands continued to work their magic as the last beam of sunlight disappeared. Tranquility and warmth filled the room. Everything between them felt so natural. Effortless

and dare she think, *right*. Fun, too, when he dropped his
guard. Had he ever let his defenses down before? She imagined he had to be wary of women because of his name and
money. To a certain extent, she knew the feeling. And she
understood his desire for independence.

"Let's grab something to eat," he said.

"Does that mean this massage is coming to an end?" she
teased.

"Just an intermission." His hands slipped around her
sides to her belly and he brought her flush against him, his
chin on her shoulder. "I can think of a few other places I'd
like to massage later."

She turned her head so her lips grazed his jaw. "Okay,
then. But no way should we leave this room and that kitchen.
Think it's stocked?"

"You like to cook?" He nuzzled the spot behind her ear
that tickled and tingled if he so much as breathed on it.

"I like to bake. I've had a few incidences when trying
to cook." She really didn't want to move out of his arms,
but his stomach grumbled. "I think together we can manage
something. Come on."

He followed on her heels and she felt a rush of power
from her head to her toes. Mr. Control seemed to slip when
she put a little extra swish in her walk.

Charlie opened the fridge. Too stunned to say anything,
she stared.

"I called ahead just in case," Connor said, nudging her
out of the way. "We've got baked herb-crusted chicken,
roasted potatoes, asparagus, strawberries and," he winked,
"a little something for dessert."

She sighed and watched him turn on the oven and put

the chicken and potatoes in. He uncovered the glass dish with the asparagus and pinched one stalk with his fingers. "I think we eat this cold," he said. Then he moved around the room and pulled out plates, utensils, and napkins. "You gonna stay quiet the rest of the night, Goldilocks?"

The little something for dessert had her mind in a tizzy. At least a dozen Violet Crumbles were stacked inside the refrigerator. Staying quiet seemed like a good idea since she was having a hard time processing this latest gesture. And when her thoughts got jumbled, well, she often blurted out the wrong thing.

Things like *I love you*. Which was ridiculous. She liked Connor. A lot. But love? She'd gushed those three little words twice before and both times had been a huge error in judgment. She thought if she said it first, she'd hear it back. Wrong.

She stepped between his legs and gently laid her hands on either side of his neck. In his eyes she saw compassion and generosity. And maybe...maybe something more, but she didn't want to be wrong about it so pushed it away. She pressed a soft kiss to his forehead. Kissed his eyelid when he blinked. Found his cheek next, then his jaw, his earlobe. With each tender touch, his breathing slowed.

When her mouth met the corner of his, he wrapped his arms around her waist and eliminated any space between them. "Let's have dessert first," she whispered.

He angled his head to capture her kiss full on. "You got it."

They kissed and kissed and kissed some more. His tongue curled around hers, each swipe light, sensual, like they had all the time in the world.

"Take a seat," he said when she ended the kiss. "And watch and learn."

"You have a special way of unwrapping a candy bar?" She hopped up onto the counter, her legs dangling so she could drum the fancy wood drawers with her heels.

"Dessert is a little more than that." He found a cutting board, grabbed two Violet Crumbles, the strawberries, and—oh dear Lord—a container of vanilla ice cream from the freezer. "Tell me about your kitchen disasters."

"Um, let's see. There was the time I blew up a pot of instant mashed potatoes all over the stove. And the time when I made baked potatoes, and they came out so perfect, looking crispy and a little burned on the outside. But the rest of dinner wasn't ready so I put them on the counter and covered them with a dishtowel to keep them warm. The towel got a little too close to the candle I had burning and it caught on fire. I dumped water over it, but the cabinet above was charred and my potatoes were ruined."

Connor chuckled. "Sounds like you should stay away from potatoes." He looked up from the cutting board where he'd chopped up the candy bars and now sliced the strawberries. "Keep that sweet body of yours right where it is."

"Yes, sir." Her cheeks grew ridiculously warm.

"Any other foods I should save from you?"

She stuck her tongue out at him.

"Save that for later. So?"

"Eggs. Well, don't ask me to hard boil them." She let out a sigh remembering what a disaster her attempt at egg salad had been. "I'd never made them before and followed my roommate's instructions of bringing the pan of eggs to a boil and then turning down the temp to low for a few minutes.

Then I went back to my room to finish a story. Only I didn't remember the eggs. About a half hour later I heard what sounded like gunfire and freaked. But because I'd like to think I could be kick-ass, I ran down the hall to the kitchen. Luckily, I only found that the pot had boiled dry. The buildup of heat had popped the eggshells and rocketed them across the room."

Connor threw his head back and laughed.

God, he took handsome to a new level when he found something funny. And his contagious laugh filled a room like the happiest melody. She cracked up right along with him. "Our kitchen smelled like rotten eggs for days."

He finished scooping the ice cream into bowls and topping them with the honeycomb pieces and sliced strawberries. "Live and learn, right?" His shirt stretched across his back as he reached into the fridge. She gave a quiet sigh of appreciation.

And a sigh of bliss when he pulled out chocolate syrup and poured it over the ice-cream creations. He handed a bowl and spoon to her, grabbed his, and joined her atop the counter. Their legs brushed. The backs of her knees tickled in the best possible way.

Nothing had prepared her for such a perfect moment.

She dug into the dessert. The cold, sweet goodness filled her mouth, slid down her throat. A tiny, but drawn out "mmm" followed.

"I'll take that as approval," Connor said.

"It's *o-kay*," Charlie teased.

"Here." He took a spoonful from his bowl and fed it to her. "I kept the outstanding one for myself." One corner of his mouth lifted.

He watched her as she ate the bite. He'd done that a lot this week—paid her quiet attention.

"You're right, you meanie! Yours is sick. Gimme." She smirked and traded bowls with him, loving the look of amusement on his face at her goading.

He slid off the counter, put his bowl to the side, and settled between her legs. "To get the full outstanding effect I need to feed it to you."

She handed him her bowl, spread her legs a little wider, and draped her arms around his neck. "But won't yours melt?"

"We'll get to it next." He slipped a bite between her lips.

A shiver that had nothing to do with the ice cream and everything to do with Connor stole its way down her spine.

"If you weren't in heritage protection, what would you be?" she asked. Her fingers played with the soft hair that lightly brushed his shirt collar.

"An architect," he said without hesitating. He fed her another spoonful, his gaze on her mouth. "I'd work on the world's tallest buildings."

"What swayed you?" Her lips parted when he used the pad of his thumb to wipe the corner of her mouth.

"An environmental studies professor I had in college." He took a huge bite from the bowl.

"Hey, mister." She swiped at his hand and the spoon clinked his teeth. "No bites allowed."

He put the bowl down. "Really? None? Not even here?" He leaned in and nibbled her earlobe.

"Maybe there."

"What about here?" Lovely vibrations danced across her skin as his mouth hopped to the curve of her neck and then down to her shoulder. He sank his teeth in with just the right amount of pressure. She squirmed.

"There is okay, too."

"Do you have another assignment waiting when you get back to LA?" he asked out of the blue. He dropped a kiss to her collarbone and then lifted his head to pierce her with intense dark eyes.

"Umm…" Did she? She didn't think so. But even if she did, she didn't want to work for her father anymore. "No. I don't believe I do."

"Then stay with me another week, Goldilocks."

Chapter Ten

When Charlie mentioned a blindfold, Connor had imagined things going a little different than this. They'd had an amazing time together the past five days, talking for hours, laughing, getting sideways every chance they got. He'd liked Charlie, the reporter, a lot more than he thought he would. But Charlie not in reporter mode took his breath away. Now, the last night before they arrived at McCall and Lucy's house, he'd hoped to spend it getting a naked workout with her.

Instead, she'd put him in the car and taken the one silk tie he'd brought to wear to the rehearsal dinner and covered his eyes. *No peeking*, she'd whispered, and he'd obliged for the fifteen-minute car ride. *And relax,* she added.

That proved to be more difficult. Having her drive when he could see was one thing. Trusting her when he couldn't, quite another. He hated feeling vulnerable. But the second she'd taken his hand, everything inside him calmed down. He'd agreed to be blindfolded because he did trust Goldilocks.

His last visual had been mountains bumpy and scarlet against the ruddy Colorado sunset.

He had no idea where they'd arrived, only that they were outside and her hurried pace and firm grip on his hand meant they were late for something. Since he couldn't see anything, he kept picturing Charlie's smooth bare skin all laid out for him to feast on. He couldn't get enough of her.

He'd definitely face an inquisition during the wedding festivities. McCall and Lucy hadn't minded the last-minute request to bring a date, but Connor sensed that was because they were more curious than put out.

And no doubt Clay had filled them in on his sexy reporter since arriving several days earlier. Texts with only five words—*ready for my car delivery*—had been coming from Clay daily. To Connor's surprise, he didn't mind paying up.

He tripped over a bump in the concrete. "Hey, Speed Demon, slow it down."

"Sorry. It's just I'm a little lost and we're already late. I should have parked at the other end of the mall. I think."

Connor chuckled. She'd gone the wrong way on a stretch of highway in Kansas when he'd let her drive so he could rest. She'd also managed to get lost on a quick trip by herself to a convenience store a mile from their hotel. By foot would have been faster, but she'd finally made it back.

His beautiful girl had zero sense of direction.

His girl.

"I could take off this blindfold and help—"

She stopped. "Don't you dare." With a hand on his cheek, she kissed him softly on the mouth. "I want this to be a surprise."

"Okay. Lead the way." He suspected this was her way of thanking him for the fancy hotels and dinners and hot-air ballooning. Her appreciation and down-to-earth personality had made it easy to spoil her.

The *mall* had to be closed, given the late hour and the quiet as they speed-walked, so whatever she had in store for him included privacy.

Maybe the blindfold wasn't such a bad idea after all.

"There it is," she said, a little out of breath and her grip on his hand tightening. She ushered him into a store and held him in place just inside the door.

"Charlie?" a man asked.

"Yes. I'm so sorry we're late. Thanks for waiting. Okay…" She took Connor's hands in hers. Her soft voice told him she stood close enough to lean in and touch noses. "You ready to build that skyscraper?"

He frowned. She giggled, then untied the blindfold. He couldn't stop the gigantic smile from taking hold as he scanned the Lego store and immediately spiraled back to his childhood. "I'm here to build," he said, excitement in his voice.

"Yep." Goldilocks grinned. "This is Ted." She thumbed over her shoulder. "He's going to get you started."

Connor lifted Charlie into the air and squeezed her tight. "This is unbelievable. Thank you." He loosened his hold so her soft curves slid down his body. It took effort to release her—he wanted to *show* his appreciation. Roam his hands over every sinuous slope and then push into her until she unraveled in his arms. Instead, he kissed her cheek. "How'd you pull this off?"

She shrugged and pursed her lips like she had a secret

and no intention of sharing it. "Maybe I know a few people in high places. All that matters is that you get to build the tallest building this shop has ever seen. Well, at least as tall as you can get in the next four hours."

"You're building with me." He stepped around her. "Come on, Goldilocks, we've got work to do."

Ted started them out with a base about five feet high and placed bins full of Lego pieces at their fingertips. What he thankfully didn't offer was guidance, which meant this baby belonged to Connor.

Charlie followed his lead and instructions using gentle hands, worried, he guessed, that she'd knock over the growing tower.

"You never watched *Scooby-Doo*?" she asked incredulously, continuing the discussion on their childhoods. "I thought that was like the number one cartoon for boys." She turned and accepted a step stool from Ted, their building rising above her head now. Connor watched as she placed the stool close to the base, moved it back, then inched it a tiny bit closer, so it sat in just the right spot.

"Unfortunately my sisters monopolized the TV, which was how I got started with Legos. And when I wasn't doing that, I wanted to be outside."

Her arm brushed his as they both reached toward the same spot. They'd accidentally touched numerous times and he'd thought he'd gotten over the heady sensations the light sweep with her skin created, but nope.

He wanted her. Right here in this store.

"You probably camped a lot as a kid." She pulled her hand back to let him place his brick, but he saw her lips twitch. She knew exactly what she did to him with all these seemingly innocent touches.

"A few times. But we didn't exactly rough it. Big cabin. Boat on the lake. But we were all together and my parents did everything with us. Fishing. Hiking. Swimming." He chuckled to himself.

"What?" Charlie asked.

"I put a fish in my sister Mary's bed once. She didn't speak to me the rest of the trip. It was great."

Charlie tilted her head and looked at him. Her full lips puckered and attraction darkened her blue eyes. "You are a bad boy, Connor Gibson."

He dropped the Lego in his hand. His body hardened. "I'm about to be really bad."

She raised her eyebrows as if in challenge. Oh yeah, he most definitely planned to play dirty now.

In his periphery, he noticed Ted walk out with another step stool. "Ted," Connor said, his gaze colliding with Charlie's in a contest of desire. "You need to run down some coffee for me and Charlie."

"I can't leave—"

"You can," Connor interrupted. "Here, take my car." He pulled the key out of his pocket and tossed it over.

"Um, uh…"

Charlie broke eye contact to look at Ted. "It's parked on the other side of the mall. White convertible Audi. Thanks, Ted." She smiled and Teddy boy was toast.

"Don't rush back," Connor said.

"O-okay. I won't be too long." He hurried toward the glass door.

"Ted." Connor's firm tone stopped the guy. He looked back. "Take your time." Ted nodded and left the store. The *click* of the lock sliding into place echoed off the walls.

"So, bad boy, whatcha wanna do?" Charlie hopped off the step stool and twirled a piece of her shiny blond hair around her finger.

"You." He trapped her in his arms and captured her mouth in a hungry kiss.

Her hands fisted the back of his shirt as she kissed him back and he nudged her with crooked steps until her back hit the wall. Their mouths stayed locked while they worked on getting each other naked. Fingers searching, bodies pressing closer, they broke apart to pull off each other's pants and shirts. Her bra hit the floor a flash later.

Connor dropped to his knees and tugged down the scrap of leopard-print material between her legs. Her palms slapped the wall when he kissed his way up her satin skin, pausing to latch onto her nipple. He licked and sucked until she cupped his face and lifted him up. Their eyes locked, and he thrust inside her.

He lifted her leg over his arm and cupped her ass. Her hands moved to his shoulders to keep herself steady as he took her hard and fast. He'd had her against a wall before, but this moment felt different. His control had completely slipped. And she liked it, her breaths coming out quick and shallow, her nails digging into his skin.

"Come with me." He knew she was almost there, her muscles squeezing his cock so tightly he groaned, getting close to climax himself.

One sexy moan, then another fell from her lips. He rotated his hips a little and moved inside her until she strained against him and together they gasped their way to completion.

He touched his forehead to hers, awash with feelings so strong they could only mean one thing. No woman had ever stolen his heart, not like this. He wanted to hold her hand, talk about nothing, kiss her sweet lips…every single day.

He loved her.

Charlie wore the pale blue dress she'd bought this morning at a little shop off the main highway. Connor said he loved the way it looked on her, and he especially liked the way it made her eyes the prettiest blue he'd ever seen. Heavenly Blue he'd named the color.

She'd overheard her last boyfriend tell his friend her eyes were green.

Was that what Connor was now? Her boyfriend?

As they walked up to his friends' front door, he held her hand like that's what he was. And the invitation to bring her to McCall and Lucy's wedding meant more than a casual thing, right?

Trees surrounded the beautiful two-story French Colonial style house, and rolling green hills peeked above the roofline. The wraparound porch had a swing and standing birdhouse with rustic metal accents.

This wasn't just a house. It was a home.

Charlie ran her free hand down the side of her dress. In a minute she'd walk through the door and meet Connor's closest friends. She prayed they didn't see the big L stamped on her forehead.

LIAR.

Could Connor hear the pounding of her heart? She

willed the overactive thing to slow the heck down.

Stay with me another week, Goldilocks. Hearing the name he alone called her, she'd somehow justified keeping her real name to herself. She melted every time he said it, warmth and need flooding her bloodstream. With each passing day, it grew harder and harder to tell him the truth. And after she'd emailed Ash to cancel her flight home, she'd sort of forgotten all about the little omission.

Until two days ago, when Connor had spoken with his mom and found out lawyers were involved in her dispute with NW. Since Natural World refused to print a retraction, Sandra Swanson had decided to sue the magazine. Sue her father.

If she really wanted something with Connor, she had to tell him the truth.

He pulled her to a stop before they took the steps up to the porch. "There's something I need to tell you," he said, crashing into her thoughts with the exact words she should be saying.

"What?"

"It's not a big deal, but Clay will no doubt bring it up, so I wanted you to hear it from me first." He noted her frown and gave her a quick kiss. "It's nothing to take personally. Although, I guess the best way to take it would be as a compliment."

"Spit it out already."

"Last month Clay and I made a bet about which one of us would get involved with a woman first. Loser pays up."

"By loser you mean the one with a naked woman in his bed?"

The mischievous smile that bloomed across his face started a riot of quivers that spread over every inch of her skin.

"Well, when you put it that way it sounds like I'm the winner." He gently moved the hair off her shoulder.

"Of course you are," she teased, trying to ignore the way his touch swept so much pleasure over her, she almost threw herself at him. She needed to keep her cool. She didn't want his friends to see how much she…

Loved him.

She loved Connor.

"I am quite the prize," she continued, blanking her expression as best she could. She loved him. Loved how he made her feel safe. How he believed she could be anything she wanted to be. Loved how they laughed together and how he listened to her talk even when she knew he wished for some quiet.

"You are that," he agreed.

"In fact, I've even been on the auction block." She gave a small smile, remembering how ludicrous the whole thing was. "My sorority did one of the those Win A Date fundraisers and you're looking at Delta Gamma's most expensive date." Connor raised his brows. "Fifteen hundred dollars. It was crazy. How much do you owe Clay?"

"I owe him a Porsche Spyder."

She choked.

"Price tag one million."

And then she was pretty sure her eyes bugged out of her head.

"I should clarify we were drunk when the bet took place."

The last bet Charlie had made was for a dollar. Not that she couldn't afford more, but Connor still didn't know that. "You do realize there are plenty of charities that could benefit from that kind of money?"

"I do, and I give. Generously." A hint of annoyance crept into his voice.

"I didn't mean—"

He pressed a finger to her lips. "What did this date get for fifteen hundred dollars?"

Jealousy edged out the annoyance and delight perked up the corners of her mouth. "Dinner and a movie."

"One-time deal?"

"Oh no. We did it ten times. No wait." She angled her head in mock thought. "More like fifteen or twenty. The guy was hot and I couldn't wait to get him off"—anger didn't just simmer in Connor's narrowed eyes, it boiled over, his mouth a grim line. "—my back!" She burst out laughing.

Connor's expression relaxed and then his hands were all over her, attacking all her ticklish spots. "You're going to pay for that," he teased.

She struggled against him, giggling and loving his attention—until the front door swung open.

They abruptly parted like two kids who'd just been caught going at it under the high school bleachers.

"Hey, Lucy." Connor jumped up the steps and greeted his friend with a hug. "We're here."

"I can see that," she said. "Heard it, too. Well, Clay did. The guy runs security no matter where he is." Lucy poked her head around Connor's shoulder. "You must be Charlie. Hi."

He'd told his friends her name was Charlie. The knot of tension between her shoulder blades eased slightly. "Hi." She stepped to Connor's side. "It's nice to meet you."

"Gibson, you got my car with you?" Clay said, coming up behind Lucy.

Connor put his arm around Charlie's waist and tugged her close. "You drove it last. Where did you say you left it, sweetheart?"

Lucy shook her head. "Do I even want to know what that's about? Come on in."

Charlie let out a nervous breath as they followed Lucy inside. The butterflies in her stomach lasted all of five minutes, though, because the small group gathered for lunch made her feel comfortable right away.

Clay sat to her left, Connor to her right, at a large round table on the backyard deck. Stuck between the two was like sitting in the middle of a who-can-be-more-charming duel. She knew Clay paid her attention just to get Connor's goat, but Connor's touches and kisses to her neck and shoulder felt like more than possessiveness. He couldn't seem to help himself.

McCall had drawing power down, too, but his consideration remained solely on Lucy. Put these three handsome environmentalists on the cover of a magazine and women would be all over heritage protection. Keats McCall had been president of field operations for WHF before handing the job over to Connor when he got engaged to Lucy last fall. McCall and Connor had traveled to a ton of interesting places on behalf of heritage protection, including the tiny village on the Bandiagara Cliffs in West Africa that McCall was teasing him about. "I'm telling you," McCall continued. "The tribal woman wanted to keep Connor as her personal diviner, his chanting was that good. Did I mention the diviners wore nothing but—"

"That's enough," Connor broke in and a blush spread across his face.

Cutest thing ever. For the first time, Charlie enjoyed listening more than she did talking.

Lucy stood and reached to pick up a plate, but McCall grabbed her around the waist and tugged her into his lap. "Leave it. I'll clean up later." He nuzzled her neck and a smile bloomed across her face.

"How did you two meet?" Charlie asked.

"Fate," Owen said from across the table. Owen McCallister was like a father to Lucy—the only family she had, Charlie had learned. And he looked at Lucy with such pride and affection it made Charlie's heart hurt a little.

Clay made a coughing sound like it was a lot more than fate. Lucy glared at him with a playful smirk.

"This gorgeous woman and I met at one of my sites."

"Actually we met on a boat." She wrapped her arms around his neck.

"Minor detail," McCall said.

"McCall likes to forget about it because Lucy lied to him and then made him look like a fool," Connor said good-naturedly.

"And then I kept lying to keep him away, but he didn't go for it." Lucy locked eyes on her fiancé. "I'm so very glad you didn't let me go."

McCall touched his forehead to Lucy's. "I didn't know I could love someone as much as I love you."

Charlie dropped her gaze to the wood deck, overcome with emotion and worried that if she looked at Connor, he'd see *everything*. Her love. Her lie.

Her hope.

If things had worked out between Lucy and McCall, maybe they'd work out for her and Connor, too.

Chapter Eleven

All eyes were on McCall and Lucy as they stood in front of the man-made waterfall on the second-floor terrace of the rustic lodge and exchanged vows. Connor had worn the monkey suit three other times over the past ten years, standing proud and happy for his sisters as they married the men they loved.

This was the first time he'd stood beside a friend, and he'd never seen McCall happier. The guy beamed. Lucy glowed. Connor knew love wasn't palpable, but some deep-rooted emotion sure as hell floated in the air like steam.

He swallowed and stole a glance at Charlie sitting among the guests. She took his breath away. Her sleeveless pink dress showed off her classic beauty. Soft blond waves fell down her back, and she wore only a touch of makeup. God, he loved her genuineness.

The past two days she'd proven to be something else, falling into easy camaraderie with the friends and family gathered in celebration. Connor owed Lucy big-time for including Charlie in all the girl stuff, and Charlie had especially bonded with Samantha. Sam and Dean Malloy had arrived yesterday morning. Dean was one of the best-known and well-liked heritage preservationists in the world, having left WHF to start his own company. Connor had admired the guy since his first day on the job at WHF and now Dean's team was partnered with WHF on the Route 66 project.

Charlie's gaze met his—her eyes bright and full of so much emotion his stance faltered. He'd never wanted to make someone his as much as he did Charlie. Never felt this primal desire to possess someone, body and soul.

They needed to figure things out before tomorrow when he had to hightail it back to Idaho and WHF's main office before he jumped on a plane for Peru.

Clay subtly elbowed him and whispered, "You'd better let me do a background check."

His friend's words cut through his preoccupation.

"You're not serious," Connor whispered back.

"Of course I am. You've known her for two weeks and fallen hard."

Connor cut him a brief glance.

"Everyone can see it, not just me." Clay's eyes stayed on McCall and Lucy as he quietly spoke. "Let me check her out."

"She's not after my money."

Clay stayed quiet. Connor's gaze drifted to Charlie again. She'd been watching him, her brows furrowed like she wondered what had been so important that he and Clay had to talk during the ceremony.

He flashed her a smile, hoping to erase the strain on her

beautiful face. It worked. Or maybe it was the declaration of Mr. and Mrs. that the preacher called out.

Applause sounded and the hundred or so guests rose to their feet to watch the bride and groom and wedding party march down the aisle.

An hour or so later, after pictures had been taken and the married couple had danced their first dance, Connor searched the reception area for Charlie. He found her talking with Samantha near the open French doors that led out to the terrace. He snuck up behind her, put his hands on her waist, and kissed behind her ear. "Hey, beautiful."

One simple touch and she melted against him. "Hey."

"Mind if I steal her away for a dance?" he said to Sam.

"Not at all. I was just about to go grab Dean. I love this song."

Connor didn't recognize the music, but it was slow, the rhythm sultry, and he wanted Charlie's body pressed against his. He led her to the center of the small square wood floor and took her in his arms. They moved in perfect sync, their hips in a subtle sway.

"Have I told you how gorgeous you look?" He slid his hands from the sweet curve of her waist to the even sweeter curve of her rear end.

Her breath hitched as she leaned into him more fully. Her arms tightened around his neck. "You look pretty good yourself." Softness shone in her eyes that he hadn't noticed before.

"You okay?"

"Never better," she whispered and put her head on his shoulder.

They danced as close as two people could be on a

public dance floor, and he found himself lost in a wonderful, pleasurable bubble, Charlie the only thing that mattered in his world.

He should tell her right now that he loved her.

No, he'd take her outside where they could watch the sun set behind the mountains. He'd tell her he wanted to be the last face she saw at night and the first smile she saw in the morning.

The song transitioned into a faster-paced tune. Charlie lifted her head and turned him inside out with those incredible blue eyes of hers. He ignored the music, the people dancing with quicker steps, and cupped her chin.

Her arms relaxed and her soft, warm hands cradled his neck.

He ran his thumb along her full bottom lip.

Passion, friendship, lust, affection...love. He saw it all flicker across her face and knew his own expression mirrored the same. His lips grazed hers with the lightest of touches because if he dared take more, he wouldn't be able to stop.

"Let's go outside," he murmured. He clasped her hand and they made their way to the sundeck.

An outdoor fireplace blazed and candles in large glass hurricanes cast a glow as evening settled on the horizon. Rose petals covered the wood planks. Other couples stood arm in arm, watching the sunset.

Connor found a semiprivate spot near the railing. He hugged Charlie's back to his front and looked over her shoulder at the breathtaking landscape of forestry extending as far as the eye could see.

"These past two weeks have been amazing," Connor said.

A shiver vibrated through Charlie. "They have."

He quickly pulled off his jacket and wrapped it around her. "Here." He'd already ditched the annoying tie.

"That's really not—"

"I take care of what's mine." He secured his arms around her once again. "What I feel for you, Goldilocks, I've never felt before."

"Oh, Connor." She tried to wiggle out of his hold.

"Let me finish. You're beautiful and kind and funny and you've taught me some things about myself. I'm crazy about you. I—"

"Wait!" She put all her weight into turning around to face him. "Please." She blinked over and over again. Her breaths came out in quick pants. "Please let me tell you something I should have told you sooner."

He took a step back. His chest hurt like he'd just swallowed a Molotov cocktail. *It's nothing*, his mind told the rest of body. It couldn't be anything important.

Because he *loved* her.

Charlie took Connor's hands in hers. She stared into his fathomless slate eyes and almost cried at their lack of warmth.

"I love you," she said, and watched as something flickered back to life in his gaze. "I love you so much, but I—"

"There you are," a loud male voice said over Connor's shoulder.

He turned. "Bill," Connor said.

Two men approached, their strides confident. Charlie looked from one to the other. She didn't know who they were, but the one on the left looked a lot like an older version of Dean Malloy. Which meant "Bill" was William Malloy, Dean's father. Connor's boss. The head honcho from World Heritage Fund.

"Charlize Beckett?" the other man said.

Her heart stopped. Seriously stopped, like it had never been there in the first place. She couldn't catch a breath. Nor did she particularly want to.

The way Connor's lips twisted in confusion cut right through her.

Regret spread under her skin like thick, black sludge.

"Thought I'd track you down to meet the wonderful woman you told me about, but I'm confused." Bill Malloy looked at Connor. Looked at his companion. Looked at her. "I thought I was meeting Ashley Morgan."

"That would be me," Charlie said weakly. The mess of all messes had landed at her feet and while it would be easier for the ground to swallow her, she never shied away from her mistakes.

The mixture of tension and anger rolling off Connor killed her. But if there was one thing her father had blessed her with, it was the fortitude to never be weak in front of others.

"I'm also Charlize Beckett." She looked at the unknown man. "I'm sorry, I don't believe we've met."

"We met last year at your father's sixtieth birthday party, but I'm not surprised you don't recognize me. I've lost quite a bit of weight. Howard Davis." He extended his hand.

"Reporter for *National Geographic*." Now she caught some resemblance to the old Howard. And realized her stupidity. She should have at least considered the possibility that since WHF operated in some of the same circles as

Natural World, she might run into someone she knew.

Connor sucked in a breath like he'd just put two and two together. She looked at him out of the corner of her eye. Pain, betrayal, hostility—she saw them all.

"I apologize for the misunderstanding," she said to Mr. Malloy. "It's a long story. But rest assured Natural World's piece on Route 66 is going to garner your organization some very positive feedback. It's been a pleasure to see the work up close and I'm in awe of all that you do."

"Thank you," Bill said before he looked at Connor with concern and affection. "We'll catch up later." He and Howard gave her a polite nod and walked away.

Caught in a lie was never good. Caught in a lie that made the man she loved look foolish magnified the fib hundredfold.

She stood frozen to her spot, not sure if she should speak first or let Connor. When after a few seconds neither one of them had made a move or sound, she shifted and stared at his profile.

Jaw tight, lips flat, he didn't so much as glance her way.

"I'm sorry." She put her hand on his arm.

He jerked it away. "Not here." He took off down the deck. She followed behind, trying to keep up with his brisk pace. They took the stairs down to the lobby, took another flight of stairs up to the second floor of the lodge, and entered their suite.

She slipped Connor's jacket off her shoulders and laid it over the couch. "I'm sorry," she said again. "I'd like to explain."

He stood across the room and jammed his fingers through his hair. "Your father is Thomas fucking Beckett isn't he?"

"Yes."

"Jesus Christ." He paced around the furniture like an animal trapped in a cage.

Charlie's heart *hurt*. Every beat hurt like it was being pounded into the ground with a mallet.

"We weren't supposed to meet like this," she offered. "And I didn't plan to fall in love with you, but I did."

His pacing stopped. "Don't even go there," he said in barely contained anger. "Who is Ashley Morgan?"

"She's my best friend. She was supposed to be your reporter. At the pool, when I told you I was with someone it was her. But that night her appendix burst, so she asked me to do the story.

"I'd been trying to prove to my father I could handle more than the fluff pieces he gave me and this was my chance. I had every intention of telling you my real name when we first met in the lobby, but I couldn't bring myself to do it after I'd already made a fool of myself. It was stupid, but I can't change what I did."

"I trusted you," he ground out.

"And I didn't break that trust. I am Charlie. I am that girl. Nothing I said or did was a lie, Connor. The only thing I didn't do was tell you the truth about my given name."

He shook his head. "I don't know what to believe." With a defeated sigh, he sat on the couch across from her. Elbows on his knees, he dropped his head into his hands.

"Believe in us. *Please*."

"You could have told me numerous times." He looked up. "I told you about my family and my mom and you didn't say a word."

"I didn't know how."

"You rarely stop talking and you didn't know *how*? How about, 'This is really hard for me to say, Connor, but that lying piece of shit you hate so much is my father.' Huh, not too difficult to get out." He pressed his shoulders back, flexed his hands.

Anger percolated inside her, but she couldn't keep her posture from shrinking. Connor's rising to do battle was a war she didn't wanted to play. "I had a job to do, too. If I'd told you the truth, there's no way you would have continued the interview with me."

"You got that right." His cold tone sent goose bumps over her arms.

"So can you really blame me?"

His eyes narrowed in defiance. "I don't see anyone else in the room."

"Connor. We can figure this out," she said softly. She didn't want to lose the best thing that had ever happened to her. She'd get him to see this wasn't a make-or-break situation.

He got to his feet. "I already have. Pack up your stuff and be gone by the time I get back. I've got a wedding to get back to."

"Wait. Please talk to me."

"Time for talking is over. I've no idea who you really are and have no plans to be made a fool twice." He brushed by her as he grabbed his tuxedo coat off the couch.

Tears pricked the back of her eyes. "You had the real me the whole time," she said to his back.

"No." He glanced over his shoulder. "I'm not sure that I did."

When the door shut behind him, Charlie sank to the floor and cried.

Chapter Twelve

Women had lied to Connor his whole life. Told him what they thought he wanted to hear. There was always an angle. Meet his mother. Snag an invitation to a special event. Sleep with him. Hang onto him for his money.

Charlie had done it to get her father's notice.

Her bastard, sack-of-shit father who knew damn well his reporter had fucked up on the piece about his mother, but refused to admit it. Would he get Charlie to twist the story on WHF once he found out who Connor was? Insist she drag his personal life into it? And Jesus, she knew about the lawsuit between his mom and her dad and had still stayed quiet. His stomach churned, the back of his throat burned.

He took a seat at the empty head table, grateful to be alone for a moment. He looked around the room, but couldn't focus on anything. It was like he sat behind a giant film of plastic and could only make out the blurry edges of movement.

Had Charlie lied about wanting to write children's books, too? Was her hobby a convenient way to keep her secret at a distance?

Every minute with her flashed through his mind. They'd been stellar minutes, the best he'd ever had.

He started to get up. It was a dick move telling her to leave like that. He should at least make sure she got a ride to another hotel or the airport or wherever she planned to go.

But he couldn't. She stripped away his control when close, and he didn't want to see her. No woman had hurt him as much as she just had.

"Champagne?"

Connor glanced up at the waitress holding a bottle of bubbly in her hand. "Sure." He grabbed his glass off the table and handed it over. Lifted the next closest glass while she poured and gave her that one, too.

She smiled. "Is that an invitation?"

He blinked, and she came into focus. He should say yes and tell her to meet him later. What better way to get Charlie off his mind?

"No. Just thirsty." He wouldn't get over Goldilocks for a long fucking time no matter what he did.

"If you change your mind, I'm off at ten." She handed him the second glass.

Hearing someone take the chair next to him, he downed the champagne before turning to say hello. For the rest of the evening he planned to be the perfect groomsman. His problems weren't anyone else's and this evening was meant to be special for McCall and Lucy.

"Since when do you down champagne?" Clay said, putting a scotch in front of Connor. He tipped his own glass in cheers before taking a drink.

"Pretty girl offered it so I said okay." Connor chased down the expensive wine with the aged whiskey.

"And since when do you notice pretty girls?"

"Since just now."

"Where's your beautiful date?"

Yeah, there was no comparison between the waitress and Charlie. "She's leaving." He ran his thumb across the rim of the crystal tumbler.

Clay got comfortable in his chair. *Great*. Mr. Badass Navy SEAL wanted to talk. When had Connor given off the vibe he liked to chitchat?

"We can do this the easy way or the hard way," Clay said, calm, cool.

Connor laughed. And maybe that had been his friend's intention. *There are people you can talk to. People you can trust besides your family.*

He trusted Clay with his life.

"I just found out Charlie is Charlize Beckett. She's Thomas Beckett's daughter. The prick owner and publisher of Natural World."

"I know."

WTF? Connor sat taller and leveled his friend with a glare. "How the hell did you know? And why didn't you tell me?"

"It's my job to know who's getting close to the top brass at WHF. And given that we're friends, I take extra steps."

"How long have you known?"

"Since I met her in New Mexico."

The muscles in Connor's back clenched. "You should have told me."

Clay's sharp as steel eyes studied him. "There was no reason. She was doing her job."

"And then she was doing me."

"And you were the happiest I've ever seen you." Clay kept his assessing gaze in place. "I didn't know you were going to turn it into another week. But when you did, I did some more digging. I found nothing to indicate she was working some angle on the story on her father's behalf."

Connor scratched the back of his head. "Doesn't change the fact that she lied."

"True. But I've watched the two of you this weekend. She got past your defenses. You going to let a stupid thing like her name get in the way of that?"

A lie is a lie, Connor thought. "It's more than that. I can't get past who her father is and what he's doing to my mom."

Clay nodded. "You can't blame her for the actions of her father."

"Maybe not, but I can't deal with the constant reminder."

"Then I guess you've made your choice." Clay lifted his drink off the table.

"Yeah, I have."

Charlie tiptoed into her townhouse after midnight. The familiar scent of strawberries took a tiny edge off her misery. The comfort of home after hours of heartbreaking travel warmed some of the cold places inside her.

She flicked on the light in her bedroom and dropped her bags. Like a robot, she went through the motions of showering and putting on her pajamas. When she finally crawled into bed the clock read 1:24.

Was Connor asleep? She'd wanted to text him several times since leaving the lodge to apologize again. He'd been about to tell her he loved her and that had to be worth another try.

But she didn't have his cell number. She'd never thought to ask for it considering they were together 24/7.

Things were over.

"Charlie?" Ashley poked her head into the room. "Everything okay? I wasn't expecting you until tomorrow. Well, later today."

Charlie pulled the covers up to her chin and shook her head.

Ashley rushed to her side. "What happened?"

"I blew it." And then with big fat tears rolling down her cheeks, she told Ashley everything.

"I'm sorry," Ash said, now snuggled up beside her. "But if Connor can't see what an amazing person you are, then he doesn't deserve you. You told one little fib that in the scheme of things is *nothing*. It's on par with 'Did you eat some vegetables today? Why, yes, Mom, I did.' See? Totally inane."

"Your mom isn't Sandra Swanson."

Ashley sighed. "I see how that complicates things, but it's only a problem if you guys let it be." She sank a little further into the covers. "And I guess he's letting it be."

"His family is important to him. When he talks about them you can hear how much he loves them. I would never want to come between that. In all honesty, I believe Sandra. We both know my father can be a stubborn ass. Jed might be one of his top reporters, but he's never been the best at checking facts. Wasn't there some story a couple years ago that he got called on?"

"You know, I think you're right."

"It makes me sick to my stomach to think about it."

"Morale at the office has been lower. I think everyone is starting to feel some tension. You're going in this morning, right?"

Charlie had done a lot of thinking on the plane ride. Mostly about Connor, but also about how she wanted to live her life and she didn't want to live it working for Natural World anymore. She wasn't sure she wanted to live it around her father anymore, either.

"Yes."

"Good, because I know it's probably not what you want to hear right now, but your dad was really happy with your story."

"You mean our story."

"No. I mean yours. I gave him what you wrote and only added a few little things after proofing it, nothing to warrant any credit."

Charlie closed her eyes. That's what she'd wanted. To prove herself and gain her father's respect. But, she suddenly realized, taking charge of her own life meant more. She'd thought her father's respect would make her happy, yet the only thing she felt was relief.

She could finally move on.

"I'm going to quit tomorrow," she said.

Ashley bolted up. "What? This is what you've wanted." Her eyes softened. "Isn't it?"

"It used to be. But deep down I don't want to be a reporter. I never truly have."

Ash smiled. "You will kick ass as a children's book author and skyrocket to the top of the bestsellers lists."

Charlie wrapped her in a quick hug. "Thank you. And after I quit, I'm going to tell my father to print a retraction." Ash's eyes widened. "If he doesn't, then we'll no longer have a relationship. I can forgive him for making the mistake. I can't forgive him for standing by it. My relationship with Connor aside, I believe his mom. If he doesn't apologize publicly, then I'm giving my piece on World Heritage Fund to another publication. I wasn't officially put on the job, so if he prints it without my consent, he's going to have a big problem."

"You're my hero." Ash raised her hand for a high five.

"Let's just hope he goes for it."

A few days later Charlie sat in a red beanbag chair in her favorite bookstore with her laptop open to the headline from Natural World announcing its sincere regret over their error in taking Sandra Swanson's words out of context.

It seemed Charlie did matter to her father. So much so, he'd broken down in his office and confessed that the magazine had been suffering financially and he'd worried that a retraction would discredit them even further.

They talked for two hours. For the first time in her life, they spoke honestly, and while it didn't fix everything wrong in their relationship, it gave them a starting point.

A *ding* sounded, alerting her to a new email message. She clicked on the icon at the bottom of her screen. Her pulse sped up at the subject line and she quickly opened the message.

Dear Ms. Beckett,

Thank you for your query. I would very much like to speak with you in regards to your submission, WHAT DO YOU SAY FINLEY QUAY? Please let me know a good time to talk.

Best,

Fiona Moore

Moore Davis Literary Agency

She pounded her feet on the carpeted floor of the bookstore in sheer delight, and maybe let out a little squeal. She'd sent a dozen queries to agents for her picture book over the past couple of days and already received two rejections. This reply rocked so much better.

Children's voices grew in volume and quantity. Charlie shut her laptop to focus on the preschoolers assembling in front of her. She tucked her computer into her bag and ran her hand over the picture book selected for story time this morning.

One day she'd hold her own book.

The tiny, smiling faces staring at her brought a smile in return. Blue eyes, brown eyes, green eyes, so full of innocence and silliness and honesty, they reminded her how wonderful it was to imagine and dream and feel free.

Plans were good, but they weren't foolproof. It had taken her a while to figure out the flaw with her intentions. In wanting to please her father, she'd forgotten something very important.

That the only way to live honestly was to see with her heart.

Sometimes things didn't work out. She missed Connor so much it was a physical ache. A pain that reached into her bones and made them brittle. But she'd been lost before and she always found her way.

A little boy tugged on the leg of her pants. "You gonna read now?"

"Yes," she answered, blinking back into the present.

She read to them and talked with them and she was happy.

Chapter Thirteen

Connor sat in his office at World Heritage Fund and stared at his computer screen. His mom had called with the good news, but he needed to see it for himself. Not only had Natural World published a retraction but Thomas Beckett had offered a personal apology as well.

He fell back into his leather chair. Relief washed over him. Whatever had possessed Thomas Beckett to right his wrong, Connor was grateful. While talking to his mom, she'd mentioned forgiveness and his admiration for her grew. She didn't hold a grudge. Come to think of it, his father didn't either. And with the fortune and platform he'd amassed, that spoke of the type of character Connor had tried to emulate.

So the weird sense of calm he felt toward Charlie's father shouldn't surprise him.

Charlie.

Every time he thought about her, he wondered if he'd done the right thing. He hadn't been willing to forgive her had he? She'd apologized more than once, been willing to fight for what they had. And he'd turned his back on her.

His heart pounded. Why had he done that?

It had taken him the past few days to figure that out. For the first time in his well-ordered life, all hell had broken loose in his head and heart and it had scared the shit out of him. Falling in love hadn't been part of his plan and when he saw a way out, he took it.

Like a coward.

Like an idiot.

The love he had for Charlie hadn't diminished in the least after he'd learned the truth. If anything, being away from her had made him love her more. He'd had time to think about all the ways she fit him better than he'd ever imagined. She'd opened up to him, especially late at night when they lay in bed together and shared memories and stories and confessions. And she'd gotten him to do the same.

She'd confided her mistakes, her experiences, the chances she'd taken. She had been real. The most real thing he'd ever been lucky enough to have.

Could she forgive *him*?

He studied his calendar. A couple of conference calls tomorrow and a flight to Peru in two days with no return date. One of his VPs could take his place. After that—

His office phone rang and he hit the intercom button. "Yeah, Gloria?"

"Mr. Malloy would like to see you in his office."

"Will do. Thanks." Half a minute later, he knocked on his boss's door. "Come in," Bill said.

Connor took a seat at Bill's desk. "What's up?"

"I received a review copy of the article Natural World is

running next week." Bill rubbed his jawline. "I don't believe it's something they normally do, but Ms. Beckett mentioned wanting to get your approval before it's finalized."

With all the crap going on in his head, Connor had forgotten about the article.

"I've read it." Bill turned his computer so Connor could see the screen. "It's good."

Connor gave a tight nod and started reading. The further into the piece he got, the faster his heart beat. Charlie's words were like magic. She shared her journey and painted such a detailed and animated picture that he felt like he'd been transported back to all the places they'd visited. If this didn't make people want to see the Route, nothing would. She also sang his praises, making him out to be a rock star in the heritage protection world and keeping his personal life out of it.

"It's more than good." Connor spun the computer back around and cleared his throat. Bill studied him like he was waiting for him to say something more. "Sir?"

"Would you finally quit with the sir?"

"Probably not." Connor cracked a smile.

"Thayer is itching to spread his wings, so I thought we'd let him go to Peru instead of you. He'll swing by your office in an hour or so and you can fill him in on what's going on."

Connor rubbed at his ear. He couldn't have heard that right. "Do I need to be somewhere else?"

"That's up to you." The older man, wise and happily married for over thirty years couldn't be playing matchmaker, could he? Because Connor got the distinct feeling Bill was implying he quit acting like an ass and go see Charlie.

"I won't be missed if I take a long weekend?"

"You'll be missed, but go anyway."

He got to his feet. He didn't need to be told twice. "Got it."

"Good luck," Bill said, before putting his head down and reading something on his desk. Connor couldn't be sure, but he thought he heard him mumble, "First Dean, then McCall. These boys are dropping like flies."

Connor hoped so.

The real Ashley Morgan turned out to be a cool chick who talked almost as much as Charlie and wanted all-in with helping Connor surprise her.

Standing out of sight outside the Route 66 Classic Grill in Los Angeles checking his watch every thirty seconds, he hoped like hell Charlie could forgive him.

While putting things together the past couple of days, he hadn't stopped thinking about the sweet gasps she made against his lips when they kissed and how he wanted to kiss her again. If she let him, he'd kiss her for the rest of her life.

The sun hung high in the blue sky, the spring air smelled like oranges and fresh tilled soil. A steady stream of customers had been turned away with a voucher for a free meal—courtesy of Connor—the next time they visited.

Ashley's car, a white convertible VW bug just like she'd described over the phone, finally pulled into the parking lot. She jumped out and hurried around the hood to open the passenger door. He smiled when Goldilocks stepped out wearing a blindfold. With no worry of discovery, he moved out of the shadow and looked his fill. God, she was beautiful.

"Ashley, enough already," Charlie said. "I'm surprised, okay? I've no idea where we are and you didn't have to go to all this trouble on my half birthday. Which by the way, technically isn't until tomorrow. Why is it so quiet?" She stretched an arm out in front of her, moving it slowly from side to side.

"You'll see in just a sec, okay?" Ashley held onto Charlie's elbow with one hand and gave him a wave with the other.

"What are you really up to?"

"No good, of course." Ashley let go of her friend. "You trust me, right?"

"*Ash*." Charlie reached for the blindfold.

His pulse ran wild.

"See you later, *chica*! Or not." Ashley jumped back into her car and started backing out of the lot.

Charlie pulled the blindfold off and yelled to her friend. "What are you doing?"

Ashley waved an arm out the window. Connor owed her one.

It took Charlie only a second to twist back around. He couldn't make out her exact expression, but heard the huff of breath she released before checking out where she stood. She saw the lone red '66 convertible mustang parked right in front and took tentative steps toward it.

He knew the minute she saw the open glove box and Violet Crumbles inside it because her face alighted with anticipation and her head whipped around like she expected someone to jump out and yell "surprise."

Not yet.

She stood still for a minute before sliding her hand along

the open windowsill and looking closer into the interior. He couldn't wait to get her inside that car and do dirty things to her.

The door to the restaurant opened and the café's owner, Stan, appeared. "You Charlie Beckett?" he called out.

Charlie lifted her arm to shield her eyes from the sun. "Yes," she called back.

"Welcome to the Route 66 Café." He gestured her over. "Come on in."

Her body startled, like maybe realization had hit. The restaurant. The car. She looked left and right before a cautious, but lively gait took her toward the café's entrance. God, he loved her. How fearless. Fun. Trusting. *Forgiving?*

Connor hightailed it around the building and entered through the back. He got to his spot next to the counter just in time to see Charlie enter.

And watch her hand fly to the center of her chest. She blinked over and over again, her lips parted.

A large three-dimensional map of the Route featuring their initials—C&C—and mounted on a piece of wood sat on an easel in the middle of the café. A five-foot tall Ferris wheel made out of Lego bricks stood off to one side. Dandelions filled small glass vases on every table. And giant teddy bears holding hearts that said I love you sat in every booth but one.

"This way," Stan said, leading Charlie to the lone unoccupied booth.

She followed and slid into the black vinyl seat. Stan handed her a "menu" and made himself scarce.

Connor slipped into the spot beside her. She looked up, hands shaking on the handmade book in her hands. "Hi," he said.

"Hi," she said, breathless. Her gaze dropped back to the book.

"Open it."

Her breath hitched. With a gentle touch, she rubbed her fingers over the cover. 66 Reasons Why I Love Charlie, it said.

Connor's first—and last—stab at writing and illustrating a book. His drawing talent left a lot to be desired, but hopefully his words made up for it.

Charlie opened the book.

Dear Charlie,
I fell in love on Route 66.
Here's why...

He watched her read the first page, the second, the third. A smile took hold of her lips on page four.

When you talk, I don't just listen. I hear you. And the sound is nothing short of extraordinary. You've opened my world to beauty and opportunity and choices.

A drawing of a dandelion accompanied the sentiment.

She glanced at him. "There's really sixty-one more reasons?" Her soft voice sounded skeptical.

"There is. There is so much I love about you, Charlie Beckett. I'm sorry I walked out on you like I did." He took her hand, needing to feel physically connected. Her delicate palm trembled under his touch.

"I'm sorry I didn't forgive you back in Colorado. I was an idiot. And I know you're probably thinking that the only reason I'm here is because of what your dad did, but that's not true. I would've come for you anyway. My world looks better through your eyes, and I want it all with you. Good, bad, happy, sad. You're my due north, and I want to take this journey with you and no one else."

Electricity sizzled between them. The intense attraction that had been there since the day they met by the pool became a living, breathing thing. It took every ounce of willpower he had to take this slow when what he really wanted to do was kiss her senseless and touch her everywhere.

She sucked in her bottom lip.

"I love you," he repeated. "The bears can vouch for me."

Affection and a gorgeous smile bloomed across her face, calming the frantic beat of his heart. "I'm sorry, too. So sorry for not telling you the truth sooner. And I love you back."

He cupped her cheeks and kissed her with all the passion and love that had been steadily building inside him since the moment she'd come into his life.

She pulled on his shirt to bring him closer and their lips and tongues gave and received until they both needed to come up for air. Her eyes sparkled with want and fire and love. "You love me."

"I love you," he repeated.

Her eyes shut for a brief moment like she wanted to relish those words. When they opened she looked around the restaurant. "This is incredible."

"Thought we could give the bears to your favorite charity."

"I'd like that."

"The car out front, though. It's a '66 Mustang and it's yours."

"*What?*"

"I plan on taking lots of road trips with you."

"Oh, Connor." She put her hands on his face and kissed him. "And you wrote me a book." She picked it back up. "It's amazing. And thoughtful. And…" She waved a hand in front of her face. "I'm gonna cry."

"Hey." He laced their fingers together. "How about we eat instead?"

She nodded. Connor gave the signal to Stan and a waitress came out from the kitchen and took their order. Burgers, fries, and milkshakes. He loved that Charlie liked to eat.

"God, I've missed you," he said.

"I've missed you too." She laid her head on his shoulder. "I quit my job," she added.

"Congratulations. How did your father take it?"

"Pretty well. We talked about a lot of things, and I think we'll be able to have a better relationship moving forward."

He squeezed her hand. "I'm glad to hear that."

"So where do we go from here?" She looked at him sideways, a shy lilt to her voice that made him love her more.

"I came here planning to figure out a way to see each other as much as possible, but since you're no longer employed, how would you feel about moving to Idaho? It's where I live." He ran this thumb across her knuckles.

She turned to face him. "You want me to move in with you?"

"Hell yes. I don't want to be away from you for longer than necessary. One less flight to be with you would be fantastic. But, I'd understand if you wanted to stay close to

your family and friends since I'm constantly out of town."
He held his breath. He was asking a lot, but the minute the
invitation had left his mouth, he wanted it. Badly.

She looked into this eyes for what seemed like forever.
"I'd love to move in with you. What you do is one of the
reasons I love you. I'll miss you when you're traveling, but
just think about all the sex we'll have to have to make up for
your absences." Her lips lifted into a sexy smile.

He groaned. "Now that's all I'll be thinking about." He
palmed her neck with his free hand. "You're sure?"

"I'm positive. Plus, that leaves me plenty of time to write
and draw without any distraction."

He kissed her square on the mouth, intending for it to be
quick, but it turned into an openmouthed assault. He tasted
her thoroughly, pouring his heart and soul into the kiss so
she would know how much she'd just gifted him with and
how proud he was of her.

"Ahem."

They pulled apart. Charlie giggled and wiped a finger
along her well-kissed bottom lip while the waitress dropped
off their food. "You could come with me, too," Connor said.

"Sorry?" Lines creased her forehead before she bit into
a French fry.

"To my monuments. We can always use an extra pair
of hands." He had a strong feeling she'd fly anywhere and
everywhere with him. Her eyes lit up like the brightest stars.
"I would love that."

"Since I'm the boss, you'll have to do everything I say."
He smirked. "And I mean everything."

The sexy slant of her mouth told him she knew he might
let her have *some* say. "I think I can handle that." She fed

him a fry, reminding him she had him wrapped around her finger. "I can't believe this is happening. I'm so happy."

Connor tucked a lock of hair behind her ear. "Believe it, Goldilocks. You're my everything, and not a day is going to pass that you don't know how much I love you."

She angled her head closer, lips hovering just out of reach. "You going to tell me, or show me?" she whispered.

"Both."

Acknowledgements

First to Wendy Chen, for always knowing what I meant to say and helping me say it better. You're the best. Thank you for your always kind words, too.

To the gang at Entangled, you all rock!

To all my writer pals, thank you for your kindness, inspiration, support, and overall awesomeness. Hayson, Roxanne, Paula, Maggie, Charlene, your friendships and emails always make my day. A special shout-out to Samanthe Beck, for being extra amazing. One day I'm going to veer off the romance track and write a book titled, Thursdays With Sam.

So often I have my face buried in my computer and my thoughts on my characters and my husband and sons still love me, hug me, smile at me, and root me on. Thanks guys, for sharing this journey with me. I love you so much.

And as always, thank you to my readers. I truly appreciate you more than I can say.

ONE NIGHT OF RISK

Entangled Publishing, LLC
2614 South Timberline Road
Suite 109
Fort Collins, CO 80525

Visit our website at www.entangledpublishing.com.

Indulgence is an imprint of Entangled Publishing, LLC.

Edited by Wendy Chen

Manufactured in the United States of America

First Edition September 2015

To Wendy Chen. Thank you for loving my heritage protection guys as much as I do. It's been a blast writing their stories for you.

Chapter One

Malia Davis didn't break rules, but desperation made a girl fly in the face of right and wrong. "Please be in this spot," she whispered to the sacred ground beneath her knees. "If you make this easy, you'll be prolonging a life. I know you will."

She wiped her arm across her forehead, catching the perspiration before it slipped into her eye. A deep breath followed. Then her hands, dry, rough, and caked with dirt, went back to work. Obviously acting on impulse wasn't her strong suit because the small garden shovel she'd brought with her had not performed the magic ditch digging she'd hoped for. *Doesn't matter.* She'd dig around the entire perimeter of the ancient Hawaiian temple to find the Peridot crystal if that's what it took.

Anything to help her mom.

Her heart continued to thump against her rib cage in a crazy, erratic fashion so she closed her eyes and visualized the green volcanic gem in the palm of her hand. As her shoulders relaxed, she felt the low hum of spiritual energy on the royal grounds vibrate through her. Her eyes flew open. That little signal told her she'd made the right choice in coming here.

She took in the lush emerald hillside, sighed, and her overactive nerves calmed. She might be breaking the law, but she did so for a good cause. That had to count for something. If her sisters knew the real reason she'd flown to Kauai, they'd scoff. Her bossy older sister did whatever she wanted without repercussion. Her younger sister batted her eyelashes and everyone tripped over themselves to right any wrongdoing.

But Malia kept everything bottled up inside and never so much as stepped a foot out of line. The "good girl" everyone called her.

Not anymore.

The pull of the sea drew a glance over her shoulder. A vibrant blue-green Pacific glittered under the late afternoon sun. As a child, she'd spent hours in that ocean, out-swimming her sisters and snorkeling until her mom told her the fish weren't going anywhere and she could dive back in tomorrow. When her family moved to her father's home state of California and too far from the sea for her liking, she'd been so mad she refused to go in the water when her parents took them to the beach.

Her happiest memories were of their vacation home back on the island where her mother was born. A flash of tanned skin, muscled biceps and dark unruly hair flashed in her mind. She blinked him away.

Men's voices sounded to her left and all the tension

she'd managed to dial down came roaring back. The ruins were off-limits to the public. But given the scaffolding, and other equipment lying around, she wondered if some sort of restoration project were underway.

The idea of getting caught trespassing flung her heart back into hyper-mode. Her chest did some unwelcome cramping that she worried might stop the flow of oxygen to her lungs. A cold, nervous sweat covered her from head to toe. She might be about to have a heart attack.

Slow the heck down. This is you panicking, nothing else.

She took a very deep breath.

The voices grew louder.

She could talk her way out of this. Jump back on her bicycle—which also stood in clear view—and ride away with a lie she'd gotten lost. Only she'd never been able to talk her way out of anything.

God, the non-plan plan she had suddenly seemed really stupid. And so unlike her. She literally had no clue what to do next. Except freeze like a fricking statue.

A radio or walkie-talkie made a loud, crackling noise, followed by a very clear "Trespasser six o'clock."

Malia took in her position. Adrenaline and the universal fight-or-flight response kicked in. She sprinted to her bike, hopped on, and raced down the mountain.

"Hey!" She heard the shout from somewhere behind her and pedaled faster.

What in the world had she been thinking? That she'd sneak onto protected land, dig up a crystal, and casually ride away without anyone noticing?

She squeezed the handlebars to steady herself on the bumpy hillside. Her butt bounced up and down on the seat.

If she got caught and her sister had to bail her out of jail, Malia wouldn't only be humiliated, she'd be crestfallen. She'd come to the island to get the crystal and she had no plans to leave until she had it.

Just up ahead the road came into view. She veered right toward the visitor center and small parking lot and got a little air as she barreled over a mound of dirt. Once she hit the pavement, she swallowed the fear stuck in her throat and after a quick look behind her, turned onto the highway and hightailed it back to her family home.

Only when her wheels met the familiar street that led to her favorite place in the world did she slow down.

She shouldn't have raced to the temple five minutes after getting to the house from the airport. A little strategy would have come in handy. A little preparation. Just because she was worried about doing this alone and chickening out didn't mean she should jump headfirst into something blindly. She *could* do this.

She'd been on her own for…for always. Growing up in a loving home with wonderful parents and two sisters was great, but she'd never been one for group projects, team sports, or asking for help.

That last one really riled her family.

And after her dad passed away when she was just nineteen, she took on the role of caregiver, helping to raise her younger sister. Her mom had been devastated, her older sister in her last year of college, and so Malia buried her grief because she didn't have time to be weak or needy.

Outside the garage, a jeep sat parked on the driveway. She got off her bike and slowly walked by the car, wondering if Kalani had called someone to leave a few groceries. Her sister liked to be in control, even from the other side of the island.

Malia leaned the bike against the side of the house and walked to the sliding French door she'd left unlocked. She dumped her backpack on the floor of the laundry room, put her shovel in the sink, and quickly washed her hands. Then she stepped over the suitcase she'd dropped off earlier and headed toward the kitchen for a glass of water.

As she strode into the open, airy room, her breath caught. Tanned skin. Muscled biceps. Dark unruly hair. Wearing nothing but a pair of low-slung board shorts.

It couldn't be.

He turned from the counter at the squeak she made and her knees almost gave out. Their gazes collided. She hadn't seen him in ten years, but there was no mistaking the gorgeously masculine man in front of her. He'd stolen her heart and then he'd broken it.

"Shit," he said.

Not the first words a girl wanted to hear out of the mouth of the only man she'd ever loved. If they hadn't been standing in *her* home, she would have turned around and offered him nothing but her back as she slammed the door on her way out. Instead she said, "Hello, Clay."

That voice.
That face.

Clay Doherty had dreamed about both—and a hell of a lot more—too many times to count. Malia might be older now, but he recognized her unmatched beauty immediately.

He also knew if he didn't drag his gaze away from her exquisite dark eyes and tend to the cut he'd just given himself, he'd bleed all over the countertop. "Give me a minute."

She hurried to his side. "You're bleeding."

"Hence the 'shit.'" Their fingers grazed as they both reached for a paper towel at the same time. She pulled her hand back, stepped away, and wrapped her arms around herself. He sensed her struggle—she didn't owe him any help, that was for damn sure, but it went against her nature not to give assistance.

He applied pressure to his finger, far too aware of the woman standing beside him. She smelled like a breath of fresh air. Light, floral, exactly how he remembered.

"I thought the 'shit' was directed at me." She unfolded her arms and almost reached for his injured hand. Almost.

"It's been ten years and you think the first word I'd say to you is 'shit'?"

"It's the first word that popped into *my* head." Hands at her sides, she leaned against the counter, a small measure of ease relaxing her shoulders.

"Liar."

She looked up at him. His body tightened, his heart beat a little faster. He stared down at gorgeous mahogany eyes that had once drawn him in like nothing else, and still did by the way heat licked at the back of his neck. "You forget how easily I can read you?"

"That was a long time ago," she said, her jaw tight.

He was even better at it now. Getting into people's heads. During his years as a Navy SEAL, he'd learned how to decipher expressions without error, and the look on Malia's face when she'd first laid eyes on him shouted surprise, yes.

But also pleasure.

"And I remember every second of it."

She took a shaky breath and her tongue darted out to lick her lips. He gulped, felt a tug in his stomach. Her dark hair was pulled back into a ponytail, but wayward strands fell around a face that could stop traffic. Smooth, tanned skin, high cheekbones, perfect little nose, heart-shaped mouth. She'd gotten more beautiful, more sexy, and just like that, all the years apart disappeared and he wanted to pull her into his arms.

"Don't." She shook her head and took a step back. "Hold still while I grab a Band-Aid."

Grateful for a minute alone to get his shit together, he reined in his thoughts and focused. He'd been at the Davis house for two weeks for a working vacation that few people knew about. His assignment required some secrecy, but when he'd told his mom he was headed to Kauai, she'd insisted on arranging for him to stay at the Davis house. She'd been their housekeeper for almost twenty years before Clay bought her a house and told her she didn't have to work another day if she didn't want to. She loved the Davis family, though, and felt indebted to them for their generosity in employing a military widow with a son who was more than a handful, so she still helped out from time to time.

He'd agreed to stay here because of the happiness he'd heard in his mom's voice. And because the house was the perfect place for him to hide out.

No one told him he'd have a guest.

He wondered if anyone had told Malia.

And shit. Having her here—close to him—put her too close to risk. He'd stayed away to keep her safe and now here she was. He needed to make himself scarce.

"Here you go," she said, stepping back into the kitchen with the grace of a ballerina. He'd always been mesmerized by the way she moved.

"I'm good," he said, removing the paper towel and eyeing the gash. He'd suffered a hell of a lot worse.

She took his finger and examined it. "It's a pretty bad cut."

All common sense fled as she held his hand. She'd dropped some of her defenses and the innocent touch put way too many far-from-innocent thoughts in his head. For a moment his memories hurdled back to all the forbidden nights they'd spent touching, kissing, loving.

Jesus. He had to get a fucking grip.

"I'm fine," he repeated, but like a moron he didn't pull his hand back.

The young girl he'd loved had been good, pure, and so far out of his league they'd hidden their relationship from everyone. She came from money. He came from squat and was messed up for years over his MIA father. Back then, he knew part of his appeal had been his rebellious reputation, but the truth was she'd had him wrapped around her little finger since the second he'd laid eyes on her at seven years old.

"Humor me." She unwrapped the bandage while still holding onto him and then covered the cut. "There."

"Still taking care of people, I see."

She dropped his hand like it burned her. Their gazes met head-on. Pain, anger, and defeat all swam in the depths of her remarkable eyes and he wished, not for the first time, things could have been different.

"What are you doing here?" She moved around the granite counter to stand across from him.

"Making a sandwich. Want one?" He picked up the knife and resumed cutting the slippery tomato.

"That's not what I mean, and you know it."

He'd meant to keep his attention on the tomato, but damn if the irritated tease in her voice didn't have his gaze flickering back to her. He put the knife down before he cut a second finger. She blew his concentration out of the water with her fresh face and kissable mouth.

"What are *you* doing here?" he asked.

She crossed her arms over her chest and stared at him. When they were younger, she'd been the only one to get him to talk with that move, and dammit, he felt himself ready to tell her whatever she wanted to know.

Except the whole truth about why he'd left her.

"I'm on vacation and…a work assignment," he said.

"Alone?"

Ah, that one little word tossed back so quickly said so much. Too much. Because now he wanted to drop *his* defenses. "Yes. I'm heading up a security project on the island. My mom insisted on making my arrangements and that's how I ended up here." They'd successfully excavated almost all of the Peridot crystal from the ancient Hawaiian temple grounds, but a ring of thieves led by a man with a vendetta against Clay still threatened the site. Which was exactly what he and the US government wanted. "I'll pack up my stuff and head to…and figure something else out now that you're here." He couldn't stay anywhere public, so he'd have to find another private home.

"Is that going to be a problem?" Lines creased the

smooth, olive skin of her forehead.

"Shouldn't be." *Might be.* He knew the Davis house like the back of his hand and finding a new place that met his requirements for confidentiality could be problematic.

She eyed him with far too much comprehension. "I could go stay with Kalani if you need a day or two. She manages the Grand Hyatt and I'm sure…" Her teeth sank into her bottom lip and he almost groaned. *She still does that.* "I'm sure she'd rather me be under the same roof."

The way she tilted her head told him she had something else on her mind, too. Her family? They'd always been important to her. "I'm sorry about your mom," he said. Guilt he hadn't felt in a while squeezed his chest. Her father had passed away a year after he'd joined the military and Clay should have reached out to Malia then, but he hadn't wanted to add to her pain. He'd also still teemed with resentment. The man had never approved of him. And Clay's enlistment was a source of pride he refused to have soiled.

"Thanks." Her soft voice reached the deepest part of him. The part no one else had ever gotten close to.

For a long beat they just looked at each other, and hell if that pull between them wasn't still there. *This is bad.* He didn't let anyone penetrate his walls. Ever.

She put her elbows on the counter and leaned forward, drawing him in like the tide to the shore. Her gaze dipped to his chest and back up. "Do you think you could put on a shirt or something?"

"Too hot for you in here?" he teased. Teased. *WTF? Leave now, dude.*

She rolled her eyes and went to the fridge. Pulled out a bottle of water. "Good manners dictate we eat with shirts on."

Clay couldn't take his eyes off the sexy slope of her neck as she guzzled down the water. He'd had his mouth on every inch of her, fumbling his way to learning a woman's body when they were teenagers. He'd gotten good at it by the time he left, but was an expert now. And the urge to show her just how much pleasure his touch could bring hit him with unwelcome force.

He wasn't good enough for her back then.

And while he might be good enough now, the millions he had in the bank, the meaningful job, and the fact that her father no longer stood in their way didn't change the danger that still surrounded him. He'd left the military after promising his best friend he would. Neal had died in Clay's arms, and his last words had pressed for Clay to finish their tour and be done. To get out so his mother didn't lose a son like she'd lost a husband. Clay had kept that promise, but he'd traded one dangerous job for another. Many of the places he traveled to, as head of security for World Heritage Fund, were in areas of conflict or neglect, and safety was always an issue. He'd made a few enemies—like the ruthless prick after the Peridot.

Clay's vow to keep people safe meant keeping his heart locked away. He'd kept his distance from Malia to protect her. Loving her would have put her at risk for loss and uncertainty and after seeing what that had done to his mom, he wanted no part of it. Now, he kept his guard up because letting anyone too close also meant a weakness that could be exploited by those with a grudge. It would kill him to lose someone he loved because she loved him.

He lived alone for important reasons and liked his life

the way it was.

"Still following the rules, huh?" He grabbed his shirt off the back of the kitchen chair and pulled it on.

"Still breaking them?" she fired back.

"Not a one." He pulled out four slices of bread and piled on enough turkey, cheese, and lettuce to make two large sandwiches. "I've reformed. At least with things that matter."

She let out an unhurried breath as she leaned against the counter opposite him again. "I can't believe you're here," she murmured. "That we're both standing in this kitchen again. You're the last person I wanted…"

"To see?"

She nodded.

"I never planned to see you again either."

Hurt clouded her eyes and he wished he hadn't said that out loud. But he'd given up any right to get reacquainted with her the minute he'd walked out of her life without explanation. No, nowadays he soothed his need for a woman with a revolving door of quick lays and zero attachment.

He and Malia might be reunited, and the island might be small, but as soon as he walked out the door, he'd never see her again. His reputation could still hurt her. His determination to keep her safe was still too big an obstacle—especially given his current assignment.

Avoidance was key. And he knew exactly how to do it. He'd been doing it for ten years.

Chapter Two

Malia hated him. Hated how he'd left her without so much as a good-bye. She'd loved him with her heart and soul and then one morning she'd woken up to Rosie making breakfast in their Beverly Hills kitchen and telling her mother Clay was gone. He'd enlisted.

She'd felt so gutted she'd rushed back upstairs and thrown up.

How she'd missed the signs still ate at her. His father had been in the marines and died in an explosion when Clay was five. For years Clay had held out hope that his dad was just missing in action and they'd find him. They never did recover his body.

"I'll just finish my sandwich and go," Clay said, breaking into her memories.

"Fine."

He pushed a sandwich toward her. She didn't touch it.

Clay's amazing green eyes watched her. Combined with

his dark hair, bronzed complexion and rock-hard body, his looks were devastating. His mixed Irish-Hispanic heritage had always made her a little woozy. Couldn't he have gotten uglier instead of hotter? He'd slipped his shirt on not a moment too soon. She'd been uncontrollably close to running her hands over his muscled chest and abs to see if he still felt like warm honey.

Her head and heart hated him, but her body had other ideas.

"Tell me about your life, Malia." She frowned at him. "I've got a few minutes and I want to know," he said, his tone so genuine that the tight knot in the pit of her stomach uncurled.

She tore a piece of turkey off the edge of her sandwich and ate it. She could handle a civil conversation with him before he walked out the door and she never saw him again. "I'm a yoga instructor. Have my own studio in Brentwood."

"Live there, too?" He leaned against the counter, his focus entirely on her. He'd always done that. Given her his full attention like nothing else in his world mattered but her.

"Yes."

"Boyfriend?"

"That's a little too personal, don't you think?"

"It's just a question."

She hated the dare-you tone he used. She'd been putty in his hands when they were younger, but not anymore. Her heart pounded like it missed that message from her brain. "No. What about you?"

He smirked. "No boyfriend."

"Ha, ha."

Heat flared in his eyes. "No girlfriend either."

The way his gaze ate her up, if he wanted to get her naked right here, right now, she wouldn't argue. Her skin tingled, her breasts grew heavy, she throbbed between her thighs. Being this close to him again had her body reacting entirely inappropriately and she wished it would stop.

"You still swim?" he asked when she stayed quiet.

"When I get the chance. I guess you're a pretty good swimmer now."

He raised an eyebrow.

"Fantastic swimmer?"

He threw his head back and laughed. "I'm flattered to hear you kept tabs on me."

She wished she hadn't. Separated by distance and new lives, she could forget how disarming his green eyes and soft lips were and how they made her want to do very dirty things with him. But right now, her body seemed to order her to live in the moment. *Shed that good girl part of you with a man you can trust.*

Only she couldn't trust him. Not anymore.

"Confession. My mom's told me a bit about you, too." He reached across the countertop and took her hand. "And she's mentioned how worried she is about you. Always the one to put the weight of her family on her shoulders."

Malia looked down at his thumb rubbing across her knuckles. His hand was so much bigger than hers and comfort, warmth, and curiosity mingled to remind her of how much power his touch had once held. With each pass of his calloused finger she softened toward him a little more.

She pulled her hand away. Tears threatened the backs of her eyes so it took her a minute to answer. She didn't want him to make her feel better. "I'm fine."

He'd always made her *feel*. So, so much.

"Your turn," she said, lifting her eyes back to his with steely determination. "Since your mom hasn't told me *that* much."

"No? Okay, I'm head of security for World Heritage Fund, one of the biggest nonprofit organizations dedicated to heritage protection. Home base for the office is Idaho, but I'm hardly there, instead traveling all over the world."

Her mind immediately raced to the Halia Alika Temple and her trespassing on protected land. The scaffolding and other equipment. If the sacred site was part of his working vacation, he could ruin her whole reason for being here.

"That's not all you do, though, right?" she asked to steer the conversation away from anything that involved conservation. She felt torn enough about what she had to do.

Again he raised an eyebrow.

"Your mom did mention something." He stayed quiet, studying her, and her legs wobbled. She held onto the counter. "About you writing code for an app."

"Yes, but it requires very little of my time now." He moved casually along the counter.

"You always had killer math skills. What does your app do?"

"It locates cell phones through Google maps." He stopped beside her—their bodies not quite touching, his clean, masculine scent surrounding her.

She'd worried about him hundreds of times after he'd left to join the navy, and seeing him now, whole and healthy and oh, so sexy, she'd be lying to herself if she said she wasn't happy he stood close enough to kiss.

"So it finds someone who might be in trouble. Or

missing." She didn't need him to explain what had driven him to create such a program. His father had been his hero.

"Yes. Although I don't personally do the finding."

Protecting. That's what he'd always done. She was proud of him—for all his accomplishments. But even if he hadn't achieved his high level of success, she'd still feel things for him she'd never felt for anyone else. Something about him, something she couldn't name, had *always* made her feel like she belonged to him.

Stupid, she knew. So, so stupid. She reminded herself to keep her guard up and her heart closed off. He'd devastated her once. He'd do it again. *I never planned to see you again,* he'd said.

"That's a shame."

He grinned and the potency of it stole her breath. His dimples should come with an advisory label: *Will cause hearts to flutter and panties to spontaneously combust.* "What about you?"

"What about me?" She swallowed the lump sitting in the back of her throat.

"You haven't told me why you're here."

She took a step back. His intuitiveness made her jumpy. But worse, his nearness made her light-headed and warm in places she shouldn't be. She seriously thought about stopping the conversation by flinging her arms around his neck and kissing him until talking was the last thing he wanted to do.

Which would be a huge mistake. She may secretly crave to be a little bit bad, and remember how good being bad with Clay had felt, but right now, given the situation with her mom, her emotions were too raw. She was too vulnerable.

"I'm here for a little R&R and to spend time with

Kalani." That's what she'd told everyone. With a busy studio and all her free time spent with her mom, she did need a little mental break. A few days to lose herself.

You could lose yourself in Clay.

He narrowed his eyes and eliminated the space she'd put between them. "You also here to excavate?"

What?

His smug smile made her mad…and somehow hotter. Dammit, why did he have to make her feel stuff? Then he licked the pad of his thumb and proceeded to wipe the corner of her forehead. "You've got a little dirt here," he said, his voice and touch equally seductive. "And"—he dropped his arm—"under your fingernails."

She stared at him. For several long, agonizing seconds.

He could probably tell her what color her bra and panties were with his insane powers of deduction.

"Still the strong silent type when things get uncomfortable." The annoyingly sexy turn of his lips grew a little bigger. "How about we go for a swim? If I win you tell me everything going on in that pretty head of yours, and if you win I'll tell you everything going on in mine." He leaned forward and dipped his head so his mouth practically grazed the side of her neck. "Although you might not like the things I'm thinking about."

Her breath committed some type of stop-go action that had every cell in her body turned on *and* scrambling to stay calm. She squeezed her thighs together. "I thought you were leaving."

He pulled back and she was lost in the angles and planes of his drop-dead-handsome face. "You chicken?"

"No." She shook his good looks from her rattled mind.

Years ago, her father had put a bright yellow buoy out in the ocean as a marker for her and her sisters not to swim beyond. On the several occasions Rosie and Clay came with her family to the island, she and Clay would race around the buoy. He might have been bigger and stronger, but he hadn't been a swimmer and she usually beat him.

"I'll give you a head start."

A part of her wanted to run. Remind him to finish his sandwich and go. But another part of her, a bigger part, wanted to play this game. Wanted to throw caution to the wind and feel the salt water on her skin with him beside her. She could swim and keep her wits about her, right? God, she didn't know what the right choice was.

Until he laced their fingers together and added, "I want to be in the water with you again, *nani girl*."

Her knees went weak and trembles raced down her spine. *Beautiful girl* had been a special nickname only he used. In a matter of minutes, Clay had captured her interest, her desire, her curiosity.

Now older and wiser, she could keep her emotions under control. Her heart tucked away. She hated to let fear rule her actions. This trip was about adventure, too, and right now, today, she could do this.

She slipped her hand free. "I get half the distance to the buoy, then you start."

His jaw clenched. "It's not often I take orders anymore, but for you I'll make an exception. Get your suit on and meet me on the sand in ten."

"Yes, sir." She gave him a salute and raced out of the kitchen. Not since her youth, and the time she'd spent with Clay, had so much excitement thrummed through her blood.

Spontaneity didn't come naturally, but it had landed her here. In this moment. She needed more spur-of-the-moments in her life. More opportunities to be reckless. She just hoped she wasn't making a huge mistake.

Clay had done a lot of stupid shit in his life but thought he'd gotten past it. The last twenty minutes, however, were...stupid. Shit.

He stood on the private beach outside the Davis home and wanted to drop and give himself twenty for letting lust instead of logic rule his decisions. He didn't give up control. Ever. Except with Malia, and that should have been his first fucking clue to leave her alone. *She's not safe around you. Cut her loose.*

Instead he'd thrown out a swimming challenge, knowing she'd take the bait, and knowing he couldn't walk away from her until he knew the real reason she was on the island.

Malia didn't play in the dirt.

She read books and played solitaire and watched old movies. Her only outdoor hobby was swimming, so the dirt thing tied his stomach in a peculiar knot.

Maybe she's changed, dude.

Or maybe she's hiding something. He couldn't shake the idea that she'd been up to something she shouldn't be. The alarmed look on her face when he'd wiped the dirt from her forehead had given her away.

He dropped to do fifty one-armed push-ups, a damn pain in the ass in the sand. But stupidity came at a price and sometime in the last few minutes he'd lost his mind. He'd only cause Malia more pain, inevitably push her away, but he couldn't seem to let those thoughts override the others.

"Seriously?" she said, coming up behind him.

Forty-eight, forty-nine, fifty. He jumped to his feet, wiped his hands on his board shorts. And almost fell right back into the sand.

Holy hell she was breathtaking. Her pink string bikini accentuated curves more generous than she'd had before and that alone would render most men brain-dead. But combined with the sparkle in her eyes and wet-dreams-are-made-of-this mouth, he was done for.

Her gaze swept over him with definite appreciation, too. "What are you going to do after we swim? Pull-ups with the other arm?"

"I could."

She put her hands on her hips. "You're not human."

"Neither are you."

"I beg your pardon?"

"Ethereal comes to mind." Her ponytail hung over her shoulder and he reached out to run a few silky, soft strands between his fingers. Christ. What was he doing? Saying?

A blush overtook her bronze complexion before she stepped around him. "Let's do this, bad boy."

Watching her walk down to the water, this boy wanted to be very bad. From the front. From behind. From the bottom. From the top. And because five was his lucky number, up against the wall.

She didn't stand a chance of beating him, and he hadn't yet decided if he'd let her win. Pushing her to open up had been a stupid, selfish move, but he had to know if she was up to something that could get her in trouble. He couldn't turn off his protective instincts, regardless of the consequences.

He wanted her to confide in him again, share her secrets. Even though they'd both be better off if she didn't.

Because Clay kept people safe, but he didn't get emotionally invested.

Chapter Three

Clay let her lead all the way until the last stroke. He'd always loved watching her swim and found he still did. She glided through the water, barely making a ripple in the tranquil sea this afternoon.

Things were less graceful when they scrambled out of the water and raced onto shore. He turned and ran backward to keep an eye on her, a move Malia hated by the scowl on her face.

He smiled and raised his arms in victory.

She pushed him in the chest in a surprise move that stole his balance and he landed on his ass in the sand.

Not to be outdone, he reached out and grabbed her ankle when she tried to pass. She kicked to shake him off, but her twisting gave him just the purchase he needed. With his free hand he grabbed her waist and pulled her down on top of him.

"Let me go!" She squirmed and pressed her hands into

his shoulders for leverage, but he liked having her in this position and had no plans to relinquish his hold just yet.

When she realized her efforts were wasted, she stilled. Or maybe it was when their eyes connected and a jolt of electricity and familiarity passed between them. Their last Christmas here, he'd taken her on this beach. Covered her with his body and then rolled them over so he could watch her ride him.

"Clay," she said on a sigh.

"Yeah, *nani girl*?"

She smiled—against her will he suspected—but pleasure gripped him all the same. "What are you doing?"

"Me? I'm the one pinned against the sand, baby."

And it felt fucking fantastic. They lined up in all the right places, her breasts pressed against his chest, her waist molded to his, her thighs bracketed one of his so her center touched the front of his hip.

A swallow worked its way down her throat.

Jesus. What the hell was he doing, playing with her like this? He could not give in to his attraction. She needed to stay far, far away from him.

His hands, however, didn't get the memo, and slid to her perfectly round ass.

"Clay."

"Right here."

She closed her eyes as if enjoying the sensation of his hands on her backside. "When are you leaving the island?" she whispered, her thick, dark lashes lifting.

"Maybe a week." During which he didn't need a beautiful distraction. His goal was to catch a criminal. Sergio Benoit and his men were expected to arrive in Kauai in the next couple of days.

But when something passed over her features that looked surprisingly like displeasure, his ego took a hit. "Too long for your liking?" he said.

"Yes."

"Because…"

She shrugged as if her answer was insignificant.

He needed an explanation. He rotated his hips and roamed his hands over her ass and up her back. Time to loosen her up and get her to—

"Uh, Clay?"

Not the lust-filled, I'll-tell-you-anything tone of voice he'd been hoping for.

"There's a very cute young boy standing right there." She nodded over his head.

Clay lifted his chin and looked behind him. Sure enough, little Alex stood over them in bright orange trunks that reached his ankles and a temporary shark tattoo on his chest.

"Hey, buddy," Clay said, carefully moving Malia to the side before twisting to see what his small friend wanted. Clay had tried to keep his distance from the neighbors, but Mrs. Stein had recognized him after he'd come in from a swim and invited him over. He couldn't say no.

"Why was she on top of you?" Alex said.

A cross between a gasp and a giggle spilled from Malia and she slapped her hand over her mouth.

"She tripped."

"And you catched her?"

"That's what a gentleman does." Clay ruffled the kid's hair. "And a young man doesn't leave the house without his mom. You run right back."

"Shake first?"

Clay put his arm out and they performed the secret handshake. Alex grinned and ran back home. When Clay returned his attention to Malia, her eyes sparkled brighter than a brand new penny.

"Busted," she said. "You pretend to be all rough and tough, but on the inside you're a big softie."

"I guarantee you there is nothing soft—"

She slid her palm down his chest and his skin burned. "It's not the first time I've seen you be nice to someone younger than you."

In an attempt to clean up his image and make his mom proud, during his senior year of high school he'd volunteered one Saturday a month at the Boys & Girls Club. He'd never forget the feel of Malia's arms around him when she found out. *I'm proud of you,* she'd whispered in his ear. Truth was, the kids there gave more to him than he gave to them.

"Who was he?" Malia asked. "Wait." Her gaze moved to catch one last look at Alex before he disappeared into the house. "Is that Mrs. Stein's *grandson*?"

Clay nodded. "His name's Alex. He and his parents are visiting." A faraway look crossed her face that stirred some unnamed emotion deep in his chest. "When was the last time you were here, Malia?"

"It's been almost five years."

"And what really brought you here now? With your mom sick, I'm surprised you'd leave her."

The gleam in her eyes vanished and her shoulders sagged. He waited until she got comfortable, arms wrapped around her bent legs, before sitting next to her. His arm grazed hers as they stared out to the sea, the sun on its way to greeting the horizon.

Silence lingered for several minutes. Not uncomfortable, but he sensed uncertainty from her. Whatever her reason for being here, he got the feeling he'd messed it up. "You know I'm not going to leave it alone until you tell me. And I did win the race."

She glared at him. "I hate you."

Yeah, he figured that. Deserved it.

He fought the urge to put his arm around her and tell her the reasons he'd left without a word. When they were together, she'd talked about forever. College, then finding a small house to live in, having a family. His stomach pinched. He owed her an explanation.

"Remember the day I got my driver's license?" he asked instead, the memory sneaking up on him out of nowhere.

"How could I forget?" She straightened her back and lifted her face to the clear blue sky. "God, I can still remember the wind on my face and the exhilaration humming through my veins."

They'd "borrowed" her father's convertible and hit the freeway late at night. Clay had wanted to show off so he'd gunned it and sped over 100mph.

"It was the first peek I got at your desire to be reckless."

She dropped her head. "I was just along for the ride."

"No. You'd gotten into a fight with Kalani and gave in like you usually did. Conceding always ate at you." He ran a hand through his wet hair. "You needed to let off steam. You needed to fly, soar like nothing could touch you and I wanted to help you get there." She had that same tightly wound unease about her now.

"You did. I was never afraid to let you see all of me."

She absently rubbed a finger across her mouth, drawing his attention there. "That night was also the first time you kissed me."

His control was about to snap. "It took me a while to get up the nerve."

Her eyes widened in surprise.

"I didn't want to blow it with my best friend."

She smiled and the years that had passed did nothing to extinguish the desire that tore through him whenever she blessed him with that sexy turn of her lips.

"I can't believe we were able to keep our relationship a secret the whole time."

We didn't.

"What secret are you keeping now?"

"I hate you," she repeated, but when he sat there to wait her out she let out a breath and added, "I might be here to get a crystal that can help heal my mom."

He silently cursed. Flexed his hands. "By 'get' you mean dig up?"

Her eyes narrowed in irritation. "Yes," she conceded.

"Where are you digging?" He was just being an idiot now. He knew all about Peridot crystal. Its healing powers were the reason it was sought after. Its scarcity and recent popularity made it valuable. Worth killing for.

"That's none of your business."

Shit. She'd just made it his business whether he liked it or not.

A group of guys and girls, voices loud and happy, came down the beach. They held towels and grocery bags. One guy had a cooler.

"We should head in," Malia said, lifting up.

Clay jumped to his feet and put out a hand to help her up. "I'll pack up and then get out of your way." Their conversation wasn't over, but he had to give some thought to it. If he could get his hands on a piece of the crystal, he'd hand it over to her right now. But he couldn't. Hawaiian officials had what they'd retrieved so far. The rest remained on the sacred grounds to trap Benoit.

Instead of releasing his hand when she was upright, though, she held on. Stepped closer. And damn if her eyes didn't darken and the air between them didn't buzz like a lit fuse on a stick of dynamite. "Don't go," she said, her voice soft, but firm. "Stay here for tonight. With me."

Malia couldn't believe she'd gotten the words out. Despite Clay's prying, she didn't want to say good-bye. Not yet. Not when her body ached with need, her nipples hardening underneath her bikini top as Clay's sexy viridescent eyes never broke contact with hers. She'd revisited the past more times than she could count, but remembering their first kiss with him right next to her had her craving to see if he still tasted the same. Kissed the same.

No other man's kiss had come close to matching the white-hot flame Clay lit inside her with his lips and his tongue, his hands in her hair, as he gave and took. Bit and sucked. He was right. There wasn't anything soft about him.

His intense stare drove her wild at the same time it worried her. "Say something," she whispered. She could see how much he wanted her, but just like their first time, he waged a battle within himself, about doing the right thing.

Only she didn't care about that. Never had. She'd only cared about him.

And now the only thing she wanted was to lose herself to his touch and his heat and feel him inside her one more time. Instead of make-up sex, this would be good-bye sex.

"I don't think…" He jammed his fingers through his hair, glanced down. "If I stay, it's going to be in your bed."

Her pounding heart relaxed, the fear that he'd reject her floating away like tiny grains of sand in the wind. "I know."

"And we're not going to sleep."

"I'm good with that, too."

He put his free hand on her lower back and brought her close. She moved into his hold with pleasure. "You have no idea what keeping you close means."

"I've missed you too," she admitted. She couldn't help it. A delicious shudder threaded its way from the top of her head to the bottom of her feet. "What do you say we forget about the past, not think about tomorrow, and live in the moment?"

"I say I'm all yours."

"Really?" She leaned into him so her breasts brushed his chiseled chest. Her stomach quivered. "Big strong alpha man like you giving me control?"

"That's not at all what I said, *nani girl*."

She sucked in a breath for the tenth time. He made her feel like she stood at the edge of a cliff ready to jump into dangerous but worth-it waters.

"I need a shower and then I'll meet you back in the kitchen," he said. A wicked gleam danced in his eyes. "You need to eat something. You're going to need your strength."

Malia gulped. She had no delusions about who held the

real power. She'd never been able to control herself around Clay and that was one of the parts about herself she'd missed the most. Only he had brought out her carefree, wild side.

His sheepish grin bracketed by those sexy dimples turned her to mush. "Problem?"

She gave him a playful push and made a run for the house. "It's a good thing I need a shower, too," she called over her shoulder.

What she really needed was time to tuck her emotions into a small, Clay-proof vault. If she had any hope of surviving this secret wish come true to be with him one more time, she had to look at tonight as just about sex and nothing else.

But twenty minutes later, the shower hadn't helped. All she could think about while she'd stood under the warm rivulets was Clay's hands on her. His made-for-sin mouth. In the past her emotions had ruled her actions. The first time she'd made love with Clay happened after she'd told him she loved him. This time meant a physical release, nothing more.

She threw her towel on the bed and looked through the clothes she'd brought. Shorts, yoga pants and T-shirts since her plans focused on digging up a piece of Peridot crystal, but she luckily packed a couple of sundresses, too.

As she picked up the yellow one with a white border and pulled it over her head, her cell phone rang. She glanced at the screen and immediately felt horrible. She'd forgotten to call her sister when she'd landed. Six. Hours. Ago.

"I'm so sorry," she said in lieu of hello.

Her sister's deep, disappointed breath came through loud and clear. "You're alive."

Malia rolled her eyes and sat on the edge of the bed. "I'm at the house and I'm sorry I forgot to call."

"How could you forget? You land. You call. It's a no-brainer, Mal. I've been worried sick and tried you a half dozen times before now. I even called Mom to see if your flight was changed or something. Now she's worried, too."

Tears pricked the back of Malia's eyes. Dammit. The last thing she wanted was her mom getting worked up. "I'm sorry," was all she could think to say again. She pressed a few fingers to her forehead and swallowed the emotion in the back of her throat.

Kalani must have heard the regret in her voice. "Is everything all right? I really wish you'd stay with me like I thought we'd agreed."

"I'm fine," she lied. She was upset about her sister calling home. She was mad she hadn't found the damn crystal. She was dizzy and aroused because of Clay. She *should* leave and go stay with her sister.

"Where have you been?" Kalani asked.

"Here at home." She had no plans to tell her sister about the crystal. Kalani didn't believe in Hawaiian culture as deeply as Malia did. If Malia brought up Mana—the spiritual energy and healing power that existed in some places, people and objects—Kalani would think it stupid. But the green volcanic crystal, known as the tears of Pele, the great goddess of the volcano, had energy and power *and* would help their mom. Malia *knew* it.

"I planned to have some groceries delivered tomorrow," Kalani said, "thinking you'd come here for dinner tonight."

Malia bit back a chuckle at her earlier guess about groceries. "I can't do dinner."

"Something *did* happen."

Yeah. Something tall, dark and sexy. Flutters kicked up

deep in her belly thinking about what she and Clay were going to do tonight. She squeezed her eyes shut and forced second thoughts away. To love someone for so long and hate him at the same time left a girl very confused.

"Mal?"

Tell her the truth? Make something up? Malia stood and looked at the clothes strewn all over her bed. She wished she'd brought prettier undergarments.

"Hello?"

"I'm just tired and want to stay in. We'll catch up tomorrow, okay?" She glanced at the papers she'd printed about the history of the temple sticking out of her bag. Not really a lie. She did want to do some more research.

"You sure that's all it is?"

"Yes."

All those years ago, she'd almost told her sister the truth about Clay a few days after he'd left. Kalani had found her under the bedcovers with tears in her eyes and demanded to know what was wrong. But instead of coming out with it, Malia said the heroine in her book had just died.

"Okay, I'll talk to you tomorrow then."

Malia said good-bye and tossed the phone onto the bed. "White or red," she said to the room, weighing the lace panties in her hands.

"Red," a deep, sexy voice said from behind her. She spun around.

Clay stood in the doorway of her bedroom wearing jeans and a black T-shirt that stretched across muscles too good to be true. His hair was damp. His feet were bare. And his heated gaze lit a torch inside her.

"How long have you been standing there?"

"Long enough to know you didn't tell your sister I was here."

"It's not polite to eavesdrop."

"Polite is the last thing on my mind." He stepped into the room and the air snapped, crackled and popped. Sooo much better than the cereal she'd had for breakfast this morning.

"I thought we were meeting in the kitchen."

"I was there. You weren't, and I couldn't wait any longer." With slow, deliberate steps he got closer. And closer.

A tag team of butterflies played in her stomach.

He lifted her hands and glanced at the panties she hadn't realized she still clutched. "Tell me you're bare underneath the dress."

She gulped. "I'm bare underneath this dress."

Gently dropping her arms back to her sides, he slid his finger down the center of her chest. Tingles shot out from the tips of her breasts and gathered at the base of her spine, between her legs. "Tell me you want me as much as I want you," he said, his voice husky.

Never had she imagined doing something as reckless as sleeping with a guy for one night. But this wasn't any guy. And it wasn't just about her getting off—God, how she needed to do that. It was about closure. Saying good-bye on her terms. It might be a bad idea, but it was the best bad idea she'd ever had.

She dropped the panties and put her hands on his chest. "I want you."

Chapter Four

"You're still the most beautiful woman I've ever laid eyes on." Clay covered her hands with his as the sweet words he spoke took her to liftoff. Pretty much anything he did to her in the next sixty seconds guaranteed her a happy ending. She was *that* turned on already.

"You're not too shabby yourself."

"Turn around, Malia."

She didn't even think about it, just did as he said.

He tucked her against his body and a moan escaped her lips when she felt his arousal. His big, strong hands slid down her waist, over her hips and down the sides of her thighs.

"I want to go slow, baby, I really do," he whispered at the side of her neck. "But I'm not going to be able to this first time."

"Thank heavens."

The warm breath from his chuckle tickled her collarbone. "How long has it been since you've been with a man?" he murmured while his fingers slipped under the hem of her dress.

Great. He could tell she was pent-up? "A while."

"Be specific." His fingertips walked up the inside of her thighs, lifting her dress as they did so.

She reached up and wrapped her arms around his neck, letting her head fall back on his shoulder. "Two years." The move left her completely to his taking.

He groaned. "Do you have any idea how sexy you are?" He pressed on her legs and she opened them wider.

She shook her head. He kissed the underside of her jaw, the corner of her mouth. Every nerve ending in her body sparked.

"Then it's become my mission to show you." Those nimble fingers of his pulled her dress up, and higher still, until he reached the sides of her very sensitive breasts. "Unhook your arms."

Malia did and then the dress was gone and she stood naked pressed against two hundred pounds of male perfection. She laced her fingers behind his neck again and her eyes drifted shut.

"Your body is magnificent," he said against the lobe of her ear. She had no idea that little spot held so much pleasure.

But when his palms found her lower abdomen and made a slow trek up her rib cage to her breasts, that pleasure burst into coils of need so strong she whimpered and rocked against the very big bulge in his pants.

"I thought you weren't going to go slow," she said, ready to beg him to hurry up.

His thumbs rubbed over her hard, sensitive nipples and

she arched into his touch. "When I'm inside you, buried so deep I'm the only thing that exists in your world, that's when I'm not going to go slow. It's going to be fast and hard because I'm going to lose my mind."

"What are you waiting for? I want you inside me now."

"Not yet, *nani girl*." His left hand stayed on her breast, cupping, rubbing, kneading, while his right hand drifted lower. "Not until I make you come first."

She turned her head so her lips grazed his jaw. "I'll come with you inside me."

"Yes, you will." He gazed down at her, their mouths brushing, and she could barely breathe. "But first you're going to come just like this."

And then finally, *finally*, his mouth fused with hers at the same time his lower hand stroked her sweet spot.

She opened to him, his kiss wild and hot and demanding. Sensation after sensation swept through her. Clay had always known exactly how to touch her. But right now? Holy mother of pearl, this more mature, slightly rough but caring assault had her on fire.

What he did with his tongue in her mouth and his hand between her legs was magic and she felt her orgasm build, her muscles grow tighter and tighter, until her entire body shook and she was flying.

Clay took her bottom lip between his teeth before letting go so she could catch her breath. He held her like he cherished her and she spun around before that crazy thought took root somewhere it shouldn't. She lifted his shirt over his head. Ran the pads of her fingers over the delicious bumps and grooves of his torso as she lowered to her knees.

"It's really unfair how attractive your body is," she said.

He stilled her hands when they went for the button of his jeans. "Get on the bed."

She scooted onto the mattress, pushing her clothes and bag aside. But in doing so the papers she'd printed on the temple fell out. Clay's eyes darted to the floor. He noticed them. He definitely did. So she quickly cupped her breasts, ran her hands over their fullness. "Isn't this the part where you speed up?" she teased. And being bolder than she'd ever been before, let her knees fall open and slid one hand to her wet, achy center.

Leaning back on one elbow, she watched him hurry to pull a condom from his pocket. "Jesus fucking Christ." He undid his pants and in two seconds flat stood naked and ready at the edge of the bed. The way his eyes raked over her body, with heat and lust and *emotion*, her arousal roared to life again. She saw her eagerness and desire mirrored back at her. Saw that maybe he'd been thinking of her as much as she'd thought of him over the past ten years.

"Hurry," she breathed. "I need you to fill me up."

"Baby, I'm gonna do more than that." He moved over her, cupped her cheek and kissed her. Not the same dominating way he just had, but with tenderness and soft brushes of his lips back and forth, with the sweetness she knew lived buried deep inside his hard, tough exterior.

She put her hands on his neck and kissed him back with every soft thing she carried inside her walls.

A moment later he broke the kiss, pressed back onto his knees and thrust inside her. She cried out at the biting pleasure of his entry. Then fisted her hands in the comforter when her body adjusted and the exquisite feel of him taking her fast and furious like he promised had her moving with him. It didn't take long for her to reach the edge of satisfaction a second time. When Clay shifted her hips higher and rubbed her in the perfect spot she fell over, his name on her lips.

He followed right behind, his eyes squeezing shut and his groan of release music to her ears.

Their lovemaking was raw and uninhibited.

Just the way she needed it to be.

"Is everything okay?" Malia asked as Clay came back into the family room, tossed his cell on the coffee table and resumed his spot on the couch. He took her feet into his lap and ground his jaw together. Even her toes were sexy.

"Depends on your definition."

She giggled when he massaged the underside of her foot. Every noise she made sounded unbelievably good. "Hmm. Sounds like someone or something is butting into your alone time." She glanced at his bare chest and every time she did that he smiled on the inside.

The easy, comfortable companionship they'd fallen into after eating and getting naked again so he could take her against the kitchen wall could definitely be considered interference, but he thought it cute she saw his phone call and not herself as troublesome.

"It's work related. I'll deal with it tomorrow." He should get his ass up to the temple, but the other security guys were some of the best and could handle things at the moment. Out of the corner of his eye, he looked at Malia. When she'd asked him to stay the night, he'd been floored. And happy.

Happier than he'd been in a long damn time. So he'd rationalized that staying with her, keeping her close, *was* keeping her safe.

The more he thought about it, in fact, the more it became clear he shouldn't let her out of his sight. If that meant staying under the same roof...

"I hope it's nothing serious." She sank a little deeper into the couch, his black T-shirt riding up her thighs as she did so and he swallowed a groan, wanting to be inside her again. He felt a pang of guilt at the rough way he'd handled her before, so wrapped in her spell he couldn't control himself.

"Nothing the team can't handle."

"Team?" her voice cracked. "What's going on?"

Damn she was cute when nervous. And now she'd know their chance meeting was a much more complicated twist of fate. "There's been some trouble with trespassers at the Halia Alika Temple."

The muscles in her feet went rigid beneath his hands.

"The temple is a historic site on protected land and trespassing is taken seriously. The monument is also under renovation and we don't want its integrity compromised while work is in progress."

She simply nodded rather than tell him that's where she'd been.

He got a sick feeling in his stomach. "I'm going to swing by there in the morning."

She pulled her legs back and scrambled up onto her knees in a very unsmooth move. He narrowed his eyes. "Something wrong?" he asked.

"No. I, uh, just need a drink of water." She started off the couch.

He wrapped his arm around her waist and pulled her into his lap. "Not so fast."

"Let me go." She squirmed. He held tighter.

"Can't." Even though he should. Even though he should put a stop to whatever this was between them before it burned any hotter. He *could* keep tabs on her from afar. That's all he should be focused on. Keeping her safe.

"You mean won't." She stopped fighting, but her coffee-colored eyes, always so expressive, held a shitload of spitfire.

"Talk." He didn't know why it was so important that she confide what she was up to except that he didn't want to pry her secrets from her. He wanted her to trust him. If she didn't and he told her what he could about the Peridot, that didn't mean she'd back off.

The damn silent treatment pressed her lips into a tight line. She crossed her arms over her chest.

"Not going to work this time, *nani girl*." He hated that she clammed up on him. Hated that every protective, possessive fiber inside him stood at attention. All for her.

A minute passed.

Five.

"Why are you doing this?" she said softly.

"Because I care." She had no idea what she'd walked into and he wouldn't let anything happen to her. A simple conversation—as much as he could share—would put this power struggle to rest, but dammit, his pride wanted to hear her confession. She'd always told him everything. He wanted—no, needed—her to tell him everything now.

The lines spoiling her soft features deepened. She blinked in slow motion. "If that were true—"

He pressed his finger to her mouth. "We agreed to live

in the moment. And right now something is bothering you. I want to help."

"There's a much better way to do that than talk."

She drew her bottom lip between her teeth and every rational thought broke into a hundred tiny pieces. His mouth landed on hers an instant later.

If this was what she needed from him, he'd give it to her.

She slid her hands into his hair and kissed him like she'd missed every day they'd been apart and wanted to make up for all of it. Wide open and giving, she swirled her tongue with his and a grenade of pleasure ripped through his muscles.

He wrapped his arms around her waist and stood. She tied her legs around him, her hot center, covered by the tiny pair of red panties he'd gotten a peek of, pressed against his button fly. Without breaking the kiss, he carried her to the guest room and laid her down on the bed. He pulled out a condom from his bag and tossed it beside her.

"This the way you want?" he asked, his voice deeper than usual. God she looked beautiful in his shirt with her dark hair falling in soft waves around her shoulders.

"Yes." Her eyes glittered with arousal and affection.

"Lift up your arms, baby."

She complied and he pulled the shirt over her head. He started with light kisses to her neck. "Your skin is like silk," he whispered, moving down her collarbone.

Her hands lifted his head and she tried to bring him down to her mouth, but he was running this show and didn't budge. "Put your arms at your sides and keep them there."

"Please," he added when she raised her eyebrows.

"I can't make any promises." She let go and smiled.

His heart stuttered. "Fair enough."

For a beat they stared at each other. He'd promised to make her feel sexy and clear her head and that's what he intended to do.

He cupped her breast and rubbed his thumb over her nipple. Slowly. Pursed his lips around her other nipple. He watched her eyes drift shut and her mouth fall open. Her breathing bumped up a notch.

"That feels…"

"Good?" He slid his tongue over to the other breast.

"So good." She pressed her shoulders into the bed, curving into his touch.

Sexy as hell.

Her breasts were perfectly round and firm and he continued to lavish them with his hands and mouth. He licked and nipped and sucked each rosy peak until she writhed and panted.

"Clay…"

God, he loved the way she said his name. He kissed down her stomach. Nibbled. Took her soft flesh between his teeth and lips and marked her. Made her his.

"Clay!"

He bit back a chuckle and blew over the love mark as his hand slipped over her panties with a featherlight touch. Her indignation immediately turned to lusty moans.

"Yes," she gasped.

"Yes?" His lips stretched into a grin. He didn't remember asking her a question.

"There. More there." She lifted her hips and pressed against his hand.

Oh, he planned to give her a hell of a lot more. He tore

her panties off with one quick pull.

Her body shuddered at the same time giggles erupted from her beautiful mouth. She fell back onto the bed. "I guess nothing comes between you and my…"

"Damn straight." He lifted her legs over his shoulders and bent his head to taste her.

"Oh God." She fisted her hands in the sheet but a second later her fingers were in his hair. Keeping him in place. Like there was anywhere else he wanted to be.

She was slick and hot. It made him so hard he had to undo his jeans. Then he reached for her, slipping one, then two fingers inside her warm, tight channel.

His tongue licked and teased her folds while he stroked with gentle, even glides and her hold tightened on the back of his head. In the next instant her entire body shook and she screamed out his name.

He didn't stop until her arms fell to the bed and she sighed in contentment.

Then he shucked his clothes, sheathed his cock and positioned himself at her opening. He kissed her shoulder, her neck. Her fingernails raked down his back, her legs wrapped around his thighs, bringing him closer.

This time he kept his control in check. He stared into her eyes, telling her without words that he'd make her feel good for as long as she let him.

She cradled his face in her hands and he let her bring him in for a kiss. Fuck if the sweet-tempered glide of her mouth against his didn't recapture his devotion. His attachment. She kissed him like he was the only man she let share this part of her and he fought the onslaught of emotions crashing over him. She'd always told him it was a kiss that captured a girl's heart.

He'd argue the same could be said for a man's.

They kissed for a long time. He relished her lips, her tongue, her breath. At some point he traced his fingers down her body until he found her center and gently worked her back into bliss.

He pulled his hand away and pressed inside her then, this time entering with a slow, steady glide that had her mouth opening wider and pressing against his like she wanted to devour him whole. *Jesus.* He swirled his tongue around hers and took back possession before she kissed him into an orgasm too soon.

Buried deep inside her, her legs tightened around him and her hands squeezed his ass. He knew just where she liked his pelvis, just how to shift and rub her body. With unhurried thrusts he took her higher, felt her clamp down around him. He lifted his head, their eyes met.

"Clay." She rocked against him, her nails dug into his flesh.

Feelings he hadn't a clue what to do with clogged his throat and he kept their perfect pace until her quickened breaths and the arch in her back signaled her climax was close.

He locked his lips with hers again. His heart beat faster. Her scent, her taste, her touch had him harder than he'd ever been in his life. He kissed her with everything he had and when her body pulsed and she shattered, he didn't let up. He didn't stop lavishing her mouth until his own release gripped him and he had to come up for air.

"That was…" She playfully nibbled on his earlobe, making the hair on the nape of his neck stand up. "Amazing."

"Amazing," he echoed. He rolled off her with a groan and cleaned up quickly, her giggle luring him back to bed.

He crawled beside her and tucked her under his arm. Without hesitation, she curled right up against him with her head on his chest, an arm across his stomach, and one leg wrapped over his.

It felt right having her there. It had only ever felt right with her.

Chapter Five

Malia woke to the sound of rain tapping the window. She stretched her very satiated muscles and before waking fully, pictured Clay. His gaze full of warmth and passion; his incredible, naked body as he pushed inside her; his smile, the one filled with mischief when he reacted to something she said or did.

Turning to her side in hopes of catching him in slumber, she opened her eyes and her heart bottomed out. She slid her hand over the cool, abandoned spot as her chest squeezed. She'd promised herself not to let him in, not to treat last night as anything special, but the tightness burning a hole behind her ribs said she'd failed epically at that.

Of course he'd hightailed it out of here this morning. He'd agreed to stay the night, nothing more, and the stupid way her heart hurt was ridiculous.

She rolled onto her back and pressed her fingers to her eyelids to push back the emotion threatening to spill out in tears she thought had dried up. She wasn't a teenager anymore and could handle this.

She didn't regret their night together. Not for a single second.

The only thing she regretted was not waking first and kissing him good-bye with a carefree attitude.

She brought her arms down and pressed her palms into the mattress, took a deep breath. She needed to put last night in the "win" column. Sex multiple times with a sexy man who had ninja-level seduction skills should probably be at the top of that column actually.

The ache started to dissipate and she smiled.

Besides, she was here on a mission and the man in her bed last night compromised that. She sat up and glanced out the window. Early summer storms usually passed quickly, but digging in the mud wouldn't be fun. And if Clay were onto her, which she suspected he was, she'd better not trespass again too soon. She wished he'd just come out and tell her he knew instead of waiting for her to come clean. Didn't he realize how hard that was for her?

She closed her eyes and allowed herself one more vision of his gorgeous everything. One more thought. When she opened her eyes she wouldn't spend another second thinking about Clay Doherty.

Only when she did lift her lids, she saw him standing in the doorway watching her. "Goddammit," she cussed.

The Clay in the doorway chuckled and said, "Good morning to you, too."

She blinked, but he still stood there. In the flesh. Her forehead fell into her palm. Her heart did a shimmy. "I thought you were a mirage."

He laughed again and the sound was altogether too delicious. "On a tropical island?" He moved into the room.

She shrugged.

"You thought I'd left." The bed dipped as he sat and handed her a cup of something that smelled like hot chocolate with cinnamon.

"Maybe."

His brows screwed up in disbelief.

"Can you blame me?"

Something flared in his eyes, but she wasn't sure what. "I did leave but I came back." He nudged the cup toward her mouth. "Let me know how I did."

She eyed him over the rim of the mug as she took a sip. The sweet drink slid down her throat and warmed her from the inside out. "You remembered how I like it."

"I remember everything." He tucked a strand of hair behind her ear. "And I'll never leave you again without saying good-bye."

She took another sip and dropped her gaze. "This is good. Thank you." She didn't know what to make of his pledge *or* his long-term memory. Trusting Clay again posed a huge risk she wasn't sure she could take.

"There's lemon poppy seed muffins in the kitchen."

Her stomach fluttered. Not entirely because of his stopping to buy her her favorite breakfast. "You've been busy this morning."

His eyebrows lifted.

"You're the one with a little dirt this time." She brushed his shirtsleeve but the smudge stayed. "Everything okay at the temple?"

"For the moment." He studied her with those damn

intoxicating eyes of his and she had to look away.

She put the mug down on the bedside table and gathered the sheet tighter around her like the thin cotton material could protect her. "That's good."

He caught her chin and tilted her head up so she had no choice but to fall prey to his handsome face again. "Is there something you want to tell me?"

"No."

"You sure?"

"Is there something *you* want to tell me?"

His jaw tensed and she tried not to laugh. Seeing him annoyed tickled her funny bone and all of a sudden she fell into a fit of laughter.

He sat there all stoic and sexy, and being near him again made her feel lighter than she'd been in forever.

When he didn't make a move, she sucked in a deep breath and got herself together.

The truth was, she could use his help. He'd probably find the crystal in no time. And if he were the old Clay, she might have asked by now. But he worked in heritage protection — was on the island to preserve the very site she was trespassing on — and she couldn't ask him to do something that went against his principles.

Or landed her in hot water.

"You're awfully chipper this morning," he said, his voice laced with a degree of cheer whether he admitted it or not.

"Sex does a body good."

His answering smile earned him the silent nickname Captain Magnificent. With his blinding white teeth and deep dimples that did serious damage to a girl's equilibrium, Malia had to press a hand into the bed to keep steady.

"I suggest a daily dose then."

"What?"

He reached out and traced a finger from her bare shoulder down her arm. Mini electrical charges detonated under her skin in quick succession. "You heard me."

"With you?"

"Not with anyone else," he practically growled before flashing the sexy grin again.

She might possibly hurl herself at him if he kept smiling like that. "I thought we were going our separate ways."

"Changed my mind and would much rather stay here to avoid the hotel crowd." He drew lazy circles on the top of her hand.

If he was trying to start a mad dash of tingles throughout her body, he'd succeeded. With a simple touch of his finger. Crap, he wasn't even close to being out of her system. "Sort of puts a kink in *my* plans." She pulled her hand back.

"Up to you."

"What does that mean?"

"It means stay wherever you want. It means…" He reclaimed her hand. "If you stay here I definitely won't complain. But I understand if you feel the need to bunk with Kalani."

He'd decided all by himself to stay in *her* house? She clenched her jaw. He had some nerve. "What exactly do you understand?"

"I make you nervous."

"No you don't." He did. On so many levels. But mostly in a good way. Which was worse than in a bad way.

"I make you hot."

She forced a laugh and said, "Maybe once, but not

anymore." She had to keep her head in this game and ignore her body. Forget attraction and affection and anything *hot*. He'd hurt her. Badly. "Last night was just about scratching a leftover itch. That's all."

One side of his very fine mouth quirked up, and one dimple teased just as annoyingly as both. "What if I said I wasn't done scratching?"

"Umm…"

"Stick around *nani girl*." He stood instead of whipping the sheet off her like she'd been secretly hoping he'd do. "The house is big enough for both of us." Then he turned and walked out of the room.

Leaving her confused and a little sullen and she hated to admit it, *hot*. He was right, though. They could both stay at the house. He could come and go. She could come and go. They didn't have to be connected at the hip or anything. Although being hip-to-hip with him… She threw the sheets off and hopped out of bed. Some low, growly, frustrated noise came out of her mouth as she threw Clay's T-shirt back on to make her way to her bedroom to shower and call her mom and sisters.

An hour later she stepped into the kitchen with a little spring in her step. Not because she'd missed Clay, but because no one made a better lemon poppy seed muffin than the little bakery in Princeville.

"You didn't get all this, did you?" she asked. Muffins sat on the counter, along with bananas and bagels, mangos and nuts.

Clay tossed the newspaper in his hand to the side. He rose from the couch in the family room and walked toward her, his gait faltering for a moment like he'd stepped on something. "No. It was delivered a few minutes ago. I put everything else away in the fridge."

"Thanks. It's from Kalani. She's worried I can't feed myself." Malia grabbed a muffin. "She, uh, invited us to the hotel for dinner tonight."

"Us?" He leaned against the counter, elbows on the granite, and she couldn't help but notice his biceps bulge underneath his navy blue tee.

"I talked to her this morning and mentioned you this time." Thankfully, Kalani had been running into a meeting and let the brief remark go without any questions. Not that Malia would have answered them.

He gave a small nod and moved around the counter. Her pulse galloped as he took the muffin out of her hand and wrapped his arms around her waist. "Hi."

"Hi?" Sweet surrender, he smelled good. And she itched to run her fingers through his tousled dark hair.

"You look really pretty this morning." He *felt* really good this morning, hard against her soft, big to her small.

She blinked at him. She had on yoga pants and a pale blue V-neck tee. "Thanks."

For a split second she thought she saw a hint of vulnerability cross his face. "You're beautiful and irresistible, Malia, and we'll do this however you want. But you should know I want all of you while I'm here."

Her pulse raced faster.

"One night wasn't enough for me. Was it for you?"

"No," she whispered, wishing it was. Huge pieces of her were dangerously close to falling under his spell again. A really bad idea considering he had the power to do major damage to her heart in a way no one else ever had.

She hadn't booked a return flight home and this morning her mom had sounded well on the phone. Happy even, when Malia had mentioned Clay. So she *could* take this one day at a time. She'd never let herself do anything like that before.

He kissed her forehead. "Come on. We'll eat on the couch and watch a movie or two. It's supposed to rain most of the day so I bought a couple of DVDs." With his fingers intertwined with hers, she let him deposit her on the soft cotton sofa.

"You got *North By Northwest* and *Some Like It Hot*?" She picked the movies up off the coffee table. Oh my God was he adorable.

"You still like classics, right?" he called on his way back to the kitchen.

"Yes, but I would've watched something more current with blood and guts." She kept *for you* from falling out of her mouth at the end of that sentence.

He handed her a muffin and put down a bunch of other food he'd carried in his arms. His step faltered again just before he sat and stretched out his right leg. "I wasn't sure what else you wanted." He had the cutest expression on his face, like he truly wanted this day to be about her.

"Are you okay?" In her peripheral vision she noticed him perch his foot on the edge of the coffee table and wince. He had on athletic shorts and shoes and his long legs were all sinewy and strong, but something seemed off.

"Perfect."

She crossed her arms and gave him a look.

He let his head fall back as he said, "I stepped on a nail when I was at the temple this morning."

"Did you clean it? Are you current with your tetanus

shots?" She'd seen the scaffolding and other equipment and they'd looked older than the dirt she'd been digging in.

His eyes softened, and so did her heart. "Thanks for your concern, but I'm fine."

"Are you normally this accident prone?" she teased.

"Never. Seems I've got something else on my mind." His gaze dropped to her mouth for a moment.

"I could kiss it and make it better."

"I can think of a few other places I'd rather you kiss."

So could she. *Gah*. If she had any hope of not totally succumbing to his charms every five minutes, she needed to get a grip.

She grabbed *Some Like It Hot* and thrust it at his chest. Jack Lemmon and Tony Curtis in drag ought to help. "Let's watch this one first."

He chuckled and she had no doubt he knew if he really wanted to start kissing her right now, she'd be on board with it. And kiss him in all the spots the sun missed out on. Poor sun.

"Marilyn Monroe's got nothing on you," he said, canting his head and letting his lips brush her ear.

She melted into the couch as she watched him start the movie. And when he sat back down and put his arm around her, she curled against him, forgetting everything else. His big, warm body felt so, so good.

They stayed huddled together on the couch for both films while the rain continued to fall outside, the pitter-patter a low hum through the open window. Humidity seeped into the house, the scent of the sea and the white hibiscus in planter boxes just outside, too. Feeling a little sweaty and sticky, Malia needed another shower before dinner.

And she definitely needed some company this time.

She got to her feet while Clay turned off the movie and television. When he turned back around and she got a look at his face, she froze.

All the color had drained from his cheeks and his hair hung matted to his forehead. "Clay? Are you okay?"

He fanned his shirt away from his stomach. "Just a little warm." He teetered and she rushed over to steady him.

"Whoa," she said, tucking an arm under his. She lifted her other arm and pressed her palm to his forehead. "Oh my God, you're burning up."

"I think I need to sit down."

She helped him back to the couch and her heart leaped into her throat when he basically collapsed on top of the cushions. "Clay!"

"It's okay," he said, his voice not at all convincing. "Something must be going through my system. It'll pass."

"Don't move." She rushed to get him a glass of water and some Tylenol.

"Still exactly where you left me," he said upon her quick return. His dim smile when she crouched down beside him twisted her stomach into a worried knot.

"Thank you. Let's sit you up a little better." But when she lifted under both his arms, he flinched and a very odd-sounding gasp met her ears. She let go and he hissed in a breath.

Her eyes ran down his body. "Shoes. Off," she commanded.

The fact that he didn't argue spoke volumes. Not sure which foot he'd hurt since he'd put a new pair of shoes on, she gently slipped both off. Then his socks.

She almost cried out when she saw the wound—red,

swollen, and a yellow-greenish fluid oozed out of it. "We need to get you to the ER."

He turned his ankle and looked down at it. "That? That's nothing." Her heart moved further up her throat, imagining the injuries he may have suffered in the past. "You're probably right, though. Only problem is…"

She put her hand on his stomach. His skin was on fire even through his shirt.

"I'm about to pass out."

Chapter Six

"Thank you so much, Marcus," Malia said, standing in the doorway of the guest bedroom. "I owe you." She smiled at her longtime friend and wished they'd connected again under better circumstances.

"How about dinner tomorrow night and I'll consider us even?" Marcus eyed her with warmth and regard as he finished zipping up his medical bag.

She smiled, not exactly sure what to make of his offer.

As a lean six-foot something with dirty blond hair and a face that turned heads, Marcus had always had an easy time with women. Add in the MD at the end of his name and she couldn't believe he wasn't already married.

She glanced at Clay tucked comfortably in bed. The emotions she'd tried to keep a grip on had only rooted themselves deeper in the last couple of hours.

"So?" Marcus said, his voice tender. "What do you say?"

"I…" She should say *absolutely*. Marcus was good-looking,

kind, smart, loved his family. He was the kind of guy a girl dreamed of catching. But he didn't ignite even the tiniest flutter or tingle anywhere in her body.

"Walk me out," he said, putting a hand on her arm and stepping around her. She followed him down the hall. "I'll call tomorrow to check in and you can let me know then."

"Okay." She opened the front door, grateful he'd taken such good care of Clay.

"The antibiotics should already be kicking in," he said. "But it could be a day or two before the fever is gone completely. Have him rest and drink plenty of liquids."

"Got it. Thanks again for coming so quickly."

He stepped onto the porch. "It's really good to see you again, Malia."

"You too." She lifted on tiptoes and kissed his cheek. "But I probably won't be available for dinner." She didn't want to leave him hanging when she already knew the answer. As much as she wished a date with him gave her something to look forward to, she couldn't make herself feel something she didn't.

Marcus gave a small, knowing smile. "I never could compete with that guy." He took a few backward steps. "If you change your mind, you know where to find me."

She leaned against the doorjamb and watched him go. What the heck was wrong with her? If she wanted a safe bet she was looking at one. But she'd come to the island to get the crystal for her mom, not start something with an old friend.

You've already started something.

As the last rays of sunshine bid farewell, the clear sky turned a royal blue. She watched Marcus drive away, sent a text to Kalani that dinner needed to be rescheduled, and then hurried back to Clay's side.

For a few minutes when he'd been barely coherent and refusing to admit he needed an ambulance, her stomach had turned inside out, her chest had constricted, and she'd gotten so mad she wanted to scream. Rationally she knew whatever he had wasn't life threatening, but it scared the crap out of her anyway. Crazy thoughts had edged out sane ones, and she would've given anything to make him feel better.

She was losing her mom. She couldn't lose him, too.

He's not yours to lose.

Somehow that made everything a hundred times worse. Too many feelings she couldn't name stuck to her like thorns on a rose, sharp yet beautiful. She hadn't felt this much since her last night with Clay. They'd snuck away to the gazebo in the backyard. A full moon and dozens of stars filled the August sky. He'd sat on the ground with her situated between his legs, his arms wrapped around her waist, her back to his front.

"You know there's nowhere I'd rather be than with you, right?" Clay whispered.

She nestled closer, wrapped her arms tight around his. "I feel the same way. You're my everything."

He kissed the top of her head. "Don't say things like that. I'm the lucky one. All my wishes on those stars somehow blinded you."

"You wish on the stars?" She tilted her head to peer up at him.

"Don't you?" The sparkle in his dark eyes was way better than any constellation.

She giggled. "Of course, but I didn't think you did. Seems sort of, I don't know, trivial for a guy like you."

"Guy like me?"

"You're the strongest person I know. But maybe like me, the stars look favorably upon you." She twisted and straddled his lap, her arms around his neck.

He grinned. *"I'm pretty sure you're my guardian angel and I have no idea what I did to keep your attention."*

"You loved me."

"I love you more than you'll ever know." His eyes clouded with something that sent a little shiver through her. *"Always remember that, okay?"*

"If you promise to remember how much I love you back."

His chest rose and fell and he closed his eyes.

"If you were to make a wish right now, what would it be?" she asked.

"To freeze time. I'd stop it right here and live in this moment with you forever." He kissed her then, slowly and softly, and as usual her heart fluttered like it had been swept up and carried away by a million butterflies. *"For the rest of my life I'll belong to you, nani girl."*

"You better have told him no."

Malia blinked with a start back to the present at the sound of Clay's voice. She slid to the edge of the chair she'd placed beside the bed and put a hand to his forehead. "How are you feeling?" His skin was still clammy, but not quite as hot as it had been. Relief washed over her.

"You better have told him no," he repeated.

"I have no idea what you're talking about." She lifted the glass of water on the bedside table and brought it to his mouth. "Sip."

"Marcus. Dinner." He sipped.

She tried not to let her delight show at his dislike for

those two words. "You heard that?"

He narrowed his eyes.

"I may have told him no, but it had nothing to do with you."

A little light sparked back into his eyes and she was happy to have put it there. "Good. You're the sexiest nurse I've ever had by the way."

Her stomach clenched. She hated that her thoughts wandered to nurses in hospitals *and* nurses in his bed. "How many nurses have you had?"

"Enough." He tried to sit up, seemed to think better of it, and relaxed. Mostly. He kicked the sheet aside and glanced at his foot. "Goddammit," he muttered. The white bandage stood out against his tanned skin.

Malia's eyes roamed over all the pure, beautiful male-ness now exposed. She couldn't help it. "Marcus gave you a tetanus shot and injected you with an antibiotic. It won't make you well faster, but it will lower the risk of the infec-tion spreading to other parts of your body. Aside from that, we'll keep it clean and wait out your fever."

He grumbled something incoherent.

"I'm sorry to say it looks like mud wrestling is out of the question for tonight."

His attention jumped back to her and one of his very sexy, very wicked crooked smiles appeared. "Not so. I'll be fine in—"

"Nice try, but you need to rest. And keep still. I'll make us some soup for dinner." She got to her feet and turned.

He caught her with his hand. "Hang on. You were sup-posed to have dinner with your sister." Tiny beads of sweat glistened on his forehead. He let out a run-down breath.

"I'll see her another night. I'm not leaving you."

"I'll be fine. You should go."

Maybe. But she wanted to take care of him. Wipe a cool cloth on his forehead, rub his back, make sure he drank plenty of water. And didn't that just muck things up further.

"Sorry Doh Boy, you're stuck with me."

You're in deep shit, Doherty.

He'd wondered what hearing her call him by her special nickname would do to him and now he knew. It felt like he'd come home.

The tease in her voice and her choice of words held more meaning than he suspected she realized.

She'd forgiven his leaving all those years ago.

Which made him want to tell her the reasons.

Or maybe it was the fever and the shitstorm going on in his bloodstream. He blinked and threw the covers all the way off his overheated body. Goddammit, he hated this.

"Hey." She sat beside him. Her hands went to his face and his torso, feeling for what he wasn't sure, since all of a sudden his head throbbed like a mother again.

"Not. Happy. About this," he said through the thickness in the back of his throat. Damn, whatever this infection was had come out of nowhere and knocked him senseless. He closed his eyes and listened to Malia's sweet voice for all of a few seconds before he fell right back under.

W hen Clay woke up his lips were dry and his back was coated in sweat, but the rest of him felt…better. He pushed up in bed, vague memories floating through his mind of Malia feeding him, pressing a cold glass of water to his lips, soothing him with soft touches and presses of her mouth to his neck and shoulder.

He glanced next to him and remembered her lying there, warming him up when he'd gotten chilled and backing off when he'd gotten too warm. On her pillow sat a tiny gold bell. He smiled despite himself. All he wanted was to get the hell up, but he rang the bell instead.

A few seconds later the most breathtaking and angelic woman stood in the doorway. "You rang?" Just looking at her demolished any pain he had.

"Thought I would."

"You look better." She sat and felt his forehead. "No fever. How long have you been up?"

"A few minutes." He took her wrist and brought her hand to lie on his chest. "What time is it?"

"Four o'clock."

"Jesus. You're kidding." He needed to check his cell. Make sure there were no new developments at the temple, with Benoit. With his free hand he brushed the hair off Malia's shoulder and slid his fingers along her neck. "Thank you." He didn't know what else to say. No one had taken care of him like this before.

"You're welcome. I, uh, should clean and re-bandage your foot now that you're awake." She moved down the bed and slid his foot out of the covers.

"Grab my phone for me first?"

She gave a small nod and lifted it off the dresser. He had

two texts, both conveying things were status quo. He focused back on Malia.

With furrows on either side of her mouth, something had her on edge. "Did Marcus stop back over?"

She kept her attention on his foot, unwrapping the gauze with a delicate touch. "No, but he did call, and depending on what I see here I may have to call him back."

"He ask you out again?"

"Would it matter?"

"I don't share, Malia. And while I'm here, you're mine."

She raised her head and glared at him with defiance—and subtle arousal—in those captivating eyes of hers. "Does that arrogance really work for you?"

"You tell me." He'd promised himself he wouldn't push her, but dammit, jealousy had kicked up its back legs and the thought of another man being anywhere near her hurt like a punch to the gut.

"Yes, it works." She sat back. "Everything about you works." She eyed the underside of his foot as if she held a magnifying glass. She was cute as hell. "It's looking better. Does it hurt if you wiggle your toes?"

"Is that some kind of test?" He wiggled. It hurt. But he wasn't about to give her any ammunition to keep him stuck in bed any longer. He'd rested. Now he wanted to be done with it.

"No. Just thought I'd ask." The corner of her mouth lifted.

"Am I allowed to shower?"

She popped to her feet. "Sure. But you still have an open wound so don't put your bare foot down on the floor. I did vacuum, but still."

He swung his legs off the bed and sat. His body needed

a chance to adjust to his upright position so he took a moment to let his gaze rake up Malia's long, lean legs to her little white shorts. A small strip of smooth skin peeked out from under her tiny black tank top. And—*gulp*—her nipples poked through the cotton material, telling him no bra. His body revved to life, a clear sign he felt better.

He grabbed her hand and tugged her close when he stood. "I like this domestic side of you."

"Don't get used to it."

"I'm pretty sure you can't help it." She cared about others. So much so, she was willing to break the law for her mom. While he admired her misplaced determination, he'd stay close enough to keep her safe and off the property.

She caught hold of his shirt and lifted her chin to look him in the eye. His arm wrapped around her waist. "I'm glad you're okay," she said quietly.

Hearing those words, recalling how she'd been there for him through the night and most of today, his insides churned with affection and the strings he'd never let tie him to anyone tugged…big time.

"You still have work to do," he teased.

"Oh, really?"

"Yep." He started hobbling toward the bathroom with her under his arm. "I need someone to wash my back."

She took his weight with one arm around his middle and the other gripping the arm he had over her shoulder.

"Probably my front too."

The sound of her sexy sigh did mind-numbing things to him. She made sure he was balanced before letting go and starting the shower.

"You going to join me?" He flung his shirt into the

corner, then pushed down his shorts and boxer briefs and kicked them to the side with his good foot.

Her eyes heated, and she licked her lips. Her unguarded perusal made him hard.

She focused back on his face and reached behind her to re-open the shower door. "You're just getting your strength back. I'll stay right here in case you need me."

He stepped to the shower, pausing to take the hair at her shoulder between his fingers once more. "Okay."

She closed the door, shut the lid on the toilet seat and sat down.

Then she watched him.

And shit if he didn't get harder. Through the clear glass he saw the lust and appreciation in her eyes and wondered why the hell she hadn't joined him. He'd never been on display like this before and the attention unsettled him as much as it turned him on.

He turned and pressed a hand to the tiled wall, let the water rain over his head. After a few deep breaths and running equations in his head, his dick settled down.

"Clay?"

"Yeah, baby?" He swallowed a few drops of water as rivulets ran down his face.

"I wish you'd let me decide what was best for me."

It took him a minute to process her words. He pressed his lips together, remembering bits and pieces of last night and talking about the past while half conscious. While Malia doted on him with warmth and tenderness, he'd let the damn fever get the best of him and his defenses had crumbled.

He'd told her his secret. Part of it anyway. Guilt squeezed his chest over how she'd learned the truth.

"All these years I thought you'd left because you didn't really love me."

He'd loved her too much. "Malia." He pivoted and swore under his breath when he saw confusion and pain in her gaze. Good thing a glass partition stood between them or he would've lifted her into the shower and taken her against the wall so she could feel how much he still—

"My father had no right to force you to leave."

He didn't exactly force me. "He loved you and wanted what was best for you."

Her back went ramrod straight and her hands pressed into her thighs. "He had no idea what made me happy."

"Maybe not, but I *wasn't* good enough for you, and I couldn't bear the idea of taking any possibility away from you."

"What does that even mean?"

"I didn't want to hold you back—from your dreams and from meeting someone who could offer you the world. Your father was right that you deserved someone in the same class."

"That's bullshit."

He jerked and clenched his jaw at her cursing. Nothing he said right now would fix how she felt so he stayed quiet and grabbed the soap.

"All that lathering is not going to clean away the past. If it were that easy I would have done so a long time ago. Not a day has passed that I haven't thought about you leaving and wondered what I did wrong to push you away."

He stopped with the soap and their eyes met. He might be the one in the buff, but the exposed, naked look she handed back to him stripped her bare.

"You didn't do anything wrong. I always…I always planned to enlist."

She sucked in a breath.

"And you deserved someone who would always be there for you." He ran a hand over his head, brushing the wet hair from his face. "I saw what losing my dad did to my mom. I saw the hope in her eyes every fucking day and then I saw it disappear and her acceptance that he was dead tore me up. I'd made the decision when I was eight years old to follow in my dad's footsteps. I just didn't tell anyone. I was going to fight for my country. But more importantly, I was going to find him and bring him home." He took a shaky breath. "Or die trying."

Malia sniffled, but Clay kept his gaze unfocused on the glass door clouded with steam and water droplets. "Things changed when I got overseas. My missions were about my team. And then I lost my best friend and I felt every definition of missing all over again."

"I'm sorry," she whispered.

"It killed me to leave you without a word. I was so close to confiding in you, but after your dad told me how he felt about us, I knew it was for the best that I just go."

"*You* were what was best for me."

"No. I didn't want you worrying about me. Waiting. Wondering if—"

"You don't think I did that anyway?" The anger and hurt in her voice snapped his attention back to her.

She stood, her long lashes sweeping down before she looked up and said, "You took away my choice and I hate you for that."

Watching her walk out of the bathroom, he hated himself more.

Chapter Seven

Malia strode into the kitchen, found a bottle of scotch that had been in the cupboard for who knew how long, and poured herself a glass. She lifted the tumbler to eye level, put it back on the counter. Added more booze.

Did a person sip scotch or down it? Did it matter? She brought the glass to her lips and threw her head back. The alcohol burned. She slammed the glass on the countertop. And proceeded to choke and cough and rub her chest in hopes the lighter fluid she'd just swallowed didn't cause permanent damage to her lungs and stomach lining. Son of a biscuit that hurt.

Almost as much as what Clay had just admitted.

He'd always planned to leave her.

And he hadn't had the decency to tell her. They'd shared everything. Or so she'd thought. She never would have held him back or tried to change his mind. She knew how much losing his father had affected him. Knew he'd sought approval and acceptance from her father and that her dad hadn't given it.

And, yes, she would have waited for him.

For as long as it took. As long as he needed. He'd left to spare her any heartache, only it backfired.

What-ifs shuffled through her mind, but she couldn't change the past. Couldn't get back all the years they were apart. His reasons for leaving were valid. She got it, even if she didn't agree with it.

But worse than finding out the truth was the way he still gobsmacked her with a simple look. Even strung out with a fever he'd managed to set those sexy eyes of his on her with enough magnetism to make every fiber of her being blush and vibrate with need.

He lit a torch inside her in more ways than one. He made her teem with energy and she liked it. She kept herself so closed off from everyone, always careful with her feelings, but Clay made it impossible to keep her emotions in check.

And just like that, she was done. They'd said what needed to be said and all the hurt and hate holding her heart hostage melted away. Memories inflicted harm as often as happiness and it was time to pull the knife from her chest for good. She pressed a few fingers to her temple, the alcohol making her a little light-headed.

"Water. I need water." She spun around and bumped right into Clay's muscled chest covered in a soft cotton tee that smelled like man and summer and soap. She shut her eyes and pictured him back in the shower with those lucky suds streaming down the hard planes and grooves of his body.

His hands went around her waist. "Where's the fire?" He lifted her away from all his yummy warmth.

She looked up at him. "In my veins."

He raised an eyebrow and glanced over her shoulder.

"You could've told me scotch burns like a mother."

His laugh warmed her further. Damn him. He quieted at her frown and took a step back. "You want to be mad at me for the scotch? Fine by me."

"I'm not mad at you."

"No?"

She was furious with him. But for no other reason than because he made her feel again, and she wasn't about to tell him that. "No."

"Didn't go down so smooth, huh?"

"I'm pretty sure the back of my throat will never forgive me."

He took a bottle of water out of the fridge and handed it to her. "Come on." He took her free hand.

"I don't think so." She tried to stand her ground and pull free of his grasp, but he didn't let go.

His abrupt pause and slow, deep breath did crazy things to her equilibrium. Or maybe that was the scotch. "I'm sorry," he said, and the tenderness in his tone told her he meant it. "Really sorry."

She sighed in acceptance. "Where are we going?"

"For a little sunshine." He led her to the patio and gestured for her to lie on one of the lounge chairs. He took the one beside her. Within seconds, the sun shone brighter, like it had been waiting for them to show up.

Malia guzzled down some water. Lifted her face to the warm rays. "How's your foot?" She noticed he had on flip-flops and hoped there was a bandage covering the wound.

"It's good." He took her hand again and kissed her

knuckles. "Thanks for taking care of me. No one's been there like that for me."

She rolled her head to the side and their eyes met. "You're welcome." His admission made her happy, but she couldn't afford to be happy around him so she added, "I would have done it for anyone." Something flashed in the warm green pools staring at her. Disappointment maybe? Her stomach pinched. The barb made her feel terrible. *That's what you wanted.*

"Are we good?" he asked.

This was the moment. The moment she voiced her forgiveness and moved forward. "Yes, we're good."

He released her hand and gave a slow, untroubled smile that she wanted to see again and again—at least as long as they were both under the same roof. The smile held as he closed his eyes and relaxed into the chair. She stared at his profile, noticing for the first time a scar along the hairline of his temple. He'd lived a whole life she knew nothing about and she found herself wanting to know everything she'd missed.

"I'm guessing you're not afraid of spiders anymore?" Weird place to start, but that was the first thing to pop into her head.

"I don't particularly like them, but thanks to you, you can count on me to slay any cane spiders that decide to make an appearance."

"Me?" Cane spiders lived on the island and could be the size of a softball.

"Whenever I come across a spider I remember the pep talk you gave me after I embarrassed myself on Christmas Eve in front of your family. You said, 'Just look right at it and remember it's far more scared of you than you are of it. Then smoosh it.'"

Sounded like something her sixteen-year-old self would say. "I'd forgotten about that." Hearing a big guy like Clay say "smoosh" did funny things to her insides.

He turned his head and gazed at her. "Did you ever go to an open mic night during college?"

"I did," she said proudly.

"What did you sing?"

She turned and tucked her hands under her cheek. "Your favorite." He used to love when she sang for him. Especially at night when he had trouble falling asleep. "Lullaby me," he'd whisper.

"'Your Body Is A Wonderland,'" he said. Then softer, "It still is."

She couldn't speak for a second. He shouldn't say these things to her. "I, um, heard your voice in the back of my head encouraging me to take a chance. I heard your voice a lot in college, actually." She didn't want to. It just wouldn't go away.

"I bet you were awesome."

"Felt that way." The entire bar had gone crazy when she finished and several guys had tried to get her number. She'd given it to one. And spent the rest of college trying to love him as much as she'd loved Clay. Didn't happen.

"You wanted to go pre-med. Be a doctor."

"I wanted to help people."

He lifted his arm and put his palm behind his still damp hair, elbow out. The move exposed a thin expanse of skin above the waistband of his shorts and she fought the urge to climb on top of him and slide her hands underneath his shirt.

"Where does yoga fit in?"

For a long beat she didn't answer, not because his question sounded rude. More like he'd given it some thought. Given *her* some thought over the years and wondered about her. She pulled in a breath, enjoying her very fine view, the sound of the waves in the distance, the floral scent tickling her nose. She didn't have quiet conversations like this, and it felt nice.

"I take it you've never done yoga."

"No."

"It's exercise yes, but at its core, it's meditative and spiritual. I've designed several of my classes for people fighting diseases. Yoga can be effective as a complementary intervention for cancer, asthma, heart disease, even PTSD."

Clay turned his head and looked at her. She saw the appreciation in his eyes, the understanding that he still influenced her decisions.

"The mind-body connection is pretty powerful," she added.

"Your birthmark," he said out of the blue.

"What?"

"The light brown spot on the inside of your thigh. That's what got me through some effed-up times. I'd picture it. Picture this beautiful mark that no one else on the planet has, and it grounded me. I imagined my lips there, making you giggle, then moan, and no way in hell could I give up or let anyone down. Most of all, you."

"Clay."

He was quiet for a long time, his gaze back out toward the sea, and she got the feeling he wished he could take back what he'd just said.

"Now I've traded one dangerous job for another."

He had? "How is heritage protection—"

"Monuments have collapsed, conflict with villagers in war-torn areas has led to injuries, death."

Malia shuddered. "I didn't know that."

"There's a lot you don't know."

His tone might have been even-tempered, but she got the message. It was time to move to a safer topic of conversation. "You've traveled all over the world."

"Yes."

"I'm still planning on seeing the Amalfi Coast one day."

He looked her way again, surprise widening his eyes. "You haven't been?"

"Not yet." They'd talked about going there since it ranked at the top of her travel list, but after her dad died, her priorities changed. "Have you?"

"I've been to Italy, yes, but never made it that far south."

"Is there a country you haven't visited?"

"A few."

"Favorite place in the world?" she asked.

"Del—" He hesitated like he wished he hadn't said that. "Mar."

Again, she didn't respond right away. Mostly because she couldn't freaking gather enough air in her lungs. The San Diego town was less than two hours away from her.

"I have a little house there on the beach." He swung around and sat facing her. Not for the first time, she saw regret cloud his expression. "I was stationed in Coronado."

She quietly scrambled to wrap her head around that. He'd been close, yet so far. "Why didn't I know that?"

"I asked my mom to keep it to herself. She wasn't happy

about it, but when I told her I needed to keep a clean break, she agreed."

"She knew about—you told her about us?"

"She knew how I felt about you." He ran a finger down her cheek to her shoulder, making her shiver.

The invisible pull between them swelled and time slowed. He gently drew her hand out from under her cheek and tugged her to a sitting position. Their knees touched. His tan fingers, intertwined with hers, stood out against her white shorts and warm, delicious stirrings between her thighs caught fire. His free hand cupped the back of her head. He moved closer.

"Again, I'm sorry."

She grabbed his arm and moved it away. She doubted he'd ever made three apologies to someone, but this new information had teeth that bit sharply. "A little late, don't you think? Why didn't you at least get in touch with me?"

"I had my reasons."

"All more important than seeing me again?"

He took a deep breath. "Yes. But I did see you. All the time." He leaned closer again, his lips hovering near hers. "In my thoughts. My dreams. Every day I remembered something about you."

"You left but you didn't leave," she whispered.

"Yes."

"But you tried."

"I did."

"Me, too."

Another inch and he'd have her mouth right where she wanted it. She could taste his minty breath, smell his shampoo, feel his heat. She reminded herself the past didn't matter anymore. This right here did.

"*Ahem*. Am I interrupting something?"

Clay pulled back on a harsh groan. Malia cursed her sister's timing.

"Since when do you cuss?" Kalani asked.

Great. She'd said that out loud. "Since yesterday." She turned and seeing the surprised smirk on her big sister's face, Malia added, "And no, you weren't interrupting." She jumped to her feet. "Hi."

"Hi yourself." Kalani wrapped her in a big hug. "Did you forget I was bringing dinner over?"

"Sort of." Look up distraction in the dictionary and there would be Clay.

"Hey, Kalani. It's good to see you." Clay stood *right* behind Malia, his hand on the waistband of her shorts, fingers curling against her skin.

Holy Toledo. He could not touch her in front of her sister. Not when her mind shut off and her body screamed for him to do wicked things to her when he did.

Kalani looked around Malia and eyed Clay up and down like she wasn't sure what to make of him. "You too." She stepped back. "Come on inside. I've got Chicken In A Barrel waiting."

Malia glanced over her shoulder at Clay. He lifted his chin and gave her a little nudge forward. "Let's go. The quicker we eat, the quicker I can get you naked afterward."

She licked her lips, glad they were back to whatever this temporary, noncommittal thing was they were doing. *Yes, please.*

Clay couldn't remember the last time he'd laughed so much. He'd forgotten what a great sense of humor Kalani had. And Malia, now that her defenses were down, spoke with unfiltered abandon to match her sister's outlandish commentary.

He took one last bite of the dry rubbed smoked barbeque chicken—the best he'd ever eaten—and leaned back in his chair at the kitchen table.

Standing in a battlefield was less dangerous than this. He didn't do homey, intimate dinners except with his close-knit family of co-workers at WHF. People who understood he had boundaries. People who took the same risks he did and had his back just like he had theirs. But hell if he could get himself to give up being with Malia.

"Wait, it gets worse," Kalani said. "My date the next night brought a sock puppet with him. A. Sock. Puppet. And he talked to me with it."

Malia cracked up and when she laughed, Clay couldn't take his eyes off her.

"It completely freaked me out," Kalani continued. "I made it through drinks and that was more than enough. I told the guy it was a good thing he had one good hand left because if this was his usual MO for dates, he was going to need it."

"Let's hope he didn't wear the puppet on his dominant hand," Malia said, the cutest smile tipping her lips as she forked the last bit of coleslaw and put it in her mouth.

Kalani tossed her napkin on her plate. "Okay, enough about me. Clay, I want to hear more about you. You work in heritage protection now?"

"Right. I'm head of security for a leading independent

organization dedicated to preserving the world's most important sites."

"I know what our head of security does at the hotel, but what does that mean for you exactly?" Kalani asked.

Clay leaned forward with his elbows on the table. "It varies, but typically I plan and implement safety precautions and procedures, given that many sites are in unstable areas of the world due to conflict, natural disaster or climate. I also keep an eye on the workforce and the executives in the field. At night I'll often stay on site to keep out trespassers."

Right now because of my military background, I'm helping to trap an international criminal.

The glass of water in Malia's hand clinked her teeth and she choked as she finished her sip. "Sorry. Went down the wrong pipe."

Yeah, the trespasser pipe.

Kalani crossed her arms over her chest and looked at him with sisterly admiration. They'd never been close, but suddenly he found himself feeling protective all over again. He wanted to knock some sense into the asshats she'd been dating.

Get your head out of your ass, Doherty. This is a temporary reunion.

"I know your mom is really proud," Kalani said, breaking into his thoughts. "Our mom, too." She glanced at Malia. "And speaking of Mom, she sounded tired today."

"I know," Malia said, love and affection in those two small words.

"I don't put much stock in all the healing remedies you believe in, but maybe more gifts like the bracelet you got her will help."

"Bracelet?" Clay said, his interest piqued. He'd come across many ancient beliefs—and artifacts—that boasted healing power and there were other forms of Mana besides Peridot. Malia had other options he'd neglected to think about.

"It's nothing," Malia said, her eyes hidden under long lashes.

"She's embarrassed," Kalani said. "Because no one believes like she does."

Clay fought the urge to cup Malia's chin and bring her eyes to his. "There are hundreds of cultures and traditions where the art of restoring health is imbued in an object or place. I've met people all over the world who believe. Tell me about the bracelet."

Malia turned and slammed him with a pair of brilliant brown gems that he knew would heal anything that ailed him. Surprise and appreciation swirled in their dark depths. "It's a Carnelian gemstone bracelet steeped with energy for emotional healing. It brings balance to the body and true happiness."

"What's going on with you two?" Kalani asked.

"Nothing," Malia said, jerking her gaze away. He didn't mind her keeping their relationship private considering it wouldn't go beyond the island. But her defensive tone hinted at a deeper attachment he liked hearing. He knew better than to lead her on, and yet he couldn't stop if he tried. It's for her protection, he reminded himself. If anything happened to her while here, he'd never forgive himself.

"Riiight." Kalani didn't buy it. She stood to refill their water glasses.

Clay picked up Malia's hand and kissed her palm.

"That's an amazing gift. I'm glad it's working."

"You don't think it's silly?" Malia asked.

"Nope."

She blinked several times. Her lips parted as if to speak, but nothing came out. This was her opening and her refusal to share the whole truth made the situation ten times harder on him. He understood her motives and beliefs, but besides the fact that the temple stood on sacred land, she'd walked into an unsafe situation that he'd keep her far away from.

He quickly dropped Malia's hand and moved his attention to Kalani before she sat back down. "Have they given you a time frame?" Emi Davis's cancer kept returning.

"It's hard to say." Kalani's mouth pressed into a thin, resigned line. "I think she wants to forgo any further treatment, though. She's had enough."

A tear slipped out of the corner of Malia's eye. His stomach cramped and his heart squeezed. It killed him to see her unhappy. Without thinking, he wiped the tear with the pad of his thumb. "No other mom has been loved as much as she has."

"Absolutely," Kalani said. "And we're not even close to being done. So, change in topic. Mal, you're coming to the hotel with me tonight. We're going to order hot fudge sundaes and watch a romantic comedy and in the morning get massages. It's not up for discussion. I've got a crazy rest of the week starting tomorrow with a celebrity couple coming in to get married and I won't be available. I'll clean up here, so Mr. Nail-In-The-Foot can relax, and you go grab a few things."

Malia cast him a worried look. "Are you feeling well enough for me to go?"

"I'm fine." He lifted her hand to his forehead. "See? No fever. You two have a good time."

"Yes, let's go do that." Kalani cleared their dishes with a sparkle in her eye that said she also planned to ask Malia about him.

"You're sure?" Malia said.

He kissed the top of her nose. "Yes. Go get your stuff and get out of here." He knew she'd be safe with Kalani because he didn't catch even an inkling of secrecy between the two of them. That meant Kalani didn't know about the Peridot, and he didn't think Malia would tell her, given the illegal nature of her plan.

She smiled at him and rose from the table. The gorgeous turn of her lips stayed with him the rest of the night as a reminder of what he'd pledged to himself. To keep his distance. To dedicate himself to his work and nothing else.

To keep people safe. No matter the cost to himself.

Chapter Eight

The next morning Malia drove straight from her sister's hotel to the Halia Alika Temple. She didn't have the luxury of time, not when her mom sounded even more fatigued on the phone this morning. She parked between two cars and wandered into the visitor center. She'd picked a busy day to make her visit. That could be bad. It could be good. Either way, she was sneaking away to the trail that led to the temple.

Sneaky being a shaky description given the wide expanse of grassland that offered very little coverage.

Her heart pounded so hard she almost turned back. She knew this wasn't a cure for her mom, but it would give them both hope. She and her mom had always shared a belief in spiritual power even if no one else did. Finding something deeply rooted in Hawaiian culture would only make it that much stronger. Her mom was proud of her roots and that's why the crystal on *this* land was so important.

If it even gave them one extra day with their mom, it would be worth it.

Clouds knit together to block the sun and a chill swept down Malia's arms. She hurried up the mountain with the new backpack she'd stopped to buy hanging on her shoulder. She'd also bought a bigger shovel. And a small canister that she'd filled with sand. If discovered, she'd tell whoever found her that she was there to fulfill her father's request that his ashes be buried on the sacred grounds.

Sweat trickled down her back. That was one doozy of a lie she hoped she didn't have to tell.

The front of the temple came into view and she gave silent thanks it looked deserted. She thought about Clay and wondered how his foot felt this morning. Wondered if he'd taken a shower yet and what he'd eaten for breakfast and if he'd shaved or left the sexy scruff on his strong jaw. She also contemplated for the hundredth time how he hadn't discounted the bracelet she'd given her mom as meaningless. That he seemed genuinely on her side with an open mind.

Maybe he would be willing to help her get the crystal once she explained how important it was.

No. She wouldn't put him in the position of choosing between his job and stealing. She saw how passionate he was about heritage protection. He had principles and integrity and she couldn't ask him to set those aside for her.

This wrong just happened to be something Malia needed to do as much as she needed her next breath. She couldn't explain it.

Crazy. Foolish. Nonsensical. For the first time in her life she was acting far outside her comfort zone, but as much as it worried her, it felt good to be doing something proactive.

According to her research, crystal was buried all around the perimeter of the temple. A "Circle of Ola" or Circle of Life that meant you couldn't have health without life, nor life without health. Hundreds of years ago when people came to the temple, they came to heal inside and out, the curative grounds that much stronger because of the Peridot.

Malia stopped in front of the steps leading to the temple's entrance and closed her eyes. Just like the other day, a low hum of spiritual energy moved through her and she knew that if she could just get her hands on some crystal, good things would come from it.

She concentrated on feeling in the moment, tuning out all sounds, and trusting her instincts. She gave silent thanks to the many respected priests who had guided visitors seeking assistance. And she prayed for the families whose ancestors were buried at the site.

Slowly opening her eyes a minute later, she had zero time to prepare for the small group of men coming around the temple. Quivers torpedoed out from her thumping heart. She couldn't swallow, her throat jammed with high-strung nerves. Where was an invisibility cloak when she really needed it?

The tallest man, the sexiest man, the man she couldn't get out of her head, noticed her immediately, like he wore a Malia-antennae. Or maybe it was the whip-sharp connection that filled the air whenever she and Clay were anywhere near each other.

He wore khaki shorts, a white collared shirt with a WHF logo on the breast pocket, and a baseball hat. Dark curls peeked out from the rim of his cap at the back of his neck. Her insides turned gooey. Sexy didn't even begin to—

"Malia."

Stern voice. Eyes narrowed. Lips pressed together. He was pissed. And leaving the group to head straight toward her.

She had no idea how her face responded since she suddenly couldn't feel anything but the pounding of her heart. She was the worst trespasser in the history of trespassers.

And hated confrontation. She spun around and started back down the mountain.

Clay's large, warm, slightly calloused hand stopped her. She looked down. His strong forearm put quivers deep in her belly. His gentle, but I-could-break-a-2x4-with-my-bare-hands touch unsettled *and* thrilled her.

For several quiet beats she stood with her back to his front, her gaze on the turquoise sea in the distance. She couldn't tell him she'd come to dig on sacred ground. *His* sacred ground. She just couldn't. He'd be disappointed. Or worse, feel betrayed. Shame made her cheeks warm.

"Talk," he instructed.

"It's a beautiful day."

"Seriously?" He stepped in front of her, blocking her view. "That's how you want to play this?"

Even angry, he was beautiful. She dropped her gaze to the ground.

"You came here to dig for crystal."

She shrugged. He wasn't stupid. Not by a long shot, but saying the words out loud? The thought stole her voice. Once she did that, she could never take them back.

"Shall I list all of your offenses?" When she stayed quiet he raised his hand to tick off her misdeeds as he spoke them. "Trespassing, stealing, lying."

"I didn't lie." She jutted her chin up. "Or steal anything." Yet.

He scrubbed a hand over the stubble on his jaw. "You know this is a national monument and off-limits to the public. The ruins are on sacred ground that is not to be disturbed — for several reasons. And you knew I was working at this site and didn't tell me this is where you'd been." His voice vibrated with frustration.

She swallowed. She could argue he had no proof this was where she'd been, but instead she said, "What reasons?"

He opened his mouth to say something, then slammed it shut. His chest slowly rose and fell. She'd managed to curb some of his anger with her question.

"The ground is unstable and the safety of the workers is at risk, as well as the integrity of the temple. It looks like preservation efforts will be put on hold until they get some engineers up here."

Malia looked over her shoulder at the ancient, weathered, but still beautiful temple. "It's not going to fall is it?"

"Not if we can help it." He sounded pleased by her concern and sure enough when she dropped her gaze back to him, the muscles in his face had relaxed. Some.

"I guess that's common over time? The soil changing?" She adjusted her backpack, her hand feeling the outline of the shovel through the canvas. Maybe the crystal was closer to the surface now.

"Yes. More so on the other islands where there's volcanic activity. But in this case, it seems that large amounts of rain combined with the digging people have done around the temple has had some impact."

She rubbed the back of her neck. Was it her imagination

or had he put extra emphasis on the word "digging?"

"Over the past ten years the site has been compromised hundreds of times by grave robbers. Since any headstones are long gone, the trespassers aren't all that careful about where they dig and the foundation has been affected." He glanced up at the sanctuary. "Recently word has gotten out that the ground is rich with Peridot crystal and everyone wants a piece."

As hard as it was, she returned his pointed stare. She hadn't told him the name of the crystal, but knew now he'd always known. Her legs shook. Because of the intensity in his eyes. Because he'd lumped her in with *everyone* and that felt…wrong. Bad. Like she was bad. Her intentions may have been good, but *she* wasn't.

"It's against the law to take anything from a protected site," he said.

She nodded. Dug her teeth into her bottom lip. Her whole body shook now.

He took her hand, his posture relaxed. "Even if she has a good heart and is doing it for a good reason."

Do not cry in front of him. Do not cry in front of him. She swallowed the lump in her throat. His sweet words and understanding nearly undid her. If he'd caught anyone else up here, he'd be all badass and unsympathetic.

"There's more going on here than I can say. I need you to promise me you're not going to sneak up here again," he said.

"I'm not very good at sneaky."

"No, you're not."

"I didn't realize how popular Peridot was."

"There's not much of it left and you're standing near the

only spot where it's in abundance."

She only needed a small piece. What harm was there in that? The good far outweighed the bad in her situation, didn't it?

"Clay?" one of the men called from over her shoulder.

"Do not move," Clay said. "I'll be right back."

Malia focused her attention on his backside as he joined the others at the base of the temple. He was definitely the guy in charge as they walked around the temple, surveying the land with hands raised to shield their eyes from the sun. Off in the distance she noticed several jeeps she'd swear hadn't been parked there before. The hairs on the back of her neck stood up. She got the feeling she was being watched.

"Time to go," Clay said, coming to a stop in front of her.

"Everything okay?"

"Yep."

She didn't believe him. His voice sounded clipped, his mouth was set in a grim line again. Tension radiated off him, making her nervous. "What's going on?"

He took her upper arm and started down the mountain without an answer.

"Clay?"

"Fuck," he muttered under his breath. "I can't tell you what's going on. It's complicated. And classified."

"Who would I tell?"

He cast her a sideways glance that said, *you've yet to tell me anything, why would I tell you even if I could?*

"Have you ever taken something from a site you've worked on?"

His eyes narrowed. "No. But…"

"But?" She needed that but like a fish needed water.

Because as he'd spoken with his team, she'd wondered if she pushed him to help her, would he?

"My buddy McCall broke, well, bent protocol last year at an Aztec village in Arizona."

Malia wasn't sure what to make of Clay's disapproving yet thoughtful tone, but decided to ask, "Why?" anyways.

"The short version is he fell in love."

She quickly turned her head and took in what looked like consideration in his profile, creases etched around his eye and the corner of his mouth. "I need the medium version at least."

He puckered his lips before letting out a long breath. "McCall was president of field operations and overseeing things at the site when Lucy showed up. Lucy was an archeologist, and she was after a sixteenth century gold sculpture that was buried in the walls of the village. She had a good reason for wanting it and they figured out a way to make it happen. Lucy got the sculpture and donated it to the Museum of American History."

"And she and McCall?"

"Got married a couple of months ago."

Malia sighed. Love truly conquered all. Clay didn't love her anymore, but maybe he cared enough that he'd bend the rules to help her, too.

His cell phone chirped and he pulled it from his pocket. He stepped away and spoke in a hushed tone.

She watched him, riveted by his broad shoulders, lean waist, and strong legs. He'd taken such amazing care with her once upon a time. Could she ask him for a favor, one last time?

But as he spoke on the phone, his authority and

confidence evident in his stance and mannerisms, she reminded herself she couldn't put him in the position of even choosing. That wouldn't be right. *He's already made it pretty clear where he stands on this, Malia.*

No. She'd have to figure out a way to sneak back up here. Then hurry home to her mom. The sooner the better.

Clay hadn't been completely honest with Malia. It was WHF's digging that had caused the most damage to the soil and compromised the temple. To catch an SOB, they'd risked it, and undermined the progress they'd made in preservation. He slipped his phone into his pocket and clenched his hands. If any part of the historical monument fell it was on him.

At least they'd learned Benoit was on the island. That meant they were much closer to their efforts paying off. But Benoit didn't walk into traps. Clay and his team had kept under the radar, yet excavation didn't go unnoticed, even in the dead of night.

He glanced at Malia. She quickly looked away like she didn't want to be caught watching him. Her sheepishness bothered him. Hell, everything she did occupied his mind far too much. A few days with her and he'd become addicted all over again. Not good.

Especially when she still hadn't confessed her intentions or promised to stay away. She'd looked at him with heat and passion one minute and tension and apology the next, conflict grooved between her eyebrows, but he knew once she set her mind to something, she didn't back down.

He also knew a part of her was excited by all this. He'd noticed the spark in her eyes, felt the adrenaline on her skin.

If she wanted a thrill, he'd give it to her.

"Come on," he said, picking up her hand and leading her along a trail. The rightness in their joined hands plowed into him as an electric current shot up his arm.

She stumbled for a moment and the backpack hanging over her shoulder slipped. He let go of her hand, reached around her back to grab it. His fingers met with something hard and sharp before she flinched and hugged the bag to her chest. He stifled a laugh.

"That's okay. I've got it," she said.

It would have taken her hours of digging with the small shovel he'd felt inside the knapsack. Make that days. Her novice—and he guessed spur of the moment—tactic shouldn't have erased the strain in his back and shoulders. But it did.

"What's so funny?" she asked.

"Nothing." He bit the inside of his cheek to keep from smiling. Sped up their pace. A puff of wind gusted by, tossing Malia's light floral scent right under his nose. He inhaled and held it. She smelled fantastic.

"Where are we going?"

"For a drive."

She stopped in her tracks and squared her shoulders. When she lifted her chin in defiance, he fought the urge to suck on her mouth. "Where to?"

"Worried I may be taking you to the authorities?"

"No." She pressed her lips together. Her brows knit together. "You aren't, are you?"

"I should."

Those perfect lips of hers pressed tighter. He slipped his arms around her waist and brought her close. "I'm kidding." He wasn't letting her out of his sight for a second. No more sleepovers with her sister. No more of anything that didn't include him. Not until Benoit was arrested and Clay's job done. Then he'd... He didn't want to think about it.

She pushed away and resumed their trek on the dirt path. "That's good because I'm innocent."

Her definition was a lot different than his.

They walked in silence until the small outbuilding and all-terrain vehicles came into view. "Uh, Clay. I can't drive one of those," she said.

"You're not. You're riding." He'd give Malia a little adventure and do some surveillance of the land at the same time. There were a couple of spots he needed a visual on that their security cameras didn't reach.

He didn't have to worry about Benoit or any of his guys showing up now. Daylight wasn't their style. But handing Malia a helmet to wear, a sudden jolt of restlessness sliced through him. He'd protected people for a long time. None more important than the woman next to him.

Somewhere too close to his heart, he felt a wild I'd-do-anything-for-you thump. Seemed he couldn't turn off his emotions as easily as he thought he could. He'd set this chain of events in motion, though, and would put an end to it.

Soon.

He climbed onto the ATV. "Hop on, *nani girl*."

She grinned and straddled the seat behind him. Her arms wrapped around his waist and she laid her chin on his shoulder. "How fast can this baby go?"

"Let's find out."

They rode over rolling hills and flat ground, covering more acreage than necessary. Clay gunned it, the rush of the wind pulling a grin from Malia. He couldn't see it, but he could feel it in the way she snuggled closer and gripped the front of his T-shirt.

He'd underestimated how much her body pressed against his would affect him. He felt alive, free. Like it was the two of them against the world. Temporary, this high is temporary, he told himself.

"That was awesome," Malia said, a little out of breath, the helmet dangling in her hand after she'd dismounted a little while later. She ran her fingers through her wavy hair.

Clay didn't let on that watching her right now, it took every ounce of strength he had not to take her against the ATV. The pinkish flush of her cheeks, the sparkle of excitement in her eyes. Damn, she was magnificent.

"What? You're looking at me funny."

He shook his head to clear the inappropriate thoughts he obviously couldn't hide from her. Dumbass. "How am I looking at you?"

She put the helmet down on the seat of the vehicle. "Kind of like you want to go all caveman on me. Throw me over your shoulder. Drag me somewhere private." She tilted her head. "Or maybe not so private."

His dick jumped to attention. "Baby, I'm all-in with whatever you like."

She playfully smacked him in the chest. "You're ridiculous."

"And you're turned on."

"Not even close," she fired back, but he noticed her shudder so he knew better.

He bent his head and said in her ear, "Challenge accepted."

She let out a sexy sigh that almost had him throwing caution aside and stripping her naked.

"You like kids parties?" he asked instead, leading her back down the mountain, toward the visitor center.

"Is that a trick question?"

"No. It's Alex's birthday and I've been invited to his beach party. Thought I'd bring you along."

The small tug on her lips had him almost tripping over his feet. Sometimes the smallest curves of a mouth were the most potent. "I'd like that. I've been meaning to stop by and say hello."

He slung his arm around her shoulders. "Great."

"Don't get any ideas while we're there."

"Ideas?"

"Yes."

"About...us?" He reminded himself they were getting physical, not opening themselves up to any long-term connection.

Tucked against his side, she shivered. He could attribute it to another breeze that swept by, but he'd rather think it was his use of "us."

She shrugged out of his hold. "We're going to a kids party and that is not the place for any sort of flirting or whatever you think you want to do with me."

Clay grinned. "I know exactly what I want to do with you."

"But I don't." Her honesty hit him like a hard blow to the solar plexus. Time to make this about carefree fun and nothing else.

So a couple of hours later when Alex and his brother and cousins ambushed him on the beach with their Uzi water guns and he noticed Malia smirking, he raced over to use her as a shield.

"Hey, let me go," she said, trying to wiggle out of his hold.

"Turnabout is fair play, *nani girl*."

"What are you—"

Alex nailed her right in the face with a stream of water. She sputtered.

"I know you sent the troops after me," Clay said, easing up on his hold so she could run away. He ran with her, the kids laughing and chasing after them.

"I did no such thing," she called out.

"Not according to the nod I just got from Alex's dad." Clay tapped knuckles with Dave Stein as they jogged by the small group of adults.

"Traitor," Malia called out.

The group of munchkins, led by Alex, charged after them, shouting and laughing, their water weapons practically bigger than they were. Malia changed directions, dodged and weaved; let the youngsters get close, then put more distance up.

There were no words to describe how beautiful Malia looked playing and giggling as she kicked up the soft sand and sought to stay semi-dry. Even with the bottom of his foot still a little sore, he could run around with the kids for hours and not tire, but watching her took his breath away.

She turned and ran backward, furiously pointing at him with both hands. "He's who you guys need to get."

The boys and one girl—cute as hell with pigtails sticking straight out—aimed at him. He stopped, spread his arms wide, and stood his ground. They blasted him top to bottom with giant grins on their faces.

Malia kept an eye on the action and shouted out a few areas where the kids missed. By the time the water ran out, they'd gotten him good.

"Reload," one of the older boys shouted and the group took off.

Clay didn't waste any time stalking over to Malia and wrapping her in a bear hug.

"Hey, you're getting me all…" She sighed and stopped wriggling. Smart girl.

Pretty soon all her sexy parts were wet and rubbing against his parts and this plan of his suddenly didn't seem very wise given one of his parts had decided to reach out and touch someone. Namely her.

She gave a little gasp, no doubt feeling his reaction to their clinch.

But when something—or rather someone—caught his attention out of the corner of his eye, the fun and games were over. He turned his head to find a man in sunglasses standing about a hundred meters down the beach watching them. A man who from a distance looked a lot like Sergio Benoit.

Clay tensed and quickly moved to block the man's view of Malia. "We need to get inside," he ordered. He wrapped a protective arm around her and hurried toward the Davis house, forgetting about the party. He didn't know for sure if it was Benoit, but he didn't want any attention brought to the Steins.

"What's wrong?" Malia asked.

"Nothing."

"Cake time!" someone shouted.

The announcement didn't deter him. He picked up their

pace away from the party.

"Clay. What's going on? You're hurting me."

Fuck. He eased up on his grip. "Sorry. Just had enough sun for one day." He glanced back down the beach. The man had disappeared.

Malia tilted her face up. Her eyes shimmered with warmth. And worry. "Are you sure that's all it is?"

"Yes."

"We doing cake?"

"No."

She dug her feet in the sand, bringing them to a stop. "Something spooked you." When he didn't answer, she turned her attention to the kids hustling inside for cake. "Alex pointed out which piece on the superhero cake belonged to you. Don't you think he'll be upset if you miss the candles?"

"You saw that?"

"I may have kept my eyes on you. We could always take your special piece to go," Malia said, her soft voice just what he needed to settle down.

He took one more peek down the shoreline. Nothing. The guy was probably just a homeowner out for some fresh air. Clay's nerves calmed further.

"Yeah. Okay." He didn't want to disappoint Alex. Didn't want to draw unwanted attention to his absence.

"Ever had cake in bed?" This time Malia's voice took on a sexy, let-me-help-you-relax tone.

He gulped. "No, and we definitely need to remedy that."

Chapter Nine

Clay's fiercely intense expression, not to mention the heat rolling off him, took the burning hot desire inside Malia and multiplied it by a thousand. The buildup over the past hour had been excruciating and God, she hoped no one noticed the permanent flush in her cheeks.

"I thought we'd never get out of there," he said, opening the sliding French door to the living room for her.

The second she stepped into her family's home, the flames licking at her intensified. Clay had kept whispering all the naughty things he planned to do to her when they got back here and she wanted him to start Right Now.

The door lock clicked into place and she turned.

He held a plate with a large piece of cake in one hand. With the other he pulled his shirt over his head, did a quick change of hands with the dessert, and let the tee fall off his arm to the floor. "Your turn."

His muscled chest and six-pack abs made her toes curl.

Gazes locked, she crossed her arms and lifted her top over her head.

"The bra, too, babe."

She obliged and the second his stare dropped to her breasts, her nipples hardened.

"So beautiful," he said, his voice rougher than usual. "Now the shorts."

Power slammed into her. The rise and fall of his chest and the effort he took to keep his stance still when his eyes smoldered darker made her forget any inhibitions. She felt his look all over and shivered in anticipation of his touch.

Her fingers found the button and zipper of her shorts and she very slowly pulled them over her hips and down her legs. Kicked them away when they hit the floor. Clay gulped, his hot gaze tracking up her legs, pausing at her lace panties, and continuing up. He reached over and put the cake plate on the nearby side table.

Malia tried to imagine some music, something slow and sexy to sway to, but the low growl that came from Clay caused her brain to short-circuit. She thumbed the sides of her panties and gave him her back, her head turned to look over her shoulder.

"Jesus," he rasped, his attention on her butt. Not a lot of material covered it. "Did I say beautiful? I meant unbelievably beautiful."

Yoga had kept her in shape, but she'd never felt more confident, more pretty, than she did now. His appreciative regard stirred all kinds of crazy, wonderful sensations in her belly, on her skin, down her sides.

She inched the tiny slips of material down the tops of her thighs, lower, and lower still, until she had to bend over to continue. Intense desire marked the angles of Clay's handsome face and she bit her bottom lip. He groaned. She reached her ankles, stepped out of the lingerie, spun around, and flung the tiny bit of lace at him rubber-band style.

He didn't catch it, instead picking up the cake and stalking toward her. "Bedroom. Now."

A giggle slipped between her smile as she hurried to his room since it was closest. And oh, how she needed him close.

"Lie on the bed," he instructed next.

"Like this?" She stretched out on her stomach, arms above her head, and rubbed against the bedding. "Or like this?" She rolled over, arms still overhead, knees together and legs bent to the side.

"I *like*." His husky tone left no mistake he liked both. At the foot of the bed, he ogled her as if deciding where to start first. A second later he straddled her hips, dipped his thumb in the frosting on the cake, and spread it over one very tight, aching nipple.

He carried out the same dip-and-spread to her other nipple. The sugary sweetness of the frosting tickled her nose. The creamy consistency soothed at the same time it inflamed. "Lick me. *Please*." She arched her back, pressed her shoulders into the mattress.

Clay stared at her breasts like they were a work of art. "Oh, I'm going to lick you. I'm going to lick every inch of you."

"Please hurry."

"Feels good does it?"

"Yes."

"Want it to feel better?"

"Yes." She squirmed and wasn't above begging if he

didn't get on with it.

"I've got a lot of frosting left. Maybe I should—"

"Frost more later," she said, sounding all breathy and needy. Which she was.

He flashed that devilish smile of his, dimples and all, and finally—*finally*—put his mouth on her. His expert tongue lapped up the frosting and then he sucked. Bit. Kissed. She ran her fingers over his shoulders as he lavished one breast then the other.

After that she lost track of everything but the feel of his hands and mouth as they worked in tandem all over her body. He frosted her neck, her stomach, the insides of her thighs. When he brushed the last bit of frosting just above her throbbing center, lifted her legs over his shoulders and tasted her, the onslaught of pleasure burned so bright she screamed out his name as he took her over the edge.

To her surprise, instead of dropping his trunks and getting inside her, he continued to circle and glide his tongue over her swollen flesh. And sweet coconuts, she found herself right back on that edge. She bucked against his mouth and clawed the sheets. Exquisite pressure built once again, she panted louder and louder, until the perfect stroke sent her right back to heaven.

Clay kissed his way up her body. Soft kisses. Kisses that cherished, didn't rush, like he wanted to memorize her feel and taste because he didn't plan on keeping her. This intimacy had a time frame, they'd said as much. She squeezed her eyes shut and banished thoughts beyond this moment.

"I'll never look at cake the same way again," he whispered in her ear.

She turned her head and their eyes met. His were heavy-lidded but greedy, and then he kissed her. He switched between light nips to her bottom lip and a full-fledged assault on her tongue. She loved both.

They kissed and touched and writhed and moaned. Finally, still keeping his mouth and one hand busy, he got rid of his shorts with the other. The feel of him, so hard and hot on her stomach, had her spreading her legs in invitation, but Clay only tortured her with more petting and kisses. When she thought she'd die if he didn't get inside her, he slid on a condom and with a slow, deliberate thrust filled her.

Braced on his elbows, his hands on either side of her head, he set an unhurried pace that she matched by wrapping her legs around his thighs. Her fingers brushed through his soft hair, over his shoulders. He moved in and out, grinding against her most sensitive spot until she fell apart staring into his eyes.

"God, Malia," he groaned, his body straining and then shuddering in his own release before he collapsed on top of her.

She relaxed her legs and skimmed her hands down his back as their heartbeats slowed.

Clay pressed up on his elbows, keeping them connected below the waist. "I'm thinking I'll run back next door for another piece of cake."

Malia giggled. "I'm happy to reciprocate."

"No. I need to spend some attention on your backside."

Oh. "If you insist."

"Actually, you're sweet enough. And the last thing I want to do is leave this bed. Roll over."

She did. He got busy. And they both fell into bliss over and over again.

"Jesus," Clay whispered the next morning, his hold tightening around her naked body. He'd woken her from a bad dream. The same one that plagued her every few weeks. Aware of her whimpers, this was the first time she'd had someone hold and comfort her. She hadn't been prepared for how good that felt and took a quivering breath.

"I'm just glad he didn't know I couldn't scream for help," she said.

Two years ago a masked intruder had broken into her home. She'd been playing solitaire on her bed, iPod earbuds in place, and gotten up to get a glass of water. When she rounded the hallway and saw the stranger her heart had slammed into her chest and she'd wanted to scream. But she couldn't do it. She couldn't make a single sound. In her nightmare, the same masked man comes to her door and she can't yell. As hard as she tries, and no matter how hard she concentrates, her vocal chords freeze.

The intruder had taken a step toward her when he suddenly bolted. At the time she had no idea why he'd turned and run out her back door, only later realizing it was the doorbell. She'd been saved by a UPS delivery.

Clay's warm, naked body is protecting you now. His breath fanned the side of her neck. "That's a normal reaction, honey. Did the police find the guy?"

"No."

His muscles went rigid. "You changed your locks, had a security system put in." It wasn't a question.

"Yes."

He relaxed slightly. "Your mom must have been a wreck." He pressed a soft kiss to her shoulder, slid his palm to her abdomen.

"I never told her. I didn't want to worry anyone."

Some sort of growly sound came from Clay. She didn't need to see him to know he had a frown on his face.

"I'm fine being on my own and don't need anyone's help." She'd played the quiet, independent sister her whole life and didn't know how else to be.

Except with Clay. With him she was different.

"You're having nightmares," he bit out. Then he took a deep breath, his chest pressing against her back. "Let *me* help."

Malia's eyes drifted shut and she reminded herself this was temporary. Being with Clay was a distraction from real life and real problems. A chance to say good-bye the right way. Without regrets. She'd taken care of her family and herself for a long time, and still would. His offer, she was sure, was a slip of the tongue. He led a life far away from hers and nothing was going to change that. Not her mom's illness, her father's absence, or the bad things that sometimes happened.

"You are. Holding me helps."

"I can help better." He drew lazy circles around her belly button. Rocked his hips against her bottom. He kissed behind her earlobe, moved his hand up to cup and knead her breast. When she moaned, he slid his hand down her torso to the curls between her legs. She rolled toward him and spread her legs. "I love how quickly you respond to me," he whispered. He sat up and back against the headboard. "Come over here."

She rose to her knees. He handed her a condom packet

and she delighted in rolling the protection over his thick, long length. *Yep, feeling loads better already.*

He took hold of her waist and maneuvered her over his lap. His hands palmed her bottom, positioning her right where he wanted her.

Eyes glued to each other, Malia lowered onto him inch by glorious inch. She'd ridden him before, but this time something was different. She couldn't name it, only that the connection touched every single cell in her body. When she took him as deep as she could, he swore softly and then his greedy mouth clamped onto hers, sucking her tongue and taking possession.

The steady, all-consuming rhythm Clay set with each intoxicating surge of his hips took her to the brink of orgasm. She broke the kiss, needing to suck in some air. He filled her so completely she didn't ever want him to stop. In silence they moved together, slow and mind-blowing, anchored by more than attraction. Something beyond compare had always existed between them and it filled the room with sparks of energy. Clay's eyes, dark and seductive, but tender, too, as he thrust inside her, were special and amazing and they pushed her over the edge. He followed right behind, and when their breathing returned to normal and he hugged her head to his chest and buried his face in her hair, she knew if she let herself be swept up by Clay a second time, it would rip her heart to pieces all over again.

Clay had lived by a code for the past ten years—protect, serve, honor—and he'd thought that was all he needed.

All he wanted. So the sudden vulnerable feeling inside him was new. And very inconvenient. Malia had him twisted in knots on top of knots and his head spinning when he should be focused on work.

"I could stare at the ocean forever," she said, wrapping her arms around his waist from behind and putting her chin on his shoulder.

"I could, too." Nothing but the sapphire sea surrounded them this afternoon. Clay had chartered a boat for the day to get Malia off the island for a while, his desire to be with her and keep her safe overruling everything else. He knew how much she loved the water, remembered how she'd loved to sail when they were kids.

"It's moments like this I wish…"

He turned and cradled her in his arm, brushed away the hair that had slipped out of the sloppy bun on top of her head. Her sun-warmed body relaxed against his, but her gaze went somewhere behind him.

"Wish what?"

"Nothing."

"It's not nothing." His heart drummed that rare stop-and-go beat he'd come to realize belonged to her.

She laid her hand on his chest, rubbed her thumb across his sternum, and looked up into his eyes. His skin heated. Could she feel the crazy-ass palpitations going on underneath her palm? "That things were different."

Words failed him. He'd wondered a million times if he'd made different choices if they'd be together, be married, have a family, and now he knew she'd wondered, too.

But wondering didn't change the circumstances they lived in now. Seeing that guy on the beach yesterday, thinking the worst, he'd almost lost it. So, he fought the urge to tell her he did, too, instead stepping around her to grab a cold drink from the cooler.

His silence hurt her. She pulled her T-shirt over her head, covering half of her bikini body, and sat on the cushioned seating with her back to him, arms around bent legs. Legs that had been wrapped around him an hour ago as he'd made love to her.

For the last time.

"You need to go home," he said. "To California."

Malia wheeled around. "Excuse me?"

"You came here to get a piece of Peridot and since that's not happening, there's no reason to stay any longer."

She flinched at his harsh words and damn it all, he wished he'd chosen a softer approach. He stepped toward her to… He didn't know what exactly. She lifted her arm, palm up. *Do not come any closer.*

He stopped, grateful one of them had some common sense. The last thing he needed was to be close enough to whisper a take-back in her ear.

"You have no say in anything I do."

"When it comes to the temple and the site, my word is the last one. You know that." He braced his legs a little wider apart as the wind picked up and the boat bobbed in the water.

She beetled her brows over eyes glittering with anger. "Peridot carries the strongest form of Mana. I can't go home without it."

"There are other kinds of crystals with similar—"

"This is my mom's birthplace. It has to be this one." Her level gaze held challenge. Fortitude. But then she bit her lower lip and he knew deep down, she wasn't as tough as she wanted him to think she was.

He watched a swallow work its way down her throat.

Clay had learned over the years with WHF that heritage played a big role in beliefs and healing power. He lifted the baseball cap off his head, pushed his fingers through his hair, and put the hat back on. "You know it's not a cure."

Hurt clouded her features and she looked away. When her eyes came back to his, they were cold, almost vacant. "You're right. It's hope."

Her soft, desperate voice killed him. How the hell was he supposed to send her away without hope when he knew exactly how she felt? He'd clung to hope for years, wishing for his dad to be found. Hoping for him to come home.

He sat down, close enough to brush her arm with his when he did. "I get that, but you can't go back to the temple." Her safety meant more than anything and if she hated him for it, then fine.

She scooted away. "But you can. You…" She pressed her lips together and stared at the deck. "You could get it for me."

He'd thought about that. Of course he had. Once they caught Benoit and he was out of the picture, Clay had toyed with the idea of getting her the crystal. But with the foundation of the temple already in jeopardy, they couldn't risk any amount of digging. No, the Peridot that remained at the temple had to stay buried.

"I can't."

"You mean won't."

"I mean both."

Chapter Ten

Malia jumped to her feet. Disappointment burned through her, but it wasn't all directed at Clay. She'd known asking for his help would lead to an answer she didn't want to hear. And put him in a no-win situation in her eyes.

He hadn't chosen her ten years ago and he wasn't choosing her now. How naive to think that would change.

"Hate me all you want," he said, reading her mind. "But you're getting on a plane and going home tonight."

"I knew you were a lot of things, but I hadn't realized bully was one of them."

"Guess that just proves we don't know each other very well anymore."

Crushed. He'd just crushed her all over again, ruining every minute they'd spent together over the past few days. Her legs shook and she grabbed the railing to keep from falling to her knees.

"I guess not."

Something flashed in his eyes. Regret? Shame? She blinked and looked harder. Apology? She did know him, and he was pushing her away.

He doesn't really care about you. He only cares about himself.

He crossed his arms over his bare chest. She wished he'd put a shirt on. And grow a tail or something. Fall overboard. But she had no idea how to sail a boat, so there went the crazy thought of pushing him.

"For what it's worth, I do wish your mom the best," he said. "If there was anything else I could do—"

"Asking for your help was stupid. I don't need it." *Or you.* She raised her chin, determined to show him she made her own decisions.

"Goddammit, Malia." He uncrossed his arms and looked like he wanted to punch something. "What the hell does that mean?"

"I don't have to explain myself to you. Can we head back now please?"

He stood and she quickly took a few steps back. "If you're thinking about sneaking back up there, you will get caught. Or worse."

"What do you mean or worse?" The sun felt a thousand times stronger all of a sudden. The isolation out at sea a thousand times lonelier.

"I've made sure the best security guys are up there and they've got orders to use force if necessary to keep trespassers away."

"Why would you do that?"

"It's my job to safeguard national monuments and the land they stand on."

And there it was. Confirmation that he cared more about his work than he did her. That he always would. She pressed the back of her hand to her nose. "Take me back. Now."

They didn't say a word to each other on the boat ride or in the car on the way to the house. As soon as Clay cut the engine, Malia practically fell out of the passenger door, so eager to put distance between them.

"Malia," he said, catching her by the arm.

She tried to pull away, but when she looked up into his warm, concerned eyes, she stopped fighting him. "Save your advice," she whispered.

"This isn't—" His cell rang for the third time in the last hour. "Shit. I need to answer that." He stepped away and she took the opportunity to escape, running to her room and locking the door behind her.

Shutting Clay out wasn't very mature, but she wasn't feeling very levelheaded at the moment. She hated being out of her league and helpless.

"Malia?" Clay's strong, deep voice carried concern through the door.

She walked into the bathroom and turned on the shower.

"Don't shut me out. We need to talk." The door handle jiggled.

That's what she did, though. What she'd always done. She stopped talking and withdrew into herself. It was easier. Safer. She undressed and stood under the warm sprays of water hoping to wash away her sadness. All the months of research and coming to Kauai ruined. All the healing her heart had done, also ruined.

She lifted her face and ran her hands over her head and through her wet hair. She didn't like herself very much at the moment. She'd basically wanted to take from Clay and give to her mom. His loyalty and integrity in exchange for her hope. Asking the man she loved to sacrifice himself had been a terrible thing to do.

She squeezed her eyes shut. She loved him.

Had fallen for him all over again the second he'd called her *nani girl*.

God, she was stupid. She grabbed the soap and scrubbed her body clean of any island reminders. A man like Clay lived for travel and adventure. Danger. Solitude. Lying in bed last night he'd told her about the friends he'd lost. His anxiety and pain still sat alive and well inside him.

He was a do-gooder man of action in the heritage protection world, and crystal aside, as her time with him drew to an end, it had hurt to think he'd leave with ease. But that's what he did. He came and left. Never stayed. Didn't make promises he couldn't—didn't want—to keep. He thrived on the short-term. This time he'd tell her good-bye, but when she wanted so much more, that was hard to swallow.

She'd tried not to lose herself heart and soul again, but she'd been helpless to stop it. And once again, he'd broken her heart. She turned off the shower, dried quickly and crawled into bed.

Somewhere around two a.m. she sat up, exhausted from tossing and turning, unable to sleep. Maybe it wasn't Clay's help she wanted, but his permission. Without it, she couldn't go through with even trying to dig up some crystal.

She slipped out of the covers, packed her stuff and got into her rental car. The emotions that had clouded Clay's eyes on the boat were varied and confusing, but she knew she'd hurt him when she had the gall to ask for his help and then throw it back in his face. As if asking him to compromise his principles for her didn't bother her in the least. But it did. It pained her more than he'd ever know that she'd reduced herself to that.

Even if Clay had wanted to continue their relationship, he deserved someone better than her.

Driving to the airport, she'd never felt more alone. She took a deep breath and thought about Clay's arms holding her close, his teasing breath on the side of her neck. Her memories had always been a double-edged sword straight to her heart. One end poisoned with what-ifs and sorrow, the other infused with love and happiness.

She eased her foot off the gas pedal as the dark, deserted, two-lane road curved. Life was full of bends in the road. What mattered was how she dealt with them.

The sun had yet to rise when she got to the airport. In the quiet glow of a streetlight, she sat in her rental car outside the company's small office to wait for someone to arrive and accept the return. She pulled out her cell and bought her airline ticket for the first flight back to the mainland. Next, she texted Kalani. Her sister's irate voice at seeing the message rang in her ears. *You left without saying good-bye. Who does that?*

Apparently, she did.

Sometimes saying good-bye hurt too much.

She'd done it. She'd left without saying a word.

Clay didn't need to look further than her bedroom, empty of clothes, empty of warmth.

He leaned against the wall, not sure how he felt about it. Adrenaline still pumped through his veins over the capture of Benoit and his men. He'd had to leave the house right after Malia had gotten into the shower, okay with his hasty exit because if she showed up to the temple, he'd be there.

Thankfully, she'd never shown. Which meant she'd heeded his request and flown home or she was with Kalani.

Either way, she was safe.

His stomach clenched. Last night had been hell for a few hours with Benoit determined to go down fighting. But in the end Clay's setup had worked and his team had come through with only a few bumps and bruises. The same couldn't be said for Benoit's.

He headed downstairs for coffee. He should get some sleep, but he knew he couldn't do that until he found out where Malia had gone. That she was okay. He wanted to tell her about Benoit. He wanted to hear her voice.

Two seconds later, his cell chirped. He quickly grabbed it, hope tightening his chest that Malia had somehow tracked down his number, but it was Connor.

"What's up," Clay said.

"Wanted you to be one of the first to know she said yes." Happiness unlike anything Clay had heard from his friend and WHF colleague sounded in Connor's voice.

"Yes?"

"I proposed to Charlie you schmuck."

Clay collapsed onto the couch and rubbed his chest with his free hand. Jealousy scorched him even as joy for his friend filled him, too. "Congratulations."

"It's not a death sentence, man."

Shit. Clay sounded like an asshole. "Let me try that

again. Congratulations, dude. That's fantastic. You're a lucky sonofabitch and she's pretty lucky too."

Connor laughed. "Yeah, I'm definitely getting the better end of this deal."

"I'm happy for you."

"Says the man who sounds about as happy as a fish on a hook. What's up? You should be on cloud nine this morning."

Clay was usually the one who asked that question. "Hang on a sec," he said, putting the phone down on the couch cushion. He leaned his head back, closed his eyes, and all he could see was Malia.

What was up?

He'd fallen in love.

Malia had taken root inside him over twenty years ago—from the very first time they'd met as kids—and being with her again nourished every fiber of his being. He hadn't expected this. Wasn't looking for it. But he'd fallen for her all over again.

With Malia, it was like touching the sun, the moon, and the stars while standing on top of a rainbow.

Until Connor had met Charlie, talking about women had entailed a sentence or two about their one-night escapades, end of story. But Clay didn't want his story with Malia to end and maybe it was time he let a friend help him figure things out.

Clay picked the phone up. "You got five minutes?"

"For you, I've got ten. Spill."

When he was through Connor let out a sigh that said, *about fucking time.* "You need to go after her."

"I want to, but—"

"No buts, man. I hear you on the danger part of your

job, but you're the biggest badass I know. Besides, you could walk across the street tomorrow and get hit by a bus. There are no guarantees. Let Malia decide how she feels about it.

"I also know how hard it was to tell her you couldn't help with the Peridot, but you did the right thing." Connor's dedication to heritage protection and his commitment to history went unmatched.

"Thanks. I'm going to make this right though."

"Want to tell me how?"

"Not yet. I've got a few things to put in place first." He hoped like hell they worked.

He'd made the mistake of walking away from her once before and would move heaven and earth to prove to her she could trust him this time. He had a feeling her leaving without a word was some kind of payback, but he'd pushed her away and she didn't know the truth behind it. She owned him heart and soul and it was time he told her.

"Why do I get the feeling these things concern WHF?"

"And who says I'm the only one with good intuition?"

Connor laughed. "I'm not sure I like where this is leading, but I get it."

"Life threw me the curveball, dude."

"Yeah, and you'd be an idiot not to hit it for a home run."

Home. He'd never wanted that more than he did now. "I'm going to catch the first plane out of here. See you in the office tomorrow."

"You're flying to Idaho?"

Clay stood and looked around the large room, mentally running through what needed to be done. "I do have a job there."

"Yeah, but I thought you might be needed elsewhere first."

"Not necessary." He filled Connor in on the new details concerning Benoit since he'd last texted several hours ago and ended the call, only to have his phone ring again. A second wave of hope crashed into him when he eyed the caller ID.

"What did you do, Clay?" Kalani's big sister bark held enough heat to raise the hair on the back of his neck. "The little snot *texted* me that she's on her way home. So what the hell did you do to make her hightail it out of here?"

"What makes you think it was me?" What else had Malia texted?

"Because I've only ever seen her glowing like Luke Skywalker's lightsaber twice. The time you two were sneaking around as teenagers—yeah, she confirmed that with me—and the other night when she finally told me everything about you."

"Did you just use Skywalker's lightsaber as a metaphor?"

"Clay! What is going on?"

It wasn't Clay's place to tell Kalani why Malia was really on the island, but he needed her help with the plan that had taken shape in his head over the past hour. "Here's the deal…"

Silence rang across the phone line when he finished talking. "You still there?" he asked.

"Yes," she said, a little out of breath. "I shouldn't have brushed off her beliefs like I have, then maybe none of this would've happened."

"I'm glad they happened."

"You're a good guy, Clay. I'll do what I can to help."

"Thanks. I appreciate it."

"Good luck," she said. "And don't mess this up or I'll have to mess you up."

Clay laughed. He really liked Kalani.

As he packed and cleaned up the house, his thoughts never strayed from Malia. When they were young, he'd wanted her to be happy. Was willing to do anything and give up everything for her to live her best life. He'd wanted her safe and secure. But he hadn't given her a chance to choose her happiness. To have a say in her future.

This time he'd let her choose.

And fight for her, too.

Chapter Eleven

Malia walked into the kitchen of her parents' house after a long day at the studio and almost tripped over her own feet. Her mom and Rosie sat at the breakfast bar with...*cocktails* in their hands? Malia couldn't remember the last time her mom had indulged in a drink. From the looks of it, Rosie had mixed her favorite—orange juice and vodka with a splash of cranberry juice. And they were using the crystal her parents had gotten as a wedding gift.

"Looks like you started this party without me." Malia could use a drink. Or ten.

"Hi sweetie," her mom said, patting the barstool beside her. "Sit down and join us. How was your day?"

Malia had been home from Kauai for a week, but tonight Emi Davis had a brand new shine about her. Seeing a glimpse of her mom's old self calmed her ever-present worry.

"My day was fine." Those were the same four words that

had rolled off her tongue every night these past seven days even though they were far from accurate.

Truthfully, every day blended into the next in a Hawaiian haze of heartache.

She sat and kissed her mom's cheek. "What's with cocktail hour?"

Rosie picked up an empty glass beside the bottle of vodka and mixed another drink.

"I've decided to start living again," her mom said.

"What do you mean?" Malia ran her finger over the rim of the glass Rosie handed her.

"I mean I'm tired of being a Debbie Downer. I'm going to drink. I'm going to eat chocolate and fried foods and I'm going to go horseback riding."

"All at the same time?" Rosie piped in, clearly on board with this plan.

"If I want to." Mom clinked glasses with her long-time friend and took a drink.

"What about—"

"There is no 'what about' anymore. I've accepted things are what they are and you and your sisters need to do the same. I want to have fun again. I want to enjoy the rest of my life on my terms. Not a doctor's. Not a disease's. You, my darling daughter"—she cupped Malia's cheek—"have done so much for me, but now it's time we do things my way."

Malia blinked back tears. From fear and joy and affection for a woman who had always set an amazing example. "That sounds awesome, Mom. You know how much we want you to heal and if this is what will make you feel better, then I'm on board."

"I'm a little surprised to hear you agree so readily."

So was Malia. A month ago she might have reacted differently, but now she wanted to live one day at a time. She didn't want to think about the past or think too far in the future.

"Let's just say I'm evolving."

"I'll drink to that," her mom said, lifting her glass. "Cheers."

The sound of glasses clinking filled the kitchen with merriment that had been missing for far too long. Maybe it wasn't hope her mom needed, but purpose—a reason to get up every morning. Sometimes the most obvious answer wasn't the easiest to see.

"I want to go skydiving," her mom said.

Malia spit her drink across the countertop.

Her mom patted her back. "Is the drink too strong? I may have given Rosie the secret eye to make yours with a little more vodka. You've been so tense this week."

Secret eye? Who is this woman?

"I'm fine." Malia cleared her throat and put her glass down in case her mother said something else to shock her. "You just caught me off guard. I'm glad to see this braver side of you, but jumping out of an airplane? This is a pretty sudden change."

"Not really, sweetheart. I've been thinking about it for a while, just kept it to myself."

Didn't Malia know about *that*. Her mom had asked about Kauai and Malia had said as little as possible.

Not a minute passed that Malia didn't think about Clay. The damn man took up waaay too much room in her days—and nights—and she didn't want to sound like a girl in love when she shared more about her trip. Plus, she was still pissed. At him for basically being born and at herself for still wishing he'd helped her get the crystal.

Imagine what the gem could have done in combination with her mom's new attitude. She took a large gulp of her drink. Bartender Rosie got an A+. Why hadn't Malia thought to drink the ache out of her chest sooner?

"So, what else are you planning to do?" Malia asked, her strong voice a surprise. The doctors had said her mom had time—months for sure, maybe more—but this seemed to put a limit on her life. Once her mother checked off some new adventures, would she be ready to go?

"Well, since you asked…" Mom pulled a piece of paper out of her sweater pocket. "Rosie helped me come up with a few things."

Malia unfolded the paper and read her mom's scribbles.

Meet Pierce Brosnan

Her mom had had a crush on him forever and he lived in Malibu. Malia could definitely figure out a way to make a meeting happen. She inwardly smiled.

Skydive

Also very doable. Crazy, but easy enough to arrange. A flutter in Malia's stomach told her she might like to join her mom. Maybe it was time to let the little daredevil inside her out more often. She could still feel the incredible sensations of riding the ATV with Clay.

Golf at Pebble Beach

Her parents had loved to golf together and a stab of

nostalgia hit Malia. When she and her sisters were little, they'd take turns riding in their dad's lap as he drove the golf cart. He let them steer while their mom complimented their excellent driving skills.

Eat every single flavor of Ben & Jerry's ice cream

Malia silently appointed herself partner in crime, starting with Candy Bar Pie.

Spend time at the house in Kauai

The air whooshed out of Malia's lungs. Her mom hadn't wanted to travel, hadn't wanted to be too far from her doctors. But now that she did, Malia lost her voice for a minute.

Wish come true

She swallowed and looked up at her mom. "Wish come true?" She handed her mom the paper. "What's that mean?"

"That one is up here." Her mom pointed to the side of her head, her thin lips pressed into a secretive smile.

"How can we help if we don't know what it is?"

"Some things are meant to happen when the time is right." Her mom glanced at Rosie. "Right Ro?"

"Right Em." Another conspiratorial look passed between the two women. They lifted their drinks in tandem and finished them off. "Another?" Rosie asked.

"Don't mind if I do."

"Why do I get the feeling you two are up to something?" Malia took another sip of her drink. If there was extra vodka in it, she didn't notice. But then everything had pretty much lost its taste this week. How would vodka and Candy Bar

Pie taste together?

"It's high time Rosie and I got ourselves into a little mischief. Hey, maybe we should do that?"

"What?" Malia and Rosie asked at the same time.

"Get high. I can get a prescription for some medicinal—"

"Mom! You can't do that." An alien had taken over her mother's body. There was no other explanation for her loony, happy, and fun-to-watch behavior.

"Party pooper."

Rosie slid her mom a new drink. "I'd like to make a toast," Rosie said. "To one of the best women I know. A woman who has always treated me as a friend. And to her beautiful daughter, whom I love like my own."

The three of them raised their glasses. This time Malia couldn't stop a tear from leaking out of the corner of her eye. She loved Rosie like a second mom and one day far too soon, Rosie would be all she had.

Talk turned to Malia's sisters and Tuesday night tacos and who had a better butt, Hugh Jackman or Brad Pitt. Laughter filled the room. Joy. Smiles from ear to ear. Malia took it all in, tucking it away some place safe and treasured.

With her mom in good hands, Malia slid off her barstool. "I'm going to head out." She wrapped her mom in a tight squeeze. "I'm truly in awe of you, Mom. Love you."

"Love you, too."

On the drive home, with the sun dipping behind the mountains, an orange glimmer on the horizon, Malia couldn't help but picture the sunset in Kauai. Recall being on the beach with Clay.

She heard his voice a hundred times a day. With every blink she saw his smile. Remembered his touch and kisses with such clarity that she'd swear he was *right there*.

She'd thought about asking Rosie for his number so she could call or text him. Shame kept her from doing it. She'd left Kauai like a coward because she was one. Afraid of more rejection, afraid her heart would never recover from Clay's refusal to help her. Afraid he'd hear the love in her voice and say nothing of it.

No doubt he'd already moved on. As he should, since she'd done the leaving. A man like Clay didn't grovel or give chase. He was probably on another continent, not giving her a second thought.

She got home and went straight to the bathroom for a long soak in the tub. A warm bath and the suspense novel she'd started with a military bad guy—who Malia hated with a passion—would take her mind off Captain Magnificent. It was time she moved on, too.

Clay stepped out of the limousine parked outside Malia's yoga studio and for the first time in his life, his nerves gripped his heart in a choke hold. He ran his hands down his cargo pants. Goddamn perspiration slid down his back. He'd been to war-torn countries and to the most desolate places on the planet and not been this anxious.

He glanced over at the second limo pulling up to the curb. This was it.

The past two weeks had been hell without her, his only saving grace the new direction of his future. He hurried up the walkway, eager to get his hands on her, the tips of his fingers tingling with anticipation.

"Mr. Doherty?" the young woman at the small reception desk said.

"Betsy." He'd talked to her a couple of times to set things up and recognized her voice. "Thanks for your help."

"My pleasure." She jumped to her feet with a big grin on her face. "She's right through there." She nodded toward an arched doorway. "Class just got started."

"Great. You'll keep this place running, right?"

"Absolutely. Malia actually just hired another instructor so the timing is perfect."

He smiled and went to get the love of his life.

She stood in front of the class, her eyes roaming over the numerous students as they did some yoga pose bent at the waist. She spoke in a calm, soft voice that soothed and encouraged at the same time. He stood frozen for a moment, lost in the sound she made and the fluid way she moved with small steps to the left and then to the right.

Mine.

Her attention jerked to where he stood and their eyes met. Hers widened in surprise before something else filled their dark depths—hope maybe? He couldn't look away, caught in their beauty and praying like hell she saw love and respect and desire in his.

The serene, quiet vibe in the large room morphed into an electric and intoxicating combination of air molecules that got Clay's feet moving. Malia never took her eyes off him as he weaved through the class to get to her. She stopped moving, her lips parted slightly. He'd swear he could hear her breathing. Unaware of what anyone else around him did, he marched right up to her.

At a couple feet away, her light floral scent hit him. He

inhaled through his nose, the corners of his mouth lifted. Someone cleared their throat. Whispers filled the room. Malia kept looking at him like she wanted to kiss and hit him at the same time.

He'd gladly let her do both.

When he got close enough, he put his hands on her waist and lifted her up and over his shoulder.

"Hey! What are you doing? Put me down." She squirmed and pounded on his back but he wasn't letting her go until he had her in the limo.

"I'm taking the woman I love and leaving."

Gasps sounded as a path cleared for him to make his way. He caught sight of Betsy at the back of the room and a second later she started to clap. The rest of the class followed her lead, the applause loud.

Malia didn't stop fighting, though. "You cannot come in here and take me."

"I just did."

She wiggled and he liked it entirely too much. "I've got a class to teach."

"Taken care of."

"What do you mean—ow!" Her foot connected with the doorframe when he turned.

"Keep still, babe. Or I'll be forced to kiss it and make it better in front of everyone." He pushed through the glass front door and bright sunshine smiled down on them.

She stilled and lifted her head. To see where they were headed, he guessed. The limo driver opened the back door. "Clay…"

"Yeah?"

"What is…" She stopped, breathless, as their moms and

her younger sister Lina clapped furiously outside the second limo.

"Go, Clay!" Lina shouted.

Clay palmed Malia's head and wrapped an arm around her back as he placed her in the sleek black car. She scooted over as he followed right behind. The driver shut the door.

Shock led the emotion on her face now. "What's going on?" She looked around the elegant leather interior, her shoulders tense, her legs pressed together.

He inched closer, dying to connect with her mouth.

"What are you doing?" Her hand met his chest and he knew she felt his heart pounding because everything about her softened. "Clay," she whispered.

"There's so much I need to say to you." He'd never talked so much with a woman in his life, but with Malia the words flowed. "Starting with I missed you."

The pulse at the base of her neck quickened. "I...I assumed you'd moved on. Which I would understand. I'm sorry I left like I did. It was thoughtless and I was confused and—"

"Apology accepted."

Her lips curved slightly. "That was easy."

"Know why?"

She shook her head.

"Because I love you. I've never stopped loving you. My heart beats for real when I'm with you and"—he gently palmed her cheek—"I'm here to ask you to have faith in me. In us."

"Clay..." She leaned into his hand. "I want to so badly."

"But?"

"I'm scared. And hurt. And mad at myself for hurting

you. I never should have asked you to—"

"You didn't hurt me. But I know I hurt you. And I'm sorry. I've only ever wanted you to be safe and my job comes with danger and I—"

She kissed him. Hard. Quick. With promise. "It's okay."

"What's okay?"

"All of it."

"I need to tell you all of it." He took her hand and laced their fingers. "A lot happened on the island you don't know about, but first I want to tell you I'm starting a new job with WHF. It's been in the works, but I sped things up. I'm starting a brand-new position I call tech genius."

"Genius?" she questioned, like it sounded bogus. But the playful slant to her mouth betrayed her tone.

"This genius is very good at things he's yet to show you, so you'd better watch it."

She put her free hand on his thigh. "Tell me more."

"I'm working on an app that will help people find historic sites all around the world. We're also revamping the website to make it interactive and adding components that can be used as a teaching tool. WHF has always been at the forefront of advocacy and cultural legacy and I'm taking us into the future."

"I meant tell me more about the things you want to show me."

He laughed. His work excited him. This new endeavor had his blood pumping. And with Malia by his side, his life couldn't get any more perfect.

"But that all sounds amazing, too. Congratulations."

"It still means travel, but no more security."

"Wait," she said softly. "You love your job. If you're

doing all this because of me, don't. I can handle it. I could even travel with you. If you want. You've sort of piqued my interest in heritage protection."

Clay grinned. Malia was made of sterner stuff than he'd given her credit for. "Baby, I'm gonna show you the world. But this new gig also means I can work from anywhere." He wrapped his arm around her waist and guided her onto his lap so she straddled him, her sweet curves brushing his front. "And I'm thinking about making my favorite place my home now if a certain girl agrees… Wait, I'm getting ahead of myself."

Malia's eyes sparkled with surprise and passion. Her body shook underneath his touch. "You are?"

"Yeah, about the crystal first, *nani girl*."

She sucked in a breath, her lips parted.

He pressed two fingers to her mouth. "I've made arrangements for your mom to have access to the grounds. As long as she's accompanied by one of the caretakers for safety and preservation reasons, she can visit the temple. We both know standing on sacred land is powerful to those who believe and your mom can spend as much time there as she wants."

Malia's bottom lip quivered and she closed her eyes for a moment. "I-I don't know what to say. That's amazing. Thank you. Did you know my mom wanted to go back to Kauai?"

"Not until I talked to my mom and told her my plan. We're headed to the airport. A private jet will take us all to the island." He kissed Malia's forehead, her eyelids.

A tear slipped out of the corner of her eye.

"The choice to go is yours." He wiped the wetness from her cheek with the pad of his thumb. "But there's a catch."

"A catch?" she whispered.

He kissed her. A soft gliding of lips to tell her how much he cherished her. Then he got down on one knee and pulled the diamond ring out of his pocket. Her breath caught.

"Malia, you're the only woman I've ever loved. You make me laugh. You fill me with gratitude. You're kind and beautiful and smart and you've taught me the importance of family. Everything I've done and everything I've learned is so I can be worthy of you. Will you marry me and allow me the honor of loving you for the rest of my life?"

She fell to her knees and flung her arms around his neck. "Yes. A million times yes." Her mouth fused with his, tongues tangling, breath catching. He felt the kiss all the way to his bones and in a certain spot below the waist. "I love you," she murmured against his lips. "I love you so very much."

"Sir?" sounded over the intercom from the driver.

Clay pulled back with a groan. "Yes, Walt?"

"I'm sorry to interrupt, but the ladies in the other car would like to know…the status, sir."

Malia giggled. "Should we torture them and make them wait?"

"Did you hear that, Walt?"

"Yes, sir."

"No, wait. I'm kidding." She looked down at the ring still in his hand. "Do they know about this?"

"No. I wanted you to be the first to know." He slid the ring on her finger.

"It's beautiful." She stared at the square-cut diamond for a long beat before meeting his eyes again. "So the catch was I say yes and you let me come to Kauai, too?"

"Yep."

"That's a pretty underhanded catch."

"There's more."

"Are you waggling your eyebrows at me?" she asked.

"I don't know. Am I?" He lifted them some more. Malia brought out a playful side he never knew he had.

She giggled again and shook her head in good-natured fun. "Stop before I jump your bones right here."

"Mic is still on, sir."

Malia buried her face in his shirt. "Oops."

He lifted her chin. "Would you rather tell them in person when we get to the airport?"

"I think so."

"Tell them the status is good, Walt, and we'll fill them in when we're in the air." Walt gave agreement and it was just Malia and him again. "I want us to get married in Kauai. I think your mom would like that. Just family and close friends. At the house or Kalani's hotel, wherever you want."

"When?" she said breathlessly.

"Tomorrow. Next month. It's up to you." He got back into the seat, bringing her with him and tucking her against his side. "But soon."

"I'd love that."

"God, I love you."

"I don't think my feet are touching the ground." She looked up at him under long dark lashes.

He brought his mouth to hers. "I plan to keep it that way."

Epilogue

Three months later...

Malia stood on the wet sand and stared out at the turquoise sea, the final rays of sunshine twinkling like stars on the tranquil water. Her dreams of this day hadn't even come close to the reality. Nothing had prepared her for the sight of Clay in his tuxedo at the end of the aisle, his impossibly bright green eyes on her like he was the luckiest man in the world. Their family and friends surrounding them on the beach, her mom... Her mom telling her that this was her secret wish, to see one of her daughters marry.

"You are unbelievably gorgeous from the front, Mrs. Doherty, but my God, you take my breath away from the back, too." Clay wrapped his arms around her and put his chin on her bare shoulder.

She leaned against him. Her entire body thrummed with anticipation for their honeymoon and the clothing optional stipulation he liked to remind her of.

"I can't wait to get you naked."

She chuckled. "I was just thinking the same thing."

"Anything else on your mind?" He brushed a tendril of hair off her neck and kissed the curve of her skin. She shivered.

"Today was magical, Clay. Perfect. Thank you for making it so."

"Kalani gets most of the credit. Come on." He took her hand and turned them away from the sea. "There's a party going on and I want to dance with you again."

"You hate dancing."

"Not with you."

"Have I mentioned how much I love you?" She peeked at his handsome, clean-shaven face from the corner of her eye. He'd ditched the tuxedo jacket and wore just the white shirt over his pants, top two buttons undone, the sleeves rolled up to his elbows.

He stopped and kissed her. With passion and wildness, sweetness and love. So much love she felt it beyond her heart and soul. It reached the heavens. "I love you, too," he said.

They strode up the sand, feet bare, the sand cool and soft between her toes, to the house where tiny white lights, candles, flowers and music transformed the inside into a wedding wonderland.

"Champagne?" Kalani handed them each a glass the second they stepped onto the patio. She'd been attentive all day, Malia's very special wedding coordinator.

"Thank you," Malia said. "For everything."

"Do not get that glassy-eyed look little sister or I'm going to have Clay spank you."

"Do it," Clay teased, heat and affection in his gaze.

"Who's spanking who?" McCall said, coming up behind Kalani with his wife Lucy. The couple had joined them on the island several days ago, along with Connor and his fiancée Charlie, and Dean and Samantha Malloy.

"I think you need your hearing checked," Clay said.

"Or a good spanking." He grinned at Lucy, who rolled her eyes.

Malia laughed and Kalani said, "My work here is done. Let me just go grab you two some champagne," she said to McCall and Lucy.

"Oh, no thank you, I'm good." Lucy gave her husband a sly grin. He beamed one right back at her.

"I'm telling you Las Mundas is the best place on the Route," Connor said, joining their group along with Charlie, Dean and Samantha.

"No," Dean said. "It's Twin Arrows. Hands down."

The two men had recently finished work on a Route 66 venture, Dean's company partnering with WHF on the huge preservation project.

Malia had loved listening to the stories the four men shared about heritage protection and their travels. She'd loved hearing about how the guys had met their significant others. But best of all was seeing the friendship between the foursome. Clay might not have any siblings, but these men were his brothers.

And they'd accepted her immediately, made her feel a part of their family, teased her just like they did the other women.

"Oh," Samantha said, putting a hand on her beautiful pregnant belly. "Junior's got the hiccups again."

Dean put his arm around Sam and palmed her stomach, too. "I can't wait to meet this little guy." He kissed Sam's cheek and the love between them dazzled.

Lucy watched Sam's stomach before lifting her gaze to McCall and smiling again.

Malia looked at Clay at the same time he looked at her. They had the same suspicion.

"You two have something to share?" Clay asked.

The sheer happiness on McCall's face could light up a football stadium during a power failure. "We've got our own bundle of joy set to bless us in seven months."

"Congratulations," rang out. Hugs. Handshakes. Clay took Malia's hand and squeezed it tight. They planned to start their own baby-making project tonight.

"While we're making announcements," Connor said, looking happy, but a little restless too, "mark December thir-tieth down on your calendars." He brought Charlie closer to his side.

"For our wedding," Charlie added.

Clay chuckled. "So much for sneaking away, huh?"

"The parents want to make a big deal out of it," Connor said. His mom was a famous TV personality and his father a British entrepreneur and environmentalist worth billions. Charlie's father was a millionaire magazine publisher. Malia guessed "big deal" meant on par with Hollywood celebrities.

But Malia had also gotten to know Connor and Charlie. Their wedding might be big and fancy, but not pretentious.

"We'll be there," Clay said, patting his friend on the back.

"Of course you will. You three goons are in my wedding party. Along with my three brothers-in-law, two nephews, three nieces, and probably a couple of cousins I don't know about." Connor glanced at his bride-to-be. "You sure we can't elope?"

Charlie put her hand on Connor's chest. "You know I wish we could." Charlie was an only child so Malia imagined all the attention and extended family could be pretty overwhelming.

While the conversation continued around her, Malia thought about how her own life had changed in the past few months. Asked to hold an impromptu yoga class during a windsurfing expo on the island when she'd first come back to Kauai, yogis had squeezed into every corner of the studio. Things took off from there. Locals wanted more and she wanted to give it to them. So two weeks ago she opened a studio for workshops and retreats when she was in town.

And thanks to photographs Clay took of her seaside yoga poses and posted to Instagram, she'd attracted over ten thousand followers in a little over a month. She captioned them with feel-good quotes like, "Believe in yourself because what you have on the inside is everything you need."

That exposure led to interest from a world-renowned health and longevity center in San Diego that wanted her to teach at their facility. With Clay's help and expertise, she agreed, but under her own name, operation, and time frame. Her first classes last month had sold out.

Clay had taken her dream and magnified it, never once stepping beyond her comfort zone. His business savvy and admiration for her work had given her the courage to take her passion beyond her imagination.

She watched him talking with his friends, so at ease and confident. Sexy. And she thanked her lucky stars a tiny green crystal had brought them back together.

Thanked him every day for the gift he'd given her mom. She'd been to the temple numerous times to feel the delicate soil with her bare feet and absorb the healing energy of Mana. Emi Davis believed in it and she'd looked better than she had in years.

Her mom must have felt her brainwaves, because there she was. "You don't mind if I steal these two for a minute, do you?" Emi said, squeezing in between Malia and Clay with an arm around each of them.

The group nodded their okay and the three of them took a little walk in the sand. When her mom stopped and turned to cast affectionate eyes on them, Malia blinked back tears.

"I just want to tell you both how much I love you." Emi took each of them by the hand. "I'm so proud of you, Malia. So lucky and blessed to have you for a daughter. And Clay, you're the best son-in-law a mom could ask for and it gives me much peace to know you'll always take care of my sweet girl."

"Forever," Clay said, his voice thick.

"Thank you for everything you've given me. And I'm not just talking about the temple." She took Clay's face in her hands. "You're an amazing young man and I always knew it."

Clay blinked several times, swallowed, and Malia fell in love with him a little bit more. Watching her short, slender mom turn her big, tough husband to mush was a sight to see. "Thank you, Emi."

"And you." Mom moved her focus to Malia. "You take care of this man, too. Love him even on days when all you want to do is throttle him."

Malia smiled. "I will."

"Love and you'll be loved," her mom said before kissing them each on the cheek and going back inside.

"Come with me," Clay said, his big, warm hand covering hers and leading her away from their reception. "I've got a surprise for you that's killing me not to show you already."

"Another one?" He'd already surprised her with a trip to the Amalfi Coast next month.

"I'm going to surprise you a million more times." He flashed his dimples at her and hurried them down the beach to a small alcove where a tent was set up. "After you, *nani girl*." He swept his arm through the linen flap.

Her heart stopped when she entered. More tiny white lights, hanging across the top of the tent. Flowers in glass hurricane jars. And a bed covered in beautiful white linens with rose petals strewn across it. She spun around. "How did you—"

Clay silenced her with a finger to her lips. "Get on the bed, Mrs. Doherty."

"Now?" she murmured. It came out a question, but she absolutely wanted it now, hot desire swirling in the pit of her stomach and between her legs.

"I can't wait another minute."

"But—" She walked backward, obeying the gentle push of his hand and body against her.

"But our guests can wait."

The back of her knees hit the bed. "Well in that case, kiss me," she said as he dropped his hand. "Slowly."

His grin turned her legs to jelly. "Are you giving me an order?"

She grabbed his shirt and pulled him down on top of her as she fell back onto the firm mattress. "Yes."

He pushed up onto his elbows. His lips brushed against hers. "Just so you know, I'm going to take those orders for the rest of my life."

Malia wrapped her arms around his neck to bring him closer and never ever let go. "Count on it."

Acknowledgments

Thank you to my real-life hero for being my everything and always up for any outdoor adventure. Thank you to my amazing editor Wendy Chen, whose guidance and wisdom I appreciate more than I can say. It's been so fun being on the road, up in trees, out at sea, and to so many other fun outdoor places with you and my heroes for this series. To my awesome writer pals, thanks for truly blessing me with your friendship. A big shout-out to the gang at Entangled—Stacy, Liz, Melanie, Heather H., Debbie, Tara, Katie, Jessica, Heather R., Ellie, MK, Julia, and Anita—I'm so grateful for all that you do. Thank you! (And I really hope I didn't forget anyone.) Thank you to Ada Hui, the winner of my Name A Character contest. I loved your choice of "Kalani" for Malia's older sister! And lastly, big hugs and thanks to my readers. You guys are the best.

About the Author

When not attached to her laptop, USA Today Bestselling Author Robin Bielman can almost always be found with her nose in a book. A California girl, the beach is her favorite place for fun and inspiration. Her fondness for swoon-worthy heroes who flirt and stumble upon the girl they can't live without jumpstarts all of her story ideas. She is a 2014 RITA Finalist, loves to frequent coffee shops, and plays a mean game of sock tug of war with her crazy-cute dog, Harry. She cherishes her family and friends and loves to connect with readers. Get the scoop on Robin, her books, and sign up for her newsletter on her website at http://robinbielman.com